THE JEKYLL REVELATION

THE JEKYLL REVELATION

ROBERT MASELLO

47NORTH

Published by 47North, Seattle

www.apub.com

Amazon, the Amazon logo, and 47North are trademarks of Amazon.com, Inc., or its affiliates.

ISBN-13: 9781503951198
ISBN-10: 1503951197

Cover design by Damonza

Printed in the United States of America

Fear is the strong passion;
it is with fear that you must trifle,
if you wish to taste the intensest joys of living.

Robert Louis Stevenson, 1886

26 November, 1894

From: Robert Louis Stevenson, Vailima House, Samoa
To: W. E. Henley, 18 Maybury Road, Old Woking, Surrey, England

Dear Henley—
What I must tell you now, I tell you with dread.

It has happened again.

What we thought—what we prayed—we had left behind us in the back alleys and darkened doorways of Whitechapel has, I fear, awakened from its awful slumber.

It has struck again, right here, in what I had foolishly thought might be Paradise.

And I have been the unwitting agent of its malevolence.

To you alone, my oldest friend—you who know so much of the story and played such a brave and crucial part in it—can I entrust this final account. I will send it to you by way of the next packet boat to leave the island. Who else, I must ask, would believe it?

Last night, as I sat on my verandah, lighting a pipe and contemplating the face of the full moon—sometimes, Henley, it hangs so close to this mountaintop, it is like having a silver pocket watch dangling in front of my eyes—I saw a flicker of light emerging from the jungle and making straight for the house. For a moment, I thought it might finally be one of the aitus—evil spirits—that the natives believe haunt the tangled slopes of Mount Vaea, but then it resolved itself into the burning end of a torch. Someone was running across the cleared land, torch held high, and I could hear, above the soughing of the wind in the banyan trees, a voice shouting, 'Tusitala! Come quick!'

Tusitala—teller of tales—is how I am known in the native tongue, and now I could tell that it was the voice of one of my boys, Malaki, who has helped clear the brush and dig the well. He arrived panting at the foot of the porch—his bare brown legs are crisscrossed with so many tattoos that they look as if he wears lace breeches.

'Keep your voice down!' I warned. 'The house is asleep.'

'Come quick,' he repeated, though in a lower tone. 'And bring gun.'

'Why?'

Pausing to catch his breath again, he merely said 'gun', and it was then that I took note of the stain on the drooping folds of the pareu wrapped around his waist. In the moonlight, it had at first appeared to be dirt or perhaps red wine—though the Samoans have no taste for wine—but its crust and gleam now revealed it to be dried blood.

A sight that you and I, my friend, know all too well.

'Are you hurt?'

He glanced down at the scrap of yellow cloth covering his loins. 'Blood not mine.'

Asking for no further explanation, I hurried inside and up to the eyrie in which I write. As you know from previous letters, the house has no doors, the better to let the trade winds play through its many rooms, but the servants sleep willy-nilly on the floor, wherever they choose to throw down their grass mats, and so I had to tread lightly, and with care. In my haste, I stumbled over one or two of the houseboys, who grumbled and rolled over, and once in my study, I unlocked the case that holds my Colt rifle. Unreliable as it is, it still affords the best and only means of protection from threats more dire than a hot word or native curse. I loaded the black powder and two .44-caliber rounds into its chambers—my fingers fumbling, I am not ashamed to say—and by the time I had returned to the porch, Malaki had saddled the horse and was holding the reins.

Mounting, I asked if he would like to ride, too, but Malaki shook his head, as I had suspected he would, and trotted alongside us, torch in hand, as we took to the jungle trail.

The villagers, who built this path for me in gratitude for past services, call it the Road of the Loving Heart. Even in the daylight, it is not easily navigable, twisting and turning, as it must, down the steep and overgrown hillside. More than once, Malaki had to wait impatiently as I—in my loose canvas trousers and shirt, the rifle slung across my back by a leather strap—had to guide the horse around a rocky outcropping, fallen tree trunk, or particularly tenacious liana vine. Had it not been for the beacon of the torch, I might have lost sight of him in the darkness altogether.

Before long, however, I could detect the crashing of the surf, and I knew that the most arduous part of our journey must be coming to an end.

But what awaited me then?

Breaking free of the suffocating trees and brush, we came upon the crescent strip of sand, strewn with pebbles and shells, which runs along the harbour front. I dismounted, looping the reins around a slender palm, as Malaki, hardly winded, gestured for me to come closer. Lowering the torch towards the sand, he pointed out what were unmistakably two sets of footprints—one made by dainty bare feet, the other by a man's tackety boots, hobnails protruding from the heels. As we tracked them down the beach and in the direction of the dock, I could not help but judge from the impression of his steps that the man must have been a bandy-legged sort. That, or an ape had donned a pair of boots and gone for a nocturnal stroll.

'Where are we going?' I whispered. 'What did you want me to see?'

Malaki just shook his head and waved me on. 'Follow. Follow.'

As we drew near the pier, he bent low and ushered me under the wet timbers. Stooping over, I crept after him, the smell of kelp and rotting fish joined by something else, something that transported me, however reluctantly, to that grim little room I once visited at 13 Miller's Court.

'See,' Malaki said, slowly waving the torch, its flame nearly extinguished, over a tide pool where a clump of long and dark strands, which at first I took for seaweed, washed back and forth in the water.

It was then that I saw the bright pink hibiscus blossom tucked—as the married women do with it in these islands—behind the left ear. She was lying with her face in the water, and when I moved to turn her over, Malaki stepped back in fear. From bosom to hem, her puletasi had been ripped wide open—as had she—and though in my heart I knew it to be impossible, all I could utter in horror was, 'Did you do this?'

He vigourously shook his head in denial. 'I turn body. No more.'

A crab scuttled over her shoulders, pincers extended, and I brushed it aside. 'Let's get her out of the water.'

But Malaki would not help.

I dragged her, as best I could, above the tideline. She looked like a girl of twenty or so, someone I had seen once or twice weaving baskets in Apia. I drew the ragged ends of her dress together and unwound a ghastly necklace of sea grapes from around her throat. The trail of the hobnailed boots ended at the waterline—plainly, her murderer had followed, or perhaps lured, the girl here—but they picked up again on the dry sand. Though the torch was out, by the light of the moon I could see that the prints continued towards the customs house, which was mounted on caissons not forty yards off.

'You stay here,' I whispered, though there was little enough chance of his following me into any greater danger.

Crouching low, I followed the telltale prints to the foot of the ladder, stealthily climbed the rungs, then skirted the barrels of copra and coffee beans clustered on the narrow deck. Positioning myself outside the door of the house, I unslung the rifle from my back. There was a small, smudged window encrusted with salt spray, but through its quarter panes I could discern a vague silhouette shifting about.

Putting my ear to the warped wood of the door, I heard sounds, too—muffled and low, but anguished nonetheless. The moaning of a tormented creature locked in a cage.

I cocked the rifle, and had no sooner readied myself to break inside when the door was flung open so violently that I instinctively fell back. The weapon was knocked from my hands, the cartridge exploding in the chamber with a shower of orange sparks and blue smoke, as a force like the wind toppled me over the railing. I landed on my back, stunned, as something dropped with a thud onto the sand at my side, and then, righting itself, shot past me. All I could see of it was a blur, black and swift as a bat, escaping into the maze of empty fish stalls and weighing stations.

But it was enough, old friend.

Enough to tell me that the nightmare had not ended in the squalid streets of Whitechapel, but had travelled halfway around the globe, ten thousand miles, to resume its dreadful enterprise.

PART I

TOPANGA CANYON— CALIFORNIA

Present Day

Piloting his jeep up the old abandoned fire road, Rafael Salazar could see all around him further evidence of the terrible drought that was afflicting not only the Santa Monica Mountains, but all of Southern California. Great plumes of dry soil rose around the tires, enveloping the vehicle in a cloud of dirt and dust as it bounced its way over the rocks and potholes, past the trees with their melancholy branches hanging low, the scraggly chaparral, the withered grasses. As a field officer with the Environmental Science Service, a perpetually underfunded division of the Bureau of Land Management, he had seen the canyon in all kinds of conditions, but he had never seen it this bad.

The forecast, unfortunately, was for more of the same. One errant spark and the whole thing could ignite like a torch.

As he came around a grove of leafless willows huddling together like conspirators and approached the top of the road, he saw a red pickup truck, parked in a rare patch of shade. He knew whose truck it was, though he'd yet to determine how or where they'd circumvented the chain and padlock that sealed off the bottom of the road. He also knew why, even in this blazing heat, they would be up here. The only question was, had they already gotten what they came for, or would there be time for him to stop them?

Pulling the jeep as far off road as he could go, he got out, slung his binoculars around his neck and his backpack over his shoulders, and started toward the truck. His legs were stiff and his butt was sore from all the jouncing in the jeep, but he knew there might not be any time to waste. He also knew that he could lose his job for this. It wasn't the first time that he'd had to consider that possible outcome.

It wasn't the first time that he had dismissed it, either.

He approached the beat-up old truck warily from the back, and only when he had determined that no one was in it did he get close enough to look into the flatbed.

To his relief, all he saw were some ropes and tackle, empty Dr Pepper cans, a busted fishing rod, and a Styrofoam cooler.

But which way had they gone?

He went to the top of the hill and swept the binoculars around the surrounding range and deep ravines. Running along the Pacific Coast and stretching forty miles from the Hollywood Hills to Point Mugu in neighboring Ventura County, the Santa Monica Mountains comprised a wilderness habitat unlike any other abutting a city as large and sprawling as Los Angeles. Canyons cut through the rolling hills and jagged peaks, and tiny towns were nestled here and there, but for the most part these undulating hills and winding gullies were still untouched and untamed, home to thousands of wild creatures, from foxes to raccoons, mule deer to brown bears, rattlesnakes to coyotes. It was the coyotes that had brought him here in the first place; even now, a pair of them, wearing the radio collars he had affixed, roamed these tinder-dry mountainsides.

He saw no sign, however, of the two men, virtually inseparable and known locally by just their first names—Seth and Alfie. Seth was the tall one with the scruffy gray beard; Alfie was built like a fire hydrant (and was just about as bright). But even they would know to go where the water was, or at least where it had been, so Rafe started down the other side of the hill, the loose pebbles and grit from the trail skittering under his hiking boots. Two or three times he had to put his hand down to the parched ground to arrest his sliding out of control. He should have topped off his canteen before he'd gone out on his patrol—standard protocol—but it was too late to do anything about that now.

When the land leveled off, he followed the rudimentary track that animals had used since time immemorial to make their way down to the lake—more like an overgrown pond—where they could drink. The closer he got, the worse it looked, and smelled. In fact, when he finally arrived on its banks, he saw that the water level had dropped lower than he had ever seen it. At least a dozen yards of ground that had once been underwater were now visible, the gravel and desiccated weeds exposed to the bright sunlight, the remaining water still and fetid. The tips of rocks that had not seen the light of day for centuries or more protruded from the surface of the pale-green water, and the rusted frame of a mountain bike lay where someone must have once flung it into the lake.

Rafe stopped to catch his breath and take a swig from his canteen. A little farther out, he spotted something even more unlikely. It looked for all the world like the corner of an old green steamer trunk. Who would have dropped a thing like that all the way out there? With the binoculars, he was able to make out a row of tarnished brass bolts running along its rim, but that was all. If he wanted to retrieve the damn thing, he'd need a raft and another pair of hands.

Watching his step, he walked around the perimeter of the lake, but before he saw anything else odd or suspicious, he heard it—scratching, a feeble humph of air. All his senses went on alert, and he dipped into a crouch, twigs and thorns catching at his khaki shorts and scratching the bare skin below. The cuts and scratches were nothing; bumping into Seth and Alfie would be a whole lot worse.

Following the sounds, he entered a clearing and saw a clump of hardy chamise that had lost its normal russet color, fading to a pale pink, but managing even in this drought to remain thick and alive. That alone would have served as a lure, offering some shade and protection to a parched animal passing by. The contours of the metal cage were concealed among the branches. Without even seeing its prisoner yet, he knew what the trap contained.

He was right.

As soon as he bent over and parted the branches, he was met by a pair of yellow eyes, horizontal and unblinking. The animal was on its side, panting softly, dragging one paw across the bars, over and over, hoping for escape, but in all other ways resigned to its fate. How long, Rafe wondered, had the bobcat been in there? He could see a blue plastic water bucket, entirely drained, and the bait—strips of beef jerky—still littering the ground in front of the cage and on the floor inside it.

But how was he to release it, and could he get it done in time? He could only surmise that Seth and Alfie had gone first to check their more remote traps, and would even now be on their way to this one to claim their prize. It was one of the little-known, but more controversial, aspects of the forestry service's land management programs. Bobcat trapping was legal in California—and Rafe had been required to recognize that inconvenient fact, among many others, when he was sworn in—but that didn't mean it was right.

Which meant, in his view, he didn't have to honor it.

Creeping closer, he studied the upper latch on the cage; it was a simple trigger device, and all he had to do was raise it.

But there was no telling what the animal would do. The bobcat had raised his head now and bared his fangs. But it was waiting. With limited reserves of energy, it was husbanding whatever strength it had left for the fight it knew was about to come. Animals were smart that way, much smarter than they were commonly given credit for. People always liked to say that only human beings understood the concept of death; Rafe always wanted to make them come with him on his patrols and spend some time with these supposedly dull-witted creatures.

Especially at times like this, when the animals were prepared to fight like hell to preserve the life that they were barely supposed to understand they had.

Off in the distance, Rafe heard a whistle. It might have been Seth signaling Alfie to come that way. Maybe they'd had some luck with another trap.

It was now or never.

He knelt down and stared into the animal's eyes, but all he elicited was a snarl. The bobcat's lips were cracked and dry and dripped none of the saliva they would normally have done. Still, he held its gaze for several seconds more.

"I'm going to let you go," he said in a deliberate and even tone. "I'm going to open this cage, and you are going to run for it. Do you get it?" He was trying to establish some kind of connection, something to calm the animal a little bit.

The cat scrunched down, its powerful shoulders hunching, and snarled again, revealing worn and broken teeth. It was not a youngster.

"Don't give me that," Rafe said. "Just get going. And under no circumstances tell anyone I did this."

When he went to the back of the cage, intending to reach forward and raise the gate from behind, the animal squirmed around to keep him in view.

"Wrong way. What did I tell you? Wrong way."

There was another whistle, and then a voice, closer than before. It was Alfie, calling out, "Nope, not a damn thing."

"One more to check," Seth replied. "One more and we quit for the day."

Rafe whipped out his canteen, unscrewed the lid, and poured the remaining water through the top bars of the cage and into the bobcat's startled face. It was enough to confuse the animal.

"Now!" he said, softly but urgently, dropping the canteen and yanking the gate up with one hand, and with the other tilting the trap from the back.

The bobcat all but tumbled out of the cage, the blue bucket rolling after him, and scrambled for its footing. Depleted as it was, it found its feet, and with one look back—was it defiance, or gratitude?—sprinted off in a lopsided gait, its tail flicking, and vanished into the brush. Its coat was the dun color of the soil, and it was no sooner out of sight than Rafe saw Seth coming into view.

Seth saw him, too.

"What the . . . ?"

Rafe straightened, wiping the dirt from his uniform, and pretended to be studying the trap.

"You know you have to check these at least every other day," he said. "No animal can be left inside one for more than forty-eight hours."

"I know the rules," Seth said, the end of his long gray beard plastered to the top of his sweat-stained T-shirt. "I don't need you to tell me the rules, Salazar."

"Maybe you do."

Alfie plodded into the clearing now, an empty canvas sack draped over his back, and stopped when he saw Rafe. He looked at Seth to find out what was up.

"You want me to show you my license?" Seth said to Rafe. "Again? I can take four bobcats this year, one bear, two deer, and as many damn critters as I can trap."

"Looks like you came up short," Rafe said, glancing at the empty bag.

"That's none of your business."

"What'd he do?" Alfie asked, taking in the blue bucket on the ground and the open gate. "Did he mess with the cage?"

Seth just glared.

"Did he?" Alfie repeated, anger rising in his voice.

Rafe picked up his empty canteen, screwed the lid back into place, and then took his sunglasses from his breast pocket and slipped them on. Even from a few yards away, he could smell the stink coming off Seth as he walked past him, then out of the clearing, and he knew, without turning around, that they were watching him go. He also knew that, much as he would have liked to keep an eye on them, it would be a mistake to turn around. Instead, he said over his shoulder, "Stay hydrated, boys." He headed toward the fire road, the binoculars swinging against his chest. "It's more important than you think."

28 October, 1881

I begin this journal in high, if somewhat desperate, hopes. I mean to make it a record of my deliverance. If it becomes something other than that, it shall have served as my epitaph. A bookmark . . . or a bookend.

The story can begin in no other spot than the coach making its slow and arduous process up the Alpine slope to the town of Davos, where I am to winter.

Riding in the rocking carriage beside me were my wife, Fanny, my stepson, Lloyd, and Woggin, a black-and-white Skye terrier as badly behaved as a dog can be. From the time we arrived in the Swiss canton of Graubünden, Fanny herself has not been well, her dark features made even darker by the altitude. At such a height as this, sixteen hundred metres above sea level, she wears a perpetual scowl and complains of headaches and shortness of breath. In her native California, she says she lived in arid lands hot as Hades and flat as a griddle.

As for Lloyd, he is as restless as any young man of fifteen might be at finding himself abruptly cut off from his school friends and familiar surroundings. Only Woggin remains unchanged, standing on his hind legs and hanging his head out the window, barking at any cow or sheep or goat that has the gall to stray from its paddock and come close to the road.

The road itself, smooth but narrowly cut, might just as well be called the Via Dolorosa of Switzerland, as most of those who travel it are, like me, invalids clinging to their last hope of a cure. Men and women, and even children, whose lungs, like mine, have haemorrhaged time and again, whose handkerchiefs bear the indelible scarlet stains of their disease, whose frames are racked by coughing fits and night sweats, and whose days are as numbered as the pages of any book. Many are the times when I have unexpectedly come upon a glimpse of myself in a mirror and seen not the bold adventurer I envision, but a walking skeleton, a pale stooping wraith with bulging brown eyes and drooping moustache. No Scottish laird here, no swashbuckling hero like those my imagination creates. I am a virtual ghost of a man, haunting the world while still alive.

I could not have come to a more suitable spot for ghosts.

The air is calm and altogether without odour—no scent of heather or bog-plant, no salty ocean mist—only a frigid stillness that makes the breath crackle and the skin grow numb. If I do not remember to keep my ears safely tucked under this fur hat (Fanny says it makes me look as if a muskrat has taken up residence on my head), I may lose them both to frostbite.

Nor, apart from the rumbling of the coach and Woggin's racket, is there any noise. It is as if all of life has been suspended. Even the crows do not caw, but silently stand vigil on fence posts and pine branches. (How is it that even these pines lend no aroma to the air?) A wolfskin hangs by its tail from a post in the pasture—as a warning, no doubt, to his pack.

But it is the light, the light, that most dampens the spirit. It is as bright and clear as the chimes at midnight—its putative healing powers rest upon just such qualities—and yet it is cold and unforgiving, white and plain, sapping the colour and vitality from all that it touches. Fanny, looking out at the snowy landscape from her window, said, 'It's as if they've stretched a shroud over everything.'

'They might just as well do it,' Lloyd snorted. 'No one comes here except to die.'

'Lloyd!' his mother remonstrated, and even he seemed to realize, though too late, the full import of his words. His cheeks, already rosy from the cold, reddened further.

'I didn't mean to say that—'

'Never mind what you meant to say,' Fanny cut him off. 'Louis, how much farther do you think it is?'

'Not much,' I replied. Indeed, I had just spotted, over Woggin's upright ears, the business district of the town—a congeries of small shops and cafés, with cobblestoned streets and crooked chimneys—through which the carriage was about to pass. Fanny's spirits seemed to momentarily lift; any opportunity to spend money and converse with strangers cheered her immensely. (Her American compatriots, I had noted, interested her the least, however; she treated them like lovers who had once spurned her.)

Though all of the establishments we passed displayed signs in German, and some in French, too, English is also everywhere present. There is, I have been told, a substantial and ever-changing community of English invalids to whom Davos has become a regular haven, and the town has accommodated itself to their tastes. One restaurant has hung a wooden placard advertising Cornish pasties over its door, and even I was buoyed by the sight of Scottish plaids adorning the window of a dry goods store. I marked those of the Campbell and the Mackenzie clans, clapped together in a way that their true owners would have most vigourously protested.

No sooner had we entered the town than we were back on the winding road to the Hotel Belvédère. Fanny, whose back was to the coachman, settled into her seat, Lloyd slumped down, eyes closed, and I alone kept watch. We were deep in the valley, the road rising between jagged peaks on all sides, when I first caught a glimpse of the great grey mausoleum that was the Belvédère. It was a brooding hulk, glowering down on the tiny town, and as we approached, I saw trails like trenches chopped through the snow, and on them several figures so thoroughly wrapped in beaver coats and woollen hats, gloves, and scarves and leather boots that one could hardly distinguish man from woman. All of them moved slowly, looking up from the ice and snow as we passed by.

As the coach rumbled under the porte cochère, Woggin fell silent—a notable event in itself—and Lloyd, awakening, stretched his limbs. An attendant lowered the steps and opened the door, and the dog shot out like a cannonball, making for the nearest elderberry bush. Fanny lifted her heavy skirt, took the porter's hand, and descended with a loud sigh. It had been a long journey, one of many, I reflected, that I had enforced upon the family as a result of my ill-health. From the South of France to San Francisco, Canada to Colorado, I had sought the one place where I might be healed of my affliction. Here, at the Hotel Belvédère, the most renowned pulmonologist of his day, Dr Carl Rüedi, had established his clinic, and so here I had come, armed as always with hope, but prepared as always for disappointment.

The bags were being taken down from the carriage when a young couple emerged from the great double doors—a handsome aristocrat with a frail but beautiful red-haired woman clinging to his arm. What it was that aroused Woggin's ire I do not know, but regardless, he made straight for the man's trousers, fixing his teeth in the cuff, growling and ripping at the fabric.

The porter attempted to intervene, aiming a swift kick at the dog, but that I would not abide. I shoved him aside, shouting, 'Woggin! Stop!'

The aristocrat, to give him his due, seemed more amused than irked, trying in vain to shake the dog off, and saying, 'There, boy! That's enough!' His companion, however, looked terrified.

With some luck, I was able to grab Woggin by the scruff of his neck, give him a rough shake, and shame him into submission.

'I am so sorry to give you such a scare,' Fanny was saying, stroking the young woman's arm, and I, too, joined in the apology.

The man looked at me rather fixedly—I am, I will admit, not the most ordinary-looking fellow—but then said, 'Are you not the author, Robert Louis Stevenson?'

'I am.'

'I had the pleasure of hearing you speak at a Crystal Palace exhibition. You made an eloquent appeal for keeping the gas lamps in London.' Removing his leather glove and extending his hand, he said, 'Allow me—I am Randolph Desmond, and this is Miss Constance Wooldridge.' Taking in our entire party and completing the introductions, he said, 'I see that you have just arrived.'

'That we have.'

'No doubt you wish to get settled; it's not an easy journey. But if you are not too tired from your travels, perhaps I can persuade you to join us tonight for dinner? I would consider it a great honour.'

Not having had time to gather our bags, much less our thoughts, I turned to Fanny for guidance. 'Yes, of course,' she said, her eyes quickly taking in the expensive clothes and refined appearance of the couple. 'We would be delighted, and we will, of course, replace your pants.'

'No one's ever promised me that before!' he said with a laugh.

As for Lloyd, he could not have fastened his gaze more intently upon one of the butterflies he delighted in pinning to a board than he did upon the alluring Miss Wooldridge.

'Where's Woggin got to?' I asked, but from the sound of a serving tray crashing to the lobby floor and a cry of alarm, I surmised that he had made our arrival known.

We were escorted to our rooms by the hotel manager, a fussy little man in a cropped jacket with red felt piping. 'If there is to be anything else that your needs require,' said Herr Hauptmann in his laboured English, 'then I am assured you shall not ask.'

'Indeed we won't,' Lloyd replied, sneaking a sly glance at his mother.

'Thank you very much,' Fanny said, tactfully declining to return it. 'We shall certainly let you know if we need anything.'

Clicking his heels and bowing stiffly from the waist, Herr Hauptmann retired, leaving us to inspect our accommodations unsupervised.

'Oh, it's very grand, don't you think?' Fanny swept from the generous parlour into one of the two adjoining bedrooms, then out and into the other. 'I think you and I should sleep in here, Louis.'

'So do I,' Lloyd said, tossing his bags through the open doorway of the room opposite. 'This one's got a view of the toboggan run.'

Woggin, nose to the floor and black tail twitching, raced from one end of the suite to the other, making sure no other dog, or— heaven forfend—a cat, was present, and determining where precisely to stake his own territorial claim.

The rooms were indeed well-appointed and commodious— plainly, we had been given one of the most choice compartments in the entire Hotel Belvédère—with wide windows opening onto towering evergreens and firs, and beyond them snow-capped mountain peaks. The sitting room boasted a marble fireplace with brass andirons, surmounted by porcelain vases painted in a floral motif; between them on the mantelpiece stood a wooden cuckoo clock, ornately carved and ticking quietly.

What I did not see, however, was a place to put a proper desk. There was a small, round table where Fanny might sit and write her correspondence, but nowhere that I could tuck myself away undisturbed. I do not like to be observed while writing any more than I wish to be distracted by anything of great beauty or distinction. John Keats said his ideal was to seat himself facing a white-washed wall and nothing more, and I do see his point—for the mind to paint its own extravagant pictures, the canvas before it has to be blank.

Fanny, intuiting my thoughts as she so often did, stopped and said, 'But where will you work?' And receiving no answer, said, 'We shall have to take an additional room.'

Aware of the bill we would be accumulating even now, and dreading the prospect of appealing yet again to my father for funds, I said, 'Surely, I will be able to find some secluded spot out of the way of the other guests.'

'Nonsense. I will take it up with Herr Hauptmann. There must be something available.'

'But the cost of another room,' I began, as Fanny brushed the objection aside.

'Leave it to me, Louis,' she said, and so I resolved to do just that. When practical matters have to be addressed, plans made and battles won, a man can have no greater ally than a wife such as Fanny. A born Yankee, brash and opinionated, with a dash of Indian blood in her veins, she is not someone easily put off. One night, when I was on the way to his London club with Henry James, he grudgingly admitted to me that if he had ever been of a mind to marry, he'd have wished for just such a lioness of his own.

'But you recognize, of course, that they can't be tamed.'

'I do,' he replied, feigning great regret, 'and thus I am fated to remain a melancholy bachelor.'

A bachelor, yes, but melancholy, I think not. Some men, such as myself, are predisposed to marry—without Fanny, the buffetings of life could swamp my little coracle at any moment—but others, of equally strong inclination, are not. To my knowledge, no experiment has yet been devised to measure the happiness, or wisdom, of the opposing states.

'So who's ready for a snowball fight?' Lloyd asked, emerging from his room as he wrapped a long scarf—my best cashmere, I noted, given to me the previous Christmas by my mother—around his throat. But only Woggin took him up on the offer, racing to the door in expectation of going out and, with any luck, finishing off that gentleman's trouser hem.

TOPANGA CANYON— CALIFORNIA

Present Day

Dusk was falling by the time Rafe finished checking for any other traps, assessing the drought damage to the native flora, and taking measurements at the lake—water level, purity, signs of life. That last item was increasingly rare. Although it was hard to believe, locals told him that the lake had once been stocked with bass; personally, he had never seen one there. Frogs, turtles, even a deadly cottonmouth or two, but no fish. A short pier, maybe fifteen feet long, that had once stood above the shore and allowed fishermen to dangle their lines over the railing was now rickety and abandoned. An old rowboat lay upside down on the dry, cracked soil beneath it.

The fire road down the east side of the mountain gave the jeep another workout, rattling the chassis and coating the windshield with so much dust even the wipers choked. A couple of the scratches on Rafe's legs were going to need a swab of antiseptic and a dab of something cool and soothing; poison sumac was as common as ants around here.

Once the fire road debouched onto the main thoroughfare of Topanga, he took a right and was driving toward the tiny town center when a horde of motorcycles, like a swarm of hornets, zipped and zoomed around both sides of his jeep. The riders wore blue denim jackets—Rafe wondered if a motorcycle gang was allowed to call itself a gang if they didn't—emblazoned with a patch that showed the logo of a floating ghost above the name Spiritz. Even the bikers who frequented Topanga had to have a metaphysical spin.

But then, that was what kept Topanga Topanga. It had always had a reputation as a haven for hippies and weirdos, oddballs and outcasts, rock 'n' rollers and stoners. The residents still played it up, since what else did they have to offer the tourist trade other than the natural beauty—now threatened by the persistent lack of rain—surrounding them?

The town center was no more than a couple of dozen storefronts— a Mexican restaurant and bar called La Raza, where the Spiritz had already parked their bikes helter-skelter; a general store called, in typical canyon fashion, the Genuine Store; a gas station with one pump; a hardware store, a vegan café, and a real estate outpost that Rafe had never known to be open. When he got close to the Cornucopia, with its hand-painted wooden sign showing a horn of plenty stuffed with grapes and flowers and berries, he slowed down, waited for a semi to rumble past on the opposite side of the two-lane highway, then crossed over and parked between the store and the rented trailer he lived in out back. A three-legged mutt named Trip—short for Tripod—scooted over to greet him.

"Hello, boy," Rafe said, extending a hand, which the dog inspected for some sign of a treat before settling for a pat on the head. "How was your day?"

Ever since he was a boy, Rafe had talked to animals—his little sister, Lucy, had called him Dr. Dolittle after seeing the movie of the same name.

"Trip had a good day," he heard from around the corner of the store. "He actually caught a squirrel."

Miranda. He found her, unsurprisingly, behind an easel, painting a watercolor of the sunset. The sky had turned a deep, almost purple, blue in preparation for going black altogether. Nights in the canyon were nothing like nights in Los Angeles, where the ambient glow of the city lights kept everything crepuscular until dawn. Here, the dark meant something.

She was wearing green flip-flops and a vintage dress, long and flowery and faded, with her long blond hair tied sloppily in a knot on top of her head.

"You know how they say even a stopped clock is right twice a day?" she said, her eyes still appraising the picture. "Well, even a three-legged dog can catch a squirrel once in a while."

The painting was good. Hers always were. Rafe sometimes wondered why she wasn't working in the city, displaying her pictures at some fancy gallery, instead of burying herself out here in the boonies. And, as usual, he found himself wondering what to say to her next.

"That's good," he finally came up with, nodding at the painting.

"You think so?"

"I do."

"Then you can have it. I don't think I can sell it, anyway. It doesn't have a unicorn in it," she said, laughing. The walls of the Cornucopia were covered with her original artwork, but the only ones that sold, she said, were the New Agey ones of fantastical beasts and rainbows and maidens. "You can take it off the easel when it's dry. Give it an hour or so."

Finally turning toward him and glancing at his bare legs, she said, "What happened to you? You fall in the briar patch?"

Embarrassed, Rafe said, "A job hazard." He always felt vaguely embarrassed around Miranda.

"Come on into the store. I've got something for that. All natural."

She padded across what had once been the lawn, her sandals flapping, then through the screen door, with Trip hopping up the steps behind her.

Inside, the store was crammed with shelves displaying everything from crystals to incense sticks, handmade jewelry to homemade jam, while the walls were covered—every inch—with Miranda's paintings, some of them ornately framed and hung, others just sheets of paper haphazardly thumbtacked to posts and door frames. Slipping behind the counter with its antique cash register, she picked up a little round bottle of something called All Organic Soothe It. She unscrewed the lid and held it under his nose; it smelled like fresh lemons.

"Smells good, doesn't it?"

"It does."

"It feels even better." And before he knew it, she had come around the counter and knelt in front of him, slathering lotion up and down, from his knees to the top of his hiking boots. Rafe felt his whole body go on alert, but this was so Miranda. She did everything on impulse, and half the time seemed unconscious of, or oblivious to, the effect it might have on other people. He really didn't think she was trying to flick his switch; she was just taking care of a problem.

"Would there be any way," she said, "you could pay your rent a little early this month? With the drought and all, not so many tourists are coming to the canyon."

"Sure."

His legs were tingling—and not just from the unguent—when the wind chime hanging near the door tinkled and Miranda's boyfriend, Laszlo, slouched in. A look crossed his face that suggested he wasn't pleased to find Miranda rubbing lotion into Rafe's calves, but he was too cool to say anything about it.

"I'm hungry," he said instead.

"It's too hot to cook."

"Want to go to La Raza?"

They were talking like Rafe wasn't even there, which he wished he wasn't.

"The Spiritz are there," Laszlo added.

"So what?"

"Just thought you'd want to know in advance."

"Good. Now I know. Maybe I'll cook after all."

She straightened and slapped the bottle of Soothe It into Rafe's hand.

"What do I owe you?" he asked.

"It's on the house."

"The hell it is," Laszlo said, snatching the bottle away and looking for a price tag. "How much is this, Miranda?"

"I said it was on the house."

He went behind the counter, found another bottle, and read the price off it. "It's six bucks."

"I'll add it to the rent check," Rafe said, eager to get out from between them.

Laszlo tossed him the bottle, a little harder than was warranted, and Rafe slipped out of the store, Miranda's dog hobbling after him. Even Trip could tell a squabble was brewing.

Opening the door to his trailer, which had been baking in the hot sun all day, was like opening the door of an oven. He stepped back as a gust of hot air washed over him. He'd have to give it a few minutes before it became habitable. Trip plopped on the dirt at his feet.

The lights went on in the apartment above the Cornucopia, where Miranda and Laszlo lived, and he could hear a few more words about the dinner plan before their air conditioner kicked on with a roar. He stood in the pitch dark, smelling of lemons, looking up at their windows until Laszlo appeared in silhouette and yanked the blind down.

28 October, 1881—Midnight

The Belvédère's dining room was, despite the best efforts of several chandeliers and wall sconces, a gloomy affair. Most of the tables were already occupied, the invalids bent low over their soup bowls, their companions keeping a close eye on their progress. At every elbow stood a tall glass, drained or not, of milk. Goat's milk, it was flavoured with honey and salt, and served as an essential part of Dr Rüedi's cure.

From the far end of the room, Randolph Desmond, in an immaculately cut suit, stood and waved a napkin.

As we made our way to his table, I could feel all eyes upon us. In places such as this—close and hermetic worlds where stimulation is so hard to come by—any new and novel element is a welcome intrusion. Our party made for more speculation than usual: Fanny rustling along in her full skirts, Lloyd sauntering behind with a mask of insouciance meant to conceal his discomfort, while I brought up the rear, looking, as Henley had once joked, like a scarecrow who'd escaped a field somewhere. Woggin, fortunately, had been left to his own devices with a bag of soup bones sent up to the room by the obliging Herr Hauptmann.

Desmond had already ordered escargots for everyone, and instructed the waiter to fill our glasses from the bottle of rich, dark Valtellina wine. Even Lloyd's glass was filled, and his mother, not wishing to embarrass him, let it pass. Miss Wooldridge alone did not imbibe; which I took to be an indication of the restricted diet she might be obliged to follow by the ruling deity of the place. When I asked if Dr Rüedi was anywhere to be found in the dining room, Desmond scoffed and said, 'He's not a man for pleasantries or social occasions. You'll find that out soon enough. Do you see him tomorrow?'

'Yes, I've an appointment first thing in the morning.'

'It won't be first thing for the good doctor. He'll have been up for hours. Rumour has it that the man never sleeps.'

'And what else', Fanny asked, 'does rumour report?'

Desmond, refilling the glasses and gesturing to the waiter to bring another bottle, said, 'That he keeps a menagerie of wild beasts in the cellars, where he performs secret experiments. On especially still nights, and if the wind is right, they say you can hear the howling.'

'Louis,' Fanny said, 'it sounds like there might be something worthy of a story there. The shilling shocker you've been searching for.'

'Not to mention', he added, 'he keeps lunatics in the attic, bound in chains.'

'Ah, so he is our own Mr Rochester?'

Desmond appeared puzzled, and Fanny quickly elucidated for him. 'In the book "Jane Eyre." By Charlotte Brontë. Rochester keeps his mad wife under lock and key.'

'Ah yes, of course. I do not read as much as I should.'

'I do give him books,' Miss Wooldridge put in, 'but I generally spot them, weeks later, gathering dust under a whiskey decanter on his sideboard.'

'Where they are much appreciated,' he said, patting the back of her hand.

Even upon closer inspection, whatever ailed Miss Wooldridge was not immediately apparent. She was fair and thin, but had no cough nor other respiratory impediment that I could detect. Still, there was something unwell about her—a downcast look in her eye, a tendency to lay a protective hand across her abdomen, a nervous disposition. Although I knew the clinic was renowned for its treatment of consumptives, she did not strike me as one. No, she had been escorted here by Randolph Desmond—who appeared to be in the perfect bloom of health—for some other remedy.

Even then, I could hazard a guess.

Out of courtesy, Desmond never asked after my own reasons for coming to the clinic, but then, the cause of that was not obscure. One look at my gaunt cheeks or fallen shoulders, I knew, would suffice. Dinner passed pleasantly, with several more courses—including veal with mushrooms and cream, served, like everything in Switzerland, on a heaping bed of rösti—and I know that Fanny was won over by Desmond's determined inclusion of her son. 'Have you ever tobogganned?' Desmond asked, and when Lloyd said he had certainly been on a hurley, Desmond replied, 'A hurley is to a toboggan as a mule is to a thoroughbred. Tomorrow I'll prove it to you.'

'Will you be coming, too?' Lloyd eagerly inquired of Miss Wooldridge, the wine having gone to his head, but she smiled and said, 'We shall have to see what Dr Rüedi says.'

I had the impression that Dr Rüedi was the oracle to be consulted, by one and all, on every decision, however trivial. We were the subjects, I surmised, in a kingdom of his invention, or, perhaps more to the point, unsuspecting prisoners of his own bastille.

29 October, 1881

'Fill your lungs as deeply as you can,' Dr Rüedi said, laying the end of the auscultation device, called by its practitioners a stethoscope, to the hollow of my bare chest, 'and hold it in.'

He bent his head low, and I could not help but be reminded, by the thick wave of pommaded brown hair that crowned it, of a coxcomb. There was something of the rooster in his demeanour, too—head held haughtily high and a strut to his walk. His every gesture was quick and certain, his hands darting from instrument to instrument, bottle to bottle, making tiny notes in a concise script in a journal half the size of any that I might employ. All in all, I found his attitude to be as cold as the end of the stethoscope, a revelation that was perversely comforting; surely, a man as remote and charmless as this must be very good indeed at his profession, or else he would long since have had to find some other sort of employment. Of bedside manner, he had none.

He listened now for fully a minute, until, no longer able to hold my breath, I exhaled in a gust—the exhalation followed by a racking cough that necessitated a handkerchief to the mouth to catch any droplets of blood or phlegm that might have accompanied it.

'Let me see that,' the doctor said, as soon as I had finished wiping my lips, and then, like some ancient priest seeking augury in the entrails of an eviscerated bird, raised a magnifying glass to study the cloth more closely.

'A minor emission'—was his verdict—'but how often does this occur?'

'Last night, three or four times.'

'That is to be expected. You are going to need several weeks simply to acclimate yourself to the mountain air.'

Several weeks. There was not only the cost to be dealt with, but the prospect of many more nights like the one that I had just endured. To spare Fanny the worst of it, I had retired to the sitting room, where, wrapped in two shawls and a woollen blanket, I had huddled in an armchair with a spittoon between my slippered feet and Woggin, ever the faithful companion, lying on the cold hearth, head atop his paws and sleepy eyes fixed on me.

'And how do you like it here, Woggin?' I had asked. 'Were the soup bones to your liking?' Though they have not the capacity to reply, I refuse to believe that our pets have no comprehension.

'And what was it about Mr Desmond that you took such exception to? You know that we are going to have to buy him a new pair of pants now.'

Woggin looked untroubled, his tail giving one tired thump.

'I should find a way to make you work off the debt.'

His ears pricked up, as if at the injustice, and then his head went up, too, on alert to something I had not heard. Bounding off the hearth, he ran to the window and stood up, his front paws on the sill, staring out at the night.

'What is it?' I asked, getting up from the chair and, swaddled in my blanket, stepping close to the glass.

Woggin was vibrating like a tuning fork that had just been struck, and though I placed a hand on the back of his head to calm him, he seemed not even to notice.

I leaned close to the glass, but because of the glow from the gas lamp in the room, I could see little beyond my own reflection. I extinguished the light, and returning to the window, I could see a salt lick, like a silver anvil, sitting squarely in the middle of a snowy field. The ground around it had been trampled down to the dirt by the hoofs and paws of a thousand wilderness creatures. Beyond the field, a thick forest of green-needled trees marched, like Great Birnam Wood upon the high hill of Dunsinane, towards the back of the hotel.

From that thicket, I heard a lone cry, long and low and melodious. Woggin growled.

The wolf cry came again, this time echoed by a second from some other and less distant quarter. Then a third.

Woggin barked, and I hastened to quiet him, lest he wake up Fanny and Lloyd, or some other recuperating guest of the clinic.

But Woggin could scarcely be contained, his short tail stiff and shaking as the howls came closer. There is something in the cry of a wolf at night, its mournful cadence and hungry undertone, that awakens in the soul of man an atavistic memory . . . and fear. One can barely hear their cry without feeling a corresponding chill and a desire to kindle a blazing fire, or arm oneself with club or rock or rifle. What did it inspire, I wondered, in Woggin? The will to do battle, to protect his master at all costs . . . or to join forces and run free with a savage and ungoverned pack?

Slinking close to the ground, a grey wolf emerged from the cover of the trees, its powerful shoulders hunched, its long and narrow snout—narrower than those of the wolves I had commonly seen on the North American continent—sniffing at the ground. On either side behind it, two black wolves crept out, too, for all the world like hench-men guarding their lord and master. Their ears were pricked up, their heads turning back and forth to survey the open ground for any threat, or quarry. The grey wolf approached the salt lick and lapped at it, while its companions kept watch. When it was done, they took their turn. But just as I expected them to retreat again into the woods, their sovereign, Lord Grey, raised his eyes to the window and stared, with the intensity of a judge who has donned the black cap of condemna-tion. For several seconds, our mutual gaze remained unwavering, and I felt a form of communication I had never experienced before with any other creature, not even with Woggin. Whatever the message might have been was unclear as yet, but I had no doubt some link had been forged. Before I could think of what next to do, the wolves suddenly turned their attention in one direction, as if responding to a call only they and Woggin, who whined piteously, could hear, and trotted around the corner of the hotel, out of my sight.

The night was silent once more.

Woggin dropped his paws to the floor and, much subdued, resumed his vigil at the hearth. What had the wolves heard and to what had they responded? I thought perhaps Dr Rüedi would have the answer, but when I mentioned the nocturnal visitors to him now, he did not look up from the observations he was jotting in his notebook. 'The Alpine wolf has been exterminated in Switzerland.'

'Not from what I saw.'

'It is possible that a few have miraculously survived the orga-nized slaughter.' It was plain where his sympathies lay.

'Three at least.'

'You have nothing to fear from them, regardless. They hunt only at night.'

'These were not hunting. They seemed to have been summoned.'

Snapping the notebook shut, as if to close this irrelevant topic, he plucked the pince-nez from his face and said, 'While you are here at the clinic, you will observe a daily regimen, to which I will admit no departure.'

As I am not a man fond of rules and regulations—what writer, or artist, of any sort is?—my natural inclination was to bridle, but as I pulled on my shirt, I stifled it.

'Your lungs are much damaged—the lower left lobe in particular—and your pulmonary capacity is, as a result, severely diminished.'

Nothing unexpected there.

'First, you will embark upon a strictly administered diet, accompanied by a series of treatments designed to clear away the malady. Once that is done, we shall undertake the necessary procedures to reconstruct your constitution along more salubrious lines.'

'Of what are these treatments and procedures to consist?'

Shaking his head, he said, 'I know that you are a literary man, Mr Stevenson—I have even gone so far as to read a number of your stories in preparation for your convalescence here—and I realize that you have made something of a name for yourself in the greater world beyond these mountains.'

Although his words should have been a compliment, he uttered them in a tone that suggested nothing of the sort—it was as if I had committed an indiscretion he was willing to overlook, for now.

'As such, you are no doubt accustomed to asking questions and living by your own lights, but here that is not encouraged. Indeed, it is forbidden. I cannot cure what I cannot control.'

'I seldom cede authority over myself.' Though I could imagine, even as I spoke, Fanny's rejoinder if she had overheard that.

'Yet you will, and you must. Else, there is no purpose to your stay here.'

In the uneasy pause that followed, the deal was struck. I was to bend to his will, and he was to heal my ravaged body.

Was this a great bargain, I wondered as I left the examination, or had I made a deal with the devil?

TOPANGA CANYON—
CALIFORNIA

Present Day

Rafe awoke to the buzzing of a bee around his nose. He waved it off, then opened his eyes to another cloudless blue sky. Rain was only a distant memory.

On nights as hot as the last, he didn't even bother to sleep in the trailer. He'd toss his sleeping bag up top and lie under the moon and stars in nothing but boxer shorts and a Nirvana T-shirt. Truth be told, he liked it better that way. He'd never been fond of confined spaces—the memory of too many foster homes and state facilities, with locked doors and fluorescent lights and communal showers that stank of Lysol, haunted him—and given any choice, he'd always opt for freedom and the open air.

Climbing down, he went inside to take a shower, in a stall so tiny he had to keep his elbows cocked into his sides; make some strong black coffee; and put on a fresh uniform of khaki shorts and short-sleeved shirt, along with all the other gear—canteen, flashlight, compass, sunblock, epinephrine syringe. Normally, he carried a flare gun, in case he had to signal a helicopter where to pick up an injured hiker, but in this kind of drought, he'd never risk shooting off a flare and starting a fire.

The night before, he'd waited until he was sure Miranda and Laszlo were eating in—he could hear the wok sizzling—before ambling across the road to La Raza. It wasn't that the place was especially good. It was simply there. And since the Spiritz were occupying the bar, harassing the cute bartender and making a lot of noise, Rafe went outside to the wooden picnic tables, where strings of lights shaped like bright red chili peppers dangled over the patio. Before he could order, Amalia, the waitress, said, "Two cheese burritos, rice and black beans, and a Dos Equis. I get anything wrong?"

"Yes."

She looked surprised.

"I'll start with a side of guacamole."

"Is that for your legs?" she asked, glancing down at all the scratches and cuts.

"That's what the Dos Equis is for. Make it two, in fact."

Only a couple of other tables were occupied. At one, a father with a gray ponytail and a tie-dyed shirt that said Keep on Truckin' was sitting with a kid who looked a lot like him, only thirty years younger. Rafe wanted to tell the old man that *Keep on truckin'* was, to the best of his knowledge, just an expression, and that it was okay to stop now. At a table on the other side, a family of Midwestern tourists—blond, sunburned, with a guidebook and a map spread out between their plates—were sneaking furtive glances all around, no doubt taking in the local color. It was nice to see a map, Rafe thought; as part of his training, he'd had to learn to read them carefully and thoroughly, but who really used them anymore, when you could just pull out your cell phone and ask Google to figure out where you were and how to get to the next stop? He wondered if the sightseers had had a chance to visit the Cornucopia and buy one of Miranda's paintings—which reminded him that he had forgotten to retrieve the watercolor she'd left for him on the easel.

He'd get it on the way back.

What she saw in Laszlo eluded him. Sipping his beer and dipping his chips in the homemade guac, he mulled it over for the millionth time. Sure, the guy was sort of good-looking, in a vulpine way, and from what Rafe could gather, she'd picked him up at an ashram or something, where he'd convinced her that Topanga was the ticket to the alternative lifestyle. He must be a very good salesman.

"His ancestors once lived off the land in these canyons," she'd told Rafe.

"Too bad they didn't buy any."

"They were run off."

He didn't ask by whom; the whole story was probably phony. As far as Rafe could tell, that was the key: Miranda felt responsible for Laszlo the same way she felt responsible for Trip, a dog she'd found run over by the side of the road. People were forever abandoning their unwanted pets in the canyon, rationalizing that they'd go off and live a wild and natural life. What they led, as Rafe had seen over and over, was a short and terrified existence until a car, or the coyotes, got them.

The same coyotes whose habits and travels were the subject of his ongoing research.

Before he finished his meal, the couple he called Mr. and Mrs. Pothead slipped in. Both were in their late thirties and, despite the hot sun up in the canyon where they lived entirely off the grid, looked and moved like a pair of ghosts. They went toward the last table in back, as far from everyone else as possible, but as they passed Rafe, Mr. Pothead nodded his head and almost imperceptibly dropped a baggie onto the bench beside his thigh. Rafe knew perfectly well what it was—he stuck it in his pocket as unobtrusively as he could—and why he'd been given it. More than once, Rafe had passed by the little cannabis patch they were growing up in the hills, but he had never turned them in to anybody. Live and let live, he'd always believed—*live* being the operative word.

Not that he wasn't aware of nature's often bloody ways. Red in tooth and claw, as Tennyson, one of his childhood favorites, had put it. At most of the group homes where Rafe had been briefly parked, there'd been bookcases, usually stocked with moldering copies of other old classics—Kipling, Dickens, Conrad, Melville, Robert Louis Stevenson—donated when somebody died. No one but Rafe ever wanted to read them, but he did, voraciously. Others tried to escape incarceration by climbing walls and breaking windows, but he fled his sagging cot and metal footlocker on a sea of words. Even then, he knew that linoleum floors and concrete walls were no way to live.

This morning, he was heading off with his aerial antenna to do some triangulating on the coyotes' present positions. The animals were in constant motion, migrating wherever the food supply led, and digging their dens wherever the spirit moved them. The problem was, they kept bumping up against freeways and garbage receptacles, and had gradually lost more and more of their fear of humans. It used to be, coyotes would slink away at the first sight of a human. Then it got to the point where, if confronted by a hollering and rock-throwing human, they'd simply stand their ground and wait it out.

At what point would they decide to stop waiting?

Stepping out of the trailer, he was just climbing into his government-issue jeep—a hundred and ten thousand miles on it but still going—when a Volvo station wagon pulled in, pretty much blocking his exit. A customer, he thought—maybe Miranda would ring up an early sale today.

But instead, a girl—not more than twenty-one or twenty-two—got out in a uniform just like his, only with the wide-brimmed hat smartly positioned on her head. She waved like she knew him and walked over to the jeep.

"Hey, Rafe."

"Hey." Did he know her?

"We met last year, at the land management conference in Anaheim. Heidi Graff. I'm your shadow."

"You're my what?"

"Didn't you get the e-mail? I'm supposed to shadow you. I'm still in my training rotation."

Rafe was bad about that; he checked his e-mails only every few days, claiming to his superiors that Internet connections in Topanga were spotty.

"Today?" he said. "Now?"

"Uh-huh." Her eyes flicked to the passenger seat where he'd stashed the antenna. "Tracking? That's great. I've never done it. Be right back."

She grabbed a backpack—brand-new, with shiny leather straps—from her car, and after gently depositing the antenna in back, tossed her pack in after it, and buckled in up front.

Rafe, nonplussed, just sat there in the driver's seat.

"You forget something?" she asked.

"Nope."

She waited, then said, "Your seat belt?"

He buckled it.

"Good," she said, now looking straight ahead and tucking a wisp of light brown hair under the brim of her hat. "I'm excited."

He put the car in gear, and pulled it around her Volvo. This day had just taken a brutal turn for the worse.

"By the way," she said, glancing at his scratches, one of which had turned purple overnight, "what happened to your legs?"

29 October, 1881

'Please place your shoulders between these,' the nurse said. Lying back on the chaise longue, I allowed myself to be cradled between two bags of sand, which she expertly tucked around me. Plainly, they were meant to discourage any movement. As if that were not impediment enough, she then swaddled the rest of my body in a scratchy striped blanket, all the way down to the toes of the warm woollen socks that had also been prescribed by the good doctor. Finally, she plumped up a pillow shaped like a fat sausage and filled with buckwheat shells, and wedged it under my neck, so that my face was angled upward towards the bright sun. I quickly understood why, despite their failing health, so many of my fellow invalids had complexions the colour of burnished gold. We were baked like biscuits in the Alpine sun each day.

'I daresay you'll get used to it,' the recumbent man beside me observed. Turning my head carefully so as not to displace the neck pillow, and opening my eyes narrowly lest the sun blind me, I saw a long face with a lush brown beard flattened atop the hem of his own blanket.

'John Addington Symonds,' he said. But before I could make my own introduction, he added, 'Your arrival, Mr Stevenson, has been the talk of the Belvédère.'

'Good talk, I hope.'

'Talk. Up here, you'll discover, everything has to be turned over this way and that a dozen times in search of something titillating.'

'Ah, but there I must have fallen short.'

'You would be surprised what provides fodder for the dinner table conversations. You have a dog, yes?'

'Woggin.'

'The very same. Portrayed in various accounts as a vicious mastiff, the size of a lion, that has attacked, among others, Mr Desmond.'

I had to laugh.

Symonds smiled, though his lips were hidden by the bushy moustache that joined with his beard to conceal fully half his face.

'But I know you, too,' I said, 'or perhaps I should say I know your work. I have read, and thoroughly enjoyed, some of your essays on the Italian Renaissance, though I cannot claim any great acquaintance with the artworks you so intimately discuss.'

'Then that we will remedy,' he said. 'Every other week, I give a lecture in the grand salon on some topic or other. Last week it was Leonardo's inventive genius.'

'And this?'

'I have not yet decided, though I am leaning towards the poetic expressions of Michelangelo. Please come, and bring your wife, Fanny, and stepson, Lloyd.'

'You do know a good deal already, don't you?'

'As I suggested, gossip is the most valuable currency there is up here. You will soon be trading in it yourself.'

'I doubt I'll have time to glean much. I have a new book in hand, and I hope to spend my time working on it.'

'That, like everything up here, will largely depend upon Dr Rüedi. He is the unchallenged despot of this realm.'

'So he told me himself, in no uncertain terms, this morning. And in perfect English, I might add. Isn't he Swiss?'

'Yes, but he studied medicine for years in America. In the city of Philadelphia.'

'That would explain the faint whiff of an American accent I detected.'

'It would also explain his willingness to break with orthodoxy on such issues as care for the consumptive. He cares nothing for received wisdom. For better or for worse, he's a man who goes his own way.'

'As do I.'

'Which means you will either get along like a house afire—'

'Or wind up drawing pistols at dawn.'

Before we could utter another word, we were interrupted by a celestial visitor from on high—a snowball, perfectly round and aimed with precision, striking my chest and exploding like a lady's overloaded powder puff.

'A direct hit!' I heard Lloyd shout. 'A direct hit!'

'You are the best gunner in the fleet!' Desmond congratulated him.

They were standing at the top of the toboggan run, with Miss Wooldridge wrapped in a fur coat, its collar turned up around her porcelain cheeks, her hands buried in a matching muff.

'Ah, I see that, despite the canine imbroglio, you are on cordial terms with our Mr Desmond and his . . . ward,' Symonds said, with an emphasis on the last.

'Watch me go!' Lloyd shouted, turning his toboggan to face downhill. 'I'm the fastest one.'

'Beginner's luck,' Desmond chided.

'Is she really his ward?' I asked Symonds sotto voce.

'If, by that, you are asking if he takes care of her, yes. If you are asking by what means he is compensated for such services, you may draw your own conclusions.'

'Can we coax you into a run?' Desmond called out to me.

'By no means may you do that,' replied the nurse who had tucked me in. Hands on her hips, she had assumed her battle position. 'And if another snowball is thrown, I shall have no choice but to inform Dr Rüedi.'

'Oh no, not that!' Desmond cried, laughing. 'Anything but that!'

Lloyd had dragged his toboggan to the starting line, and though he appeared impatient for the contest to resume, his eyes were riveted to Miss Wooldridge.

'Shall we make a wager?' Desmond said to him.

'You bet!' Lloyd replied, using one of the common colloquial American expressions I found so charming. 'What'll it be?'

'What would you like?'

Even from the terrace, I could see Lloyd's cheeks flush red, as the words he wanted to say stuck somehow in his throat.

'Well?' Desmond said.

'If you win, I'll black your boots.'

'Fair enough. And if you do?'

'I get a kiss from Miss Wooldridge.'

Desmond laughed and looked to his companion. 'It appears you have been drawn into this unseemly wager, Constance. Do you consent to the terms?'

Taking it in good spirit, Miss Wooldridge said she would abide by its conditions.

And then the race was on. Each of them climbed onto his sled, and at the word Go! from Miss Wooldridge, they shoved off from the crest of the run and went hurtling down the hill. From my lounge chair, I could not see the whole journey—they were lost from sight after twenty or thirty yards—but when they returned, minutes later, a jubilant Lloyd dragged his toboggan behind him like Achilles taunting Troy with the body of Hector.

Desmond, feigning great shame at being beaten by a mere stripling, trudged behind him. 'I demand a rematch.'

'Not before I have had my winnings!' Lloyd cried, and in a fashion bolder than I would have credited him, dropped the rope of his sled and strode to where Miss Wooldridge stood.

Smiling shyly and proffering her cheek, she awaited the chaste peck of a love-struck schoolboy, but received instead two hands turning her shoulders so that her lips were in play, and an embrace as fumbling as it was ardent. Lloyd kissed her full on the mouth, and even Desmond looked shocked.

Miss Wooldridge put a hand to his chest and pushed him away, flustered.

And in Lloyd's cheeks, the colour rose again, but was it the heat of embarrassment or the flush of conquest?

'Lloyd!' I said. 'That's quite enough.'

But he looked as if he had not even heard me.

Miss Wooldridge rapidly quit the scene, marching up the steps of the hotel.

'"Gather the Rose of love, whilst yet is time,"' Symonds recited. 'Spenser.'

But I was not amused. Davos was a small world, and the Belvédère even smaller, and I did not want my stay there to be made any more uncomfortable than the medical procedures were bound to make it, anyway. Unless I could find some other means of occupying the boy's mind, however, I believed that it would be.

4 November, 1881

Herr Hauptmann stopped on the corkscrew stair long enough for the shaking to subside.

'It is quite safe,' he assured me, as I clung to the railing with both hands. 'But I shall not spare to have Yannick come to make it more stronger.'

'I would be grateful for that.'

'Aber natürlich. We would not want one of our most notorious guests to be an accident.'

Overlooking the unintentional slander of my good name, I continued up the winding iron stair until I found myself in a room that resembled nothing so much as a tree house I had enjoyed in my youth. It was tight and spare, with wide wooden planks for a floor, rafters that grazed the top of my head, a sloping roof, and the overwhelming, but pleasing, odour of old wood and varnish. Tucked as it was at the top of the clock tower, the room commanded a view, through a pair of small mullioned windows, of both the front of the hotel, with its snowy pathways and toboggan run, and the back, where I had glimpsed the wolves at the salt lick.

'We have taken the liberties of placing the desk and chair where your wife instructed.'

Leave it to Fanny to have found and furnished just the sort of study I would need in order to finish the book I was writing, a tale of buccaneers and buried treasure. The desk was already outfitted with paper and pen, oil lamp and blotter. She had even had them place a bookcase with several of my reference volumes within easy reach of my chair, to the seat of which, she had added a feather pillow. How they had managed to wrestle all these things up that precarious stairway eluded me, but I could well imagine Fanny overseeing the task and brooking no dissent.

'I will leave you to your labour,' Hauptmann said, bowing himself back to the staircase.

After a quick turn about the premises, I sat down at my chair, dipped pen in ink—she had even thought to sharpen the nib— and set to work. In almost no time at all, I was back on the high seas, transported there on the wings of imagination, and did not even remember stopping to light the lamp or replenish the ink-well. It has been a great and fortunate gift of mine, this ability to transcend my immediate surroundings and live among my own creations. Perhaps—no, <u>assuredly</u>—it is the method which I, like many another lad of frail constitution, has employed to leave the confines of his sickbed or hospital ward and travel the world. My mind was always carrying me off to exotic ports of call, to faraway lands where slave girls told stories to stay alive, where father-less boys stowed away on pirate ships, and wild creatures roamed jungle isles. Nestled in the arms of my nanny and protector, the much-beloved Alison Cunningham, I would look out over the chimney pots of Edinburgh, blue in the moonlight, and imagine myself instead basking in the hot sunlight of a tropical clime. At times Cummy, or so I called her, would ask me, 'And where are you now, Louis?' knowing that I had left the shelter of her rocking arms and gone somewhere that the cold and damp did not affect me, where my coughing had been quelled. Seldom could I put a name to the place.

The clock tower study was unusually well insulated and warm, not merely from the heat of the hotel below rising up, but because it had been meticulously built so as to ensure that the mechanism of the mighty clock remained dry and functioning. The hum of its many parts was a constant refrain, but rather than being an impediment to my work, it provided a soothing sound, steady as the waterfall in Rogie, or the distant susurration of the ocean waves that crash along the coast of the Isle of Erraid. The Merry Men is what the local inhabitants call the breakers, though merry they are not. More sailors have been sent to the bottom of the sea by their power and malevolence than by all the cannonballs e'er shot.

Bowls of barley soup, with hunks of fresh brown bread, found their way to the foot of the staircase, accompanied, of course, by a glass of cold milk from the Belvédère's own herd. Seldom would I even hear the footfall of the servant dispatched to leave the tray or recover it later, so deeply was I absorbed in the task before me. My essays and reviews and stories had begun to make my name, but fortune still lagged far behind, and though my father has never denied a request for assistance, I was loath to ask him for anything more than the regular stipend with which he has supplied me.

I asked Fanny for some idea of what additional cost this garret had come to, but she brushed the question aside.

'Don't bother your head with that, Louis. They are glad to do it.'

'The hotel? Or my family?'

'You have brought glory to both, and if you simply bend your thoughts to your book, you will bring even more. They shall all be well rewarded.'

From my perch, I could keep a God-like eye upon all the doings of the hotel. When standing before the rear window, I could observe the staff restocking the smokehouse and taking short respites from their toil, lighting a pipe or darning a skirt, walking in the thick woods that bordered the grounds, and even—on more than one occasion—when the shadows of the mountains grew long and the stars were just twinkling into sight, pursuing some more amorous sport. For all the gloom cast by the hotel's convalescents, there was, here among the servants and nurses, a spirit of life, unquenchable and impatient.

It was a spirit I envied. My condition had continued in precipitous decline, despite the most valiant efforts by Dr Rüedi and the sanitarium's staff. My diet was under constant adjustment, with certain drink and viands reduced or eliminated, and others increased. My temperature was taken every hour on the hour, but remained stubbornly high. And my breathing, never easy, had become more laboured and draining. Nights were the most trying.

On one night, when lying flat in bed had proved impossible, I had stealthily returned to my garret to work on the tale that had been taking shape in my mind, the seafaring adventure of a one-legged ship's cook. The figure was loosely modelled on my oldest and dearest friend, William Henley, who had lost his own leg to a cancer of the bone; he would be amused, or so I hoped, to have provided such inspiration.

But as I paused to replenish my pen, I happened to witness something that had all the earmarks of subterfuge—a trait sure to quicken the pulse of any writer. I heard voices at the back of the hotel, near the cellar stairs—voices that were muffled, meant to go unheard. And as they were speaking German, I would have been at a loss regardless. But then Yannick, the handyman who had bolstered the corkscrew stairs, and two other servants lumbered into view on snowshoes, lugging first one bundle, and then another, up the steps from the cellar. The bundles were large and plainly heavy, and it took at least two men to manage each one. They shifted the bundles onto waiting toboggans, where they were bound fast with ropes and then dragged around the west wing of the hotel. Once the sleds escaped my view, I crossed the tower and, standing beside the great whirring clock, rubbed the front window clean with my handkerchief—stained with old blood—and waited for them to reemerge around the corner of the wide verandah.

The three men tugged the loaded sleds to the embarkation point of the toboggan run. Fast and exhilarating during the daylight hours, the toboggan run posed an even more formidable challenge for anyone at night, and I could hardly believe they were planning to try it. In the valley far below, a single bright light shone at the top of the church steeple, as if to provide some beacon to navigate by. I was reminded, inevitably, of the many lighthouses my family had built to help guide sailors safely to port.

Yannick, a strong fellow built like an ox, directed the other two men onto the sleds, where each of them lifted one end of a bundle, and then settled it onto their laps once they had seated themselves. It was then that it became clear, as it should have done much sooner, that the sacks, wrapped as tight as mummies, contained bodies.

After the man in the first toboggan nodded his assent, Yannick bent low, and pushing the sled hard, sent it whistling down the run towards the village. Straightening, he went to the second sled, where he paused, rubbing his heavy jaw as if something had just come into his mind. Words were exchanged, and crouching down, Yannick tugged at the cloth until he was able to insert one of his paws and fish about inside. When he withdrew his hand, he held some items that glittered in the moonlight before he stuffed them into his pocket. The other man objected, but Yannick gave him a clout on the ear that knocked his fur hat off and shut his mouth, then dispatched the second sled with a hard shove to the man's back—so hard that he lost his own balance and rolled onto his side, cursing and spitting the snow from his lips.

When he got to his feet again and turned back towards the hotel, I stepped away from the window, not wishing to be seen. My suspicions were confirmed the next morning when, lingering over my breakfast longer than usual—'Louis, should you be drinking quite so much coffee?' Fanny inquired, before quitting the dining room—I noted the absence of two of the guests who had, of late, looked particularly unwell. One, an Italian dowager always adorned with an ornate silver crucifix and awash in eau de cologne, had already missed several meals; the other, a young Spaniard not much older than my stepson, had excused himself after a coughing fit so uncontrollable, he had fled the room in shame.

Both were gone now, their customary chairs empty, their napkins neatly folded and untouched, their milk glasses unfilled. Others, too, had surely noticed their absence, but nothing was said. It did not need to be. Invalids arrived at the Belvédère every day, some with one foot already planted in the grave, and even the renowned Dr Rüedi could not perform miracles. But how best to insulate the survivors from the stark reality that might well await them, too, if not by this clandestine means? Secretly, everyone knew what had occurred, though no one wished to dwell upon it. Had they, however, ever guessed the method of their fellows' disposal? Had any of them awakened in the dead of night to witness these silent sled rides—and wondered when their own turn might come to depart the mountain in like manner?

I had witnessed it; I had so wondered. Like weeds persistently o'ertaking a garden, these thoughts would never again be completely extirpated from my mind.

TOPANGA CANYON—
CALIFORNIA

Present Day

For the first ten or fifteen minutes of the ride, Rafe kept his thoughts to himself, while Heidi burbled on about everything she planned to do for the environment, not just in California, but worldwide. It sounded like she was going to solve the problem of global warming single-handedly.

"According to a study by the Woods Hole Oceanographic Institute, the melting of the polar ice caps is going to raise the sea level as much as two feet in some places," she declared. "Say good-bye to Melanesia."

Rafe wasn't entirely sure where that was. Was it American Samoa and places like that?

"And the warming temperatures are going to cause a mass die-off of many different fishes. Just look at what's happened right here to the delta smelt."

Because of the rising temperatures of the Sacramento River water, the smelt had all but gone extinct in California. For Rafe, that was an issue that struck closer to home, and she was dead right about it.

The Chinook salmon were hanging on by a thread, too. They needed to reach their traditional spawning grounds, the cooler waters of the McCloud River and other Sacramento tributaries to the north, but the construction of the Shasta Dam and hydropower plant, not to mention the concrete buttresses of the smaller Keswick Dam, had made it impossible. Now the fish made their redds, or nests, in the shallow gravel beds downstream, and then hovered listlessly there until they—and later, their emerging fry—died. Rafe had seen it himself on a solitary trek he had taken. Sitting on the banks, he'd watched the bodies of the dead fish floating by, belly up, and wondered just how many bears were going to go hungry up north now, and what other repercussions, less obvious but just as destructive, would follow. The natural world was a tightly integrated web, and every time humans messed with it, there were as many unintended consequences as there were intentional. But that was a lesson nobody ever seemed to learn.

Maybe it was a good thing that eager young people like Heidi here were ready to take up the challenge. Although he wasn't really that much older than she was, he was already becoming way too cynical.

"I've been reading your field reports," she said, "and they're really interesting. You've got three coyotes now wearing radio collars?"

"Two."

"Oh, I thought I read three."

"We lost one." He didn't tell her that he'd found it peppered with buckshot.

"Okay, two now. And they're moving south-southeast?"

"Like everything else," he said, taking the turnoff to the fire road. A rusty chain with a padlock stretched across the entrance. "Can you get that?" he said, fishing the key from the Velcro strip on the sun visor and handing it to her.

Eager to take on any task, Heidi leaped out of the jeep, removed the chain, and waited for Rafe to drive a few yards past it. Locking up again, she climbed into the jeep, stuck the key back where it belonged, and looked at him as if expecting a letter grade.

"Good work," he said, and she all but bounced in her seat.

Just before they reached the top of the ridge, he pulled over, noting that there was no sign today of Seth and Alfie—not that they might not be skulking somewhere else in the canyon, killing or capturing anything they could get their hands on. It might be a good idea, he thought, to say something about them to Heidi. Forewarned is forearmed.

"Just in case we come across a couple of bumpkins," he began, then gave her a thumbnail sketch of each. "They're bad news, all around."

"You think they're really dangerous?"

"To wildlife, no question. To us? Let's just say I hope we never find out." After retrieving the antenna and receiver from the backseat, he took a GPS monitor out of the glove compartment and handed it to Heidi, then led her toward the crest of the trail. From their vantage point, the mountains rolled around on three sides, spliced by deep, dark ravines. To the west, the hazy blue of the Pacific Ocean merged seamlessly into the blue of the summer sky.

"You know how this works?" he asked.

"The coyote collars transmit an intermittent signal?"

"Right. And once we pick one up, we plot it along a line on our GPS."

"And then we track it?"

"I wish it were that easy." He held the antenna aloft, feeling, as he always did, like a desperate farmer holding a divining rod. "One signal gives us only one line, and the animal could be anywhere on it."

"Oh, so I get it—we need two."

"Three. We need to triangulate if we expect to get a fixed position on their movements."

"How do we do that?"

"By moving around a lot ourselves, to widely separated locations, and taking a reading each time."

The receiver he had clipped to his belt beeped, and a green light flashed on and off.

"Contact," he said. "Check the GPS. You see that pulsating spot?"

"I do."

"Hit 'Record Coordinates.'"

She did.

"Now we just have to do it two more times and we'll know where she is."

"How do you know it's a she?"

"Every signal has its own frequency, and the monitor recognizes them. That one's from Frida."

"They have names?"

"Sure. She's the alpha female of the pack—the mom—and Diego is the alpha male."

"Wait—like Diego Rivera and Frida Kahlo?"

"Don't tell." In the reception area of one of the state foster facilities, there'd been a big Diego Rivera mural that had captivated him as a boy, and he'd been a big fan of both artists ever since. In some way he could not have expressed, he felt even then that they were his people.

Rafe led the way down the hillside, keeping an eye out for rattlesnakes, which made it a practice to lie, coiled in the sun, beside the trail. He didn't want to have to explain losing a trainee to his superiors at the land management offices.

When they arrived at the lake, nothing much had changed since his encounter with the trapped bobcat, though the water level might have dropped another inch. The pier was still rotting, the rowboat was still upside down, the mountain bike was still baking on the new shoreline, and that old trunk, the one he'd noticed before, was still poking its nose out of the brackish pool.

"It stinks here," Heidi said, holding her nose.

"That'll happen when it never rains."

From force of habit, Rafe checked the bush where the trap had been hidden, but nothing was there, not even a desiccated jerky strip. Nothing edible lasted long in the wilderness.

"What's that out there?" he heard Heidi call.

"Out where?"

"In the lake. It looks like a big old trunk or something."

"It is."

"Don't you think we ought to check it out?"

"Probably."

"People are such slobs. It's like they've never heard the word *pollution.*"

She was right. He'd planned on retrieving it sometime. But just now something even more interesting had claimed his attention.

Paw prints. Recent ones.

Taking off his sunglasses and crouching down for a better look, he could tell right away that they didn't belong to a bobcat. Or any cat at all. The tracks were canine. Could they belong to a dog who'd been abandoned in the canyon, like Tripod?

On closer inspection, it didn't look that way to him. Dog prints showed more widely splayed toes than these, and a more oval than oblong shape. The nails, too, usually registered as bigger and blunter than these.

Heidi came up behind him and bent down. "Are they coyote tracks? Is it Frida?"

"Could be Diego," Rafe said, still puzzling over them. "But coyotes are pretty damn aerodynamic—they have tight toes that register deeper than the palm pad. It's because they trot along very purposefully, very alert." It was one of the many things that he admired about his charges—they knew exactly what they were doing at all times, and didn't get distracted or wander aimlessly the way that domestic dogs did. And unlike dogs, their nails were small and sharp.

These prints, however, were wider than most coyotes would leave. Most coyotes were around four feet long and weighed less than sixty pounds; even Diego, the leader of the pack, was no more than five feet long. This animal, judging from the deep impression and spacing of the prints, was bigger than that. And when Rafe compared the front prints to their mates, he noted another discrepancy.

Standing up, he put his hiking boot next to a rear print, and then, putting his own shoes toe to heel, he walked several steps.

"Are you checking to see if he was too drunk to walk a straight line?"

"Nope. I'm gauging its size, and this fella is easily close to six feet long if you throw in some tail." Rafe could hardly believe its size, but there were the tracks to prove it.

"That's big?"

"Too big. Bigger than any of the coyotes I've been studying."

"So it's an interloper?"

"Maybe."

"What else could it be?"

He was reluctant even to say it, since they had been ruthlessly hunted to extinction in all of Southern California. All he needed now was for this kid to go running back to the Land Management office, shouting that the descendants had somehow made their way down to Topanga Canyon. But the last time he'd seen prints like these had been in the Blue Mountains of southeastern Washington.

And they'd belonged to a wolf.

22 November, 1881

'The drawing that you are passing around amongst yourselves', Symonds said from the lectern in the grand salon of the Belvédère, 'is, as you will surely recognize, a rendering of "The Rape of Ganymede".'

The picture, framed, was circulating from hand to hand among the members of the audience. Randolph Desmond and Constance Wooldridge were bending their heads over it in the row ahead. I had made sure to keep our ardent swain Lloyd a suitable distance from his inamorata.

'And this,' an elderly French gentleman asked, 'it is the original?' And Symonds scoffed.

'Would that it were. The original is held by the papal curia. The eagle in the picture is, of course, Zeus transformed, the better to abduct Ganymede, the most beautiful of all mortals. Zeus wanted the boy to serve him on Mount Olympus.'

The picture had made its way to Fanny on my left, and we marvelled at its exquisite detail and line and shading. Lloyd, making no secret of his boredom, hardly bothered to glance at it.

'The picture, one of four, was a gift—what has been aptly called a "presentation drawing"—to a young Italian nobleman. Unlike mere sketches or studies, these drawings were completed works meant as gifts. In this case, it was for Tommaso dei Cavalieri, whom Michelangelo believed to be the masculine ideal of beauty. The artist called him "the light of our century, paragon of all the world".'

Fanny, nudging me gently, whispered, 'That's one way of putting it.'

'But these drawings were not his only gift to the handsome young aristocrat. Although it is seldom remarked upon, Michelangelo was more than a great artist with chisel and brush—he was also a poet of the first water.'

At this, Symonds raised his baleful dark eyes to the chandelier glowing overhead, and recited several stanzas in Italian. My understanding being rudimentary at best, I was able to glean only that the poet was expressing a wish to be a worm—a silkworm—and thereby make a garment gorgeous enough to clothe the young man's supple limbs.

'Can you make it out?' Fanny said.

'A bit,' I replied, 'though I will tell you later, when young ears are not so close.'

'No need. You just answered my question.'

'Of the three hundred poems Michelangelo penned in his lifetime, at least thirty were dedicated or addressed to Cavalieri. Most were sonnets, though occasionally he would compose a madrigal or quatrain, all of which were later altered by Michelangelo's grandnephew, who elected to publish them in 1623. Before doing so, he took the unconscionable liberty of changing all the pronouns so that the verses would appear to have been written to a woman.'

He stopped to let that sink in. Although it was no secret in society that Symonds was a Uranian himself, I was nonetheless surprised that he should express his indignation so publicly. Perhaps, I surmised, it had something to do with the venue—a remote mountain clinic, inhabited chiefly by the dead or dying. Mortality has a way of lending perspective, I have found.

'I am now changing those pronouns back', he declared, 'in an English translation. They will be incorporated into the biography of Michelangelo that I am writing.'

The lecture continued for well over an hour—Symonds was among the most eloquent extemporaneous speakers I had ever heard—but all the while, I felt my strength ebbing. The salon was warmer than usual, and though I put my shortness of breath down to the close quarters, in my heart I knew otherwise. For several days, I had been experiencing haemorrhages that had doubled me over at my desk in the clock tower. Lloyd had witnessed one while we were huddled on the floor, making a map of an island where a buccaneer's sunken treasure lay. My purpose there was twofold—to engage Lloyd in a pastime that might channel his thoughts in a more healthful direction, and at the same time to employ his youthful mind in the construction of a story aimed at an audience of similar age. Henley had informed me that he had found for me a magazine, called "Young Folks," that would be happy to entertain such a story from me. 'The pay is poor,' he'd written, 'but writers can't be choosers.'

Lloyd and I were just plotting out the necessary landmarks that the story would require—I have learned through experience that it is wise to have a clear and defined sense of the geography in a tale, lest the reader become lost or confused—when I felt a pain sharp as a dagger slipping between my ribs. I slumped forward, and Lloyd at first imagined me to be playing at some game. So did Woggin, who had been snoring softly on his old pillow in the corner.

'We haven't figured out where X marks the spot should be!' he proclaimed. 'We can't stop now.' Woggin had trotted over to see what all the fuss was about.

My face was pressed to the map, and I writhed in pain as the dagger was twisted into my left lung by some unseen but vicious hand. Blood trickled from the corner of my mouth, staining the outline of the mythical isle, and it was then that Woggin, smelling the blood, barked, and Lloyd became alarmed.

'Louis!' he cried. 'Are you dying?'

It was a thought, I must admit, that had occurred to me, though I was less than pleased to have it introduced so promptly.

I tried to reply, but all that emerged from my mouth was a fragile bubble of blood, which caused Lloyd to leap to his feet and Woggin to wail piteously.

'I'll get help!' he said, but I managed to reach out and snag the hem of his trousers before he could go. If indeed I was to die, I preferred that I not be alone, and if I were to live, I did not want Fanny to be unduly alarmed.

'Let go! I'll be right back!'

But still I clung. The bubble popped, and I said, croaking more like a frog than a human, 'Stay.'

'Why? You need help. I'll go get Dr Rüedi.'

'My pills,' I said. 'In the drawer.'

I released him, and he yanked open the desk drawer, which was filled with enough bottles and vials to stock an apothecary's shop.

'Which ones?'

'The silver pill box.'

Rummaging around, he found the box and gave it to me with a glass of brandy, the liquid closest at hand. I swallowed the pills—they felt like pebbles descending my strained throat—and waited for the relief they sometimes brought. Woggin, huddled at my side, watched me anxiously, his tail thumping hard on the floor.

'Can I go now?' Lloyd asked. 'I still think you need help.'

I shook my head. The dagger felt as if it were being withdrawn. The pain abated, but with it came a discomfiting flapping sensation, like an unsecured sail, in my chest. I did not need to guess what it was.

Breathing as calmly and steadily as I could, I waited for the flapping to slow, then lifted my cheek from the soiled map.

'We will make a new one,' I said to Lloyd, whose face was as white as chalk but whose eyes were riveted on the glistening bloodstains.

I was able to sit up, and after several minutes, hazarded standing and returning to my desk chair.

'Do you want to keep working on the story?' Lloyd asked timidly.

'Not today,' I said, and without turning round—I did not want to see again the horror I had inflicted upon the boy—added, 'Please don't tell your mother about this.'

'Shouldn't she know?'

'It is enough that I tell Dr Rüedi. Tomorrow.'

What he would then recommend, I dreaded. As these standard measures were proving ineffective, he would surely advocate again for more radical steps.

Symonds, at the lectern, was asking now for any last questions, and several hands and fans were raised. The voices came to me as if from a great distance. Even the lights in the wall sconces and chandelier seemed hazy and dim. There was a round of applause, and Fanny gathered up her skirts and stood.

'Your friend did an admirable job,' she said. Having studied art in France and Holland, she would have enjoyed a further discussion of the lecture. 'Shall we go and congratulate him?'

Nodding, I rose, hoping she would not notice that to steady myself, I held on to the back of the chair before me. It was foolish to have thought so.

'Louis,' she asked, 'what's wrong? Are you all right?'

'I just need some fresh air.'

Desmond had approached me from the other side. 'That talk might have created a scandal in Mayfair,' he said, 'but here, it will be forgotten by breakfast. I say, old man, you don't look quite well.'

'He's not,' Fanny said. 'Help me get him to the balcony. It's too warm in here.'

Hands were placed beneath my elbows, and I was escorted to the French doors, which Lloyd threw open. As I leaned upon the balustrade, I took a deep breath and felt again that loose sail luffing in my chest. I would not have been surprised if the others had heard it flap.

'What is going on out here?' I heard from the doors, in the doctor's distinctive English flavoured with both an American and a Swiss accent.

'Louis was feeling faint,' Fanny said.

'Pale as a ghost,' Desmond put in.

'I think he's running a fever,' she added.

'I am not surprised to hear this,' he said, coming close. Producing the ever-present stethoscope from around his neck—he wore it the way some men might sport an ascot—he pressed it to my chest and listened for several seconds. 'It is just as I thought,' he said, removing the instrument. 'It is time we took more determined measures.'

I could see his pince-nez glittering in the moonlight. I opened my mouth to respond—to protest—when that old familiar dagger punctured my chest, obviating any need or use for further discourse.

TOPANGA CANYON— CALIFORNIA

Present Day

After several hours of taking down coordinates and figuring out where the pack was going, Rafe was heading back to the jeep, a weary Heidi trudging close behind—right on his heels, in fact. He wondered why that was bothering him, until he realized that it reminded him of having his little sister dogging his steps, all her worldly possessions stuffed into a pair of plastic Little Mermaid shopping bags from a county-sponsored trip to Disneyland. He'd wanted to protect her, but he was ashamed, too, because he secretly wished he didn't have to worry about her. If it hadn't been for Lucy, he could have run for it, scaled any wall, slipped out of any shelter, made his own way in the world.

"How long before the sun sets?" Heidi asked.

"What difference does it make? We'll be back at the jeep in ten minutes." They were already skirting the lake.

"I think we should get that trunk out of the water."

"That trunk really gets to you, doesn't it?" he said, though truth be told, he shared her curiosity.

"It's a hazard. We should do whatever we can to clean up the lake. We should get rid of that old bike frame, too. One day, maybe this lake will be beautiful again."

It was a lovely thought, but not one that he saw coming true in the immediate future.

"Look, we've even got a boat," she pointed out.

The rowboat, lying upside down on the shore, looked about as seaworthy as a sponge.

"It'll take no time at all," she said, already trying to rock the old boat right side up.

"You sure you're up for this?" he said. What if the trunk contained something truly horrific? That was all he needed, to traumatize his first trainee on her inaugural venture into the canyon.

"Never put off till tomorrow what you can do today." She'd actually managed to roll the thing over and was inspecting its insides. "I don't see any holes."

"We'll find out when we get out there, you know."

"And there's an oar in it."

"It generally takes two of them."

"We're not going very far."

Rafe guessed it was about a couple of hundred yards off.

"Maybe we could just wade there, then," she said, shielding her eyes from the late-day sun. "It looks shallow enough."

But that idea was even worse. In some spots, the lake was actually deeper than she knew, and besides the turtles and frogs, there were snakes to contend with.

She was tugging at an old rope attached to the bow of the boat, but it hardly budged. Her tan ranger hat, so neat and trim at the start of the day, was sweat stained, and the wide brim was flopping down. She was a pain in the butt, but he had to hand it to her—she stuck to her guns.

Dropping the radio antenna and his backpack onto the ground, he took hold of the rope and helped her drag the boat into the water, where it bobbed from side to side. They watched to see if it would sink, but it didn't. Apart from a little water seeping in through a seam, it looked okay.

Heidi climbed in, and sat on a thwart. "Shit!"

"What?"

She reached under herself and pulled something out. "A splinter."

He handed her the oar, then pushed the boat farther into the lake. When the water rose to the top of his hiking boot, he jumped in, and once the rocking subsided, said, "Okay, you can give me the oar now."

Standing like a gondolier, legs spread as wide as possible, he rowed the boat through the pale-green sludge of the lake. The bottom was only a few feet down, and half the time, he was just pushing the boat along like a raft. He could see amid the mud and rocks, broken coolers, bent fishing rods, soda cans. He wondered if the Dr Peppers belonged to Seth and Alfie.

Not a fish in sight, though.

Heidi, facing the bow, said, "We're in luck."

"We are?"

"It looks like it's sitting on an underwater ledge."

Steering the boat toward the trunk, he saw that it was standing, however improbably, on one end. Even when the lake had been several feet higher, the trunk must have been barely submerged.

"How should we do this?" Heidi asked, starting to get to her feet, which threatened to capsize the boat.

"Just sit down." Using the oar as a pole, he maneuvered the stern of the boat around until it was within easy reach of the trunk. He dropped the paddle into the boat and said, "Take hold of both sides of the boat and counterbalance it."

The trunk was just a couple of feet away, and when he touched it, his fingers blazed like he'd touched a match. Why wouldn't they, he thought—it was an old green metal trunk that had been baking in the sun.

"Use this," she said, tossing him her sweaty hat. Her hair frizzed around her head like a corona. "It's gonna need washing anyway."

Folding the hat around one hand like a glove, he reached out again and managed to tilt the trunk toward the boat, but as he did so, its bottom started to slip off whatever rock it was resting on and down into deeper water.

"Damn," he muttered, and grabbed it with his other hand, too, the one that had no protection. The metal seared his palm, but he held on long enough to haul the trunk over the stern and plunk it with a wet and resounding thump into the bottom of the boat. Water streamed off its sides, joining the thin rivulet that was still seeping through the hull. He shook his hand to cool it off.

"Was it heavy?"

"Yes," he replied.

"So it's got something inside it?"

"Could just be water."

"Or maybe it's gold bullion."

He had definitely heard, and felt, something shift inside the trunk, but he doubted it was gold bars. His own thoughts went in darker directions.

Glancing at the bottom of the boat, where the water seemed to be creeping in faster than before, he said, "I think we've taken on too much weight. We're gonna sink if we don't start back. Better give me that oar again."

"You're injured. I can do it."

Rather than argue the point, he kept one hand, shielded by her ruined hat, on the trunk, while pressing his boot to the bottom of the boards where the leak seemed to have sprung. Heidi paddled and prodded the boat back to the nearest bank, and before he could tell her to look first and maybe give the water a warning swirl with the oar, she had hopped overboard. The water was only a foot or so deep here, but Rafe was still wary.

"Watch yourself," he said.

"I'm a very good swimmer," she joked.

He grappled the trunk as well as he could, then toppled it over the side of the boat. It splashed into the water, and he had to drag it across the gravel and mud and up onto dry land, where it lay like a beached green whale.

"Now what?" she said, still in the water and yanking at the rope.

"Now we have to figure out how to drag—"

"Ow!"

Heidi doubled over, her hands plunging below the surface to grab at her ankle.

"Ow-ow-ow!"

He didn't need to ask what had happened—he could see the little ripple in the water, racing away. He grabbed Heidi by the arm and pulled her onto the shore. She was clutching at the skin just above the top of her soaking boot.

He made her sit on the trunk while he wiped away the weeds and mud that mottled her shin. He could see the fear beginning to dawn on her face.

"Was it a rattlesnake?" she asked, her voice beginning to tremble.

Rafe looked closely at the skin and saw not a row of tiny bite marks, which would have been preferable, but one deep one. The other fang appeared to have hit the top of the boot, which showed a puncture wound of its own.

"Keep calm," he said. "That's the best thing you can do right now." Panic only increased respiration and blood flow, and the most important thing was to get her to a hospital before the venom managed to circulate to her heart.

"Take off your shirt," he said, and quickly scanned the surrounding ground for anything that might help. Spotting some wilted yarrow, he yanked up a handful, then ground it between his palms and slathered it onto the sticky wound.

"Tie your shirt just above your knee, tight, like a bandage." The starch in the yarrow would act as a natural coagulant, drawing out the poison. Sucking out the venom, as had traditionally been recommended, only poisoned two people instead of one, while introducing other possible infections to the wound.

"Am I going to die?"

"No trainee of mine has ever died."

"How many have you had?"

"You're the first."

It was critical that she not go into shock. If the rattlesnake had managed a full clean strike, she would already be losing consciousness; what might save her yet was the fact that only one fang had hit its mark.

"I want you to get on my back and hang there, like a sack of potatoes. Let your legs dangle."

Wrapping her arms around his shoulders, she climbed onto him. He slipped his hands back under her thighs to give her some support, then, leaving his backpack and antenna behind, hustled up the hillside, furiously calculating how long it would take him to get to the jeep and drive back down the bumpy, twisting fire road. The jostling wouldn't help her.

By the time he reached the crest, he was nearly out of breath, and after dropping her into the passenger seat of the jeep, he took a second to breathe deeply and assess Heidi's state.

He didn't like what he saw.

She was pale and listless; her eyelids were beginning to droop. Her chin was dropping down toward her black sports bra.

"Heidi," he said, lifting her chin and looking into her eyes, "you've got to hang in there for me." He strapped her into her seat belt, then jumped behind the wheel, backed the jeep up, and shot down the fire road. With every twist and turn, he put a hand on her shoulder to keep her steady, and he kept talking to make sure she remained conscious.

"You with me?" he asked, and if she murmured yes, he made her repeat it.

"We're almost there," he said, without telling her where *there* was. "You're going to be fine. You know that, right?"

There was a white froth forming on her lips.

"This is going to be some story to tell," he said, trying to sound lighthearted. His own fear was taking a firm hold on him. His little sister kept coming to mind, and that terrible day at the public swimming pool.

He had to banish the thought. Heidi would not end up like Lucy.

At the bottom of the fire road, he saw the old chain drawn across the entry, but there was no time to waste dealing with the padlock. Instead, he revved the engine, stretched one arm firmly across Heidi's chest, and barreled right through it, the chain snapping in the air like a whip, one of the posts it was attached to popping up out of the ground and skittering across the main road. The jeep did a wheelie, a passing van's horn blasted in fury, and Rafe hit the gas again and took off for his trailer. There wasn't time to get her to a hospital; the antivenom, which had to be kept refrigerated, was stored in his minifridge at home.

Heidi, only partly aware of what she was doing now, started to lift her leg to fiddle with the improvised tourniquet, and he had to push the limb back down again.

"Keep your feet on the floor," he said. "Try not to move, okay?"

"'Kay," was all she got out.

When the roadside sign for the Cornucopia appeared, he swerved across the opposite lane, hitting the horn to make sure Tripod was out of the way, steered the jeep to within a few feet of his trailer, and leaping out while the dust still filled the air, unbuckled Heidi's seat belt.

Lifting her out of the car, he saw Laszlo stepping out onto the back stairs of the shop. At the sight of Rafe carrying a limp girl in a bra into his trailer, Laszlo bobbed his head approvingly.

"Call an ambulance!" Rafe shouted.

"What for?"

"Just do it!"

Throwing open the door, he carried her inside and laid her on the single bed. She was sweating profusely, and her pupils were alarmingly enlarged. Ducking down, he threw open the minifridge, pushed the bags of carrots and cherries aside, and fumbled for the snakebite kit. He'd done this on dummies, during training, but never on a live person.

Much less one who might die if he did it wrong.

He snapped open the kit, uncapped the vial of antivenom, then ripped the plastic off the syringe. His hands were shaking, and he had to force himself to slow down enough to stick the syringe into the bottle and fill it, press the plunger to make sure there was no air bubble, then smack Heidi's sunburned forearm to bring up a good vein. She was squirming on the bed, a bit delirious.

"Hold still. This will take just two seconds," he said, "and then you're going to be perfectly okay."

He inserted the needle—it went in smoothly, he was relieved to see—and watched as the antitoxin flowed from the syringe into her vein. *Go, baby, go*, was all he could keep thinking, as if he could will it into greater efficacy.

When the syringe was empty, he gently withdrew it, dabbed a cotton ball soaked in antiseptic on the spot of blood—wasn't that supposed to have come first? he thought—and removed her boot. The skin around the wound had taken on a faint purple tinge.

Trip was barking outside the trailer door.

Heidi's breathing perceptibly slowed, which was either a good sign or a bad one, he couldn't tell for sure.

He covered her with a blanket, then slumped to the floor.

He heard footsteps rapidly approaching, and looked up just as Miranda stepped up into the trailer. "Laszlo called 911," she said. She saw the girl on the bed, the open snakebite kit on the floor. "Oh my God, is she going to be okay?"

Rafe's mouth was so dry he couldn't have replied even if he'd known the answer to that.

6 December, 1881

The two weeks following my dramatic episode in the grand salon have been a nightmare from which, I fear, I have yet to awaken. The next morning, Fanny escorted me to Dr Rüedi's examining rooms. Symonds insisted on coming, too, claiming that, as it was his speech that had brought on the attack, the least he could do was see to its aftermath. 'I do not wish it chalked up to my account that I put an end to the brilliant career of one of Scotland's most promising authors. I will not be able to show my face on the lecture circuit.'

But Dr Rüedi left him cooling his heels in the hall, and only with some reluctance admitted Fanny to the room.

On the desk was an alarmingly lifelike replica of the human torso, its rib cage and viscera fully exposed. Using a pointer, from a distance that in no way required one, Dr Rüedi tapped at the model to illustrate his thoughts as he spoke.

'As my colleague in Berlin, Dr Robert Koch, has recently demonstrated in his study "The Etiology of Tuberculosis," it is a mycobacterium that is the cause of the disease from which you suffer, Mr Stevenson, and it is your left lobe'—he tapped a blue plaster lung—'that is most affected.'

The pointer made a hollow clicking sound as it struck.

'That is why', the doctor continued, 'I intend to collapse it.'

'Isn't it nearly there already?' I asked, recalling the flapping sensation in my chest.

'Possibly.'

'But what purpose would be served by collapsing it altogether?' Fanny asked. 'I don't see the use in that at all. He has trouble enough breathing as it is.'

'The technique, a new one, is called plombage. I believe it offers the best hope. By removing a small portion of the fourth rib'—now he touched the pointer to the corresponding bone—'and deflating the lung, we can allow the organ to achieve complete rest. Rather than producing more of the tubercle bacillus, it will become dormant, which will in turn allow it to heal.'

'Won't that leave a cavity, if you will, in the chest?'

'Well observed, Mr Stevenson. And that is why we will fill the vacuum with paraffin wax.'

Fanny looked highly dubious, and no doubt so did I. Before I could ask it myself, Fanny said, 'And once the lung has been deflated and the paraffin introduced, how long before the lung is restored?'

Dr Rüedi tilted his head this way and that. 'Several weeks. Perhaps a month. Or two. Much depends upon the patient.'

Subjecting myself to the surgeon's knife has always presented itself only as a last resort—a measure to be taken in extremis, if you will, when all else has failed. But for years—nay, decades—I had travelled the Old World (from the spas of southern France to the Highland peaks) and the New (from the Adirondack Mountains of New York to the redwood glens of distant California) in search of a cure, and all of my journeys had proved futile in the end. I had washed up, like the broken mast of a shipwreck, on this unlikely shore.

'Frankly, Doctor, I do not like the sound of this,' Fanny said.

'Frankly, Madame, that is of no consequence to me,' Dr Rüedi replied.

Though it was not out of keeping with his character, I was nonetheless taken aback by his rudeness, as was my wife.

'If you have come to me for idle conversation,' he said, thwapping the pointer like a riding crop against the palm of one hand, 'I do not have time; I thought I had made that clear upon your arrival. If you have come to me to be healed, however, you may do as I say, or seek help elsewhere.'

'We may just do that,' Fanny said in a huff.

'The coach leaves at one o'clock this afternoon. As soon as you have settled your bill,' he said, 'you may use it.'

It was the mention of the bill that was the most telling, and that set even Fanny back on her left foot. We had been anxiously awaiting funds from my father in Edinburgh, but heavy snows had no doubt delayed the post, and in the meanwhile, we had accrued a sizeable debt—twenty francs a week for the suite, the same for board, and various fees for consultation and treatments. If our departure depended upon our accounts being brought into balance, then we were in effect being held hostage at the Belvédère.

As it was nearly time for my daily sun bath, I allowed Fanny, fuming, to return to the room while I went with Symonds out onto the wide verandah. He was full of genuine concern for my welfare, for which I was grateful, but I did not wish to share the grim prognosis, or plans. I spotted Lloyd, a woollen scarf wrapped tight around his throat, walking Woggin on a long leash around the snowy front lawn of the hotel. Randolph Desmond walked with him, a friendly, even avuncular, arm around his shoulder. Though the difference in their ages was not more than ten years, Desmond had taken a great interest in my stepson, for which I was glad. Lloyd's father was off in Nevada, prospecting for gold or oil or whatever other will-o'-the-wisp beckoned to him—Fanny had often described him to me as a ne'er-do-well who could not resist a shot of whiskey, a loose woman, or a bad bet—and as for me, I was a poor substitute in that regard, too. Although I did my best to broaden Lloyd's horizons and stimulate his faculties, I could not provide him with the kind of physical companionship a boy of his age desires. Some of my fondest memories were of taking long journeys to remote lighthouse sites with my father, and watching as he supervised the construction of the tall stone towers and the installation of the all-important beacons at their top. Lloyd, by comparison, would remember travelling with an invalid to a cold clinic on an isolated mountaintop.

Or, perhaps, making maps of imaginary islands where pirate treasure pretended to lie.

'Have you seen the oracle?' Desmond inquired upon seeing me.

'We have.'

'And what did he have to say?'

As I had no more wish to share the news with Desmond than I had with Symonds, I merely said he had examined me and prescribed some changes to my regimen.

'He's got Constance drinking so much of that damn goat's milk', Desmond complained, 'it's a wonder she doesn't bleat.'

Even after all this time, I had not found the proper occasion or opportunity to ask about her affliction. Although she was pale, she did not appear to me to be any more a consumptive than so many of the other young ladies of fashion who, conflating the illness with melancholy romance, deliberately affected a white complexion. Whatever Desmond had brought her here to remedy, it was of some other nature and, were I to hazard an unsavoury guess, venereal.

Woggin, bored with all this stationary talk, pulled so hard at his leash that he broke free and ran to the toboggan run where, nose to the snow, he burrowed about. Several of the other guests laughed at his antics, and even the nurse, propping pillows behind a patient as he settled in his chaise longue, smiled. Digging furiously, he nipped at something frozen to the ground, then yanked it up as if dragging a rabbit from its burrow.

But this prize glittered in the sunlight, and when I called, he trotted over with a silver chain dangling from his mouth. It took two or three attempts before he would relinquish it, but once I had brushed away the snow and ice, I could see that it was a gaudy, bejewelled crucifix. I glanced at the spot on the toboggan run where he had found it, and it corresponded directly with my recollection of that night when Yannick and his assistants had dispatched the bodies . . . and he had slipped on the snow.

'Didn't that old Italian woman wear something like that?' Desmond said.

'Yes.'

'She disappeared rather abruptly. Was it the menu, I wonder? Not enough spaghetti?'

I put the necklace, still redolent of her perfume, into my pocket.

The look on my face, however, must have communicated something more, as Desmond fell silent, then rallied to slap Lloyd on the back and say, 'What about a sled race?'

Lloyd, jubilant, ran off to claim the sleds, and I went to my customary chaise longue, where the nurse was waiting impatiently with a blanket folded over one arm. At the appropriate time, I would find an address to which I might forward the memento mori.

That evening, I found my thoughts turning in an unusually morbid direction. Though mortality had never been far from my mind— a lifetime of fevers and coughs, night sweats and chilblains will no doubt leave a mark—I had long trained myself to marshal my thoughts like the little tin soldiers that I played with as a boy. Arranging them on the counterpane of my sickbed, I had marched the figurines into battle in orderly rows and battalions, but tonight I could not do the same with my imaginative fancies. They would not assemble to the bugle call; they would not do my bidding. I tried to focus them on the old blind pirate tap-tap-tapping his way up the lonely road to the Admiral Benbow public house, where young Jim Hawkins and his mother scraped together the barest subsistence. But instead they ran amok, flitting from visions of the old Italian woman, wrapped in a shroud and sent hurtling down the dark mountainside, to corroded lungs, flat and useless as a spent bellows. Unable to sit still and write, I paced the confines of my garret, hands clasped behind my back, my red brocade dressing gown buttoned to my Adam's apple. Woggin, head resting on his paws, kept a close watch.

After one such turn, I happened to glance out the window to the back lawn at precisely the moment a great, beautiful stag warily skirted the smokehouse and approached the salt lick. It was a noble creature, head held high, crowned by an elaborate rack of antlers. Indeed, it took some manoeuvring before the beast could get them out of its way enough to allow its tongue to lap at the salt.

I watched, a handkerchief already soiled with blood balled up in one hand, for several minutes. Moonlight glinted off the fresh, powdery snow and the overladen boughs of the evergreen trees. An owl hooted somewhere in the darkness. It was a scene as tranquil as any that could be imagined. My peace of mind somewhat restored, I was just about to return to my desk when my eye caught a gleam of something among the trees.

A flash, like a mirror reflecting a bolt of sunlight . . . but moving stealthily towards the lick—and towards the oblivious stag, whose head was craned low and at an odd angle.

What would happen next was not difficult to predict.

Without further hesitation, I took to the winding stairs, an alarmed Woggin scampering at my heels, around and around, then down the main staircase of the hotel, past a drowsing night porter, through the swinging doors of the dining room, and into the kitchen. But what to grab? A cleaver lay on a cutting board, and a black iron skillet on a stove. Stuffing the handkerchief into the pocket of my robe, I armed myself with both and made for the cellar stairs.

Here, the white plaster walls gave way to rough grey stone, the oak-planked floors to damp cement. The cold, wet air filled my lungs, and I gasped for a full breath. Woggin barked in shock when, with one shoe, I knocked him backwards—no sense in endangering him, too—before throwing open the door to the back of the hotel and slamming it shut behind me.

The stag was no longer unaware of the menace. Its head was up, nostrils flaring, brown eyes wild and wide. From the border of the trees, the wolf I had seen before—and christened Lord Grey—emerged with head low and ears pricked high. The stag backed up, lowering its own horns in preparation for battle.

I wondered that it did not flee, before noting that the wolf's two black henchmen had come, too, and were lurking in the shadows on either side.

If I had come to give warning, I was too late. If I had come to wage war, I was not well equipped.

Still, I had dealt with wolves before, in the canyons of the American West, and a show of noise and bravado almost always put them off their game; they knew enough to fear man and to run off in search of easier prey. Banging the blunt edge of the cleaver against the iron skillet, I shouted and made a racket, and though they certainly took note of me, these wolves did not retreat. The deer was the most affected, now unsure what posed the greater danger, its panicked eyes swivelling from the human with the clanging pan to the wolves slowly encircling it. It snorted, its breath fogging in the air, and pawed at the slippery, snowy ground.

'Get out of here,' I shouted at Lord Grey. 'Get out!'

How I had come to feel myself the determined ally of the doomed stag might have been unclear even to me—I was certainly familiar with the ways of the natural world, sanguinary and dispassionate as they were—but the mismatch of the single, unsuspecting deer against a trio of marauders stirred in me a spirit of fair play. Even at school, my sympathies had always lain with the underdog.

So when one of the black wolves made a sudden feint at the hindquarters of the stag, I banged the pan loudly, and when that proved no deterrent, stepped close enough to swing the cleaver in front of its nose.

The wolf backed up, but the other henchman took advantage of the opportunity to make its own attack. I heard the stag bellow in pain, and when I turned, I saw that it had been expertly hamstrung, blood running down its buckling leg. It was struggling to stay upright, even to run, but the deep snow made it well-nigh impossible to find any footing.

I swung the cleaver in the other direction, and so was completely unprepared when Lord Grey launched himself like an arrow at the stag's head, clamping his jaws around the animal's snout and holding fast even as the frenzied stag shook him from side to side. Nothing, it was plain, was going to loosen that deadly grip, even as the wolf was whipped back and forth above the forgotten salt lick.

Windows in the hotel were opening now, gas lamps coming on as the guests awoke to the commotion.

I thought I heard Fanny's voice, terrified, shouting my name.

Then, I was struck from behind—a black wolf hurtling against my shoulders, its hot, foul breath scorching my cheek and knocking me to the ground. I rolled to one side, just in time to crown it with a blow of the iron skillet. The cleaver had fallen from my hand, and my fingers scrambled in the snow to find it. The wolf, stunned, snapped at my hand, and just as my fingers grasped the handle of the blade, it pounced on my chest with the weight of an anchor. I tried to lift the cleaver, but the strength had utterly left my body. The wolf's fangs rent my dressing gown and tore at the sinews of my shoulder. I was certain that the next moment would be my last, when a shotgun blast split the night and the wolf flew off me as if hit by a cannonball.

There were howls and shrieks, and another blast, and before I could even assess my own situation, I caught sight of Dr Rüedi, shotgun cradled in the crook of his arm, crunching across the clearing.

'Jetzt stoppen!' he shouted at the wolves. 'Stoppen!'

The smell of hot blood permeated the air, the writhing of the dying stag sent tremors through the ground, and then, a final shot abruptly ended even those. All I could hear was the doctor, talking to the wolves like a stern schoolmaster lecturing his unruly students, and under his voice, the strangely comforting sound of the snow crystals crackling in my ears.

TOPANGA CANYON— CALIFORNIA

Present Day

There seemed to be no end to the stack of official forms in duplicate and triplicate, stamped in red or yellow, that Ellen Latham's long, lacquered fingernails were riffling through. How many crimes and misdemeanors, Rafe wondered, could he possibly have committed since his last departmental review?

"We'll be lucky, you know, if Heidi Graff's family doesn't bring a civil suit against us," she said without looking up.

"But she's going to be all right, right?"

"Yes, but that's beside the point. You were responsible for her welfare in the field that day."

"There are rattlesnakes out there," Rafe said, "and sometimes they act like rattlesnakes." What he wanted to add was something to the effect that Latham might know this if she ever left the air-conditioned office in a downtown Los Angeles skyscraper where she shuffled papers all day and second-guessed the rangers and researchers who worked on the front lines. If she'd ever had to go out and protect the wildlife and do whatever was necessary to preserve the environment in the face of withering budget cuts and a total lack of cooperation from Mother Nature, she'd have a better idea of what she was asking.

But he bit his tongue, as a lifetime of dealing with bureaucrats had taught him to do.

"Is she still in the hospital?" he asked.

"No, she's been released. She's back home with her parents."

"Would it be okay if I paid her a visit?"

Latham sat back in her ergonomically designed chair and gave him a level look. "No, it would not be okay. Our in-house counsel advises no further contact until we're sure she's not going to sue." She pulled another paper from her pile, this one a familiar pale green that he knew was used for environmental science evaluations. Weren't computers supposed to make all this paperwork obsolete?

"Why don't we have a current field report on your coyote migration research?" She said it as if she were asking for something that had all the importance of an odometer reading.

"Because I'm having to readjust the stats based on a smaller sample of animals."

Latham looked blank.

"Pedro got shot."

"Who's Pedro?"

He'd forgotten that only he knew the coyotes by the names he had given them. "The youngest of the pack."

"You name them?" she said drily. There it was again, Rafe noted—coyotes were considered one step above vermin, even by people who ought to know better. More than once he'd thought that that was why he felt such a kinship with the maligned creatures. He'd been treated like that as a kid, and the courage, ingenuity, and resilience that the species displayed, in the face of encroaching civilization and all the barbarous means that had been used to exterminate them, made him want to come to their defense all the more.

"Any idea who shot him? Was it someone with a state license?"

If he knew who'd done it, he'd have settled the matter himself. "I have my suspicions." Seth and Alfie. "But that's all I have."

"Right. Fine. Have that report on my desk by Friday, latest. And make sure it's comprehensive and up-to-date. Turn in anything you've got, even if it's incomplete at that time."

Alarm bells went off in his head. "Why the rush?"

"In case you haven't been reading the papers, there's a drought on, and a lot of the funding we had for collateral matters is now being redirected to water management and conservation programs."

"So what are you saying? My grant is being curtailed?"

"Your grant is under review."

Rafe had been an environmental scientist long enough to know what that meant. Every time there was a crisis of any kind—a drought, a fire, an infestation of some foreign flora or fauna—the long-term studies and fundamental research that might have averted the crisis in the first place were abruptly abandoned. Ecology only moved forward in fits and starts, like an old car with a balky stick shift.

Latham's phone rang, and she picked it up and started talking to someone about a lunch reservation. Rafe, sensing an opportunity to escape before any more bad news hit him, snatched his backpack up off the floor—he'd retrieved it but had to leave the trunk until he could contrive a means of dragging it out to his jeep single-handedly—but he was too slow on the uptake. Latham lifted one finger to delay him. Damn.

Hanging up, she said, "I got this weird alert from the Malibu police department last week."

"About what?"

"Have you heard anything about a crystal meth lab up in the canyons?"

He thought of Mr. and Mrs. Pothead, the pale, harmless hippies who'd recently smuggled him the baggie at La Raza, but meth was definitely not their thing.

"What exactly did it say?"

"There's a motorcycle gang—"

"The Spiritz," he interjected, relieved to see the focus move in this direction.

"—and drugs appear to be one of their main sources of revenue."

"Could be."

"Keep an eye out on your patrols for anything that might look like an operation of that sort. That's all we'd need right now."

Although this was the first he'd heard of it, he didn't doubt it was possible—was that why the Spiritz seemed to be around so much more of late?—but if giving up a few low-life bikers was all it would take to keep him looking like a team player, it was a small price to pay—especially if he could keep the harmless Potheads out of anybody's crosshairs at the same time.

Leaving the office, he got lost in the maze of cubicles, and a secretary had to guide him back to the right elevator bank. In his brown uniform and boots, backpack slung over his shoulder, he felt like a total rube. At the lobby desk, he returned his temporary ID badge to the security guard, then stepped outside onto a wide plaza, where office workers were unwrapping sandwiches from cellophane and eating them, perched on low concrete walls surrounding a dry fountain. Exhaust fumes from passing traffic filled the air. A bus was honking its horn, a jackhammer was ripping open a seam in the street. He couldn't wait to get the hell out of there.

8 December, 1881

The pain. The pain was what brought me around.

I remembered Dr Rüedi and the night porter carrying me, my bony arms slung around their shoulders, back into the hotel, down a long, twisting corridor of rough-hewn rock, past iron doors and flickering gas lamps, then into a blazingly white and bright room. My eyes were swimming in my head, but still I took in the glass-fronted cabinets of surgical instruments and the high table draped like a catafalque, onto which I was laid.

I remembered Fanny's voice, remonstrating and hysterical, and Lloyd—what was he doing up at this hour? I wondered in my delirium—helping to remove my bloody and torn dressing gown. I remember him watching intently as the doctor raised a blue cotton cloth towards a mirrored light—a lighthouse, here, in a cellar of all places—and doused it with a sweet-smelling liquid.

'What are you going to do with that?' Lloyd asked.

'Hold him steady.'

'What is it?'

'Ether.'

The cloth was pressed to my mouth, and I do not remember much after that. When I came around again, it could have been a minute, or a day, later. I was lying on a hard cot in a small underground cell. There was a searing pain in my shoulder, and I recalled the wolf biting me there, but this pain extended all the way to my shoulder blades. Indeed, it seemed to have its origin there. I wanted to call out for help—my throat was so parched, I'd have sold my soul for a draught of cold water—but for some reason I was labouring under the impression that I was a prisoner in the dungeons of a castle and that if I were to give myself away, I'd be shackled, or, worse, put to the rack. Feeling myself a character in one of my own adventure stories, I rose from the bed, wearing a white woollen gown, and moved stealthily towards the door. The flagstones were like ice under my bare feet.

In the hall, a nurse—one of those who ordinarily made up my sun bed—was asleep and snoring, a striped blanket lying across her ample lap.

Tiptoeing past, I crept around the corner, stopping to lift one foot, and then the other, to rub some warmth into them.

In the low light of a single lamp, I saw a line of several doors, no more than waist high, with barred grates. The rattling of a chain came from one of them, though I could not tell which.

Crouching, I peered through the bars of the first, but the light was so dim it took several seconds before I could make out a sight so shocking that, even if I weren't so scantily dressed, would still have sent a shiver down my spine.

A black wolf, presumably one of those which had attacked me, hung upside down from a rafter, its throat cut and a bucket below it, now quite full of blood.

Had this been done as some sort of revenge? Despite what damage the wolf had done me, I would never have demanded such ghastly retribution.

The rattling sounded again, and this wolf, dead as a doornail, was plainly not the cause.

Moving to the next cell, I peered in again, and was greeted by a rush of wind through the grate, the screeching and snap of a chain, and a pair of infuriated eyes only inches from my own. Lord Grey, a leather strap lashed around his muzzle, had charged at the bars and been restrained by a rusty chain bolted to the back wall of the cell. One of his ears stood erect, the other drooped raggedly, grazed perhaps by the shotgun pellets. That his life had been so far spared was as mysterious to me as the slaughter of his henchman.

'What are you doing out here?' the nurse said, bustling up behind me. 'You should have told me you were awake.'

Lord Grey struggled to break the muzzle and howl, but it was no use.

The nurse threw the blanket around my shoulders and steered me away from the cell. 'The doctor wished to be notified as soon as you awoke.'

'What are you doing with these wolves?'

'That's the doctor's business, not yours,' she said, drawing me back down the hall.

'But I want to know!'

'Have no fear, they will not be bothering you ever again.'

'I have no fear of that at all.'

'Of course you do not, Mr Stevenson, of course you do not.'

Urging me back onto the cot, she said, 'I will just go and get the doctor now.' She tucked the sheet and blanket in so tightly that I might just as well have been clapped in irons. 'And no more excursions for you.'

The pain, which had trebled already, made such a feat as impossible as it was unwanted.

TOPANGA CANYON— CALIFORNIA

Present Day

By the time Rafe got through all the rush-hour traffic and back to the canyon, he felt like he'd been pummeled by crowds and cars and commotion all day long, and all he wanted was to lie on top of his trailer, look at the stars, and feel the evening breeze.

Ducking a bedsheet drying on the clothesline, Trip came hopping across the backyard and rolled over so Rafe could give him the desired belly rub. In her apartment above the store, Miranda was saying, "With what? There's nothing left in the checking account."

Rafe couldn't make out Laszlo's answer, but he'd heard these squabbles enough times before to know how they generally turned out. Miranda would be lucky if it didn't escalate beyond words.

He left the door to the trailer wide open and went straight to the minifridge for a cold beer. He popped the top, then flopped onto his narrow foldaway bed, which was as always neatly made, the white sheet and yellow blanket smooth. Everything else in the cramped interior was equally organized and tidy. A lifetime of being displaced from one foster home to another—or living with a mother who was (as he had learned from years of listening to social workers' jargon) "decompensating" from the desertion of her husband—had left him with a powerful need for order and cleanliness. The women he'd dated over the years—nobody for very long—had invariably been surprised that a rugged single guy, much less one who spent his time out in the wilderness, was such a neat freak. "I thought you'd live like a mountain man," one of them had said, vaguely disappointed. "Turns out you're OCD."

Although Rafe wouldn't go that far, she wasn't completely off.

Cleanliness was what he appreciated about the group home where his sister, Lucy, lived. Run by a former nun named Evangelina, the place functioned like a military operation, with more house rules than a casino and strictly enforced policies about personal space and belongings. But he knew Lucy was safe there, and cared for. After he'd left the Land Management office downtown, he'd driven over to the house to check up on her and drop off the monthly check, which came to half of his already meager salary.

The house was a fairly forlorn-looking thing, the color of a pink flamingo, in an area of Mar Vista that used to be cheap but was now getting gentrified, along with what sometimes seemed to Rafe like the whole damn world. Even Topanga had its share of five-million-dollar homes now.

He parked his jeep in the driveway, the concrete riven with cracks and stained with oil, and went around back where he could hear laughter and voices and a tinny radio playing rap. Evangelina had set up a bocce court, but since nobody seemed to know how to play, the residents—there were always around eight of them, disabled teens and young adults in a revolving cast—simply used it like a kind of bowling alley. Evangelina was bent over a dying plant, watering it from a can, and when she saw him coming, she said, "It's used dishwater."

"Too late. I've already called the drought police."

He handed her the check and she stuffed it in the back pocket of her jeans without looking at it. She wore her gray hair cropped close to the skull, and he was pretty sure she chopped it herself.

"Lucy's inside."

"How come?"

"It's a time-out. She got a sunburn yesterday and wouldn't put on sunscreen today."

"How's she doing?"

"Fine. She got a new roommate," Evangelina said, nodding toward a skinny girl rolling a bocce ball. "Always takes some getting used to. But they're getting there."

The screen door to the kitchen was propped open, and Rafe wiped his feet carefully on the mat before going in. The linoleum floor was worn but spotless, the plates were piled neatly in the dish drainer. Lucy's room was down a short hall, past a bathroom ripe with the smells of bleach and Lysol; towels and washcloths hung on a rack with name tags.

"Luce?"

Her door was closed, and he rapped on it gently. "Lucy?"

"Rafe?"

When he cracked the door open, she leaped off the top of the bunk bed and ran to hug him. Too hard. She was nineteen now, but she acted like she was the same spindly kid she'd been on that day at the rec center, when he'd forgotten to keep track of her and she'd lain at the bottom of the swimming pool—after being hit on the head by another kid's kickboard—for one, maybe two minutes.

That was all it took. A couple of minutes, and even after the lifeguard had resuscitated her, her oxygen-starved brain had been stopped in its tracks. She was, and forever would be, eleven years old.

"Evangelina tells me you got a sunburn," he said, gently extricating himself from the embrace.

"Look," she said, holding out one splotchy red arm to show him, but what he noticed most was that she'd gotten even heavier. She was on some meds that had that effect—she needed them to ward off the epileptic seizures, which often accompanied brain injuries like hers—but he also knew she needed more exercise. He'd mentioned it to Evangelina, but she'd told him that his sister was "as stubborn as a mule, and twice as fat." Evangelina did not mince words. "The Lord helps those who help themselves." She was big on tough love.

"Does it hurt?" he asked, examining the sunburn.

"Not if I don't touch it."

"Why don't we put some sunscreen on it, and go outside with everybody else. It's beautiful out."

"I don't like sunscreen. It makes me feel all goopy."

"Goopy is good."

Leading her by the hand, he found the sunscreen on the bathroom counter and lathered her up. "Close your eyes," he said, as he swiped some on her cheeks and nose.

Outside, she said, "That's my new roommate over there."

"You like her?"

Lucy shrugged. "She's okay. I'd rather live with you."

It was a frequent refrain of hers, but it still made him feel guilty as hell. "My trailer is hardly big enough for me."

"I don't care."

What he couldn't say—wouldn't say—was that she needed constant supervision, the kind he could never give her.

"You wanna go bowl with the others?" he asked.

He could see she was tempted.

"You won't leave if I do, will you?"

"Nope. I can stick around awhile. Go—play."

He watched as she made her way across the scrubby yard, noting that her limp—another effect of the accident—was no better, but no worse.

"You get the sunscreen on her?" Evangelina asked, her hands filled with pulled weeds.

"Yep." Lucy had just been given the red ball, and when she was sure he was watching, she rolled it down the lane.

"Rafe," Evangelina said, "she's happy here. You've done the best anyone could ever do for her."

He must not have looked convinced.

"So knock off the gloom," she said, reverting to nun mode. "Life goes on. That means yours, too." Her expression all but said *Be fruitful and multiply*.

Yeah, right, he thought now, as he rolled off the cot in his trailer and lobbed the empty beer can—a perfect swish—into the trash. *Life goes on.*

Rummaging around in the minifridge, he unearthed a burrito that was only one day past its sell-by date, and was just unwrapping it when he heard Miranda cry, "Mail call!" from the open door.

She was holding out a stack of envelopes and catalogs. "You haven't picked it up for like a week."

"Anything important in there?"

"I don't read it, Rafe."

"Neither do I."

Seeing the petrified burrito, she said, "That's what you're eating for dinner?"

He looked at it appraisingly.

"I wouldn't feed that to Trip," she said. "Give me ten minutes, then come on over to *my* place."

After she left, he microwaved the burrito until it was good and soft, and, inspired by her comments, flipped it to Tripod, who was lying under the clothesline where Miranda had pinned some sheets to dry in the hot breeze. No doubt grateful for anything that wasn't totally wholesome and gluten-free, the dog wolfed the burrito down, then looked longingly at the paper wrapper Rafe still held scrunched in his hand.

Miranda was in the kitchen when he got there, expertly chopping vegetables and greens with a long knife, then tossing the ingredients into a salad bowl the size of a hubcap. He saw tomatoes, peppers, carrots, dried cranberries, sunflower seeds, and cucumber slices flying into the mix and tumbling through the cascade of dark green leaves. Kale, too, if he was not mistaken. Whatever happened to good old-fashioned iceberg lettuce—or even spinach, for that matter?

"There's beer in the fridge," she said, "but just don't drink the Coronas. Those are Laszlo's fave."

"Where is the man of the house?"

Miranda frowned and pushed a wisp of blond hair off her forehead with the back of her hand. "Off on his scooter, chasing the Spiritz."

Laszlo drove around on a little green Vespa that aspired to be a real motorcycle.

"He won't mind my being over?"

"I wish you'd cut that out. This is my place. I own it."

"Sorry, just making a lame joke."

"Make some oil-and-vinegar dressing instead. The cruet's on the counter."

While Rafe mixed the dressing and shook it up, Miranda put two vividly painted clay plates—"I made those myself," she said, "when I was at Burning Man"—on the rickety round table carved from driftwood, next to a candle in a little red jar with netting around the outside.

"You can light that," she said, tossing him a book of matches.

Killing the overhead light, she said "Cheers" and tapped her wineglass against his bottle of Bud. He sat opposite and let her dress the salad and ladle a generous heap of it onto his plate.

She sat back, sipping her wine while he took the first few bites. "Aren't you eating?"

"Yes. I just wanted to get a buzz on first," she said.

"It's good, even sober."

"Lots of antioxidants in it."

"Love those antioxidants."

She smiled, poured herself more wine, and with her bare feet propped on the chair between them, started picking at her salad.

"Is that girl okay? The snakebite one?"

"Apparently so, though I'm sure some official reprimand has been entered into my personnel file."

"Why? What'd you do, besides save her life?"

Though that much was true, he still felt a great burden of guilt for not warning Heidi to stay clear of the shallows. He was also contending, just now, with all the strange sensations evoked by sitting in Miranda's candlelit kitchen on a warm summer night. When he raised his eyes to look at her, he tried not to let his gaze drop toward the scooped neckline of her short-sleeved top. But it wasn't easy. From the first day he'd met her, while scoping out the canyon for the cheapest possible place to live, he'd felt this undeniable tug. When he'd seen the For Rent sign stuck on the parked trailer and pulled over to check it out, she'd drifted out of the store like some kind of wood nymph in a long skirt—like the one that draped around her ankles now—and after allowing him to inspect the interior of the camper, said, "How much can you pay?"

"How much are you asking?" he'd replied.

"How much can you pay?"

"Depends on what you're asking."

Giving up on that line of inquiry, she said, "What do you do?"

He told her he worked in environmental science and would be doing some fieldwork in Topanga. "You're not here to figure out how to cut a highway through the mountains, are you, or how to subdivide the land for developers?"

"I'm here to protect the mountains and subdivide the developers."

That was what had sealed the deal. She quoted him a price a lot lower than he'd expected, and he moved his stuff in the next day—not that that was so hard. All of his stuff had fit into three boxes and a couple of duffel bags.

The candle made the cramped kitchen feel like a cave lit by a campfire, and their voices instinctively fell into that lower range used to confide secrets in the dark. Sure, they had talked before, but only on the fly, or with Laszlo lurking nearby. Tonight she asked him question after question about growing up, and though he almost never talked about it with anyone, he found himself telling her about how his dad, a fiery young Salvadoran radical, had overstayed his visa and been deported, never to be seen again. All of this he'd gotten from his mother, an impressionable and unstable grad student in Latin American studies, whose own family had pretty much dispensed with her after she'd gotten involved with Jorge. It was all very confused. His memories of his dad were all mixed up with Che Guevara, whose poster hung over his mother's bed. Did his dad wear a beret?

"I can relate to that being-dispossessed stuff," Miranda said, "even though I didn't have all the trouble you had to deal with. When I didn't fit in at the Marlborough School, where my mother and my grandmother and her grandmother went, my family didn't know what to do with me. My dad passed away a long time ago, and I got a small trust fund. I call it an arts grant, since I use it to support my painting and this store. My mother recently married her third husband."

"Third time's the charm, they say."

"Maybe. This guy's named Bentley Wright—sounds like a comic book hero, right? And he seems pretty nice. A retired curator at the

Huntington Library, which happens to be almost next door to my mother's house. But I only see them at Christmas or Thanksgiving, or at a funeral if one of my aunts or uncles dies. Topanga might as well be a million miles from San Marino."

Two very different roads, he thought, but converging, in an odd way, here. While Miranda was rebelling and getting thrown out of every fancy school she attended, he'd been working like crazy to play the one good card he'd ever been dealt—his native intelligence—to make a life worth living for himself and his little sister. With some help from a couple of insightful public school mentors, and even a grudging hand, extended once, from his maternal grandparents, he'd managed to get a BS and a master's from UCLA.

For dessert, Miranda offered a carton of lemon sorbet, but instead of bothering with bowls, she simply stuck two spoons into it and they passed it back and forth. At one point, they got the spoons mixed up, and Miranda, laughing, said, "I don't know which one is mine anymore."

"I'll take my chances," Rafe said, secretly hoping that he might get hers.

As she scraped the last shavings from the cardboard bottom, they heard the crunching of tires on the gravel out in front of the Cornucopia, and a couple of car doors slamming.

"That's not Laszlo," Miranda said, and a moment later they heard someone calling for him and banging on the front door.

"What the hell?" she said. "At this hour?"

"I'll come with you," Rafe said, already guessing whose voice he'd heard.

After trooping down the stairs and through the dark store, he saw Seth peering in through the window while Alfie stood on the porch shouting for Laszlo to come out.

"We're closed," Miranda said through the door, and Seth, stepping back, said, "We don't want you. We want to talk to Laszlo."

"He's not here."

"When'll he be back?"

Rafe interposed himself, opening the door, and said, "Why? What can't wait?"

Seth looked taken aback, and so did Alfie. They looked at each other like, *Hey, what's the story here?* Rafe could already see that they were calculating how they might be able to turn his presence here to their immediate advantage, or at the very least cause some trouble with it.

"Hey, Salazar," Seth said. "Didn't expect to find you here."

"What do you want?"

"An opinion."

"Fine. I think you should go home."

"Not from you. From Laszlo." His eyes sought out Miranda, standing behind Rafe. "We've got something we think Laszlo might be interested in." He glanced back at their flatbed, where Rafe could see a big green steamer trunk. "We dug it up and want to know what it's worth."

Rafe decided not to let on, just yet, that he already knew they were lying. How did they think the trunk had found its way onto the shore? A miracle? He felt like it had come back to him, even by this roundabout means, for a reason.

"Bring it inside," Rafe said, and when Miranda, surprised, started to object, he whispered to her, "Let them. I know what I'm doing."

Seth and Alfie stalled, unsure of their next move, but since they were not the kind of men gifted with patience and foresight, they picked up the trunk, and while Miranda turned on the lights and Rafe cleared a space for it on the counter, they carted it in and plunked it down, wiping their hands on their dirty jeans.

Seeing it inside, under the lights, covered with grime and rust, it had an altogether different aspect. At the lake, it had looked like flotsam. Here, it assumed the appearance of some ancient relic. Rafe fingered the padlock, which would never have yielded to a key anymore; it would have to be knocked off with a hammer.

"What now?" Rafe said. "What do you want to know?"

"We want to know," Seth said slowly, as if speaking to a child, "what's inside it."

"And what it's worth," Alfie added.

"Why bring it to me?" Miranda asked.

"In case you forgot, we *didn't* bring it to you," Seth replied. "We brought it to Laz. But since he's not around, maybe you and Salazar here can tell us."

Rafe was torn. Ever since spotting it sticking up out of the lake, he'd wondered what was in it himself. Who dumps a trunk in the middle of a lake in a desolate canyon? And when had they done it? How many years had passed before the level of the lake had fallen enough to reveal it?

"You got a chisel or something?" Seth asked.

Miranda shook her head.

"I've got some tools in my trailer," Rafe said, reluctant to leave Miranda alone with them for even a minute or two, until Trip showed up to guard her.

After fishing his metal toolbox out of the storage bin in his trailer and coming back, he found Alfie smoking a joint on the front porch and Seth leering at a painting of a nubile maiden petting a unicorn.

"You do these yourself?" he was asking Miranda. "Maybe I'll buy one of 'em someday."

Probably with the riches he was expecting to find inside the trunk, Rafe thought. Pulling the trunk to one side of the counter so that he could land a clean blow on the padlock, he could still make out the faintest impression of travel stickers—scraps of color and the outline of illegible letters—imprinted on its top. He had the impression that this trunk had seen the world in its day.

It took just two strikes with the hammer for the padlock to explode into a cloud of red dust, and one more for the remnants to drop to the floor. As Rafe brushed the dust off his hands and pants, Seth, unable to wait any longer, grabbed the lid and pried it up.

Even before looking inside, Rafe had to wonder what they had just cracked open. Was it, as Heidi had suggested, a treasure chest . . . or was it something more dire? Not a treasure trove, but a coffin?

9 December, 1881

And so began what I have come to regard as the period of the Great Experimentation.

I was, at once, its chief beneficiary and its most tortured subject.

I lived a divided life, half the time in the subterranean labyrinth that comprised the doctor's treatment rooms and laboratories, and half the time above ground, in my own suite, recovering from whatever the latest ministrations had entailed. My blood was let, and anaemia diagnosed, which required that I consume slabs of calf's liver nearly raw and submit myself to cold showers meant to force the constitution into rallying its forces; these were quickly followed by steaming saunas designed to leach the tubercle bacillus from the body through the natural perspiration. I was reminded of an American sweat lodge in a place called Laramie, where I had joined the Lakota Indians under a suffocating tent of buffalo hides. I had done so with an eye towards including the episode in one of the letters for which the London and Edinburgh newspapers paid me negligible sums, but I had in the end needed to be ignominiously carried out, insensible, by the tribal elders.

I could tell Dr Rüedi was no more satisfied with my progress than I was. Even the glittering of the lenses in his pince-nez seemed to radiate a sense of impatience, as if it were I, and not the disease, that was obstinately refusing to yield. Surely, I thought, he must be accustomed to such results—the midnight toboggan runs still occurred with dismal regularity, and the quaint cemetery, not half a league up the mountain slope in Davos-Dorf, was well-populated with the graves of those who had elected to rest forever in the region where they had last entertained some hope of recovery. Although I did not like to admit to such a vanity, it did cross my mind that in my particular case he was most determined to effect a cure because of my public reputation. He had already saved my life once, during the wolf attack, but were I to resume my place, untroubled by disease, in the literary world, I would provide an indisputable advertisement of his medical services to all and sundry.

I only wished that I could oblige.

Fanny, too, was growing irritable. She missed the hustle and bustle, the engagements and even intrigue, of more cosmopolitan surroundings. She had long since worn out the excitements of the few establishments in the valley, where the fashions leaned towards lederhosen and dirndl skirts, and the stock in trade was seldom replenished. At the Belvédère, she had earned the animosity of several guests with her American candour, though it must be said her native colouring alone had predisposed many of them to place themselves at one remove. I overheard a chambermaid referring to her as 'the Mexican', and though I had experienced this before, I resented it, and found myself, in consequence, harbouring no few resentments of my own.

To their credit, Randolph Desmond and his companion displayed no such prejudice, and so we found ourselves thrown into their society more and more often. So long as Lloyd's affections for

Miss Wooldridge were kept in check, these gatherings, at the skating pond or sledding hill, dining room or grand salon, were pleasantly benign. On occasion, Symonds joined us, though the conversation was plainly beneath his usual level of discourse; Desmond had scraped his way through Harrow, been sent down from Oxford after less than a semester, and made no bones about any of it. By subtle, or even overt, means, Symonds would attempt to draw me off into some separate colloquy. For some reason, he had taken it into his head that I was wasting my talents on adventure tales for boys and poetry for sickly children, when I could be better employed dilating on the moral characters first sketched by Theophrastus. 'Your gifts are a river not to be denied,' he said, stroking his beard, 'but think what a sublime contribution they could make if their course were but better directed.' I think he does not, in this respect, understand me at all.

But do I understand myself any longer? Where once I might have answered the question readily—'I am a belletrist in the tradition of Hazlitt and the gentle Lamb'—I would now careen between such undistinguished posts as chronic invalid and wandering Scotsman.

Or worse.

Increasingly, when the night nurse had fallen sleep, and my fevered brain could not be calmed, I would slip from my cot, put on my red silk robe and deerskin slippers—a recent gift from Fanny's shopping expeditions to town—and creep slowly down the stone-walled corridor. In the pocket of the robe, I kept a biscuit or a bit of beef from my dinner, and when I had reached Lord Grey's cell, I would stop and peer inside. The first time or two I had done this, the wolf had thrown himself at me in a frenzy, but as he became more accustomed to my presence and learned that my visits preceded a morsel or two of food, he had come to tolerate, and even quite possibly relish, my intrusions.

For my part, I pitied the animal. He was kept on a chain in a dark, dank cell, and though I could not fathom why, he occasionally showed evidence of having been subjected to some experimentation of his own. I could see patches of linen bandages on his limbs and a furtive look in his once fierce eye. Though Yannick was appointed his keeper, he was an oaf who, left to his own devices, would long since have starved or beaten the beast to death. I had once come upon him taunting the animal with lashes from a birch rod extended through the bars, and even with one lung artificially collapsed, I had summoned enough strength to wrest the stick from his hand.

From under his thatch of thick blond hair, he regarded me with a mask of dull incomprehension. (Which of Theophrastus's moral characters, I wonder now, would Symonds have said he most resembled?) 'Give that back to me,' he said.

Bending my knee, I snapped the rod over it and tossed the pieces onto the ground.

'Why did you do that?' he said, now with menace in his voice.

'Don't ever let me find you at such a game again.'

'It's just a damn wolf. Once the doctor has taken as much of his blood as he wants, he has promised the creature to me.'

This explained the bandages at its joints and jugular.

'The pelt is a fine one, and I can use it to make a coat for my son.'

'Why would Rüedi want its blood?' I asked, in a voice made less commanding by shortness of breath.

Yannick snorted. 'Why indeed,' he said, surveying my rickety body. 'What do you think he has been pumping into you through those needles of his? Claret?'

The doctor had taken pains to conceal the syringes from my view, a practice in which he was aided by my own aversion to the sight of a long, sharp point puncturing my skin. When I had asked about the injections, he had assured me they were composed of iron for the anaemia, mixed with the extracts of various local flora rich in nutrients. After exhausting my forearms, he had resorted to making the injections in my calves and buttocks. Coming upon me fresh from a bath, Fanny had joked that I looked as if I had been sitting on a pincushion.

The revelation that I had been infused with the blood of a wolf was enough to send me reeling, and the next day, instead of waiting for the doctor to summon me to his examining rooms, I accosted him in his laboratory, among the beakers and bottles, the surgical models and instruments. A human skeleton dangled like a marionette from a hook on the white plastered wall. Looking up from his microscope, he squinted to see who was trespassing in his inner sanctum, and when I challenged him, he sighed and said, 'Where did you hear such nonsense?'

'I have seen the evidence myself. I have seen Lord Grey.'

'Who?'

'The wolf.'

'You have a name for him?'

'What can you have hoped to gain by such barbarous experiments?'

'Progress.'

'Without so much as my consent?'

'Your consent was, and remains, implicit, so long as you are under my care. While the plombage allows your lung to rest and heal, the course of injections is designed to attack the bacillus in your lymphatic systems. Your blood is weak and febrile. The blood of an Alpine wolf is perfectly adapted to the rigours of a high altitude and harsh climate; it is richer in oxygen than any other, and the blood in the veins of your so-called Lord Grey is richer than that of any specimen I have ever seen. A wolf like that, the leader of its pack, can cover fifty kilometres in a day—can you go fifty feet without stopping?'

It was doubtful.

'That wolf can break an antler between its teeth. Yours would crack at a soup bone.'

His eyes flicked to something behind me, and I turned to see a brooding hulk blocking the doorway.

'I'm sorry, Doctor,' Yannick sputtered. 'I didn't see him go by. Do you want me to get rid of him for you?'

'What I want is for you to learn to keep your own counsel in future.'

'I don't know what you mean.'

'You seldom do. Suffice it to say, if you arouse another patient with ill-advised comments on my research, I'll sack you on the spot. Do I make that much understood?'

Yannick, fuming, grunted, and Rüedi dismissed him with a flick of his hand. If there had been any doubt in my mind, I knew now that I had just made a sworn enemy of the worst kind.

Returning his attention to me, the doctor said, 'I have drawn and distilled a more than adequate amount of the grey wolf's blood. It's being kept in an icebox. And the infusions you've been given have already made a marked improvement in your condition.'

'How would you know that?' I scoffed, though, truth be told, I had indeed felt slightly more vigourous for the past day or two, even with only the one lung working.

'See for yourself if you don't believe me.' Vacating his stool, he gestured at the microscope. 'It's a sample taken from you yesterday.'

I had certainly seen a microscope before—no one who had consulted as many physicians and scientists as I had could have avoided them—and had even ventured to put my eye to a lens more than once. Bending to this one now, and adjusting its focus, I saw a pink sea swimming with tiny amorphous creatures, gambolling like dolphins before a ship's prow. 'What am I observing?'

'Blood cells—red and white—and what my late colleague Dr Max Schultze, at the Anatomical Institute in Bonn, has dubbed "spherules". Those are the smaller and more purplish bodies.'

It was a world of wonders, as colourful and complex as anything seen through the kaleidoscope kept in the grand salon for the amusement of the guests.

'It is an English physician, a Dr Richard Hill Norris, at Queen's College in Birmingham, who has best described their purpose.'

'Which is?'

'To coagulate at the site of an interrupted endothelium.'

Although I understood the words, my expression must have said otherwise.

'They stop the bleeding where you have received a wound or injection. Without them, you would have been leaking blood like a worm-eaten wine barrel by now.'

Under normal circumstances, the doctor would not have been nearly so forthcoming, but I had gathered the impression that he wished his methods to be made comprehensible to the man who might one day help to make his name famous. I resolved to do nothing to disabuse him of that notion—not yet, at least.

'And the end game?' I asked innocently. 'How will any of this effect a cure?'

He all but rubbed his hands together with glee and confidence. 'By injecting the wolf with your own diseased blood, I have been encouraging his much stronger constitution to create an antigen to the bacillus.'

'As with smallpox inoculations?'

'Precisely. And then, by returning that fortified and oxygenated serum to your own bloodstream, I intend to root out and eradicate the bacillus wherever it may hide.'

Though being no physician, still I could see the ingenuity, and with any luck the efficacy, of the scheme.

'Your red blood cell count has already trebled,' he said, arms folded, beaming with pride. 'When we reverse the effects of the plombage, you will feel the full measure of the treatment.' He leaned back against the wall, the limp skeleton hanging by his side like a mute conspirator. It was a tableau I could not shake from my mind, try as I might, as I ascended into the hotel. The skeleton had all but grinned at me. Trudging up the winding stairs to my attic bolthole, I debated, and not for the first time, whether my intrusion on the doctor had brought me into the company of a genius, or a madman.

TOPANGA CANYON— CALIFORNIA

Present Day

Seth's grubby fingers tore into the contents of the trunk, pulling out one item after another, shaking it out, tossing it on the counter, then burrowing deeper, like a terrier pursuing a rat.

But Rafe could see he was becoming more and more frustrated as the musty old clothing piled up on the counter. The smell alone was bad enough.

"What the hell," he muttered, yanking out a flat black board that only upon shaking popped up to reveal itself as a battered top hat. Onto the stack it went with the black frock coat, the black pants and leather gloves, the silk brocade vest, the pale pink cravat—once no doubt scarlet—the scuffed high-button boots with the tips of nails protruding from the heels. "God damn, is it all nothing but this shit?"

Miranda had stepped a few feet from the counter to get away from the smell of mildew and rot, but Rafe stayed close, wondering just how long this trunk could possibly have been lying at the bottom of the lake.

He was no expert on the history of fashion, but these clothes looked to him like something people wore in the late 1800s. The only place he'd ever seen anything like them was in old oil paintings and some movies.

"Are you kidding me?" Seth said, stretching open what appeared to be a black shoulder cape with a high velvet collar. "Who was this guy—Batman?"

Alfie laughed, grabbed the cape, and despite the stink, wound it around his shoulders. "Watch me—I can fly!" he said, twirling around so fast he banged into a display table, knocking over a jar of incense sticks.

"It's an opera cape," Miranda said.

But Seth's eyes had suddenly lit up, as he pulled from the trunk a bamboo scabbard, and then drew from that a long knife with an elaborately carved wooden handle. "Now, this I can use."

Rafe didn't want to think too hard about what he'd use it for—especially as he had just noticed, at the very bottom of the nearly empty trunk, an iron strongbox about the size of a DVR.

Once Seth had finished waving the blade around in the air, he, too, spotted the strongbox and, wedging the knife under his belt, exulted, "Finally!"

Maybe it was time, Rafe thought, before the box was opened, to establish just who had really found it—that he and Heidi had dredged it out of the lake and that anything of value it might contain belonged, first and foremost, to any rightful heirs who could be found; considering the age of what he'd seen so far, however, he doubted if that would be possible. Still, even if the contents went unclaimed, they were probably the property of the state of California, since both he and Heidi were in the government's employ when they'd recovered the trunk, and on state-owned land to boot.

Seth already had the box on the counter and was fumbling at its lid, locked tight. "Give me that hammer," he said, keeping his eyes on the box but extending his hand like a surgeon expecting the nurse to slap the tool into his palm.

"No."

"What do you mean, no?" Seth said, blinking in disbelief.

"I mean, this trunk, and everything inside it, doesn't belong to you."

"What are you talking about?" Alfie exploded. "We found it! We dug it up! It's ours!"

"You didn't dig it up, and I know where you found it," Rafe said. He calmly explained just where things stood, while Seth and Alfie got madder and madder.

"What if there's money in that box?" Seth said.

"Even if there is," Rafe said, "think about it. Look at all this junk. Look how old it all is. Any currency that old will be worthless by now."

"Jewels wouldn't be," Alfie challenged. "Gold wouldn't be."

True enough, Rafe thought, so he took a chance, lifted the box, and shook it back and forth. The only sound was the rustle of something shifting from side to side. It sounded like a book, or maybe a bunch of old letters, and weighed no more than that.

"Open it up and let's see," Seth demanded.

"A hammer won't do it," Rafe said, "and I don't see a key. Do you?"

Seth stuck his head into the vile-smelling trunk and groped wildly through the remaining items—loose buttons and broken combs, scraps of cloth and bits of paper, a dented flask, a crumpled bonnet with a faded blue band. Coughing, but empty-handed, he emerged no less truculent than before.

"You're just going to steal whatever's inside it for yourself. Don't think I don't know that."

"You want a receipt?"

"A what?"

"Miranda, have you got a pen and paper around?"

She produced a pad with an elf sitting under a toadstool and a pen with lavender ink. Printing carefully, Rafe wrote out and dated a receipt. "One steamer trunk and its contents," he declared, "found by Land Management officials and transported to Cornucopia of Topanga by the undersigned." After scrawling his own signature on it, he turned the paper around and said, "Sign your names and print them underneath. You can file a claim with the state if you want."

Seth and Alfie looked terribly uncertain, but when Rafe said, "You can keep the knife—I'll pretend I never saw it," Seth grudgingly scribbled his signature on the paper and shoved it toward his partner to do the same. When Alfie hesitated, Seth said, "Just do it—we'll come back. This isn't over by a long shot."

On the way out, Seth seized the painting he'd been looking at earlier, stuck it under his arm, and waited for them to object. Miranda knew enough to write it off, and they slammed the door so hard the wind chimes rattled and clacked like bones on the porch outside. Rafe looked at Miranda, who breathed a sigh of relief at their departure and said, "Let it go. I never could sell that one anyway."

25 December, 1881

No sooner had the last candle been lit on the Yule tree than Yannick, his arms filled with firewood for the hearth, burst through the French windows and into the grand salon. A gust of icy wind accompanied him, and Fanny exclaimed, as the candles guttered in their metal jackets and several went out altogether, 'Quick—close the windows!'

Yannick kicked a booted foot at them, but it took another servant, who put down his tray of liqueurs and, bending his shoulder to the frame, bolted the windows tight against the raging wind outside.

For several days, the temperatures had been dropping precipitously, and the skies, once a cerulean blue, had turned the dull grey colour of a stagnant weir. The surrounding mountains, whose snow-covered peaks usually cut a jagged profile around the valley, had been obscured by a legion of low, scudding clouds, until it was as if the Belvédère was a ship lost in a fog bank and all its inhabitants but spectral figures caught in the same strange limbo.

But it was only at dawn on this, Christmas day, that the tempest had finally descended in all its fury, enshrouding the hotel in a white and blinding embrace. From my eyrie that morning, I had been able to see nothing but frost on the windowpanes, and hear nothing but the incessant howling of the Alpine blast. Doors rattled and loose shutters banged, draperies rustled at vagrant drafts, and fireplaces sighed through cracks in the flue. Even Woggin had lost his native zeal, huddling under the bed with his ears flattened against his head and his head cradled between his paws.

'Of all people, it was the Protestant reformer Martin Luther who is said to have first affixed candles to an evergreen,' Symonds was saying to anyone close enough to the decorated tree. 'The Northern cultures, of course, were already predisposed to the worship of various trees. The oak was sacred to the Germanic Chatti tribe until it was replaced by the fir, whose triangular shape, it was suggested by Saint Boniface, pointed the way towards Heaven.'

'We'll all be going there soon enough', Fanny said, 'if they don't keep those candles from setting fire to this whole place.'

Undeterred, Symonds continued by pointing out that among the ancient rituals there had been one where the village girls danced in a magic circle around the tree, imprisoning its imp inside, and only allowing it to go free when it had promised to give them their heart's desire. 'It is perhaps from that custom that the giving of gifts derives.'

Fanny, losing interest in Symonds's disquisition (the man is a walking encyclopaedia, but one that never closes), went to her son, who was standing close to the tree, seemingly transfixed by its gaudy lights and ornaments. In addition to the candles, a host of gilt cones and gaily-wrapped candies had been attached to its boughs. At its top, which grazed the very ceiling of the salon, a star had been wrought from holly berries and golden braid.

Watching mother and son together, I was struck again by both the similarities and incongruities. From Fanny, Lloyd had inherited a growing stockiness, along with a forthright temperament, but none of her dark colouring. In his features—his pale eyes and light hair—he most resembled his father, a man whom I had seen only in a faded sepia photograph taken in some mining camp where, once again, he had failed to strike gold. As a Christmas gift, I had given Lloyd a volume of tales by E. A. Poe, which, as it happened, I had reviewed for the Academy five or six years before. It was 'The Masque of the Red Death', when I had first read it to him one wintry night, that had been his favourite, though Fanny had discouraged me from sharing such stories with him in future without her prior assent. 'I don't need him waking from any more nightmares, thank you kindly.' As he was older now, I felt Poe's grim fantasies could do no great harm.

Indeed, as I considered it, there was something of the masque about the scene before me that night. At dinner, the guests of the hotel had worn their finest clothes; dinner jackets with velvet collars and scarlet cummerbunds on the men, silken gowns complemented by glittering baubles on the throats and wrists of all the women. My own old black suit hung loosely from my shoulders. Paper hats had been issued, too—tiaras for the ladies, crowns for their companions. The mood was meant to be one of gaiety, and all conspired to further the illusion, but in the hectic flush of their cheeks, the antic gleam of their eyes, one could not help but note among the good doctor's invalids the underlying sense of apprehension. Would their next Christmas be spent with family, gathered round the table at their ancestral home, or would they still be here, assailed by fevers, coughs, and infection? Worse yet (among those privy to the secret), would they have been dispatched by toboggan in the gloom of night?

'Oh, I see your friends have arrived,' Symonds said, gliding away before he could be subjected to what he regarded as their inane banter, 'and so I will leave you to them. I doubt they have come to hear the lieder.'

Turning, I saw Desmond pushing Constance Wooldridge in her wheelchair—a rattan-seated affair running on two great hoops—with her ankle wrapped and elevated on a sort of stirrup. 'A fall on the ice,' Desmond had explained over the roast lamb at dinner. She had also bruised her cheek, and most mortifying of all, chipped a tiny fragment from a front tooth. She had barely looked up from her plate all through the meal, and even at the best jokes had covered her smile in embarrassment.

'We're here for the dancing!' Desmond exclaimed, whirling her chair in a circle that left the poor girl clutching her stomach.

'Put me down for the mazurka,' I said.

'Done.' Surveying the room, Desmond said, 'I shan't be sorry to leave this sad bunch behind. The Sunday coach can't come soon enough for me.'

I had not known of his imminent departure, and was sorry to hear it. Noticing my surprise, he said, 'Didn't Lloyd tell you?'

'No.'

'The lad can't keep a thought in his head when our Constance is around.' He reached down to pinch her cheek, but, her bruised face no doubt sensitive to the touch, she shrank from his fingertips.

'When will you be making your own escape?' he inquired, a question I had been asking myself for some time.

'Soon, I hope. There's a bit of reconstruction to be done, on one lung in particular, but I hope to catch a Sunday coach myself.'

'Do look me up when you get to London.'

'I shall be happy to see you both,' I said, as a means of including Constance in the conversation, and in acknowledgement, she turned her face upward. Her lips still sealed to conceal the damage, she gave me a look designed to convey encouragement, but something else, too, that I could not readily determine.

There was the clap of a piano keyboard being uncovered, and as the accompanist drew his bench towards the pedals, a bony spinster approached the front of the salon, a real tiara somewhat askew on her head, clutching a sheaf of sheet music in one hand. Dr Rüedi himself, removing his pince-nez with a flourish, introduced the lady to the audience now taking its seats.

'Good Lord,' Desmond muttered, 'when does the band begin?'

'After the bel canto.'

The songs—fittingly, given the locale—were chiefly Franz Schubert, rather than the Italians, and the singer, though well past her prime, gave of her utmost. Never one to become lost in a legato, I found my thoughts wandering, addressing themselves to everything from the narrative difficulties in the manuscript that lay on my desk, to the storm pummelling the hotel on all sides with all the ferocity of the cannon batteries at Sebastopol. But beneath the shrieking of the wind and the expressive wailing of the soprano, I gradually became attuned to something else, something whose origins were not in the room. It was a low and prolonged moaning, a sigh so plaintive that, once heard, it could not be ignored. My ears virtually pricked up at the sound.

Lord Grey.

It came to me, impossible though it be, that I was hearing the laboured breathing of the wolf . . . the creature whose blood even now coursed through my veins . . . as it lay, in extremis, in its frigid cell below.

I looked around for any sign that the sound had come to others, but everyone around was attending to the concert, undistracted and undismayed. I alone was in perfect harmony with the suffering beast below.

When an opportune moment struck, I unobtrusively absented myself from the salon, stopping in the kitchen to grab some scraps of lamb, which the chef obligingly wrapped in a napkin ('Your Woggin should have a Christmas dinner, too!' he said), and then quickly descending the dimly lit staircase, where the gas lamps flickered on every landing, and into the cellars. The sound only grew louder.

Passing the recovery room where I had lain so many a night after the surgery and other treatments, I went straight to the wolf's cell, only to find the latch down and the door ajar. Wet footprints—human, and large—smudged the stone floor. I had no doubt who had made them.

Glancing into the examination room, I was greeted by no one but the grinning skeleton hanging from the wall. The doctor's fur coat hung beside it, and snatching it from the rack, I pulled it on while following the footprints around a corner, down another hall, and finally to an arched wooden doorway bolstered by iron slats. Judging from the rattle of its hinges, beyond it lay the vacant yard behind the hotel.

Bracing myself for the blast, I threw the door open, though even then I was not prepared for the strength of the gale. The footprints were nearly invisible, but a path had plainly been cut through the snow. A narrow track led into the maelstrom and towards what I surmised was the smokehouse. No other refuge could be found out here, and there could be no better place for Yannick to conduct the deadly business he undoubtedly had in mind.

Finding it, however, was another matter. Although the distance was small, no more than a couple of hundred yards, it was an easy thing to lose all sense of direction. As part of the holiday décor, every window in the hotel had been outfitted with a lantern or candle, and by the light of them, I was able to orient myself until they, too, became a blur, and I was guided more by the preternatural auditory sense than anything else. With one hand out in front of me and the other clutching the collar of the coat closed against the wind, I ploughed slowly ahead until my frozen fingers grazed the planks of the smokehouse door. I fumbled for the latch, lifted it, and ducked inside.

Slabs of meat and dead fowl dangled from the rafters. A low fire smouldered in the grate, and Yannick himself was crouched beside it, poking at the glowing embers. Lord Grey, torn bandages trailing from his limbs, the muzzle still holding his jaws fast, was now chained to the bottom bars of a rack used for stretching pelts. Though wobbling with fear and fury, he was on all four paws.

'What,' Yannick said, 'the party, it is over already?'

I shivered, not from the cold, but from the sudden warmth of the room. On the long refectory-style table, several knives and cleavers were arrayed for the task at hand.

'You look an idiot in that,' Yannick said, sneering at the paper crown that I'd altogether forgotten and that the storm had miraculously stuck to my forehead.

There being no fit rejoinder to his remark—no words indeed necessary to explain my purpose there—I brushed the hat aside and went straight to the wolf.

'You'll want to keep clear of him. He knows what's coming.'

Kneeling, I looked straight into Lord Grey's eyes, and he into mine, and in that moment, something passed between us that I felt as viscerally as I might the kick from a horse. Something stirred in my heart, something surged in my bloodstream, my limbs ached, and my skin prickled.

'Do you want to go and get that son of yours, that Lloyd?'

'Why on earth would I do that?'

'He loves to watch the doctor go about his operations, the autopsies best of all.'

This was news to me, though it explained his unaccounted-for absences of late.

'Perhaps he would like to watch me go about my own operation,' he said with a guffaw. 'He could lend me a hand, too.'

I reached towards the muzzle and unfastened the leather strap.

'That's a good way to lose your fingers,' Yannick warned, rising now and gripping, conspicuously, the handle of a gleaming cleaver.

But the jaws did not snap. Reaching into my pocket, I took out the napkin filled with lamb and laid it on the hard-packed dirt floor. Lord Grey looked at it dubiously—had his food until now been laced with some sedating agent?—then, as it had come from my trusted hand, gobbled it down.

'That won't be halfway through his gullet before it's spilled out onto this table.'

Paying no heed, I stood up and methodically unwound the chain from the rack.

'Are you mad?'

Again, I made no reply.

'Stop that!'

When the wolf realized that he was free from constraint, his eyes shifted rapidly from mine towards the door, then back again, as if begging for one further act of assistance.

'Oh no you don't!' Yannick shouted, raising the cleaver. But I had already turned to the door and lifted the latch.

The gust of wind and snow that blew into the smokehouse stirred the fire and threw a cloud of orange sparks and black ash into the air. Bandages still dangling from his fur, and staggering like a drunken sailor, Lord Grey made for the open door. The whistle of the cleaver shot past my ear and thunked into the wooden wall.

'I'll kill you!' Yannick raged. 'I'll kill you both!'

I ducked out the door and into a storm that, if anything, had only gained in fury. Even the candles and lanterns in the windows of the Belvédère were utterly obscured, and after only a few steps, I had tumbled into the snow and, scrambling to my feet again, lost all sense of direction. Whirling around, I saw nothing but a veil of white, heard nothing but my own gasping breath, but felt—and this was an astonishment to myself—a rising tide of strength welling up from some heretofore secret source.

A moment later, I was struck by a blunt force so overwhelming I was knocked halfway down the slope, rolling over and over again like a barrel. I felt hands tearing at my coat and grasping at my throat, and Yannick's angry breath swearing my destruction.

But if wolves had failed to kill me on this bleak mountaintop, no man, I vowed, would do the deed.

As I struggled to fight back, I conceded myself—a chronic invalid, a man with but one lung—overmatched. At the same time, I felt the burst of a strange energy, like lightning, crackling in every vein, and in my fingers a prehensile strength, as if they had become an eagle's talons.

'I'll kill you!' I heard again, hot spittle spraying my face.

I greeted the threat not with fear, but with a kind of mad vigour, a lust for engagement, for combat . . . for blood.

What should have been a hopeless contest became a pitched and even match, the two of us on the icy ground, ripping at each other's limbs and skin. Even my teeth ached with the desire to bite and savage his flesh, and when they found their mark and tore a shred from his cheek, he shrieked and leaned back on his knees, his hand pressed to the bloody wound.

God forgive me for saying so, but the taste of his blood was as sweet as nectar on my lips. I might have laughed at his agony were it not for the glint of a knife I now saw he had fished from the back of his belt and raised like Abraham about to sacrifice his son.

I fended off the first blow, and the second, the blade slicing through the thick sleeve of the coat, but as the knife came up again, a dark force hurtled out of the snowstorm, catching Yannick unawares and, like Ganymede suddenly swept aloft by Zeus, he was carried off. I heard a prolonged scream, descending in both its hold on life and in the sheer distance from which it came. Whatever savagery Lord Grey was inflicting—and it could be no other agent—it was being rendered on the slope of the hill, then down towards the fringe of the forest, and finally into the dense ravine that plummeted another thousand feet towards the valley floor. Several seconds more elapsed before its echoes were swallowed up altogether by the night and the storm and the driving snow.

To my own astonishment, I raised myself to my feet, lifted my face into the stinging spray of ice and sleet, and, with no shame or hesitation, howled in triumph.

TOPANGA CANYON—
CALIFORNIA

Present Day

The roar and sputter of Seth's truck had barely dissipated down the canyon when Miranda turned to Rafe and said, "What do we do with all this stuff now?" Even in a store as eclectic as hers, she knew there was no way she could sell these things. The smell alone would kill the sale.

"The strongbox I can take to the firehouse on Kanan Road. They're used to picking locks on abandoned cars and campers."

"And the rest?" she said, surveying the musty clothes.

"I don't know," he confessed. "Halloween?"

"You're no help," she said. "Go get some sleep. You look wiped."

"I am."

Once he'd gone, Miranda started to pile the clothes back into the trunk, then thought better of it. What they needed first was a good airing out. And even sorting through them now, she could see that these had once belonged to a gentleman; a tattered label in the tailcoat read Henry Poole & Co. The gloves were kid, and the opera cape had a black velvet collar with a silver clasp at the throat; the brocade vest was lined with silk; the trouser buttons were bone. The top hat was lopsided, even when she had punched it completely out, but made of beaver, and its brim was encircled by what had once probably been a deep crimson ribbon.

The stink was pretty unbearable, though, and it was to the smell that she attributed the goose bumps she felt erupt on her skin as she gathered the clothes into a bundle. Turning her head, she carried them at arm's length out to the yard, where she dropped them onto the ground beneath the clothesline. Trip came over for a quick sniff, but even he backed away.

"That bad, huh?"

The light in Rafe's trailer was out—he must have gone right to bed—but the moonlight was enough to work by. Taking the dried sheet off the line and draping it over her shoulder, she pinned the old clothes up one by one—even the hat—until she had the pieces of what looked like a whole Victorian gent on the line. In the Santa Ana breeze that was blowing through the mountains that night, it looked like he was dancing a silent, eerie jig, and despite the warmth of the wind, she found herself wrapping the sheet around both shoulders . . . and her eyes shifting to the door of Rafe's trailer.

She hadn't wanted that dinner to end—much less with a visit from the canyon's two most scurvy characters. Not for the first time, she wondered how she'd wound up in just such a place as this, living the life she was living. Sure, she'd had plenty to run from—classes and cotillions, privilege and possessions, encumbrances and expectations, all of them things that only made her feel more unworthy and fake—but maybe, just maybe, she'd run long enough, and far enough, to stop. If she'd had some point to make, hadn't she made it by now? Was it time to wave the white flag at her forebears, declare a truce, and come to some middle ground? Or was it too late for that?

The answer arrived on a grumbling green Vespa that Laszlo nearly crash-landed beside the porch. Climbing off, he plopped onto the ground, laughing. He was stoned, drunk, or some combination of both. Laszlo had been her single greatest act of defiance; she'd picked him up, or maybe he'd picked her up, at a naked hot springs resort in Baja. He'd told tales of life on the wild side, wooed her with the stories of Carlos Castaneda, and introduced her to everything from magic mushrooms to coke. Although he'd also used a needle on occasion, she'd stopped short of that, like a horse rearing up at a snake in its path. But that was about all she'd stopped short of. In bed (or out of it, for that matter), he'd made her feel things she could never have imagined, things that those prep school boys from Pasadena and San Marino could never have dreamed of. She'd felt like a pile of dry kindling, and he had been the match.

Spotting her in the yard, he called out, "Guess where I was?"

"La Raza."

"And guess who else was there?"

That wasn't hard, either. "Seth and Alfie."

He clambered to his feet, brushing the gravel off his jeans. He still had that long, rangy body that had first driven her crazy, but these days it wasn't as hard as it used to be. He was even starting to develop a potbelly.

"Is that the stuff?" he said, gesturing at the clothesline. "Looks like a lot of crap to me."

"Maybe."

"Or maybe," he said, "it's just what the doctor ordered." He started toward the clothesline, ready to remove the top hat, but she wanted none of it. Nor did she want to have Rafe hear, or worse yet witness, some scene between the two of them. Taking him by the arm—he reeked of beer and dope—she steered him back toward the house, with Trip bringing up the rear.

"And didn't I hear something about a box of gold and jewels?"

"No, you didn't."

"I think I did."

"You're so stoned you don't know what you heard."

"I'm not *that* stoned," he said, letting one hand slink over her shoulder, still swaddled in the sheet, and onto her breast. She let it stay, figuring it would help get him up the back stairs and into the house.

Which was about as far as it worked. As soon as they got inside, he swerved toward the fridge, took out a Corona, and slumped into a chair, his hands cradling the cold bottle, his chin nearly resting on his chest.

"Sit down," he said, his words starting to slur. "Have a drink with me."

Fat chance, she thought, though with any luck, he'd fall asleep at the table. With even better luck, he'd stay right there all night.

In the bedroom, she turned up the window air conditioner—its roar might just cancel out the snoring she was sure to hear soon from the kitchen—and put the fresh sheet on the bed. In the shower stall, she positioned the tin bucket to catch some of the runoff, and when she was done, ruffled her hair dry while standing at the window onto the yard. The gent was still doing his creepy jig on the clothesline, and she yanked the blind down.

Falling into bed in nothing but a long T-shirt, she felt the last ounce of energy drain from her limbs. She'd had too much wine with dinner. And it had been a tiring day—running a store was a lot harder than it looked—capped by that bizarre visit. Before long, her mind had drifted, too. She hadn't moved a muscle on the bed, even to untangle the loose wet ends of her hair from the pillow, before sleep overtook her. But it wasn't a deep or relaxing sleep; her dreams were strange and discomfiting—she was late for some event, but couldn't leave until she'd found a pair of white gloves, and everywhere she looked for them she turned up other odd things from her past, like stuffed animals, field hockey sticks, and the wilted corsage from her prom. She was vaguely aware that this wasn't real, that it was all just a dream, and that if she could only wake up, she wouldn't have to worry about the white gloves at all.

The room was cool from the old air conditioner, but the racket was getting intolerable. And so was Laszlo's snoring. She really should force herself to wake up and get out of bed and fix the situation. Her wet hair would be a hopeless tangle the next day. The light coverlet that she had drawn up over her body was being drawn down again, and her fingers tried to catch it and keep it where it was, at least until she'd located those missing gloves.

Besides, it was too cold in the room to sleep in just the T-shirt.

There was a bad smell in the air, too. Foreign, but familiar. Could it be the rotting corsage? Her eyes opened, blearily, and made out something just above her, weaving back and forth in the moonlight cutting through the slats of the Venetian blind. But what was it? It was squarish at the top and black all over, and when it moved, there was a rustling sound, and another wave of the foul odor washed over her.

Wake up, she told herself, while something else, in the back of her head, said, *But you* are *awake, Miranda.*

She felt the coverlet descending again, and the thing looming above her bent down, and now she thought she could see that the squarish shape was a top hat, and the blackness was a cape with a wide collar, and the terrible smell was from those old clothes in the trunk. But the blanket was down at her ankles now, and the bottom of her T-shirt was coming up, and the fingers lifting it were hard and cold, and with a jolt like electricity her mind snapped into consciousness—*you* are *awake, Miranda.* Her hands flew up to push back at the body trying to clamber on top of her, its fetid breath on her face, its crumpled hat tumbling onto the pillow.

She opened her mouth to scream, but she had no breath in her, and what she heard instead was a low chortle. She kicked the blanket off her feet and struggled to turn on her side, but a voice said "Don't fight" and she was pushed onto her back again. "Don't fight," the voice repeated, though she squirmed in the other direction. Cold hands groped at her waist, and she managed to kick out, feeling the soles of her feet connect with a hard thud and send the intruder reeling back against the window. Something clattered to the floorboards. The blind rattled and crashed from its rod, and when she'd landed upright on the other side of the bed, she snapped on the lamp and saw the Victorian gent slumping down, one hand to his chest, the other planted on the windowsill.

"Shit, Miranda," Laszlo gasped. He looked stunned, as if the kick had shaken him out of some trance. "It was only a joke."

A joke?

"You could have killed me," he complained, massaging his sternum.

She could hardly believe what had just happened. "You're lucky I *didn't* kill you. What the fuck were you thinking?"

"I was *thinking*," he said, "that it might turn you on."

"Turn me on?"

"You used to be kinky. Remember?"

Her mind was still reeling, blood pounding in her temples.

"I think you might have broken one of my ribs."

"I hope I did," she said, storming into the bathroom and locking the door behind her. Putting her hands on either side of the sink, she stared at herself in the mirror, taking slow, deep breaths. She ran cold water over her wrists, then soaked a washcloth and held it to her face. She heard Laszlo, bitterly complaining, tromping out of the bedroom. In the kitchen, a chair got kicked, and the refrigerator door slammed shut. Thank God it was well stocked with Coronas. A few more and he'd be unconscious till dawn. If she slept at all that night, she was going to do it in the tub.

3 January, 1882

There was no funeral for Yannick, no formal obsequies of any kind to mark the passing of the man. It was clear to me that Dr Rüedi preferred it that way. He wanted nothing to put the guests of the Belvédère any more in mind of mortality than they already were. As it was, death was always just around the corner, or even in the next room of the hotel. In this Alpine castle, the music of the danse macabre played on forever.

But I had resolved to quit the masque, just as Desmond and his Miss Wooldridge had done, and had booked three seats on the next Sunday coach to the train station in town. When I shared the news with Symonds, as we lay wrapped in our blankets on the outside verandah, he looked positively stricken.

'But whom shall I talk to?'

'Surely there is no shortage of other convalescents,' I replied, though flattered at his consternation.

'None whose mind provides quite such fertile ground.'

'You make me feel like a fallow field.'

Robert Masello

'And that you are!' he said, turning his long face and doleful eyes my way. 'I have been tilling this soil, cultivating this crop, ever since you arrived.'

'Time, then, that you brought in the harvest.'

'I'm not yet done,' he declared. Looking off towards the valley, so filled with fresh snow it looked like a bowl of milk, he said with great resolve, 'I shall simply have to return with you.'

'Are you well enough?'

'No, but I never shall be. And making the arduous journey back into the world will be much easier if I have travelling companions who may, should disaster strike, be able to offer aid.'

How Fanny would react to having been turned into an ambulance service was not something I looked forward to with any relish, but I could hardly refuse. Already, I had aroused the ire of Dr Rüedi, who had vehemently opposed my departure and nearly refused to undo the effects of the plombage.

'It is too soon to reinflate the lung,' he had insisted in his office.

'But you yourself have said, and seen, that I am much better.' The results of my blood tests had been improving, and even more to the point, the bout with the now-departed Yannick had confirmed a newly restored constitution. Indeed, it felt as if the fight had miraculously invigourated it.

'But there are better results yet to come. If you leave prematurely, you will undo everything we have accomplished.' By 'we', I thought for one moment that he was referring not to me, but to the grinning skeleton hanging behind him on the wall.

'I will have to hazard that.'

'It will be on your own head, not mine.'

'I accept that charge.'

Reluctantly, he agreed to perform the necessary surgery that same afternoon, removing the paraffin through a small but painful incision between my shoulder blades, and then using a rubber nozzle to guide fresh air, blown down my throat through a device that resembled a miniature accordion, into the collapsed lung. Feeling it expand again in my chest was among the strangest sensations I have ever known, like having a bird awaken in its nest and spread its wings beneath your skin. I coughed several times, Dr Rüedi watching intently, before I could regain my equilibrium and give him a reassuring smile. I did not let on that each cough had been accompanied by an exquisite jab of pain.

The news that we were leaving brought nothing but joy to Fanny, who had long ago exhausted the stores and diversions of tiny Davos, and Lloyd, who missed everything from the streets of London to the lovely Constance Wooldridge. Her charms had never worn off; indeed, at one point, Fanny had caught Lloyd stealing a bit of her monogrammed lacery from a laundry basket left out for the maid.

Even Woggin seemed to have intuited the news somehow, and though he had come to enjoy the treats from the hotel chef, he followed us from room to room as the packing was done, tail wagging, making quite sure that no one went anywhere without him. In my attic study, he stood by his pillow on the floor, head up and barking, until I had proved to him that it, too, would be brought along. I took one last look from the window onto the rear of the hotel, thinking I might catch some glimpse of Lord Grey lurking at the fringe of the forest, but saw nothing. The salt lick was unvisited. The smokehouse was as dark and silent as a tomb . . . which, I reflected, it might well have become. Could I really have died in such a remote place, a hut for curing dead game, and in such an ignominious fashion? Hacked to pieces by a murderous Swiss peasant?

Symonds was already ensconced in the coach under two blankets by the time the rest of us climbed in. It was another cold and overcast day, and I saw him glance fretfully at his pocket watch.

'The train leaves at three o'clock.'

'It will wait if it has to,' Fanny said, already exasperated and settling several boxes around her feet. She left so little room that I had
to stretch my legs above the boxes and across to the opposite seat,
between Lloyd and Symonds.

There was no send-off committee to wish us well. The porter,
having secured the bags atop the carriage, tipped his cap, stepped
back, and the coachman cracked his whip. With a jolt, the carriage
left the shelter of the porte cochère, and as it came around the curve
of the hotel drive, the bell tower tolled. Symonds checked his watch
again, and from the corner of my eye I saw the odd tableau of a
stout woman with a striped kerchief tied under her chin, sitting on
a plough horse, the reins held by a sturdy blond lad in lederhosen
and a crumpled hat with one red feather.

And then the Belvédère, and all of those whom it housed,
disappeared.

The coach grew quiet as each of its occupants descended into
separate reveries. So much had transpired in this place, it was
no wonder. For myself, I could not view the narrow pathways cut
through the snow without thinking of the doomed souls who took
their lonely exercise there, or the toboggan run without recalling
the cargo I had seen dispatched on it by moonlight. I was fortunate
indeed to be leaving under my own steam, of my own volition, and
in more robust health than I had arrived. For all his eccentricities,
Dr Rüedi had proved himself to be my saviour, and I looked forward
now to resuming my work and retaking my place among the literary
mob of London. W. E. Henley's was, of course, to be my first stop;
no one would be better able to bring me up to date on the latest
news.

As if by some tacit agreement, the doctor and I had never dis-
cussed Yannick's death—it was put down to a wolf attack—nor did
we address the missing occupant of the subterranean cell. I suspect
he knew I had had a hand in Lord Grey's escape, but what was done

was done. All the doctor asked of me was that I keep him informed of my progress, and, if I remained well, make some mention of the magical Belvédère (and its resident Prospero!) to anyone who might ask—particularly if the interlocutor was of a prominent station in life. In return, he gave me a supply of the elixir to which he attributed much of my improvement.

'But as this remedy still carries no patent, and is in the experimental stage, I have taken the precaution of disguising it,' he said, handing me two bottles of what appeared to be the local Valtellina wine. 'Be sure you do not lose it among the other vintages in your cellar.'

'No fear of that,' I replied. 'I have no cellar. But if I am to inject it as you have done, do I not need a lesson or two in that procedure?'

'I have diluted it for just this reason. Direct intravenous injection is a delicate operation and carries with it too great a risk of misapplication. A small dose of the liquid will offer the benefits of the drug without the inherent dangers.'

The bottles were now thickly swaddled in the bottom of the handbag I had tucked beside me in the coach. With only one brief detour, to skirt the corpse of a frozen cow, we made steady progress towards the town, arriving at Davos with plenty of time to spare. Fanny employed the coach to make one last round of the stores— the shopkeepers were sure to weep at her departure—while Lloyd took Woggin for a quick romp in the snow. And then we were off again, rumbling the rest of the way to the valley floor and the train station, where Symonds promptly took a seat on the bench closest to the fire, while I made mental notes for a travel essay I was contemplating. If one were to keep up one's name among the public, it was necessary to contribute pieces on a variety of subjects to as many different periodicals as possible.

It was after an hour or so, and while making these observations, that I noticed, through the window of the station, the stout woman in the kerchief again, now waddling along the platform and turning her head this way and that. She had watery eyes and fat cheeks red as apples. Under one arm, she carried a bundle the size of a baby. Thinking no more of it, I made some jottings in my notebook, and when the train blew its whistle and the conductors called for the passengers to board, I gathered up my tribe and we made our way to the first-class cars.

Our compartment was soon filled with luggage, and as the air inside was stifling from whoever had last travelled in it—one could only imagine that they had been devouring onions—Lloyd took it upon himself to lower the window all the way to the sash and hang his head and shoulders outside.

'Make sure you come back in before the train starts up,' Fanny said. 'I came here with a full boy—I don't want to leave with just a half.'

On Symonds's face, chin huddled down into the upturned collar of his coat, I detected no great unwillingness to leave with half.

The conductor called again for those holding tickets to board the train, and loud jets of steam plumed from the undercarriage and into the air.

It was from that swirling fog that the woman with the bundle emerged again, scanning the train frantically. At first, it appeared that she was trying to enter the first-class car, but when she was barred from doing so, she went back to marching up and down the platform, as if searching for someone. The blond boy appeared at her side, said something with a hand cupped to her ear—even idle, the noise of the engine was quite deafening—and, to my surprise, pointed up at Lloyd.

She looked uncertain; then, when he had assured her, she ran to the train, which was just beginning to roll, shouting something in German. Lloyd shrank back just as her hand reached out to snag his sleeve, and Symonds said, 'For God's sake, close that window!'

But it was already too late. As the stationmaster struggled to hold her back, she threw the bundle as hard as she could and with unerring aim. It came straight through the window, rebounded off the luggage rack, and banged me on the knee. She was still shrieking something as the train picked up speed and left the platform behind.

'Good God, what is <u>that</u>?' Symonds said.

Woggin's ears pricked up.

It was round and wrapped in rags, old pillowcases that carried the monogram of the Hotel Belvédère, and as I unwound them, I felt my heart sinking in my chest. This would be no gift, I knew. But the full measure of horror had not yet dawned. As my fingers peeled the last rag away, I saw staring up at me a pair of yellow eyes, dull as copper coins, and a muzzle of broken teeth, twisted to one side. The crown of his head, where the grey fur had sustained a deep gash, was matted with blood.

'How ghastly,' Symonds said.

'What's it mean?' Lloyd said, as if this gory prize were some clue in a game.

But Fanny, whose German was even worse than mine, asked the question I was wondering myself. 'What was the old woman shouting?'

'She was calling you a murderer,' Symonds said.

'Me?' Fanny said.

'I believe it was directed at Louis.'

'Why in the world would she shout such a thing at my husband? Much less hurl that awful thing through the window!" Reaching for it, she said, 'Throw it back out, right now.'

But I kept hold of it. Whatever torture had already been inflicted on Lord Grey, I could not undo, but I could keep any further indignities from occurring. The whistle of the train blasted the air and echoed around the valley. As gently as if I were diapering a baby,

I wrapped the rags around the head again and, to Fanny's open-mouthed astonishment, petted the skull.

'Louis, have you lost your mind?'

The woman, I could only assume, had been Yannick's wife. And the boy, his son? The one who was to wear a coat made of the wolf's skin?

'Now I have seen everything,' Fanny said, slumping back in her seat.

And though I said nothing to correct her, I knew, to my own sorrow, that she had not. The world, I have learned, always has something more in store.

TOPANGA CANYON— CALIFORNIA

Present Day

Rafe had been running late all day, which was no surprise, given his alcohol intake with Miranda the night before.

After retiring to his trailer, he'd heard Laszlo coming home on his Vespa and, glancing out his window, watched Miranda steer him away from the yard and back toward the house. The old clothes from the trunk, he saw, had been pinned on the clothesline.

But by the time he left the next morning, the clothes were gone, except for a pocket watch that he spotted glinting in the morning sun. It must have fallen out of a pocket. The watch and its chain were tarnished silver, and when he was able to get the spring to work, it opened to reveal an antique, though crushed, face, and on the inside of the dented lid the initials SLO, elaborately etched under the manufacturer's name, Asprey Ltd. He had no idea if it was worth anything, especially in this dilapidated state, but until he knew, mentioning it to Seth and Alfie would probably be a big mistake.

He stuck it in his backpack, which he threw into his jeep, along with the radio tracking equipment and all his camping supplies. He was planning on a two- or three-day jaunt, tracking the coyote pack before his grant was cut or the animals disappeared altogether. At the last minute, he remembered to take the sealed strongbox.

At the Kanan Road firehouse, one of the firefighters took one look at it and whistled. "How the hell old is this thing?"

"Maybe a hundred, hundred and fifty years?"

The firefighter shook it gently. "Is that the sound of money?" he said with a smile.

When Rafe shrugged, he produced a slim and pliable pick, and after two or three attempts and a lot of wriggling, he was able to release the lock. "Want me to keep going?" he said, and when Rafe said, "Be my guest," he lifted the rusty lid.

Inside, its edges worn and ragged, was a worn leather book.

"Sorry, pal—no dough."

Rafe was relieved; it was one less headache. If everything in the trunk amounted to nothing much, he could hand it all over—the pocket watch included—to Seth and Alfie, with his blessing, and without the bother of filing any report or paperwork at the field office downtown.

"What is that stuff?" the firefighter said, running one finger over the finely mottled surface. The book had no title printed on its cover, and was made of a pale-green skin.

"Shagreen."

"Sha-what?"

"Shagreen," Rafe said. "Sharkskin. The little bumps are calcified papillae."

Now he looked even more puzzled.

"Scales," Rafe explained. "They're placoid scales, probably from a baby shark." Part of his training as an environmental scientist had been spent at the aquarium in Monterey.

"Huh."

"Yeah." Rafe didn't know much about the value of old books, but he sensed that this one had been expensively produced.

Opening it, however, he was surprised to see no printed text, but instead page after page after page of fragile, crinkly paper, densely covered in a loose scrawl of black ink.

"Does it say who killed Kennedy?" the firefighter joked.

Rafe would have been hard pressed to say what it said—the writing was faint, and so idiosyncratic it was hard to decipher at first glance. But what he could make out were some dates, and they were all from the late nineteenth century. Apart from any monetary value it might possess, maybe this thing would prove to be of some historical importance—though how, and why, it wound up in a locked trunk filled with a bunch of old clothes, then dumped in a lake in Topanga Canyon, was likely to be even harder to explain.

The answer would have to wait awhile. He had planned to be well up into the canyon trails by now, so he slipped the journal into his backpack, threw the box into the back of his jeep, and drove on. At one of the more remote and hidden access roads, he turned into the wilderness, drove as far as he could go, and when the road gave out, parked and locked the jeep up in the shelter of some trees.

Toting his gear on his back—counting the nylon pup tent, it must have weighed thirty or forty pounds—he marched into the canyon. He hadn't gone more than a half mile before he came across a tiny, ramshackle house almost entirely hidden by trees and brush. With a sloping tin roof, a crooked chimney, and a Dutch door hanging by one hinge, it was something out of a fairy tale. The witch's house, most likely.

But the woman whose eyes he spotted checking him out from the open portion of the door wasn't a witch. It was Mrs. Pothead, as she was known not only to Rafe but to every ranger and firefighter in the region. She and her husband were the classic living-off-the-grid couple, doing without electricity, making their own clothes, drawing their own water from a well, raising their own fruits and vegetables. By all rights, they should have been rousted out long ago, but nobody had the heart to. They were completely harmless, a couple of misfits who, as it happened, also served a purpose. They owned a cell phone, and though they had to walk a piece to get within range of any tower, they were what Rafe and the others who knew about them considered an early-warning system. If a lightning strike started a blaze deep in the canyon, Mr. and Mrs. Pothead could be trusted to call it in pronto. If a hiker got hopelessly lost in their area, they could be notified to keep an eye out for him.

In return, Rafe turned a blind eye to the other crops—the cash crops—growing out back in their wild and scraggly garden patch. Two or three times a month, when they made a run down into town, they converted some of their top-quality weed into just enough money to buy seeds and sodas and plant food, after which they treated themselves to a plate of tamales at La Raza before burrowing back into the brush again.

"It's just me—Rafe!" he called out, in case she hadn't determined that yet.

"Hi, Rafe," he heard from off to his left, and only now noticed Mr. Pothead, thin as a rail and still as a statue, standing between two trees with a hoe in hand. He looked like that guy from the painting—*American Gothic?*—the one holding a pitchfork.

"Hey," Rafe said.

"What brings you up here?" Mr. Pothead said, in a soft voice that sounded unaccustomed to use.

"Tracking my coyotes."

Mr. Pothead nodded.

"You see them lately?"

"Always see coyotes," he said, pronouncing it "ki-oats." "Yours any different?"

"Got tracking collars on 'em."

He shook his head, then called out, "Sarah, you see any coyotes with collars on?"

She laughed, a little hysterically, and Rafe wondered, as he often had, just how strange a relationship these two had.

"I guess not," Mr. Pothead said. "You wanna come in for a cup of tea?"

"Thanks, but I've got to keep moving. You take care now."

"You, too, 'specially if you're going that way."

"Which way?"

He lifted his chin toward the east, where Rafe was headed.

"Why?"

"I mind my own business," Mr. Pothead said. "I'm just sayin', keep a lookout."

He could feel their eyes on him as he set off again—he was probably the only person they'd seen up there in months—and he wondered what in particular he should be keeping a lookout for. Once he was well out of their sight and had found a good clear spot to begin his triangulations, he raised his antenna and looked for a signal from the coyotes' radio collars. When he'd found it—he was picking up the transmission from Diego, the leader of the pack—he recorded it and moved on, trekking several more miles before looking to get a second reading on his GPS. But he knew it might not be easy. The drought had changed everything. Coyotes were territorial, and under normal conditions, with an abundant supply of food and water, a pack like this could stake out a fairly small area and stick to it, finding everything they'd need within its parameters; in California's verdant coastal range, that meant they could usually make do with an area comprising one to three square miles.

But in these parched conditions, they might have to roam over as much as fifteen square miles in search of adequate resources. Omnivores of the first order, coyotes could—and would—eat anything from nuts and berries to rodents and insects, along with carrion they came across in the course of their extensive travels. Even when wary farmers left guard dogs to protect their flocks of sheep and goats and calves, the coyotes got around them; sometimes, the dogs themselves became prey. In Rafe's experience, a coyote would try eating anything at least once.

Except, maybe, a wolf.

He hadn't forgotten the print he'd seen on the trail, days before. Reading tracks wasn't an exact science; the soil didn't provide perfect impressions. But he couldn't forget the chill he'd gotten when he'd studied and measured the print he'd seen. He knew he had a good eye for these things, and if he was right, then he'd made a significant discovery. If he shot off his mouth too soon, however, and was later discredited, he could give the bureaucracy one more reason to defund his research.

By the time he reached the next crest, the sun was dropping toward the horizon and the shadows of the trees were lengthening. For now, it was time to set up camp while there was still some light in the sky and he could see what he was doing. He pitched the solo tent and debated which of his canned rations to have for dinner, cold; in view of the drought conditions, lighting a fire to heat anything up was way too risky. Sitting on a log, digging his spoon into the mac and cheese, he gazed up at the stars and wondered, as he pretty much always did, how there could be so damn many of them. When you were in Los Angeles, or any city for that matter, you could see a few. When you were out in the backyard of the store in Topanga, you could see a lot more. But when you ventured into the wilderness, miles from any city and its ambient glare, the sky seemed to take on an altogether new dimension. The stars were strewn everywhere overhead, twinkling so brightly it was as if they were in motion. Rafe remembered many a night, growing up, when he'd stare out the window of some temporary refuge and take comfort in the sight of the moon and the few stars that he could discern. Instead of making him feel insignificant, or his problems no big deal, they made him feel a part of something bigger and more beautiful than he could ever comprehend. He just wanted to be out among them.

And now he was. Alone, in the mountains . . . with just his thoughts, which kept turning to Miranda. What would have happened, after all that wine and the candlelight and the ice cream, if Seth and Alfie hadn't shown up at the door? What *could* happen, so long as she was shacked up with Laszlo?

To distract himself, he crawled into the tent, and by the light of the Coleman lantern, took the antique journal out of his backpack and flipped through it. Some of the pages were more legible than others, but the nineteenth-century dates and exotic headings alone—Davos and London and Samoa—were enough to transport his imagination in the same way that gazing at the stars had once done. All those years ago, in all those places Rafe had never been, a man—and he just assumed that it was a man—had sat hunched over this book, with its then-blank pages, and written the story of . . . what? His life? His adventures? His philosophy?

Plainly, there was only one way to find out.

Turning to the first page, and slowly deciphering the distinctive scrawl, he began to read. A coach was traveling up a snowy road in Switzerland, with a dog named Woggin, of all things, hanging his head out the open window . . .

PART II

22 February, 1885

40 Cavendish Square, London

As God is my witness, I had never expected, nor wished, to open this journal again. It was to be a volume whose story closed on the Continent.

But stories have not only a will of their own, but a secret well-spring, too. My own come to me as dreams, cobbled together by an army of what I have dubbed my Brownies, those anarchic spirits whom I willfully muster, every night, as my little boat sets sail upon the sea of sleep. Their task is to bring me a tale of derring-do, of intrigue or adventure, a shilling shocker to capture the imagination of the public and make my name, and fortune. When I awake, I do so slowly, taking care not to shake my head or address the events of the coming day lest I disturb whatever strange cargo they have brought me. I sift through the remaining impressions, the images and incidents and ideas, as if they were dry goods piled in bins, and if my Brownies have done their job, there is invariably something to reward my search.

Symonds, to whom I have confided my secret, tells me that smoking opium has an equivalent effect, and that many of his most penetrating aperçus have come to him while reclining on a silken divan in the darkest dens of Whitechapel. 'What Dr Rüedi prescribes is medicine for the body,' he says, 'but opium is the balm for the soul.' Although he has encouraged me to join him on one of his 'mystic excursions', I have so far declined the honour. 'What need do I have of Oriental powders', I told him, 'when I have my obedient Brownies?'

'That is precisely why you need the pipe,' he said. 'It doesn't know a thing about obedience; no true artist should. The unruly impulse is the one to indulge. What is it Wilde wrote in that Dorian Gray book? "The only way to get rid of a temptation is to yield to it."'

Tempting as the offer was, and much as I agreed with what he said in theory, in practice my constitution remained so precarious, my lungs so fragile, that I feared taking any step whose outcome was too uncertain. The distillation, secreted in the bottles of Valtellina, I husbanded carefully against the day it ran out. That day could not be indefinitely postponed. Since leaving the Belvédère, I had suffered several setbacks, sudden onslaughts of pulmonary distress as severe as any I have known. On one morning, Fanny swears that she found me as cold and stiff as a marble slab—'Anyone else would have given up and called for the undertaker'—and that it was only her immediate ministrations, her vigourous rubbing, and scalding bath, that brought me back to this world. 'You English would have packed it in,' she said, 'but Americans don't give up so easy.'

'Scots,' I corrected her.

'Have it your way, Louis.'

The house we have taken, on Cavendish Square, is cold, drafty, and grander than I believe we need; for all her democratic and egalitarian ideals, Fanny is at heart a snob, and to her, a fashionable London address is de rigueur. The furnishings are as gloomy and cumbersome as the house—a Georgian manse with a stately façade and a red-brick wall surrounding a small, scrubby garden at the back—and it requires at the very least a housemaid, a cook, and a butler to run it. In that, we have been fortunate, finding a family, the Chandlers, who can apportion all such duties among themselves. Mr Chandler, a veteran of the Royal Fusiliers, is prepared to undertake any task, from cleaning the coalscuttle to decanting the brandy, while his wife tends to all things that belong to the kitchen and infernal regions of the house. Their daughter, Sally, a plump young creature of sixteen summers, is as lazy as they are industrious, but if reminded enough times, will eventually focus her efforts sufficiently to finish polishing the silver or dusting the library shelves. On one occasion, I discovered her there, still as a statue, her dust rags tucked under an arm, the other holding open a book.

'You may read anything here that you wish,' I said, and she was so startled she dropped the book, then, stooping to pick it up, dropped the rags, then, straightening, dropped the book again. I laughed, though she did not share in my amusement. 'Just try not to bruise them.'

She scuttled out of the room, head down and blushing furiously, before I could explain that, as an author, I prized nothing so much as readers. When I saw what she had been perusing—a new novel, "Far from the Madding Crowd," inscribed to me by Thomas Hardy—I was even more impressed. That she could read at all was commendable—that she would make such a good selection was even more so. When Fanny and I had paid a call on him at Max Gate outside Dorchester, Hardy was as flustered as a guinea hen, but gracious and welcoming. When I told Henley about the visit, he declared, 'The man may be the critics' darling, but I'll take one of your boisterous yarns over one of his yawners any time!'

The London air is thick with Japanism. The opening of the Japanese Village in Knightsbridge has become all the rage, and a clever new musical production, called "The Mikado," has been filling the Savoy Theatre every night. It was always Henley's wish, and remains so, that we write something for the theatre together. There is something about the sight of the nobs with their tickets in hand, pouring in through the open doors of the gaily lighted house, that thrills him to the core, though I suspect it is more about the money than it is the artistic acclaim. We have tried our hand already, and probably shall again (over Fanny's objections), but the stage remains a prize we cannot capture. Messieurs Gilbert and Sullivan have nothing to fear from us at present.

Nor do the Japanese. By virtue of his current position as editor of "The National Observer," Henley was able to procure several much-coveted tickets to the formal tea ceremony, held each afternoon at the exhibition. 'I could have wished for better company than him,' Fanny said, 'but you can't look a gift horse in the mouth.'

Rather than remonstrating with her yet again, I let it pass. This twitchy discord between my wife and my closest friend, both rivals for my attention and affection, is simply something to be borne. Henley and I have been friends now since 1875, when Leslie Stephen, the editor of the "Cornhill Magazine," suggested I come along to pay a visit to a friend of his who was undergoing a long and painful ordeal at the Royal Infirmary of Edinburgh.

'A braver man, and a greater stoic, you will never meet.'

What he had not prepared me for was the veritable force of nature that greeted us as we entered the ward. 'What is it this time, Stephen?' Henley bellowed. 'Am I late submitting my review?' Gesturing at his lower trunk, he added with a laugh, 'I'm not getting around as I used to.'

That he could endure what I saw—one leg had been amputated just below the knee, and the other was swaddled in bandages and elevated in a sling—was surprising enough, but that he could make light of it, and maintain such a buoyant spirit, was miraculous indeed.

'And who is this scarecrow you've brought along to gawk at me?'

Stephen introduced us, and Henley put out a meaty hand to shake. 'I know you by your scribblings,' he said. 'All you need is a good editor to trim your excesses.'

'Perhaps I just found one.'

'A bright lad,' Henley said to Stephen, though the man could not have been more than a year or two older than I.

The rest of our conversation revolved around the wretched life of the writer—an endlessly popular topic among members of this caste—and once Henley had been released from the hospital, where an enterprising physician named Dr Joseph Lister had been able, after multiple surgeries, to salvage the remaining leg, we continued in that vein, and many others. Stumping about town on his one leg, a wooden crutch thrust under his strong right arm, Henley became a notable fixture on the London literary scene, forever popping up like some jack-in-the-box, as editor of one publication or another, or penning an unforgettable ode. Out of that dreadful sequester at the infirmary, where the complications of tuberculosis had claimed his leg, he wrote the poem 'Invictus', a cri de coeur whose last stanza has become the rallying cry of all who must face impossible odds: 'It matters not how strait the gate, How charged with punishments the scroll, I am the master of my fate: I am the captain of my soul.'

In my own darkest hours, I have had occasion to recall those lines, even as I struggled to assert them.

Lloyd being away at school, it was only Fanny and I who rendez-voused with Henley at Humphreys's Hall, within whose cavernous confines the entire Japanese Village had been erected. It was a great feat of engineering—my father would have been much impressed—and succeeded brilliantly in transporting its patrons, who came by the thousands, from a dreary stretch of London to a rural hamlet in medieval Japan. The organizer of the exhibition, a Mr Tannaker Buhicrosan, had populated his mythical village with over a hundred Japanese men and women, all attired in their national garb, going about their native crafts in tiny shops and houses, all laid out in the most picturesque fashion, along winding walkways, past ornamental gardens, and over delicately wrought, rustic footbridges. At its centre stood a red-and-gold Buddhist temple, fantastically decorated and illuminated by a flotilla of Japanese lanterns. Fanny, I could see, was quite taken, even going so far as to try to engage some of the workers in a commercial transaction—she had her heart set on a silken kimono being woven before her eyes—but was gently discouraged.

'You'd think they would try to turn a profit,' she harrumphed.

'That's a very American concept,' Henley could not resist putting in. 'Sometimes, things are done simply for their cultural value.'

The battle was joined yet again.

The teahouse itself was a humbler affair, but deliberately so. Hewn of bamboo and wood left unpainted and unvarnished, it was entered through a small anteroom, where coats and scarves and boots were exchanged for simple homespun robes with wide sleeves, and thin cotton slippers. This was the first of many problems to confront poor Henley, who sat on a stone bench to wrestle off his one boot, then pull on a slipper before holding up its mate and asking, 'Anyone need a spare?'

After a pretty young maid, whose chevelure of jetty black was pinned with pink blossoms, instructed us, in halting English, to perform a ritual purification by rinsing our hands in a basin of cold water, we were guided to a low doorway, through which we had to virtually crawl in order to enter the inner sanctum. Henley was once more nonplussed, but plunked himself down and scooted backwards into the room, tooting like a locomotive whistle. Judging from the expression on the face of the tea master who waited within, I had the distinct impression that we had committed a gross faux pas.

'Beg pardon,' Henley said.

The master, an elderly man with skin the colour of old ivory, bowed silently, and once we were each seated on a thickly woven tatami mat, began the ceremony, explaining each step, and even each utensil. Nothing, it appeared, was left to chance or accident—everything from the scroll on the wall to the placement of the brazier carried some greater meaning. The cup was not at all what I might have expected; it was neither fine nor delicate, but rough pottery, the colour of mud, and with many imperfections. These irregularities, we were told, were to be admired; the goal of the ritual was to encourage serenity and reflection, to focus the thoughts on nature and not on ornament. Even Henley's ebullient demeanour had soon been tamed, and he gave himself over to the admiration of the foreign that I have always felt.

For her part, Fanny was polite and attentive, but as I could tell from the way she kept shifting her weight on the mat, increasingly impatient. The measured progress of the event, so unlike the sweets and chatter of an English tea, began to wear on her. No doubt she was eager to return to the narrow lanes outside, where she still harboured hopes of buying something.

By the time the ceremony had been brought to an end, she was all but rolling towards the little doorway, scrambling through to the anteroom and pulling on her shoes. 'Thank you, thank you so much,' she said to the maid in the kimono, even as she thrust her arms back into her coat. 'A wonderful experience, quite wonderful,' and then she was out of the teahouse altogether.

Henley, still wrestling his boot on, said, 'I think I've got enough material for a very fine column, maybe even two.' As the maid, bowing, ducked back into the tearoom, he drew on my sleeve to bring my ear closer and whispered, 'And what do you make of that little lotus blossom?'

'Quite lovely.'

'Good God, man, is that all you can say?'

'All I dare say here.'

'Well, I dare say she's as pretty as any chorus girl mincing her way across the stage of the Savoy.'

'I heard that Gilbert and Sullivan brought the Mikado cast here, to study the gestures and comportment of the true Japanese.'

'Damn their eyes, those two. There's no reason they should have yet another bonanza, while you and I crank out poems and stories and newspaper columns that vanish the next day.' Slapping his crutch under his arm, he said, 'Have I told you my latest inspiration?'

'There are so many, I'm not sure.'

'Treasure Island.'

'What of it?' The novel, shepherded by Henley, had first appeared in serialized fashion in "Young Folks Magazine" three years earlier, and, once it had been published as a book, has gone on to great success, with editions published—though often unpaid for—all over the world.

'As a play!' he exulted. 'We could adapt it! Think of the money it could make if presented as a Christmas treat! Better than the pantos! Louis, we're sitting on a gold mine.'

And sit on it, we shall, I thought. I had already travelled down this road with Henley—our play about the burglar Deacon Brodie had opened, and swiftly closed, in Edinburgh the year before—and had little intention of doing so again. Fanny saw Henley's attempts to turn me towards the stage as a waste of my talents, and a means of simply binding my rising fortunes to his. On the first score, she may have been right—such abilities as I have do not seem to lend themselves to the limited scope of a proscenium arch—but on the second, I felt she had unjustly impugned the man's integrity. Henley is an enthusiast, not a conniver.

Outside, the crowds were still milling about, but across the pathway, Fanny was in an animated conversation with a couple whom I could not distinguish at first.

'By the by, Oscar Wilde is up to his old tricks again,' Henley remarked. 'Did you see his piece in the "Pall Mall Gazette"? It's unsigned, but unmistakably his.'

I had not, but as a trio of women in hats the size of sofas finally moved past, I saw that the man, a dashing figure in a dark-blue cutaway, was none other than Randolph Desmond and that the flame-haired woman on his arm was Constance Wooldridge. I had not seen them since the Belvédère, and found, upon encountering them now, a welter of conflicting feelings arising in my breast. Glad to see old comrades in arms, as it were, but at the same time sorry to have this reminder of my long-standing debility.

'Louis!' Desmond called out, raising a furled umbrella in salutation.

Introductions were made all around, and Henley, quite unbidden, treated everyone to a preview of the columns he would write about the tea ceremony before excusing himself to gather more 'local colour' for the article.

'You look fully restored,' Desmond said to me, though it was far from the truth. I could not exactly return the compliment, however, as it had never been clear what was wrong with him, or his consort.

'Is this your first visit to the exhibition?' he asked.

'It is,' Fanny replied, 'though it won't be our last. There's been so much to take in.'

'We've been three times,' Desmond said, 'though I'll confess that the last one was under duress. Constance swears by the green tea they serve in the pavilion.'

After several minutes of comparing our impressions of the Japanese Village, Desmond happened to mention that Lloyd, too, was looking well these days, catching me quite off-guard. Fanny, too, it seemed.

'Didn't he tell you?' Desmond said. 'I was in Bedfordshire a week or two ago, and dropped by to make sure he was applying himself to his studies.' He smiled, adding, 'Perhaps he's been too diligent to write you. That must be it.'

I will confess to getting a slightly uneasy feeling about what should have been quite anodyne news. Randolph Desmond was a gentleman, from a wealthy and well-respected family, and it should have come as pleasant tidings that he had looked up young Lloyd.

'As he was on a school break, I took him on a brief jaunt to the sea,' he added, bolstering my misgivings. 'Please don't tell me he deceived me about the break.'

'I'm sure not,' I said, though I was anything but.

'Will you join us for the green tea?' Desmond said, gesturing towards the pavilion at the rear of the great hall.

'Please, do,' Constance said. 'And invite your friend to join us, too.' She looked around, in search of Henley.

'We'd love to,' Fanny said, 'but I'm afraid I am already awash in tea.' And reuniting with Henley was the last thing she would want.

'But you must come and see us,' Fanny added. 'We're at Cavendish Square now. Number forty.' Stating the address gave her evident pleasure.

On the way out, and to Fanny's dismay, we bumped into Henley again, who said to me in passing, 'That friend of yours—'

'Yes?'

'Has a visit been paid to the House of Cyclax?'

Located on Bond Street, Cyclax was a popular purveyor of ladies' skin creams.

'Oh, you mean Constance,' I replied, though it seemed impossible, as her face was such a translucent white that the veins stood out in blue.

'No, no, I mean the fellow.'

'That hardly seems likely.'

'Then it could have been a trick of the lamplight in there,' Henley said with a shrug. 'That, or perhaps he runs in that crowd of fops with our outrageous Mr Wilde.'

Although I took his meaning—it was hard to miss—I knew he was mistaken. But not altogether wrong. For all his breeding, there was something unmistakably louche about Desmond, something I feared was already rubbing off on the impressionable young Lloyd.

TOPANGA CANYON— CALIFORNIA

Present Day

Rafe had been up and walking since the first rays of the sun hit the top of his tent, making the blue nylon shine. In weather like this, you wanted to get as much traveling done in the early morning hours as possible. The noonday sun would be unbearable.

Besides, he needed to get the rest of Diego's triangulation done as quickly as he could; the coyotes were always on the move, and already he'd left more time than was advisable between gathering all his coordinates. Luckily, it turned out that he was closer than he thought; the signal was clear, and when he'd finished his calculations, he discovered that the pack was not far off. Now it was just a matter of hauling himself and his supplies—enough for one more night—within striking distance. He had his binoculars around his neck and his cell phone camera at the ready.

Keeping a close eye on the ground for any signs of prints or scat, he found his thoughts turning to the mysterious journal he'd been reading the night before. Between the difficulty of deciphering the idiosyncratic handwriting and the bone-deep weariness that came from an entire day of trooping through the canyon, he hadn't been able to get through much, but the pages that he had read, before turning off the lantern, had been fascinating. They reminded him of all those old books he'd devoured, from the dusty shelves of the shelters and facilities. They were all classified as books for young readers, or some such, and most of them looked like they'd been donated by rich old white people who'd read the books themselves when they were young. But the illustrations in some of them—*The Last of the Mohicans, Ivanhoe, Kidnapped*—had enchanted him, and a lot of them he could still envision, in every detail. Those stories had been even better than the constellations at transporting him to a faraway place.

Before the accident, Lucy had enjoyed them, too.

The Santa Anas were blowing again today, making the hot dry air even hotter and drier. Sitting in the relative shade of a nearly leafless tree, he leaned back against the trunk and took a swig of Gatorade from his canteen. Warm, it wasn't nearly as palatable. He was tempted to take the journal out of his backpack and read a couple of pages, but his hands were so dirty and sweaty he was afraid he'd smudge the pages and run the ink. After slathering himself with another coating of sunscreen, he closed his eyes, tilted his cap down over his face, and rested awhile. Flies buzzed around him, but he was just too tired to wave them away.

He must have dozed for as much as an hour, because when he woke up, the sun was behind the hills, the air was a trifle cooler, and from somewhere in the distance he could hear the sound he'd been hoping for. The high-pitched yapping of a coyote. Caroming off the hillsides, it was almost like a yodel, and he jumped to his feet, listening carefully to determine its direction, but it wasn't easy; a coyote's cry can travel up to three miles under the right conditions. Song dogs, the Native Americans had called them, and for good reason.

When the howl came again, he determined it was emanating from the west, and slinging on his backpack, he headed off toward the setting sun. The sky was streaked with pale pink clouds, and as he crested the next ridge, he stopped in his tracks, knelt on one knee to be less conspicuous, and grabbed his binoculars.

Two coyotes—Diego and Frida—were converging from opposite directions. If it weren't for their long snouts and bushy, black-tipped tails, they might be mistaken from this distance for small German shepherds. They trotted along purposefully, and in Frida's mouth, Rafe could see something limp and dangling—a dead rabbit, or some other prey. Coyotes killed with a clean, knifelike bite, usually to the head or neck, using their razor-sharp carnassial, or cheek, teeth. But what was most exciting to Rafe was that she was surely carrying this quarry back to a den, and her cubs.

It was like hitting the jackpot.

Afraid of alerting them to his presence, and uncertain about where the other members of the pack might be, he scooted behind a clump of jojoba bushes; most of their leaves, which normally stood vertically so that only the tips received the brunt of the hottest sunlight, had turned gray and lifeless, and hung listlessly on the branches. Still, the shrubs provided some cover. Taking off his backpack, he laid it flat on the ground as a kind of bulwark, then, clearing a view through the base of the bushes, propped his elbows on top of the pack to hold the binoculars steady. The two coyotes circled a patch of ground several hundred yards in diameter, noses to the dirt as if checking for the scent of any intruder, and then, after a long and wary look around, came together at what looked to Rafe like no more than a shadow in the side of the hill. Adjusting his focus, he could see now that it was a burrow, concealed behind a fallen log.

He could also see something slightly puzzling—that prey in Frida's mouth looked distinctly like a Subway wrapper, still holding the mustard-smeared remnants of a sandwich. It wasn't that a coyote wouldn't go for a sub; the question was, how the hell had a sandwich, even a half-eaten one, gotten this far into the wilderness? It was unlikely that Frida had carried it all the way from a fast-food Dumpster off in Topanga or Malibu. Either way, this would be worth a photo for his fieldwork, and he fumbled under the flap of his backpack to get his camera. He'd no sooner screwed on the telephoto lens than he saw Diego's ears stand up, his tail extend, and a second later he and Frida had vanished into the den.

Had they heard the tiny sound of the camera being readied? Rafe wondered. Had they picked up his scent? A few seconds later, the mystery was resolved when he heard voices and footsteps approaching. Had Mr. Pothead been following him? And whom was he talking to?

The voices came closer, but slowly; the talkers were tired, and slogging along as if they were dragging something on the ground. Rafe stayed perfectly still, relying on the fading light and the tangle of jojoba brush to keep him concealed.

"I'm too old for this shit," one of the men said. "Next time I'm gonna tell Axel to get somebody else."

The voice was familiar. It was Alfie's.

"I want to be there when you do," the other one said. Seth.

"You don't think I've got the guts?"

"Oh, you've got the guts. I'll see 'em coming out the hole where he stabs you."

They were passing right by the jojoba now—wearing sweaty T-shirts and red bandanas around their brows, dragging what looked like a big flat snowshoe covered with a net. Under the net were white plastic jugs and a slew of cardboard boxes.

"Hang on," Seth said. "I need a break."

Not even daring to lift his head another inch, Rafe waited and heard the sound of a match being struck, then smelled the cigarette smoke.

"You set fire to the canyon and I'll kill you myself," Alfie said.

"Who gives a shit."

It was all Rafe could do not to leap up and brain the bastard. But he held on to his temper, and his mounting curiosity.

Seth exhaled, a plume of smoke wafting over Rafe's head. "Why'd he have to put it so fucking far in?"

"Yeah, you be sure to ask him that, too."

"Fuck you."

"No, fuck you."

Seth chuckled at the wit of the exchange, and after a few more drags on the cigarette, tossed the butt over the bush. It landed on the dirt, just inches from Rafe's nose.

And then they were trudging off again, dragging the load like sled dogs.

When he was sure they had to be at least twenty or thirty yards away, he dared to lift his head higher, but to his surprise, he saw nothing. He raised his eyes higher, and still saw no sign of them. They had been moving so slowly, it seemed impossible they'd disappeared so fast. He stood up as the sun, a fiery ball, sank below the horizon, and by the time he'd followed in their tracks to the top of the ridge, the shadows had grown so long the only way he could have picked them out would have been if they were wearing neon.

But at least he knew now what Mr. Pothead had been warning him about.

3 March, 1885

Lloyd, as I have since discovered, was not on a school break at all, but had been sent down, in all but body. After he had enjoyed his brief sojourn in Margate with Randolph Desmond, he was allowed to return to the Bedford School only long enough to wind up his affairs there, make certain amends to the masters he had wronged, and, with funds of an uncertain origin (I suspected his mother), pay restitution where it was warranted. When it comes to gambling and drink, he is apparently following close in his father's footsteps.

But if I had expected him to come home with his tail between his legs, I was quickly disabused of that notion. Far from evincing disgrace, Lloyd, at nineteen now, displays nothing but confidence. He feels that school has become an obstacle to what he has suddenly perceived to be his true calling.

'I'm an author!' he declared, only minutes after Chandler had carried his bags up to his room. Standing before the fire, legs spread like Lord Byron straddling the Hellespont, he said it as if it were the most obvious thing in the world and he expected Fanny and me to applaud.

'An author?' his mother said. 'Have you written something?'

'Not yet,' he admitted, 'but I will. Now that I no longer have those silly schoolboy chores to attend to, I can do what I was destined to do.'

Perhaps noting the perplexity on my face, he said, 'Surely, you didn't think that all of those hours I spent watching you at your desk, or helping you to map out the geography of Treasure Island, or listening to you read your stories aloud in the parlour, were idle time for me. I was learning my craft. I've seen how you do it, Louis, and it's what I'm going to do, too.'

There was no denying that the boy had watched me like a hawk, noting, it seemed, everything from the stroke of my pen to the blotting of each page, but where to start with him now? For the better part of an hour, his mother and I attempted to explain the rigours of such a life, the preparation (which he had already abandoned) that would be required, the devotion (which I doubted he could show) that it would demand. For every query, he had a ready retort, and by midnight, I could no longer keep up the barrage. Excusing myself, I went to my study, locked the doors, and then, with the key I kept on my watch fob, unlocked the cabinet in which I kept the last bottle of the purported Valtellina.

All that day, I had felt my energy flagging, and for the past week, my handkerchiefs had been spackled with tiny crimson droplets. To keep Fanny from knowing, I had rinsed them thoroughly before dispatching them to Mrs Chandler to be properly bleached and laundered downstairs. But as my last entreaty to Dr Rüedi had not yet had a reply, I took the smallest draught possible. The liquid had coagulated over time, and where it had once been the colour of rose, it was now a thick ruby-red, almost a paste, and carried the bouquet of rotting fruit. Once I had choked it down, I sat at my desk and quickly penned another missive to Davos, reiterating the dwindling of my supply, and sealed the envelope for Chandler to post first thing in the morning.

When I went to bed, the lamp was out in the bedroom, but I knew that Fanny was awake. As I slipped between the cold sheets in my nightshirt, she said, 'The apple doesn't fall far from the tree.'

'Why, did Sam fancy himself a writer, too?'

'Never wrote a thing, apart from IOUs. But he sure as shootin' gambled and drank and whored around.'

'When was the last time you heard from him?'

'Not for two, maybe three, years now. He was in a town called Bakersfield, in California, but he could be dead, for all I know.'

Despite the dismissal, I could detect in her voice a small, but persistent, concern for the man.

'Now it looks like Lloyd is going to head off into the wild blue yonder, too,' she concluded. The bed frame squeaked as she turned towards me in the dark. 'Did he ever show you anything he wrote?'

'Once or twice, a snatch of a story or poem.'

'Were they any good?'

'He was only a child.'

'Louis, I'm asking you, were they any good?'

If ever a man was put in an untenable spot, it was this—how to sum up, to a mother, a son's potential? 'It's too early to tell. My own juvenilia would not have promised much.'

'That's not an answer,' she said. 'Or maybe it is.'

In the darkness, I could feel her turn away and draw the blankets up to her chin. There was no moonlight filtering through the curtains tonight, and the only sound was the slow and lonely clip-clop of a horse's hoofs as it drew a hansom cab. I lay in the bed, trying not to disturb Fanny by stirring about, but I was restless. The taste of the serum was still on my lips, and I was sorry I hadn't thought to bring a carafe of cold water to the bed stand.

Instead, I tried to will myself to sleep, and closing my eyes to the pitch darkness, summoned my Brownies. They were some time in coming, but when they did, I gave them their marching orders, as was customary, and then set them loose. For weeks, I had been casting about for a new plot, a story that could capture my own imagination and ignite a fire of quick composition; that shilling shocker Fanny is forever nattering on about, which will for once and always settle our financial issues. "Treasure Island" has been an undoubted success, but I sold it cheap, and the money from it has run through our hands like water. (At least there will be no more bills for room and board at the Bedford School to contend with.) And a slim volume of poems—'A Child's Garden of Verses'—has recently made a happy and profitable impression on the public, but poems have a more limited appeal. What I needed was a rollicking tale, a story so original in its conception, so violent in its telling, that it would create a great clamour in the press and among the public.

The room was icy-cold, the window sashes being unevenly sealed, and so I was reluctant to get out of bed, even to appease the growing thirst I felt, or the aching in my limbs. Though still in that twilight sleep where I did so much of my best imagining, I was aware of a nervous impulse in my legs—a desire to stretch them loose and run—and a nagging hoarseness in my throat. Was it a premonition of yet another respiratory ailment? That, I could not abide. I needed to husband all my strength to write. I felt an anxiety, not only from fear of another decline, but over my missing Brownies. Where had they gone? Even if I had opened my eyes, it would have been too dark to see the clock, but I thought I had heard the bell strike two in the All Souls Church steeple, and I wondered how much longer I could endure this gnawing thirst and pent-up energy. I was on the very point of rousing myself when to my mind came a sudden flood of unconnected images, so surprising and vivid that I lay back, perfectly still on the pillows, to receive them. I saw two gentlemen looking up at a window at night—a window like my own—and remarking on something or someone hidden within. In a separate image, I saw another man, small and swift and odious in some undetermined way, charging through the gas-lit streets, wielding a cane as if it were a cudgel, coming around a corner and colliding with a child so hard he trampled her underfoot, without so much as looking back. And then I saw that man in a private cabinet, behind a red baize door (identical to the door of my study), drinking from a flask that smoked as if it were on fire, and clutching at his own throat . . .

It was then that I must have cried out in my sleep.

'Louis!' Fanny was groping for my shoulders in the dark. 'Louis! Wake up! You're having a nightmare!'

I was furious. 'You shouldn't have awakened me! I was dreaming a fine bogey tale!'

'You were waking the whole house!'

I threw off the blankets and put my feet to the cold floor, searching for my slippers.

'Louis, stay in bed! You'll catch your death!'

But nothing was going to stop me from recording the impressions the Brownies had bestowed. There was the making of a great tale in it—of that I was sure. Once the slippers were on and I'd thrown the belt around my flannel robe, I scuffed out of the room, brushing my hand up and down the bedroom door just to find the handle, and hurried down the hall to my study.

Twice I banged into the furniture, though Lord knows I should have been able to navigate this familiar geography without a thought. For the life of me, I felt I could not fully straighten up, either; my robe was sweeping the floor. I must have grown stiff in the bed, too, for every bone in my body ached, and every joint felt as if it had been given a wicked twist.

My desk, however, I knew in every particular, and in a matter of seconds I had found a matchstick and lit the oil lamp by which I worked at night. It flared a pale green before turning to white, but, in that sickly burst of light, I saw myself—or what should have been myself—in the mirror above the desk. In horror, I leapt back, away from the gnarled, grimacing face that glimmered in the glass. The black hair was mine, the hollow cheeks, the drooping moustache—but the mad gleam in the bulging eyes was not, the cruel curl to the lip was not, the hunched shoulders were not. My fingers rose to touch my face, but even they felt foreign—their tips were blunt and coarse, their nails long and jagged. The back of my hand, normally a fragile alabaster, was dusky and spotted. I slumped down into my chair, afraid to look any longer, afraid that my wits had forever slipped their moorings.

It was not until the tolling of the next hour from the bells of All Souls that I even dared to move a muscle or limb. When at last I arose enough from the chair to see into the mirror, the reflection, though murky, was reassuringly my own, flickering in the light from the sputtering lamp. With a sigh of relief—no man had ever entertained a more hellish hallucination—I sat down again, but my hands—now white and smooth once more—were so numb that I could barely hold the paper or the pen. My fingers trembling, I wrote just long enough to leave some account of what the Brownies had brought me, and to limn the dreadful creature I had dreamt in the glass. The name for such a monstrosity, a man whose company no one would ever willingly seek, came instantly to my mind. Mr Hyde.

TOPANGA CANYON— CALIFORNIA

Present Day

"Another round," Laszlo said, slapping his hand on the top of the picnic table so firmly Miranda jumped.

"On the rocks, with salt?" the waitress asked.

"The works," Laszlo said. "I'm buying."

For days now, Laszlo had been trying to get back into her good graces, but for him to pick up a check, even at a place as cheap as La Raza, was downright shocking. He considered it a mark of honor to grift his way through any situation. But the stunt in the bedroom with the old clothes had been beyond the pale, and he was working hard to make up for lost ground.

"Not for me," Miranda said before the waitress left.

"I thought this was a party," Laszlo said.

"Nobody told me," Miranda replied. "What are we celebrating?"

He took a second, then offered up exultantly, "The new moon."

More like a blue moon, she thought, given that he had offered to pay. But she'd noticed he was wearing new boots, too much of some unfamiliar cologne, and he'd even taken his Vespa to a car wash. She just hoped he wasn't swiping the money from the till at the Cornucopia.

Not that there was much to steal. The week before, a bus carrying a high school band from Corvallis had pulled in and the kids had swarmed all over the store, buying candles and crystals and beaded headbands, but other than that, there'd been very little business. It was lucky she had the rent from Rafe, insubstantial as it was.

The waitress put the fresh margarita down in front of Laszlo, but before she could take away the old glass, he licked the rim for any remaining salt.

What was she doing here, Miranda wondered, with a guy like this?

"I've been thinking," Laszlo said.

Never a good development.

"Why don't we set up like an outdoor area to sell some other kinds of stuff? Bigger stuff."

"Like what?"

"Lawn stuff. Chairs, tables, benches. These outdoor heaters," he said, gesturing at the glowing stanchions around the open deck of the restaurant. The night had grown cold.

"And where do you propose we put this outdoor market?"

"Out back, to the side of the store."

Precisely where the trailer sat. Now she got it. "Oh, so you think I should evict Rafe and sell the trailer?"

Dipping a chip into the salsa bowl, he said, "It's got nothing to do with Salazar."

As far as Miranda was concerned, it had everything to do with him.

"We could just make a lot more money using that space for something else."

She never failed to notice that when he referred to her store, it was always *we* and *our* business.

"He can always find some other place to squat."

Miranda was already wondering if he had. There'd been no sign of him for the past couple of days—Tripod generally barked like crazy the minute his jeep pulled in. Not that that was entirely unusual. He sometimes went off on field trips, tracking his coyote pack, and there was no real reason for him to keep her posted. It's not like they were an item or anything.

"While we're at it, why not sell the store, too?" she said facetiously.

But Laszlo didn't take it that way. "You'd do that?"

"Why?"

"Because I could definitely get behind that if we did. Sell the store, the trailer, then take the money and head south. I hear a lot about San Miguel de Allende. It's got a lot going on."

Maybe the road really was in his blood, as he often claimed. Like a lot about Laszlo, the absolute truth was up for grabs. "Who's talking to you about San Miguel de Allende?"

He didn't answer that, but then, it wouldn't have mattered if he did, because four or five of the Spiritz tore into the parking area in front of the restaurant, their mufflers roaring, tires spitting gravel every which way. God, what a throwback, she thought. These guys had seen too many movies.

When they got off their bikes, pretending not to notice all the commotion they'd caused, and tromped into the restaurant, their leader, Axel somebody, broke off and strode toward the outdoor deck. To her surprise, he headed straight for their table, where Laszlo sat up like a student about to be singled out by the teacher.

"Laz," Axel said, plunking his helmet onto the tabletop and slouching into a chair. He was built like a bulldog, and wearing a denim jacket with a pro-life button on the lapel. "Muriel."

"Miranda."

"My mistake."

What on earth was he doing at their table? He'd been in the store exactly once, to buy a lighter.

"I got something for you," he said to Laszlo. "You got something for me?"

"Here? Now?"

"No, not here. Not now. Tomorrow." He glanced at the margarita and said, "That still cold?"

"Yes," Laszlo said, pushing it toward him so quickly it sloshed over the side of the glass. "Help yourself."

Which he did, draining what was left of it in one long gulp. Then, getting up, he took a long unabashed look at Miranda's breasts and, touching the brim of an imaginary hat, said, "Miriam."

"Miranda."

"My mistake." Smirking, he headed into the restaurant.

Laszlo looked like some kid who'd just gotten an autograph from his idol.

But Miranda had the awful feeling that she'd just found out not only who had been talking about San Miguel de Allende, but whose money was indirectly paying for their drinks. How, she wasn't sure, and she was even less sure that she wanted to know.

Laszlo ordered a refill, and they ate the rest of their meal listening to the raucous laughter and shouts of the bikers inside. When the check came, Miranda had to remind Laszlo that he was treating.

At home, he fell onto the bed in a stupor before she could properly grill him on what was going on between him and the Spiritz; she hadn't wanted to do it at the restaurant for fear of being overheard.

But she didn't want him in the bed with his dirty jeans and boots—new though they were. She had just changed the sheets. In fact, now that she thought about it, she'd changed them the day before, too. It was like she just couldn't banish the smell, the sight, the sound, of that one terrible night fast enough or thoroughly enough.

The boots hit the floor, and then she had to unbuckle his belt and reach under him to wriggle the jeans down. At some point, eyes still closed, he roused himself to laugh and mumble "Go for it" as she wrestled them past his ankles. A bunch of stuff fell out of the pockets, scattering around the floor. Coins, keys, a couple of joints, the free peppermints that sat in a bowl by the door of La Raza.

One of the mints rolled under the bed.

"Shit," she mumbled. If she didn't get it now, the ants would.

She tossed the pants onto the wicker chair in the corner, then bent down and groped under the bed. Her palm was quickly coated with dust, but no hard candy. She reached farther and found something, but it wasn't the candy. It was hard and sharp, and drawing it out from under the bed, she saw that it was one of her kitchen knives. The one she used to cut up stuff for her salads. It took her several astonished seconds before she remembered the clattering sound she'd heard that night, right after she'd kicked out at Laszlo and he'd crashed up against the blinds. When it had seemed he was almost in a trance.

"So," he said, still lying there in his socks and underwear, "you gonna do me, or what?"

10 April, 1885

So lost was I in the work at hand, my pen flying across the foolscap pages at such a gallop, that I did not hear the jangling of the doorbell. The feverish pace had not abated for the better part of the month—the whole household tiptoeing about so as not to disrupt the madness of invention—when I could not help but hear the voice of Henley, raised in indignation, booming in the foyer below.

'I'll see the man', Henley bellowed, 'or damn well know the reason why.'

'I've told you before,' Fanny remonstrated, 'and I'll tell you again. Louis cannot be disturbed.'

'I'll hear it then from his own lips.'

'You've heard it from mine, and that will have to suffice.'

Before the damn thing came to blows, I threw open my study door and called down the stairs, 'Come up, Henley!'

'Louis, you said you were not to be distracted for anything,' Fanny cried.

'Well, now I have been, so let it be!'

There was a low exchange of words between them, the rustling of paper, and then the unmistakable sound of Henley stumping up the stairs on his wooden leg. I had just time enough to straighten my dressing gown and throw a lock of hair from my forehead before he appeared with a parcel under one arm and the crutch under the other.

'Good God, man, you look a sight,' he said, lumbering past me and into the room, 'and have you never heard of the salutary effects of fresh air?'

He dumped the tattered box atop the pile of manuscript pages teetering on the desk, and then yanked the curtains aside and opened the window. 'It's a fine day outside,' he said, 'and you ought at least to look at it.'

Blinking from the sunlight, I shrank back. Henley brushed some crumpled and rejected pages from the seat of the leather armchair and plopped down into it.

'What on earth have you been up to?' he said. 'I've stopped by several times on my way from the office, sent notes around, and never got past your Cerberus at the door.'

'I have been working,' I said, barely able to contain my exuberance, 'and I think it is the thing that will make my name.'

'Working on what?'

'A story.'

'A short story? Something I could run in the magazine?'

'No, it is longer than that.'

'A novel then?'

'Shorter.'

'Come to the point,' he said, out of patience.

'It is something my Brownies brought me, the best gift they have ever made.'

'You and your damn Brownies. Talk to Conan Doyle about nonsense like that. Talk sense to me. What's it called?'

'I'm calling it, "Strange Case of Dr Jekyll and Mr Hyde."'

'The Strange Case of what?'

'No, not "the"—simply Strange Case.'

Plainly, he didn't like that. 'We'll worry about the title later. You're terrible at titles. Let's not forget that if you'd had your way, "Treasure Island" would be called "The Sea Cook." I fixed that one, I'll fix this. So what's the damn thing about?'

Ah, how to explain it. It is a story so protean in nature that to describe it is to see it change its shape before one's very eyes, a story so singular in conception that I marvel no one—even the master Poe, whose 'William Wilson' had touched upon the fringe of its garment—has ever composed anything like it. There are depths to it that even I, its creator, cannot plumb, nor do I wish to, for fear of robbing it of some of its mysterious potency.

And of course, at its core lies the one secret that could never be revealed—that the fundament of the thing is true.

In brief, I sketched out the tale—a London doctor, of late middle age and impeccable reputation, who discovers, in the course of his medical experiments, an unholy concoction through which he is metamorphosed into an abject creature of the basest appetites and desires. A creature that terrorizes the town, and eventually the doctor himself when he realizes that he is no longer, to borrow the phrases from Henley's own famous poem, the master of his fate or the captain of his soul. The power that this Jekyll has unleashed spirals out of his own control, and in the end, the good doctor is consumed—subsumed, one might say—by the monstrous thing to which he has given birth.

'Ah, so it is a doppelgänger story!'

'No, not that! This thing—Mr Hyde—is not the spitting image of the man, but a foul distillation of all that is vile and repressed and hidden in the human soul.'

'So, then, he is a slave to some sexual depravity?' Henley said, still grasping at the conceit.

'No, not that either! You know how I feel about that! That a man's lust for a woman should be considered a sin is the most absurd of all the bourgeois notions, and those who inveigh against it the most fiercely are as thwarted as they are hypocritical. No, my Mr Hyde is no simple voluptuary; he bears in his countenance—in his loathsome features and stunted posture—all the outward marks of human cruelty and pure evil.'

Even saying it, I was reminded of that vision in the mirror above my desk. And subsequent visions, more horrible than that. My eyes inadvertently flicked to the cheval glass that I had ordered Chandler to bring to my study, so that I could observe in its full-length glass the complete effects of the unbidden transformations.

For unbidden they are, and all the more terrifying for that. As my illness has returned and I have attempted to ward it off with the last of Dr Rüedi's elixir, the choice has become more harrowing each time. To renounce it is to surrender to the consumption, but to imbibe it is to undergo, at the peril of my very soul, a transformation so radical that simply to behold it threatens the sanity.

No one, not even Fanny, has any notion of what transpires in the confines of my study on those nights when the change occurs.

'Has anyone else read this story yet?' Henley, ever the editor, asked.

'Fanny and Lloyd.'

'And they've told no one else?'

'I'm sure not. Indeed, Fanny hated it,' I said, gesturing at the fireplace where the last ashes of many pages still lay. Sally had been banned from cleaning the room until further notice.

'You burned it?'

'She felt that I had missed the point of my own tale, that it was an allegory, and I had made a mere sensation out of something that should have been my masterpiece.'

'And you listened to her?'

'I rewrote it,' I said, indicating the stack of pages that lay beneath the package Henley had carried upstairs. 'It is once again well in hand. But what have you brought me?'

'Damned if I know,' he said. 'Your wife shoved it under my arm and said if I was going to ruin your work, the least I could do was deliver your mail.'

For the first time, I looked more closely at the box, much damaged and loosely bound up again with twine, and at the postal marks. Switzerland, and France, and a stamp from the local delivery service. My heart leapt in my chest as I tore at the string and the scraps of brown paper still clinging to the sides of the box.

'Don't tell me,' Henley said, 'it's the latest Paris fashion.'

The top flaps of the box looked as if they had already been torn open, but inside, the contents were still snugly wrapped in thick towels bearing the Belvédère imprint. They were not the Valtellina bottles I had expected, though, and as quickly as my heart had risen in my chest, it now began to plummet.

The towels held metal flasks, firmly shut and engraved with the two-headed face of the Roman god Janus.

Was this a joke of some kind? A rebuke?

A letter in a pale blue envelope lay below the flasks, and paying no heed to Henley, I ripped through the sealing wax that closed it and read:

'Dear Mr R. L. Stevenson, The medication that you have requested will be, after this shipment, in very limited supply. As I have attempted to explain, its means of production is extraordinarily difficult and the reservoir from its source highly attenuated.'

Lord Grey's severed head hurtling through the train window sprang to mind.

'Furthermore, I was not at all confident that, given the vagaries of intercontinental transfer, glass bottles would make the journey unbroken.'

There, he was most certainly correct.

'In consequence, as a means of transporting it safely, and without arousing any undue notice from inspectors through whose hands it might pass, I have secreted it in the flasks enclosed. What more likely goods could an author have ordered from abroad?'

It was unlike the doctor to make such a sly aside, but the next sentence suggested why he had.

'I hope that, despite your urgent requests for this aid, your respiratory health continues, and that, should the occasion arise in the course of your professional interviews and public notice, you will not fail to mention that it was at my facility where you received your most critical and essential care.' It was signed, in his precisely neat hand, 'Carl Rüedi, Doctor and Director of the Belvédère Hotel and Health Clinic, Davos, Switzerland.'

'A love letter? If it is,' Henley said, looking in disgust at the incinerated pages in the grate, 'you'll want to add that to the pyre Fanny instigated.'

Folding up the letter and thrusting it into the pocket of my dressing gown, I said, 'It's simply some supplies.'

'Looks like brandy flasks to me.'

'It's of a very high quality.'

'Since when did London, of all places, run out of decent brandy?' he said, picking up a flask and beginning to unscrew its cap. 'I'll be the judge of it.'

'No!' I protested, perhaps too vehemently, and whisked the flask from his hand.

'Good God, man, get a hold of yourself. It can't be all that precious.'

The look on my face must have said otherwise.

'Can it?' he said, before letting the matter drop.

TOPANGA CANYON—
CALIFORNIA

Present Day

Before Rafe could get out of his jeep, Evangelina came bustling out of the house and said, "Can you keep your sister overnight?"

"Sure," Rafe said, although he wasn't really prepared for that. He'd just swung by to drop off the check, and to take Lucy out for the day. "Is something wrong?"

"She had kind of a blow-up last night with her new roomie."

"What about?"

"Doesn't matter. Never does. Things just need to cool down."

Rafe was quickly reorganizing his schedule in his head. He'd planned to drive Lucy to the Malibu Pier—she liked to feed the seagulls and watch the people fishing—then take her for an early dinner at her favorite restaurant, the Reel Inn, where she could sit at one of the outdoor tables and eat clam chowder out of a bread bowl. If everything had gone according to plan, he'd have had her back at the group home, happy but pooped, just in time to turn in. Lucy liked schedules, too—he knew she looked forward all week to their outings—but the prospect of spending a whole night away from the home, and at his trailer yet, would thrill her beyond measure.

The hard part would be convincing her that she had to go back to Evangelina's the next day.

Predictably, Lucy whooped with joy when she got the news, and with Evangelina's help, packed a toothbrush and change of clothes for the overnight. On the way out of the house, Rafe noticed the skinny roommate sulking in a corner of the living room. "She going to be okay?" Rafe murmured to Evangelina.

"She'll be fine. I'm going to shuffle some of them around to different rooms."

Tough as Evangelina was, she was an angel in Rafe's book; he didn't know what he would have done if he hadn't found her.

"Can we go to the pier?" Lucy said, buckling herself into the passenger seat. "Look—I brought some old crackers to throw to the birds!"

"That sounds like a great idea."

"And dinner, too?"

"What, you think we're not going to eat?"

"And then I get to sleep in the trailer tonight?"

"You bet." Which meant that he'd be on the floor, or, if the weather stayed this warm, up on the roof, contemplating the stars from atop his sleeping bag.

At the pier, an old fisherman let Lucy hold the fishing pole for a while, and then, when they actually got a bite, instructed her on how to reel it in. Less than a foot long, the fish came up wriggling and fighting, and when the fisherman tossed it in the bucket and clamped the lid down, Rafe could see a moment of regret cross his sister's face. She was sorry she'd done it. He also caught a fleeting glimpse of the girl she'd been, a lonely eleven-year-old who'd already seen her share of trouble and didn't want to see any more—much less cause any. He wondered, as he often did, what kind of a woman she'd have grown up to be if it hadn't been for those precious minutes on the bottom of the swimming pool.

At the restaurant, they ordered their food off the wooden board mounted behind the counter, and because the guy recognized Lucy from their previous outings, he threw in lots of extra croutons—"I'm a crouton guy myself," he said, "can't get enough of 'em"—and they ate at a table outside, overlooking Pacific Coast Highway.

"Rafe," Lucy said, spooning the hot chowder out of the bowl, "is that store going to be open?"

"The Cornucopia?"

"What's that mean again? I know you told me last time, but I forgot."

"It's a horn of plenty. It just means there's lots of different stuff in there."

"That's what I like about it."

"If it's not open, I can probably get it to open," he said. "I've got some pull with the owner."

"That blond lady?"

"Right." He knew Lucy had mixed feelings about Miranda. On the one hand, she was a potential rival for his attention—Rafe deliberately tried not to pay too much attention to Miranda on those rare occasions when the three of them were together—but on the other, somewhere in Lucy's heart, he suspected she harbored some hope that he and Miranda might get married someday, and provide a home where Lucy, too, could come and live with them. As if she'd been tuned in to that very thought, she said, "I hate living with that new girl."

"Why?"

"She's ugly, and boring. All she wants to talk about is her boyfriend, and I don't even think she has one."

"I think it will all be okay by the time you get back tomorrow. Evangelina is making some changes in the room assignments."

Lucy frowned, concerned that he had missed her greater point, though Rafe, of course, had not. On the way back across the parking lot, she clutched his hand so hard he said, "That's some grip you've got there, kid."

All along the twisting road up into the canyon, Lucy had swayed back and forth at each turn, exaggerating the motion and laughing when Rafe pretended to have lost control of the wheel. It made him happy to see her laugh, reminding him that there were still some things, however small, that he could do to bring some joy into her life.

The store was not only open when they got there, but positively bustling. Four or five cars had pulled up outside, and there was a gaggle of teenage girls inside, gathering up love beads and bottles of scented body lotion. Lucy hung back, torn between wanting to join in their fun and knowing, from bitter experience, that it would not go well. Miranda, stuck making change behind the counter, waved hello and shrugged, as if to say, *Don't ask me where they all came from.*

"Can I buy stuff?" Lucy asked, and Rafe said, "Knock yourself out."

He looked around for the dreaded Laszlo, but given that there was actually work to be done at the store, didn't expect to see him. Laszlo's income, such as it was, was mysterious and, unless Rafe missed his guess, illicit. But Rafe wasn't a cop, and he wasn't about to become one. Despite the fact that the Land Management office had issued him a handgun for his protection in the wild, he kept it locked in the portable safe in his trailer.

"Whew," Miranda said when the commotion had died down. "I think I just made the rent this month."

"You own the place."

"Oh, that's right. Where'd Lucy go?"

They found her in the back of the store, marveling at several of Miranda's paintings. "Hi, Lucy."

"Hi," Lucy said, without really looking at her.

"You like any of these?"

Nodding, Lucy said, "I like the one with the boy and the dragon in it."

"The dragon's name is Puff, and the boy is Jackie Paper. Do you know that old song?"

"No."

"I'll download it and send it to you," Miranda said, taking the painting off the hook. "Here, take it."

"Really?"

"My gift."

"Come on, Miranda," Rafe said, "you've got to stop giving stuff away. I'll pay you for it."

"I'm making big money today—don't spoil it."

"Will you help me hang it up?" Lucy asked Rafe, and he said, "Just as soon as you get home."

"But that's not till tomorrow, right?"

"That's right, Luce."

Miranda, looking surprised, said, "You guys are having a slumber party?"

Rafe nodded, turning over the price tag on the painting to see what Miranda had been asking for it. Seventy-five bucks. He wished Lucy had picked something cheaper.

"I saw you do that," Miranda said, leaning close, "and don't even think about it."

When he started to protest again, she put a finger on his lips and said, "Not another word."

But the touch of her fingertip on his lips was all that penetrated.

"In fact, if you don't mind my busting in," she said, "once I've closed the store, I'll make some caramel popcorn and bring it over. How's that sound?"

Now Lucy was really torn. She wanted Rafe to herself, but the popcorn was terribly tempting.

"Then it's a deal," Miranda said. "Why don't you guys go out and play with Trip? I've had so many customers he's been ignored all day."

Holding the painting flat in front of her as if it were a pizza, Lucy went outside to look for the dog.

"Where's Laszlo?" Rafe asked. "Looks like you could have used some help today."

"He's no help even when he is here," Miranda replied, going back behind the counter to close out the register.

Why did Rafe's spirits lift at her dismissive tone of voice?

Turning around to put some topaz jewelry back in the display case behind her, she banged her shin on something and said, "Ouch."

Rafe glanced over the counter and saw the old steamer trunk squatting against the bottom shelf.

"That damn thing has got to go somewhere else," she said, rubbing her shin. "I want it out of here."

He had the feeling there was more to it than the urge to tidy up.

Closing the display case, she turned toward him again and asked, "Did you ever get that strongbox open, though? That's what they're banking on."

"Now that," he said, "is another story."

Miranda paused. "Don't tell me. It *did* hold the crown jewels."

"Not exactly. But there was a book in it—more of a diary, actually—from the 1800s. I read the first few pages. They were pretty interesting."

"They can't have been all that interesting if you could put it down that fast."

"I was out in the canyon, at night, after a long day of tracking."

"You're excused," she said, with a laugh that sounded as musical to his ears as the wind chimes that hung from the front of her store.

"When you come over with the popcorn, we can read some of it out loud. Lucy might like that."

"It's a date."

He got that same sensation he'd had when she'd touched his lips. Christ, he thought, how old was he? Before embarrassing himself further, he went outside to check on his sister and found her running in circles in the backyard; her limp was hardly noticeable, especially with Tripod hobbling along behind her. The painting was propped up against the door of the trailer.

"Can we get a dog?" Lucy shouted to him.

"Someday." Slipping the painting under his arm, he unlocked the door and went inside. The air was stifling, and he cranked the skylight open to let some fresh oxygen in, then slid the narrow window panels fully open, too. He folded the cot out of the wall and straightened the pillow and blankets, not that it would matter to Lucy. To be with him, she'd have slept on a bed of nails.

By the time Lucy had exhausted herself in the yard and gotten ready for bed, Miranda had come over with a big red ceramic bowl filled with homemade popcorn. But after she stepped up into the trailer, she said, "Whew, it's too hot in here. I think we should dine al fresco."

"Al what?" Lucy said.

"Outside," Rafe explained, wondering where exactly.

"Let's go up on the roof," Miranda said, lifting her eyes to the ceiling of the trailer. "And bring that book, Rafe."

Once Lucy understood that they were all going to climb onto the roof of the trailer, eat popcorn, and read from an old book together, there was no stopping her. The second Rafe had finished spreading the sleeping bag open over the luggage rack, she clambered up the metal rungs and, using the open skylight panel as a backrest, nestled herself between Rafe and Miranda, with the blanket from the bed wrapped around her shoulders and the pillow propped behind her back. A warm breeze was blowing through the canyon, and the stars were bright overhead.

"You want to hold the flashlight?" Rafe said to Lucy, and she readily agreed, pointing the beam at the open journal.

"Do I know this story?" she asked.

"I don't think so," he said. "Nobody does. It's a very old and private book."

"A beautiful one, too," Miranda said, admiring the deep green cover.

Turning to the page where he had left off, and making sure to keep the paper unsullied by the caramel-covered popcorn, he said, "The story is taking place in Switzerland, high up in the mountains. There's a man who isn't feeling very well, and he's married to a woman named Fanny—"

"That's a funny name," Lucy giggled.

"And they have a dog named Woggin."

"That's even funnier."

"They're going to a hospital to see if the doctor there can make the man better."

"Does he?" Miranda said. "I can't take a sad story right now."

Rafe, amused, gave her a look. "Your guess is as good as mine. Should I start reading?"

"Yes," she said, as Lucy, nodding vigorously, dug into the popcorn bowl.

"'We were deep in the valley,'" Rafe began, "'the road rising now between jagged peaks on all sides, when I first caught a glimpse of the great grey mausoleum that was the Belvédère. It was a brooding hulk, glowering down on the tiny town, as we approached.'"

It wasn't five minutes before Lucy had slumped down, fast sleep.

"'It had been a long journey, one of many, I reflected, that I had enforced upon the family as a result of my ill-health. From the South of France to San Francisco, Canada to Colorado, I had made one journey after another, seeking the one place where I might be healed of my affliction.'"

Miranda, too, was soon asleep, sprawled on the bag, with a corner of Lucy's blanket across her shoulders and her cheek resting on the edge of the pillow. The popcorn bowl was empty, and the flashlight beam was only obliquely hitting the page. Rafe read a bit further, far enough to learn that the family's name was Stevenson and that the man had given a speech about preserving gas lamps. Maybe he was a prominent businessman or local politician of the time. The flashlight beam was dimming, and Rafe switched it off, closing the journal. For a few seconds, he simply took in this unexpected tableau. So many feelings, inchoate and unexpected, swirled in his chest, that he couldn't begin to sort them out. Then, the diary cradled on his chest, he laid his own head on the other corner of the pillow and shut his eyes.

15 January, 1886

Even from across the street, I could feel the thrumming of the great printing presses in the cellars of the "National Observer." The very cobblestones seemed to vibrate under my shoes as I made my way to the entrance. The bell above the door tinkled, but who could have heard it over the Stygian roar? Compositors, heads down and fingers flying through trays of type, were laying out pages that boys, so black with ink that they could have served as their own shadows, then carted below.

'Help you?' one of them cried, as he butted me out of his way.

'Thanks, but I know where I'm going.'

Already, he had vanished down the rickety staircase, where I could hear him shouting, 'Theatre page! Final!'

Ascending past the second floor, where several wretches sat hunched over proofs in a warren of rooms the size of cupboards, and after taking a short breather on the landing, I reached the comparatively pleasant eyrie of the "Observer"'s editor-in-chief. Even here, however, the floorboards seemed to hum with energy.

Henley was on his feet—or foot, as he would have no doubt jested—at the grimy window, crutch under one arm, looking out over the chimney stacks and water towers of the surrounding streets. He was talking to a man seated before his desk, whose back was to me.

'I think you've put paid to Wilde's latest incitement,' he was saying, 'but I would suggest you go even further in your next piece. Controversy sells—let's get some going!'

'I have never been averse to an intellectual brawl,' the man said, 'but I won't stoop to invective, if that's what you mean.'

The voice was unmistakable. 'Symonds!' I said. 'You, here?'

Both men turned, expressing their surprise at the same moment.

'You've come to exult?' Henley said, as Symonds stood to shake my hand.

'Congratulations,' Symonds said. 'Henley here tells me the reviews of your new book have been favourable.'

'Favourable?' Henley crowed, grabbing the "Times" from his desk and snapping it open to read aloud from an interior page. '"Nothing Mr Stevenson has written as yet has so strongly impressed us with the versatility of his original genius."'

'That does sound favourable,' Symonds said with a sly smile.

'And then there's this,' Henley said, flinging the "Times" aside and picking up the "Fortnightly Review." '"Of all Stevenson's books, the one which has most of a dream's vivid pictorial quality is undoubtedly 'The Strange Case of Dr Jekyll and Mr Hyde.' What piece of prose is less likely to be forgotten?"'

'Enough,' I said, holding up a hand.

'Or this,' Henley said, picking up a third publication, 'which just came out yesterday. It's from the "Century Illustrated." '"There is a genuine feeling for the perpetual moral question, a fresh sense of the difficulty of being good and the brutishness of being bad, but what there is above all is a singular ability in holding the interest. I confess that that, to my sense, is the most edifying thing in the short, rapid, concentrated story, which is really a masterpiece of concision."'

Although I had not read that one, the prose alone was enough to tell me who had written it.

'You can thank your old chum Henry James for that one.'

'And who should respect concision more?' Symonds joked.

It had indeed been a remarkable time. "The Strange Case of Dr Jekyll and Mr Hyde"—for I had given up trying to elide that very first word from its title, as it was routinely included—had taken hold of the public's imagination and shaken it like a terrier shakes a rat. Overnight, it had become the talk of the town—the nation, if the reports from the publisher's sales agents were to be believed—and my little allegory of good and evil promised to pass into the common language as an abbreviation for the duality of human nature.

'To what, then, do we owe the honour of this unforeseen, but entirely fortuitous, visit?' Henley said.

'To my appointment with a physician three streets over.'

'And the diagnosis?'

'He recommended removal to a more salubrious clime.'

'Are you coming back to Davos, then?' Symonds asked. 'I return there next month myself.'

'Banish the thought,' Henley advised. 'Removing yourself from the scene, at the very apex of your career? It would be criminal, and I won't stand for it.'

There was little danger of that. I was done with Davos, done with Dr Rüedi, done with the insular world of the desperate and dying. Done with the grim shades of Lord Grey, and the murderous, murdered Yannick. Switzerland was a closed chapter, of a book I regretted ever having read at all.

'Symonds here has just turned in a capital essay suggesting that the revival of Hellenistic ideals might be a boon to the masses,' Henley said. 'If you were smart, Louis, you would give me something to run right away, while you are the apple of everyone's eye.'

'I'm afraid I can't allow myself to be distracted.'

'From what?'

'I'm working on a new novel.'

'Called?'

'"Kidnapped."'

'Huh,' Henley said. 'Is it possible? Have you actually come up with a good title on your own?'

'I'd say so,' Symonds put in.

'Still, it wouldn't do you any harm to rattle off something punchy and to the point. A short story, a critique—I can even throw you something to review if you'd prefer.'

Henley knew, like no man alive, how to play upon my instincts. Like the horse at the firehouse, I have only to hear the alarm bell and I am champing at the bit, but this time I demurred. The new book is off to a rollicking start, and I am reluctant to deprive it of my full concentration, especially as the critics have so often taken me to task for constructing narratives that lose steam as they progress.

'But it appears I've interrupted a work conference,' I said, preparing to withdraw.

'Don't be ridiculous,' Henley said. 'We were just about to adjourn for a bibulous lunch.'

'Please do join us,' Symonds said, laying an encouraging hand on my sleeve. I had the impression he was seeking support.

'And you can tell me all about this new book of yours with the intriguing title. Another tall tale of adventure and suspense? A return to stowaways, perhaps, and buccaneers?'

'Highland Scots,' I replied, hoping to cut the inquisition short with the briefest of answers. I have long been of the opinion that a writer who tips his hand too soon loses more than the interest of his audience; he loses his own. 'Where were you going to lunch?'

'A quaint little pub called the Coronet,' he said, propping his crumpled top hat on his head, 'known far and wide for the quality of its patronage.'

A wary look crossed Symonds's face, a man more at home in the clubs of Pall Mall than the public houses of Piccadilly, and Henley, spotting it, laughed and clapped him on the back.

'Never fear,' he said. 'I'm a steady customer and I've yet to have my watch stolen or my throat cut.'

Symonds looked insufficiently reassured.

'And besides, we have the toast of the town with us,' he added, herding us towards the door. 'I ask you—who would dare to challenge the man who gave us the terrifying Mr Hyde?'

TOPANGA CANYON—CALIFORNIA

Present Day

He should have seen this coming, Rafe thought.

By the time he had run Lucy back home—getting her there first thing in the morning, while she was half-asleep, was a strategic decision—and then gone back to his own place to get his equipment together, Heidi Graff was sitting at the picnic table in the yard. She had two Starbucks cups in front of her, and Tripod at her feet begging for a piece of her cinnamon bun.

"I didn't know what you drink," she said, "so I just got a basic black coffee, with cream and sugar on the side."

In deference to their last misadventure, he noticed that she was wearing her long brown uniform pants, tucked into a pair of lace-up leather boots that came several inches above her ankle. Any rattler they encountered would have to make a determined and vertical lunge this time around.

"I didn't expect to see you here," he said, "but I'm glad to see you're getting around again. You should have let me know you were coming."

"I did. Don't you read your e-mails?"

The truth was, as little as possible—and never over a weekend.

"I sent you a text, too."

Ditto.

"I still have to complete my field training requirement," she said.

She had chosen one hell of a day to do it. Rafe had planned on heading straight into the interior of the canyon to check out the coyote den he'd spotted the last time, and to figure out where Seth and Alfie had disappeared to with that sled full of supplies—and he planned to do it without spending the night under the stars. He was still stiff from those hours on top of the trailer the night before.

"This might not be the best day for it. I've got a long hike through rough terrain ahead."

"That's exactly what I'm supposed to get used to. And this time," she said, patting the leather boot, "I've taken precautions."

"You think your leg's up to it?"

"Definitely. You'll see."

That's what he was afraid of. But there was no getting around it now. "Give me a few minutes," he said, ducking into the trailer to gather up his stuff. In addition to his backpack, which always contained water, protein bars, flashlight, a first-aid kit, binoculars, and a camera, he was going to carry something else today—the Smith & Wesson he'd been issued and never once used. Taking it out of the safe, he checked it over—the weight and heft of it in his hand felt strange—before sticking it back into its holster and slipping the belt around his waist. Chances were, he wouldn't have to use it today, either, but the sight of Seth and Alfie, on their mystery mission out there in the middle of nowhere, gave him pause.

Heidi noticed it right away. "You didn't have a gun with you the last time."

"This time I'm determined to get you back in one piece, no matter what."

"I appreciate that, but the rattler was my fault. I should have watched where I was stepping."

"I should have warned you."

"By the way, what ever happened to that trunk we found in the lake?"

"I got it back down," he said.

"What was in it? Anything?"

"Nothing of any value." He'd still have to convince Seth and Alfie of that.

"Too bad. I thought we could have gotten famous or something."

"No such luck," he said, avoiding meeting her eye.

On the way up the road, she told him all about her recuperation and physical therapy—and then inquired about Diego and Frida and the rest of the coyote pack.

"That's where we're headed," he said. "I found the den. But we'll have to be very careful approaching it." For more reasons, he thought, than he had yet let on. Driving as far into the canyon as he could go—several of the slopes were so steep he saw Heidi clutching the sides of her seat like she was on a roller coaster—he finally parked at the top of a crest, and from there they trekked into the wilderness. By the time they got to Mr. and Mrs. Pothead's little homestead, he had warned her of what to expect, so she wasn't so surprised when they came upon the pair of them, naked except for shorts and sunhats, tending to their vegetable patch. Rafe performed the introductions—Mrs. Pothead not even bothering to cover her slack but prodigious breasts—and asked if they'd seen any sign of the coyotes.

"Found some paw prints out back," Mr. Pothead said. "Are they big fellas?"

"Not especially."

Mr. Pothead scratched his chin stubble. "These were big."

"Mind if I see them?"

"They're gone. I had to till that soil. Spinach."

"It's full of antioxidants," Mrs. Pothead said.

No matter how crazy they were, Rafe thought, everybody in California was a health nut.

"You keepin' your eyes open?" Mr. Pothead asked.

"Yes," Rafe replied. "I am."

Mr. Pothead nodded sagely.

"You're referring to the guys carting supplies up into the canyon, a mile or two from here?" Rafe said.

"I'm not sayin' anything more. I mind my own business, just like the government ought to do."

"No offense," Mrs. Pothead put in, bobbing her head at Heidi's uniform and badge.

"None taken," Heidi replied.

It was lucky he'd prepared her for them, but he had not mentioned the intruders on their supply run.

When Mrs. Pothead offered to brew some of her homemade tea, which Rafe knew from experience tasted like moldy bark, he knew it was time to move on. Once they were out of earshot, Heidi followed up on the guys with supplies and said, "Were these the two dudes you told me about the first time, the bobcat trappers?"

"Yes. But they might be up to something new, maybe with the help of some others." The Spiritz, but that could wait. "Just do whatever I tell you to if we run into any of them."

Heidi grew silent, then said, "That's why you have the gun today."

He didn't answer, but checked the coordinates flashing on his cell phone screen and saw that they were close to the den. Cresting the next ridge, he came upon the jojoba bush where he'd hidden—he knew it was the same one because the cigarette butt was still lying under its branches—and looked around until he'd located a fallen log with an opening behind it. Coyotes liked their dens concealed behind logs and foliage—most of the time, they actually appropriated dens that had been dug out and abandoned by foxes, skunks, or badgers—but they also liked to pick places from which they could survey a wide area. There was a good chance, even now, that Diego or Frida was observing them anxiously from a distance. Venturing down the slope toward the fallen log that provided cover for the den, Rafe remained on guard, and instructed Heidi to follow in his footsteps as closely as she could. She didn't need to be told twice.

Crouching down to peer over the log, Rafe saw an opening no more than a foot and half high and about as wide, and used his phone to snap a few close shots.

"They can get in and out of something that small?" Heidi whispered as Rafe crouched down and used his phone to snap a few close shots.

"Uh-huh. And there could be a tunnel twenty feet long, leading to the main chamber."

"Where the cubs are?"

"Possibly." But it was late in the year for that, and after six or eight weeks, the cubs would be ready to get out in the open. Coyotes were smart—one of the many reasons he admired them—and made sure their burrows had more than one escape route. They were hygienic, too, removing food scraps and bones, and changing one den for another as soon as it became infested with fleas or some other parasitic nuisance. In documenting their habitat and habits, Rafe hoped to do whatever he could to persuade the Land Management office to lay off their draconian policies—sometimes he wondered if the bureaucrats in Los Angeles and Sacramento had any feeling whatsoever for the native wildlife—and stop the wanton slaughter, and once he'd done that, to make some inroads with the public at large. The animals had been here first, and even when they came into conflict with humans, it was only because they were doing their best to survive in a world that kept encroaching on their territory and limiting their options.

"They're bound to have other tunnels around this immediate vicinity," Rafe said, "so why don't you do a circuit and see if you find anything?"

Bending lower to turn his flashlight into the darkened burrow, Rafe was disturbed by the slight, but telltale, odor of smoke. He saw no cigarette butts on the ground around the hole, but what he suspected—and feared—was that someone had tried to smoke out the coyotes. It was often done—sometimes because they were considered a threat in some way, and other times because some sonofabitch still thought he could get a few bucks for a pelt. Once, he'd come across some teenagers shooting BB guns at a lame coyote for the sheer fun of it. If he'd had his own gun with him that day, he'd have been sorely tempted to give them a taste of their own medicine.

He dictated some notes into his cell phone, noting the absence of prints or scat around this entrance, and looked up only when he heard Heidi, maybe thirty yards off, saying, in a somber tone, "Rafe—I think you'll want to see this."

She'd found another tunnel, higher up the hill, and at this one he detected the faint trace of something stronger than mere smoke—maybe tear gas. There were plenty of tracks here, and even what looked like boot heels. Worse, about a dozen feet away was the body of a scrawny cub, not much bigger than a squirrel, curled up under a dead bush. An empty canister of something lay in the dirt nearby. The cub had probably been the runt of the litter. Though the maggots were already working away, it didn't look like it had been lying there very long.

Rafe saw red. Looking in all directions, he saw no sign of Diego or Frida, or any of the others in the pack, watching.

"Who would do this?" Heidi said, and when he didn't answer, she added, "I guess it's not that hard to figure out, huh?"

No, he thought, it wasn't. Not hard at all.

31 August, 1888

'Who would challenge the man who gave us the terrifying Mr Hyde?'

Although it has been well over two years since Henley spoke those words as we left the offices of the "Observer," I remember them as if they had been uttered only yesterday.

But oh, what a tempest has swirled between that day and this. My little story has swept across the world, catching the fancy of the public everywhere from Dublin to Chicago. Indeed, the United States has embraced the tale like no other land—Scribner's informs me that close to a quarter of a million copies, if that is to be believed, have sold there—and to take advantage of the groundswell, Fanny and I and, of course, Lloyd, having long since abandoned any course of study, departed from the Royal Albert Docks on the SS Ludgate Hill in late August. Henry James had sent a crate of champagne to our cabin to celebrate the voyage, but if we had laboured under the impression that this was to be a luxurious cruise, we were quickly disabused of it. When the ship put in at Le Havre, it took on a con-signment of French horses and, to our astonishment, a menagerie of great apes and monkeys destined for North American zoos. A sorrier lot of creatures, I could not imagine.

What should have been a tranquil late-summer crossing became instead an arduous voyage through storm-tossed seas and against powerful, walloping headwinds. Fanny and Lloyd took to their beds, seasick, but for reasons inexplicable even to me, I found my sea legs and kept them under me. I would stride the decks and cargo hold in all weather, doing what I could to calm the panic-stricken horses and provide some welcome jibes to the captive apes. No one can look these animals in the face and not feel the strongest and most eerie sense of kinship. In their eyes, there is a melancholy yearning to understand, an almost palpable desire to express some thought or sensation, hindered only by the natural want of means to do so. Time and again, they reached their hairy arms through the iron bars of their uncleaned cages—so small the animals could barely turn in place—and though the crew had warned me to stay clear, I allowed their fingers to touch my own. I was, perhaps inevitably, reminded of the Sistine Chapel, and the fresco of the Almighty reaching out to channel life to the finger of the firstborn man, but I could transfer no such blessing. I could only signal a knowing complicity in our situation—passengers on a dangerous ocean journey—which would end for me in a comfortable bed in a hotel suite, but for these unhappy prisoners, only in another cage, a cage from which they would never escape.

Upon our arrival at the harbour of New York, I was met by a jostling mob, with reporters from the "Times" and the "Tribune" and the "Sun," note pads and pencils in hand, shouting questions over the heads of the hundreds vying for autographs or simply hoping to catch a glimpse of the story's fabled author. That I was not a fearsome-looking creature, in a black cape and a top hat and brandishing a deadly cane, was a great disappointment to many of them, I think.

'At the very least,' Fanny said, 'you should give the photographers a frightening scowl.'

For the next day or two, I gave them what I could, though I am, in my normal guise, more akin to the respectable Dr Henry Jekyll than I am to the dreaded Mr Hyde. When I could offer no more, I absconded for the peace and refuge of a seaside town called Newport, in the state of Rhode Island. America is a fine place for eating and drinking, and for the kindness of its people, but this raw dose of popularity was more debilitating than the transatlantic crossing had been. I longed for the quiet of my study, and to return to my work, but the fever ignited by "Jekyll and Hyde" was inescapable there, and now it has infected London, too, rekindled by the debut of the play based upon the book.

Adapted by an American named Thomas Russell Sullivan—a man whom I have never had the pleasure of meeting—it has become the sensation of the New York and Boston stage, and has finally bivouacked in my own neck of the woods. Although I do receive a small and erratic royalty from its adaptation, Henley has been beside himself—'We lost our chance, Louis, it was sitting in the palm of our hands and we might have made a fortune!' He evicted his usual reviewer from the "Observer"'s box at the Lyceum Theatre in order to invite me to join him there for the opening night.

'Fanny will be delighted,' I said.

'Are you sure she'll be up to it?' Henley said. 'I've been told that Richard Mansfield's portrayal of Mr Hyde is so shocking that ladies have fainted dead away at the transformation scenes.'

His concern for Fanny's welfare was as patently insincere as it was transparent. 'Have you ever known Fanny to shrink from anything?'

Defeated, he agreed to meet us at the theatre, where the manager—'a great friend of mine, Irishman by the name of Stoker, anxious to make your acquaintance'—would show us to the proper box.

It was a stiflingly hot night when Fanny and I stepped into a hired carriage and left for the theatre district. All month long London had sweltered, the air as hot and still as an oven, horses keeling over dead in Trafalgar Square. The houses being intolerable, the stoops and steps of every building played host to the tenants, who fanned themselves with newspaper sheets and pressed wet cloths to their foreheads. The horse plodded down the dark cobblestoned streets toward the electric lights, only recently implemented, of the West End, where the proud columns and grand portico of the Lyceum Theatre, recalling a Greek temple, stood on Wellington Street, just off the Strand. The marquee announced the play and the celebrated actor who had gained such international renown in the title role. In preparation for the debut, trick photographs, in which Mansfield was portrayed as the respectable Dr Jekyll, but o'ershadowed by a hideous Mr Hyde, had been plastered in the windows of tobacconist shops for weeks, and the very air crackled with excitement.

'Oh, how Lloyd would have loved this,' Fanny said, as the carriage drew close. 'What could be so much more interesting than this in Paris?'

'The Folies Bergère,' I replied. Lloyd and Randolph Desmond had embarked, to the best of my knowledge, on the boat train the week before.

Much as I might have hoped to pass unnoticed into the lobby, we had no sooner stepped out of the cab than a flock of pressmen descended upon us, so forcibly that a toothless woman in a blue crêpe bonnet, selling wilted flowers from a basket, was forced up against me.

'A carnation for that suit, sir?' she said, and out of a natural instinct, I was fishing in my pocket for a coin to aid the crone, but Fanny shooed her away with her fan. The woman was instantly swallowed up in the mêlée, and the carnation, I could not help but note, was crushed under the heels of the jostling journalists.

'Have you seen the play in the States?' one reporter shouted.

'Have you met Mr Mansfield?' cried another.

'What are you writing next?'

I could barely mumble a reply to one question before being peppered with a dozen more, and was relieved when a strong hand took my elbow and a voice in my ear said, 'I'm Bram Stoker, the manager here, and I'll take you through the side door.'

Fanny and I were ushered away from the main steps, around a low railing, and into the bowels of the Lyceum. Stoker, a pugnacious-looking fellow with close-set eyes and a thick Irish brogue, laughed once we were inside and said, 'I had expected a crowd, but not a rugby scrum.'

'I've encountered worse,' I said, thinking back to the docks in Manhattan.

'A pleasure to meet you,' he said. 'I told Henley that I am a great admirer of your work.'

'And so he reported. Haven't I read your own stories in the "London Society"?'

'You might well have done. But nothing so impressive as this.'

With that, he guided us up some back stairs that opened directly into a private box overlooking the stage. Henley, already ensconced there, with his crutch propped against his chair, nodded to Fanny—who returned a nod just as curtly—and then said, 'Ah, so you two scribes have met now.'

'We have,' Stoker said. 'But if you'll excuse me, I have to attend to Mr Mansfield. He requires someone to guard him from any intrusion whatsoever in the minutes before the curtain is to rise.'

'Pull your chairs up to the railing,' Henley said. 'You'll get a better view of the whole stage that way.'

Leaving room for Fanny's voluminous skirts—not her usual attire, but something she trots out for special occasions such as this—required a bit of shifting about in the close quarters of the box, but once we were settled, with me in the middle to maintain the peace, I looked out over the auditorium below, where hundreds of people were still milling in the aisles and finding their seats, all dressed to the nines, chattering away and waving to each other in anticipation of the spectacle to come. Prominently positioned at the door leading to the lobby were two husky young ushers and a nurse who was equipped, I was told, with smelling salts and compresses to assist any lady who might be overcome with horror. Henry Irving, who owns the theatre and often appears in its productions, is a master of such theatrical flourishes.

'They're all out tonight,' Henley said, 'the society ladies, the swells, even what passes for statesmen in our day.' He indicated the box directly opposite ours. A portly man in a black tailcoat, with the face of a basset hound, was holding a chair for his wife as she adjusted her own dress. 'If the prime minister's here, can the Queen be far behind? Or a knighthood?'

'Heaven forfend.'

'I don't see what would be wrong with that,' Fanny said, perhaps already fancying herself 'Lady Stevenson'.

Before the curtain opened, Stoker stepped out from the wings to settle the audience, introduced himself, and warned that 'the play we are about to present—never seen on this side of the Atlantic—is not for the faint of heart or those easily given to morbid fancy.'

A delightful chill ran through the theatre.

'For anyone overtaken by fear or apprehension at what is about to unfold, please be aware that help is available from one of the Nightingale nurses, whom you will see at the rear of the auditorium.'

Heads swivelled.

'Finally, allow me to introduce our esteemed guests tonight. Lord Salisbury,' he said, bowing toward the prime minister's box, and then, once the applause had died down, turning again, 'and the author of the book upon which tonight's entertainment is based—I give you Mr Robert Louis Stevenson.'

For this, I was not prepared, and when all heads turned again, and applause rippled through the room, I had to be urged to stand by a firm jab in the ribs from my wife's fan. Even Salisbury was clapping.

'What did I say?' Henley exulted. 'A title, for sure!'

As soon as I had taken my seat again, Stoker left the stage, the house lights dimmed, and the curtain—maroon velvet with a fringe of golden tassels—parted to reveal a gloomy laboratory where a dishevelled Mansfield, in shirtsleeves, was labouring over a counter of vials and beakers. He lifted one and swirled the greenish liquid inside, a wisp of smoke rising from its lip, and, just as he was about to drink, there was a loud rapping off-stage and a man's voice crying, 'Dr Jekyll! You have a visitor!'

'Blast it, Poole! Haven't I told you I cannot be interrupted for anything?'

'It's Mr Utterson, sir, and he says it cannot wait!'

'Wait it will! Wait it shall have to!'

He took a swallow from the smoking glass, grimaced at the taste, then hurled the glass at the fireplace, where it shattered into a thousand pieces. A woman yelped at the explosion, a titter ran through the audience, and the play sailed on.

TOPANGA CANYON—CALIFORNIA

Present Day

"But why?" Heidi said, surveying the rusty canister, the rotting cub, the disturbed entrance to the den. "What could they get out of it?"

Rafe could think of several things. Wanton, useless slaughter was right up Seth and Alfie's alley, for starters. So was the chance to make a buck with a fresh pelt, even if it was only a coyote cub. Finally, there was always the chance that they knew Rafe had been tracking and studying this pack. Maybe it was revenge for the loss of the trunk.

As Heidi wandered off in search of other tunnels, Rafe used his boot heel to scrape dirt over the body of the dead cub. It just seemed wrong to leave the little critter so exposed like that. Then, he gave the canister a good, swift kick, hard enough that it actually lifted into the air and toppled end over end down the hillside until it came to rest, with an unexpected clank, on something hard. Something that definitely wasn't dirt.

Rafe followed it down, and saw, half covered with weeds and grit, a concrete slab, maybe thirty or forty feet long. A tangle of wires and rusted metal—once an antenna, it would appear—was bolted to it, and he realized that the slab was actually the roof of a low building, buried like a pillbox or a bunker in the slope of the hill.

"What the heck is that?" Heidi said, coming down the hill sideways.

Judging from its position and the contraption on the roof, Rafe could hazard a guess. "It's probably an old conning station."

"A what?"

"During the Second World War, there were radar installations built along the coastline here, to give warning in case of a Japanese attack." This was the first one he'd ever come across, though, and as he made a slow reconnaissance around its perimeter—the whole thing was about the size of a three-car garage—he noticed that the windows, narrow and only inches above the dirt line, were all blocked with tinfoil, and the ground around the bunker was even more arid and discolored than it had been higher up the hillside. As if the soil had been poisoned. The entryway was simply a few steps of cracked concrete, leading down to a sheet-metal door of more recent vintage. It still had a gleam to its surface, and a sturdy lock with a loose chain hanging down. Putting his ear closer to the door, Rafe could hear music playing softly inside. Some rock band he didn't recognize.

Heidi came up behind him, but he held up a hand to stop her. "Stand back, and stay there."

"But I'm supposed to—"

"Just do it."

Pushing the door open as gently as he could, he peered into the interior, expecting it to be pitch black, but what he got instead was a glaring white brightness. A generator hummed somewhere below one of the dozen counters, all of which were covered with beakers and boxes and plastic bottles with tubes sticking out of their tops. A guy who looked like he was ready to go deep-sea diving, in a face mask, goggles, headphones, and blue scrubs, was bobbing his head to the music while counting out pills. He had no idea Rafe was there, nor did the other guy, stretched out asleep on a dilapidated sofa, with a fuzzy black face mask over his eyes and a denim jacket that said Spiritz draped across his chest. Rafe had seen him around La Raza—his name was Axel something, and he ran the gang.

It looked like that tip to the Land Management administrator had been right. He felt like he had just stumbled into the center of the spider's web, but what did he do about it now? He was wondering if the wisest course of action right now wasn't to simply back out again before they'd even noticed he was there.

The lab tech scratched his butt through the scrubs, then bent down to pick up something that had rolled off the counter. He paused halfway up, and then, as if not sure of what he was seeing, made a swipe at his goggles with his gloved hand.

Too late now, Rafe thought.

"Hey, Axel," the techie said.

"What?" Axel grumbled, eye mask still in place.

"Wake up, Axel."

"Why? Did you fuck up again?"

"Somebody did."

With a grunt, Axel shoved the mask up onto his forehead and rubbed his eyes. He looked at Rafe, and then at something just behind Rafe's shoulder—Heidi must have disobeyed him enough to be seen in the doorway—and said, "Well, if it isn't Dudley Do-Right."

Rafe wasn't sure what to say, but noticed Axel taking in the gun slung on his belt.

"Are you really this stupid?" Axel said, slowly swinging his feet off the sofa. "Coming in here? And with your little girlfriend yet?"

"I'm not his girlfriend," Heidi declared. "We're with the Land Management department."

Rafe would have given a million bucks to have her out of there just now, or at least as much simply to have her keep quiet.

Axel laughed and said, "Oh, yeah, I'm really sorry about that. Didn't mean to piss you off, little lady."

The techie had removed his goggles and hood—Rafe recognized him now as one of the other Spiritz he'd seen around La Raza—and was trying to unobtrusively move farther back into the lab.

"Stay where you are," Rafe said, and the man stopped, though Rafe wondered what he could have done if he hadn't. Using a gun in a meth lab would only serve to blow them all sky-high—a blunt fact of which they were all, except perhaps Heidi, undoubtedly aware.

"What do you want?" Axel asked, stretching his arms out on the back of the sofa. "This is already getting boring."

"Who killed the coyote pups?"

"Who what?" Turning to the techie, Axel said, "Hey, Roy—you know what the hell he's talking about?"

"Yeah. It was those dumb fucks you hired to haul shit. They did it. I told you not to use them, Axel."

"Yeah, well, remind me to run all my decisions by you in future." Returning his attention to Rafe, he said, "So, what do you want me to do about it now? Pay you? What's a baby coyote go for these days?"

It was strange, Rafe thought, how they had all implicitly agreed to waltz around the much greater, and deadlier, topic surrounding them—the lab counters covered with everything from crumpled pseudoephedrine packets to acetone jugs, all the random paraphernalia required to manufacture methamphetamine.

"There's no price on them at all. But gassing them is a state offense."

Axel laughed again, and pulled out a wad of bills. "Go ahead—fine me." He dug into his pocket and threw a few hundreds onto the grimy cement floor. "And then get out."

Although Rafe pointedly ignored the bills, Heidi murmured, "Do you think that constitutes a bribe to a state official?"

Axel slapped his knee with delight. "Where did you get her?"

"We're going," Rafe said, deliberately backing into her to move her toward the door. "You two just stay where you are."

He could see the rapid calculations going on behind Axel's eyes now that his secret lair had been discovered, and by a park ranger, no less.

Rafe kept them both in his line of vision. Roy repeatedly glanced at Axel, as if awaiting instructions to do something, but Axel simply watched Rafe and Heidi retreat, without budging from the couch.

Once they were up the stairs, Rafe told Heidi to run back toward the jeep.

"I won't be able to find it!"

"Then just run that way," he said, pointing back toward the Potheads' farm. "I'll catch up to you."

"But what about—"

"For once, will you do what I tell you to?"

Heidi swallowed hard and took off, while Rafe unsnapped the holster on his Smith & Wesson nine millimeter and waited. It wasn't long before Roy came scrambling out with a shotgun, the goggles still dangling around his neck, followed by Axel on his cell phone.

"Fuck this phone," Axel cursed, shaking it. The reception this deep into the canyon was virtually nil.

"What do you want me to do?" Roy shouted nervously. "He's right here, just standing here."

Axel looked up. "What do you think, Officer? Do you think we should discuss this . . . situation?" He shoved the useless phone into the back pocket of his jeans. "And I don't mean the coyotes."

"I'm not an officer," Rafe said, stalling for time. The farther Heidi could get away, the better. "I'm an environmental scientist."

Axel's expression didn't change a bit. He had thick, dirty brown hair that had been sculpted close to his skull from years under a motorcycle helmet.

"I'm not a cop," Rafe repeated.

"I get that," Axel agreed. "I know who you are. You're that poor broke asshole who chases coyotes—dead ones at that—and lives in a shitty trailer out behind a bullshit store."

Rafe let it stand. Just let him keep talking.

"*That* is what you are, my friend."

"The girl," Roy interjected impatiently. "You want me to go after the girl?"

Rafe's hand moved now toward the handle of the sidearm, and Axel noticed it.

"Don't wet yourself," Axel told his anxious confederate. Then, to Rafe, he said, "So what do you think? Are we going to be able to get a handle on this situation?"

"Meaning what?" The sun was slipping below the horizon in a fiery ball.

"Meaning, are you going to be able to shut her up, for one thing? She just might be so dumb she doesn't even know what she saw—and if you were to fuck her, and for all I know you already are, maybe you could get her to go along with anything you say."

"She's not your problem."

"That's right. She's just an itty-bitty part of it. You're my problem. And that's what I need to fix."

"I could still catch her," Roy insisted.

"What do they pay scientists these days?" Axel asked, ignoring Roy altogether.

"Enough."

"To do what? Buy a bean burrito at La Raza? You could make some money—serious money, by your not-so-serious standards."

Could Rafe convince him he was bribable, after all? Never much of an actor, he was grateful for the failing light. He felt like he had to play along, even as he felt Axel was playing a part, too. Neither one of them wanted the situation to come to a head right here, right now—not with trigger-happy Roy champing at the bit, or Heidi running loose in the canyon—but neither of them could work out the details of another plan fast enough.

"It's getting dark," Axel said, casually taking a pack of cigarettes out of the front pocket of his jacket. "If you don't find her fast, she's going to have to sleep all alone in the woods tonight." He glanced at Roy, then, significantly, back at Rafe. "And that would not be safe. I can guarantee you that."

Rafe felt that some deal was still lying on the table—in return for his silence, Heidi's life, and his own.

"And all things considered, everything you just saw," Axel said, tilting his head toward the lab, "is history. Gone. Poof. By the time you got back here, there'd be nothing left to find and no one to arrest. That right, Roy?"

Roy was shifting back and forth on his feet like a racehorse still in the gate, the shotgun in his hands.

"You got that?" Axel repeated, and Roy gave his grudging assent.

Rafe nodded, too, and moved his hand away from his gun. Then, he backed away, slowly.

Roy muttered something to Axel, who said "Shut the fuck up" and took a long drag on his cigarette. "I said no, just go inside and start packing up your shit."

By now, Rafe was moving out of earshot. Roy flipped him the bird, then stomped back down the steps as he'd been ordered. The last thing Rafe saw, before he finally got below the crest of the hill and felt it was safe to turn around and run after Heidi, was Axel, his stubby legs planted wide, staring off at the setting sun, probably planning where to set up his next base of operations.

2 September, 1888

For the past two days, all of London has been in the grip of fear.

But not, would it were so, because of the debut of the play.

True, the audience at the Lyceum was caught up in the drama, and even I, the author of the tale, found myself immersed. The performance of Richard Mansfield in the title role was a prodigious achievement. His transformation from the eminent Dr Jekyll to the malevolent Mr Hyde was something that seemed to defy the very eyes. After imbibing the concoction—a plot device for which several critics took me to task in the reviews of my novel—everything about him, from his posture to his physiognomy, altered in both radical and subtle ways. His shoulders became stooped, his legs bandied, the hair on his head appeared electrified, and in his eyes—and that is where the subtlety showed—a bottomless black pool yawned.

Henley glanced at me for my approval, and my pallor no doubt spoke to the efficacy of the actor's work. But Henley could not guess—no one could—how deeply the performance affected me, how close to the quick it cut. When Mansfield's clothes hung from his frame like wet washing on the line, it reminded me of my own dressing gown, dragging on the floor on that first fateful night in my study. When his twisted hands reached out as if to throttle someone, it reminded me of how my own hands had become gnarled and hairy and dusky of hue. When his eyes lost their human lustre and became those of a pitiless beast, I saw my own, staring back at me in horror in the mirror above my desk. It was as if the man had somehow witnessed the very metamorphosis I had undergone and subsequently utilized in my art—and which he now employed in his. Like me, he shared in the revelation that beneath a man's respectable exterior lurked a darker and more sinister side, aching to break its chains.

Perhaps that was why I felt the shudder that descended my spine, and could barely suppress the cough that erupted. Fanny, concerned, took my hand, and whispered, 'Louis, is it too much? Should we go?'

Shaking my head, I said I simply needed a breath of air, and stepped out of the box, and into the empty hall. There, I took the handkerchief from the breast pocket of my tailcoat and pressed it to my lips—it came away tinged with russet—and leaned with one hand against the wall. The craving for the magical elixir, for so I think of it now, was as powerful as it had ever been, though at the same time I dreaded its after-effects. This tug of war has become alarmingly familiar.

'Was the box too warm?'

I turned my head to see Stoker coming down the corridor.

'No, no, it was fine,' I said, collecting myself.

'What's it like, then, to see your creation transformed, shifted from a page to a proscenium?'

'Strange,' I replied, keeping my voice, like Stoker's, low. 'It's as if you were seeing a lady with whom you were once in love, now strolling on the arm of another man.'

Stoker chuckled, then quickly muffled the sound.

'The liberties with my story, I will admit, rankle.' The American playwright had introduced a romance for Dr Jekyll. 'But as someone who has written the occasional play myself, I can understand why they were taken.'

'The ladies do love their romance, and if they are to persuade their husbands to escort them to the theatre, they must have it.'

For several minutes, we engaged in a discussion of the relative merits of the various forms of writing, and I soon gathered that Stoker, despite his long employment at the Lyceum, had his sights set more upon the printed page. We shared an interest in the macabre—he had read my short stories 'Thrawn Janet' and 'The Body Snatcher', and complimented me on them—and confessed to a desire to add something of consequence to that canon one day. 'But are you, may I ask, a true believer in things of an occult nature,' he said, 'or do you merely use them for dramatic effect?'

It was a fair question, and one that I had been asked before. 'I believe only in things I can apprehend with my own imperfect senses,' I answered, 'though their very imperfection suggests I keep an open mind.'

'The answer of a diplomat.'

'Of a writer, with no wish to insult his readers. My aim was simply to write a bogey tale they would not soon forget.'

'Well, if I should ever stumble upon my own great bogey tale, I shall send you an autographed copy of the first edition.'

'Yes, do that,' I said. 'I enjoy reading them even more than writing them.'

Stoker checked his pocket watch, said, 'We should be dropping the curtain soon,' and marched off to continue on his rounds. I slipped back into the box in time to see the play conclude—at least it remained faithful to my ending—and to observe the many curtain calls for its acting troupe. Saved for last was Mansfield, who returned to the stage like a man who had just traversed the Sahara on his hands and knees. He looked as if he could barely remain upright, and acknowledged the applause—the audience leaping to its feet, amid cries of Bravo! and Huzzah!—with a bobbing of his head and the touch of his fingers to his brow in salute.

'If that doesn't send the book sales flying,' Fanny said, 'nothing will!'

'I think I can promise you a rave', Henley said, 'in the next issue of the "National Observer."'

Taking the same back-stairs route out of the theatre that we had taken on the way in, we were soon outside, where the heat of the day had only slightly abated. Cabs and carriages were jockeying for place, the horses snorting and pawing at the pavement, the theatre-goers fanning themselves with their programmes, the ladies lifting the hair from the back of their damp necks. I was searching in vain for the carriage we had hired for the night—they all looked alike in the garish glow of the electric lights—when I saw Stoker yet again, ploughing through the crowd with what turned out to be the prime minister in his wake.

'Excuse me, Mr Stevenson, but Lord Salisbury wished to express his regards.'

Fanny, I thought, might keel over with delight, while Henley, I feared, might bring up some delicate political issue. 'Behave,' I muttered to him.

He grunted his acquiescence, and the introductions were made peaceably all around.

'I'm a bit of a writer myself,' the prime minister mentioned—is there anyone in London who is not?—'and so I can appreciate the artistry of a tale well told. I have read "Treasure Island" to my children three times, and still they haven't tired of it. That peg-legged pirate, Long John Silver, is their favourite.'

Then, perhaps taking sudden notice of Henley's wooden leg, he said, 'And many other characters, too, of course.'

Henley, not one to let an occasion for embarrassment pass, said, 'Still, it's the one-legged ones that make the strongest impression. Why, my friend Louis tells me I was the very model for the man. Didn't you, Louis?'

'And how did you enjoy the play tonight?' Fanny burst in, all but knocking Henley off his crutch.

'Very much, I enjoyed it very much.' But before he could expatiate on that, a thin man in a drab brown suit and derby squirmed to Salisbury's side and whispered something in his ear. Salisbury bent his head, asked the man to repeat it, and all I could detect were the words 'fire' and 'frigates'. Now that it had been mentioned, there was indeed an acrid smell in the air.

'Yes, yes, quite right,' Salisbury said, then making his apologies, hurried back to his coach, with the Union Jack emblazoned on its door, cabriolet lamps shining, and a pair of perfectly matched chestnut mares in harness.

'What was that all about?' Fanny asked.

'Judging from the direction of the wind,' Henley said, 'I'd bet there's a fire over at the Holloway docks. I must be off—a newsman's work is never done.'

On the journey home, the sulphurous smell in the air only grew stronger, making the horse skittish and aggravating my lungs even further. And yet there was something else in the air, too, a sense of impending doom. Was it the residual effect of the play? The spectre of a fire at the docks? Possibly. But I could not attribute it solely to those causes. As we passed away from the white glare of the West End, down the narrower streets, lit only by the intermittent glow of gas lamps, and sometimes by nothing but starlight, I felt the approach of something dire.

The next afternoon, the penny press carried the first tidings of a crime so savage that even the sordid slums of the East End, long accustomed to violence, had seen nothing like it before.

'Brutal Slaying in Whitechapel!' the "Times" proclaimed. 'Atrocity Committed Under Cover of Dark!'

It was an act so heinous, so wanton in its cruelty, it might well have been perpetrated by a genuine Mr Hyde.

TOPANGA CANYON— CALIFORNIA

Present Day

Roy kept his goggles on and his head down, tending to his lab work, but all the while his head was spinning. Sure, sure, he knew he was supposed to be packing up, but he was right in the middle of mixing up a big batch, and there was no way he was going to let all that work amount to nothing while Axel found a new place to set up shop. But now that those two park rangers had found their secret lair, how long would it be before the whole gang got busted? The marijuana laws were changing all the time, but meth? Meth was still a major felony and carried hard time. He'd been to the Chino state penitentiary already—three years for auto theft—and he was not about to wind up there again.

Glancing back over his shoulder, he saw that Axel had stretched out again on the sofa, sleep mask over his eyes and earbuds firmly implanted. Nothing ever seemed to get to the guy. But what the hell? Was Axel just going to let them walk away, knowing what they knew?

Was he planning to count on their instinct for self-preservation and simply trust them to keep their mouths shut?

That was not a plan in Roy's book.

The sun had set, and Axel was still asleep (Roy had seen him swallow a couple of something—maybe Xanax—when he lay down) when he dared to stop working, gather up the stuff he needed—a flashlight, compass, hunting knife, and of course, the shotgun—and creep out of the building. At the top of the stairs, he waited, wondering if he'd hear any noise from within, but apart from Axel's contented snoring, there was nothing.

The sky was clear, and the moon was bright enough to let him see where he was going, most of the time. The ground around the lab was sere and parched by all the waste chemicals Roy and his occasional lab assistants had dumped there, but even when he'd put the building far behind him, the undergrowth was sparse and dry. He swept the flashlight back and forth, looking for footprints, but there wasn't much to see. Maybe a scuff mark here and there, stuff Hiawatha could have picked out, but Roy was going on his gut. When that girl had taken off, she'd headed off toward the Potheads' place, so that was where he headed now.

What he would do once he got there was still unclear to him. Sometimes he wondered if working around so many chemicals and fumes had kind of altered his cognitive functionality. That was a phrase he'd heard a few times from the Chino psych therapist—cognitive functionality. He'd really kind of liked it; it sounded like he had something important going on in his head. And he certainly preferred it to all the talk about irrational anger and impulse control. Once, he'd gotten so mad at hearing about how out of control he was, he'd managed to pick up three plastic chairs in a row and smash them to smithereens on the floor of the mess hall. That had taught them all a lesson; he never heard about his anger issues again—at least not to his face.

The air was cooler now, and he enjoyed being able to swing his arms without the constrictions of the lab gown. It was nice, too, to be free of the sweaty goggles and the gloves. But when he got within sight of the Potheads' shack, he slowed down and tried again to formulate some kind of plan.

Was he just going to bust in and shoot everybody on the spot?

Appealing as it was, it was pretty drastic. That many dead would definitely draw attention, and could in the end get him arrested again.

And besides, Axel would be pissed. He hadn't ordered the hit, and he liked to operate under the radar as much as possible.

A lantern was shining through what you could call the side window of their shack—there just wasn't any glass in it—and as quietly as he could, Roy crept up to it and took a peek inside.

Christ, why didn't that old bag ever cover her jugs? She was leaning over a rickety table, pouring tea into clay cups in front of the rangers and her idiot husband. Ducking down again, he heard snatches of the conversation. Bees. They were talking about bees, for some reason. "The hives are disappearing," that guy Salazar was saying, "and without them, a lot of other plants and animals are going to suffer."

Mr. Pothead said something about Washington and a conspiracy, and Salazar let him run his mouth. The girl tried to get in a word or two edgewise, but Roy had already lost interest. At least they weren't talking about the meth lab, or cops.

But shooting them all seemed like a bad idea.

He had to do something smarter. But what?

When he heard the word *jeep*, it gave him a thought. "It's dark enough now for us to head back to the jeep," Salazar said. "But thanks again for your hospitality."

"Yes," the girl said.

"Wait," Mrs. Pothead said, "I just want to wrap up some of my muffins for you."

Muffins? Man, those had to taste like shit, Roy thought. But if they'd driven the jeep up to this area, he had a damn good idea of where they'd left it.

And with any luck he could beat them there.

Slinking away from the window, he loped off across the field, over the next crest and into the patchy woods and brambles of the canyon. His brain was teeming with cognitive functionality. It was almost like he could even see and hear and smell better, too. His feet were dancing on the ground, feeling a trail, and when he picked up the dull glint of moonlight on metal—the hood of the car—it was all he could do not to let out a war whoop like some Indian.

The jeep was still pointing up and into the canyon, as far in as it could go, which meant Salazar would have to back up and then turn it around before heading home. Roy knew he would have to take that into account. A huge puddle of brake fluid on the ground might be spotted in the headlights, which, by the time Salazar got there, would definitely have to be turned on. Besides, Roy needed the brakes to work a little still, enough to get the jeep under way and to make it as far as the steep slope that ran down the crest toward the main Topanga road. That's when they would really need the brakes, and without them, run the biggest chance of accelerating out of control and hitting something. A tree, a rock, maybe even a truck if the jeep made it far enough to go rocketing onto the asphalt highway. In his dreams, Roy saw the car smashing headlong into something and erupting in a ball of flame that took both of the rangers out of the picture for good, with no questions asked and no evidence left to sift through.

But if his dreams were to come true, he needed to work fast. A practiced car thief from his many years on the streets of Bakersfield, he had popped the hood and taken his hunting knife to the brake lines in a matter of minutes. This, he thought, as he clamped the flashlight between his teeth and sawed away just enough to get the job done, was cognitive functionality at its best.

3 September, 1888

Seemingly overnight, the dining room at Cavendish Square had come to resemble the reading room at the British Museum. Fanny must have subscribed to every newspaper and penny press in London, and those that weren't spilling off the edge of the table were spread out between the cups and the bread basket, leaving barely enough room for the spoons.

'Oh, it's horrible,' she said, as soon as I shambled through the door in my dressing gown, not even fully awake. 'Absolutely unspeakable.'

That, I knew, would not keep her from speaking of it.

'I assume you refer to the fire at the Holloway docks? Two of Her Majesty's frigates, and a ship of the line, to boot.' Unable to sleep after the debut of the play, I had hailed a cab on the street, and in the dead of night gone to observe the mounting conflagration, whose acrid odour hovered over the city still.

'Very funny, Louis. You know perfectly well what I'm referring to.'

Mrs Chandler came in from the kitchen and filled my cup with thick, black coffee, a habit Fanny has inculcated in me; Americans much prefer it to tea. 'Will you be wanting eggs and bacon this morning, or just porridge, sir?'

'Just some buttered toast, I think.'

'Oh, but sir, you need more than that to make a start of the day.' She glanced at Fanny for her true orders, and with a nod, Fanny effectively countermanded me.

'They've determined it for sure now,' Fanny said, holding up the "Times." 'The woman's name is—was—Mary Ann Nichols, though it seems her friends all called her Polly. Poor thing.'

I poured a touch of cream into the coffee and watched it swirl about, then dissipate; doing so always puts me in mind of the dreams my little Brownies so assiduously assemble each night, only to have them subsumed by the demands, both petty and pressing, of the daylight hours.

'The man who first found her body—a carter on his way to work at four in the morning—mistook her for a tarpaulin, thrown up against a fencing, and went to fetch it for his own use. When he saw it was a woman, with her arms flung wide and her dress much dishevelled, he put it down to drink—a drunken prostitute. Not something uncommon on Buck's Row.'

Much of the story was already known, but each day the papers retold everything already established and added such salacious details as they had been able to muster in the interim. No recent story had received quite so much attention as this. Lord knows murder and assault were far from unusual in the East End, but the sheer malevolence and barbarity of this one had shocked everyone, from the officers of the Metropolitan Police at Scotland Yard to the ordinary citizens of the city, whether they lived in squalid Whitechapel or lofty Mayfair.

Putting down the "Times," Fanny riffled through her library, pulling out the "Star," the paper that could be depended upon to dig deeper, and dirtier, than the rest of its competition. 'The killer apparently held her by the throat with one hand—his right—and slashed with his left,' she said, summarizing the account. 'He must have sent her bonnet flying; it was a few yards away. And once he'd severed her jugular, and the woman could no longer fight or cry out, he'd used his knife on her, over and over again.'

Mrs Chandler put a plate of rashers and runny eggs on the table before me, and scurried from the room with her hands all but covering her ears.

'I think you are frightening the servants,' I said.

'There was a long gash down her left side,' Fanny went on, unperturbed, 'and a number of deep lateral incisions across her abdomen. The doctor who did the post-mortem, Dr Ralph Lees Llewellyn, says that all of these mutilations were done after she was dead, and must have taken him at least five or ten minutes to finish.'

'I think you are frightening me.'

'The way they were done', Fanny said, finally lowering the "Star," 'indicates that the murderer had some basic anatomical knowledge.'

'So now we should look sideways at our physicians?'

'We should do that, anyway,' Fanny said, 'starting with that Dr Rüedi.'

'Surely, you don't suspect him of the murder,' I joshed.

'No, not of that.'

'And as for me, I'm still alive, aren't I? Years later?'

'Yes, there's that,' she said, as if it were somehow beside the point. 'I just never liked his manner—very condescending, and particularly towards me.'

How could I tell her that it was Rüedi's elixir that was keeping me alive—much less that it was rendering me, on certain desperate occasions, a stranger even to myself?

Outside, we heard the clip-clopping of a horse's hoofs coming to rest, and when Fanny went to the window, she said, 'Oh my, it's Lloyd.'

'In a carriage, of course. Has he got any money to pay the driver?'

'Now, Louis, don't harangue him about his writing again.'

'There's nothing to harangue him about. Has he written two words?'

The hall door opened, and I could hear Lloyd rustling through the envelopes and bills, many of them his own, that tended to congregate on the foyer table. I left them there in the vain hope that he might notice how much he was spending and consider doing something one day to pay them.

'We're in here,' his mother called, and he slouched around the corner, looking much the worse for wear. 'Morning, Louis,' he said, as he went to kiss his mother's cheek.

'Where have you been all night?' she asked.

'Oh, didn't I tell you? Desmond and I went to his club to play cards, and as it was so late when we quit, I stayed over at his house in Belgravia.'

In no time, Lloyd had cultivated a taste for the finer neighbourhoods and frivolous activities of London. In Randolph Desmond, he had found the perfect tutor.

'What's that under your arm?' she asked, and he said, 'The latest edition of the "Illustrated Police News." I knew you would want it.'

And on that score he was quite right. She snatched it eagerly from his hand.

Mrs Chandler put her head in to ask if he would like anything to eat or drink, but Lloyd shook his head. 'I ate already, at the club.'

From the way he spoke, it might have been his own club he was referring to.

'I'm just going to go up to bed,' he said. 'Wake me for tea.'

Fanny watched him go with the loving, but concerned, look of a mother hen, and I attended to the last of my eggs and bacon. What I did not need this morning was another debate about what to do with Lloyd. I had done all that I could to help him in his literary aims, even going so far as to assist him in plotting and composing various dramatic ideas, but the lures of London life were too enticing, and his fundamental nature was, like his father's, too diffuse and undetermined.

'I do think it's a great help to have such useful pictures,' Fanny said, her face buried in the "Illustrated News." The engraving on the cover, which I could hardly avoid seeing, showed a toothless, middle-aged woman, in a dark bonnet, with a basket slung over one arm.

'Fanny, does it say anything in there about her selling flowers?'

'Why?'

'Does it?'

'Let me see,' she said, scanning the interior pages. 'Yes, here. It says her bonnet, blue crêpe, was a few yards off—they knew that already—and a basket of dead blossoms was strewn on the pavement near the corner. He might have knocked them from her hand before the attack.'

Leaning across the table, I lifted the paper from her hands— 'I'm still reading that, Louis!'—and studied the cover, and then the additional pictures of the victim inside. My heart grew cold.

'Don't you recognize her?' I said.

'What? Polly Nichols? Why would I?'

'At the theatre. As we got out of the carriage. She tried to pin a carnation on my lapel.'

Fanny studied the pictures again, and then said, solemnly, 'Yes, I think you're right.'

I knew I was. And what occurred to me, a moment later, was that I might have been able to alter this woman's fate—that had I simply bought a carnation or two, she might have had enough to pay the fare for a bed that night. Instead of plying the streets as a prostitute, she might have been asleep in some shabby, but safe, doss-house, and awakened the next day in no worse way than she had gone to sleep.

'Oh, isn't that awful,' Fanny said. 'But I don't suppose that information would be of any use at all to the police.'

'No, I don't see how it would be,' I replied, as we had barely noticed her at all, 'though it is surely a grim coincidence.' More than that, even, it was a reminder—one I hardly needed any more—that the workings of fate were as inexplicable as they were implacable.

TOPANGA CANYON— CALIFORNIA

Present Day

Rafe hadn't really wanted to delay their departure from the canyon, but despite her protestations, he could tell that Heidi's ankle wasn't completely healed. By the time he'd caught up to her fleeing from the meth lab, she was favoring one leg, and trying to disguise it. She needed a rest, and maybe, he'd reasoned, it would be better to travel after dark; if Axel and Roy had decided to come after them, they might have given up by now.

Now he was regretting it.

Heidi was still moving slowly, and the canyon was so dark that their flashlights hardly made a dent. More than once, he wondered if he'd be able to track down the jeep at all. The night air was cool and the sky cloudy, but he didn't relish the thought of sleeping out in the canyon. He'd already returned Heidi from a training mission in terrible shape once; he didn't want anything else to go wrong on this one.

Enough already had.

What was he going to do about the meth lab? It was his duty—absolutely—to report it to the proper authorities, but by the time they acted on the news, the evidence would be gone and all activity there ceased. Axel would make sure of that. What's more, Rafe's number would be up, if it wasn't already, with the Spiritz. The Land Management office would have an excuse, too, to cut off his funding and transfer him, for his own safety, to some godforsaken spot where he would never know what had happened to Diego and Frida.

"How much farther is it?" Heidi asked, trying not to sound as weary as he knew she was.

"Not much."

"You know where we're going, right?"

"I'll try to forget you asked me that."

"Sorry."

Not that she didn't have a point. "Maybe we should rest for a minute or two," he said, slinging his backpack to the ground. He'd put this kid through an awful lot, and he felt terrible about it. He'd have offered to give their boss a special commendation of her performance, but he was afraid that, coming from him, it would only backfire.

From the way she slumped down on the spot, he could tell she was at the end of her endurance. They squatted down on the hard ground, and instantly they were enveloped by the darkness and the silence. It was always that way—the moment you stopped hearing your own breathing and the rattle of your gear and the crunching of your boots, it seemed as if all of life was suspended. But then, after a minute or two, the sounds of the canyon came to you, as if on a frequency you had not been tuned to. He heard the distant call of night birds, the light breeze blowing through the chaparral, the chirping of crickets.

"Have you still got those muffins?" Heidi asked.

"You sure?"

"Why?"

"No reason," he said, not wanting to prejudice her. He dug the homemade muffins out of his backpack, handed one to her—it felt like a Nerf ball—and waited. Seconds later, he heard her cough and sputter.

"What is this made of?"

He hoped not pot. "All natural ingredients."

"I guess I like unnatural ingredients."

"You'll get some soon."

She started to say something else, but Rafe's attention was suddenly riveted to a sound somewhere off in the nearby brush. It could have been nothing—just the wind in the dry boughs—but he kept listening.

"Do you think we might have passed the jeep already?"

It came again—a footfall of some kind. Human or animal, he wasn't sure. He remembered the wolf tracks he had seen.

"I think we parked over that way."

A twig snapped, and even Heidi heard that. She stopped talking.

In the dark, Rafe reached out to grab her hand and urge her to her feet. She needed no more encouragement than that. Still holding her hand, he made for some trees and once they were there, picked up their pace.

Ominously, he had the sense that someone, or something, was keeping pace right along with them. He unsnapped his holster.

"Rafe," Heidi whispered, but he just shushed her and kept on.

He trained his flashlight beam close to the ground as they walked, just enough to keep them from tripping over something, but not enough to provide much of a beacon to their whereabouts. When they hit the next summit and he saw, with a huge sigh of relief, the windshield of the jeep, he said softly, "There it is. Come on."

After tossing their backpacks into the rear, he turned the ignition, and while backing up to turn around, surveyed the area for any sign of a predator.

"Were we being followed?"

"Maybe," he admitted.

"Are we now?"

"Make sure your seat belt's fastened."

Much as he would have liked to gun the engine, the terrain was too rough and uneven to do that. He proceeded at no more than five or ten miles per hour, steering between trees and rocks and trying to pick up the trail they'd forged on the way in. The jeep was balky, and the headlights penetrated only so far.

"What are you going to do about those guys and that lab?" she asked.

"Leave that to me," he said, working hard not to lose his focus. "I'll take care of it through the right channels."

"The Land Management office?"

"Just forget you ever saw it," he said, "and don't tell anyone." He glanced over at her. "Promise me that."

"I promise," she said, and he had the sense that she was glad to be relieved of that responsibility.

On the first downhill slope, the jeep was okay, but on the next one the motor kept stuttering and he had to pump the brakes more than once to slow it down.

"Everything okay?" Heidi asked.

"Fine," he said, though he knew they were not. The jeep was a relic when he'd been assigned it, but up until that night it had been pretty reliable. Maybe it had taken more of a hit than he thought when he'd barreled it through that chain on the day Heidi had been bitten by the snake. He'd have to get it checked out once he was back.

But even that was starting to look uncertain. He knew there was at least one more hillside to traverse before getting anywhere near the canyon road. He gripped the wheel with one hand and the gearshift with the other, and used both feet for the pedals. What was wrong with the damn thing, and why did it have to happen now?

It was only as he started to descend the last ridge that he felt the car going out of control. When he hit the brakes, he got nothing, and when he stamped his foot down even harder, the jeep simply screeched.

"What's going on?"

"Just hold on tight," he said, pulling the emergency brake.

The car juddered, as if hit by an electric shock, then continued to gather speed.

There were trees up ahead, and he was barely able to steer the car around them, the branches scraping the hood.

"Rafe!"

What else could he tell her to do? He whipped the wheel to the right, jouncing over a rocky ledge and slamming down on all four tires at once.

If it weren't for the seat belts, they'd have been ejected altogether.

Heidi screamed.

The car kept hurtling down the hillside, as Rafe looked everywhere for some flat ground or a place he might even bring it to rest without crashing. But there was nothing but a downhill slope of dry soil and tumbling rocks and scrubby plants, nothing to slow them down enough, much less provide a safe landing.

Except perhaps for one thing.

But where was it?

In the dark, and at the headlong pace they were traveling, he had only seconds to decide if it was to his left or right, and he could not afford to be wrong.

The wheel flew out of his hands from a hard jounce, the undercarriage of the car bumping over a fallen log, and once he'd grabbed it again, he pulled it hard to the right, then the left, slaloming down the hill in an attempt to cut the speed even by a little, before finally breaking into some clear ground and seeing, at its bottom, his only hope.

Holding the jeep as steady as he could, he shouted "Keep your head down" and—in the dim glow of the headlights, one of which was already smashed—aimed straight for his target. The tires couldn't hold onto anything anymore, and the car skidded down the hillside like a kid on a slide, before soaring off a low rise in the ground and, momentarily airborne, sailing out and over the mirrored black surface of the lake below.

9 September, 1888

Can it be that a week has passed—and the monster has struck again?

I can hardly believe it, nor can much of London. The city is in shock.

As before, the victim is a poor unfortunate, driven, by drink and bad luck, to sell herself on the street. Annie Chapman. Her name has now been conjoined forever with that of Polly Nichols. The penny press and magazines have whipped the public into a frenzy of fear and speculation. Who can the murderer be? While the "Times" and the "Daily Telegraph" have remained fairly judicious in their accounts, the illustrated papers—which have proliferated, like much of the press, ever since the abolition of the newspaper tax—have added grim pictorial elements and a good deal of reporting of a more dubious nature. The "Star" has led the way, dubbing the killer Leather Apron. And on what evidence? A slipper maker, who wore a leather apron as a part of his workwear, has reputedly extorted prostitutes in the vicinity with a sharpened knife. A man whose 'face was of a marked Hebrew type', this phantom has never been named or otherwise identified, and if what I know of human nature is true, it is just another calumny on that foreign and much-maligned race.

'I doubt the man even exists,' Henley has opined. 'They're just out to sell newspapers.'

Still, even his own "National Observer" has been unable to remain immune to the current panic. 'I'll be damned if I'll rely upon the scraps thrown to us by the official Metropolitan Police reports, however,' Henley said, insisting that he would inspect the scene of the latest crime himself. 'Perhaps you'd like to join me, and see what those of us who have to write about the real world must contend with,' he said.

Fanny, upon hearing the suggestion, reacted with dismay. 'Louis has enough horrors heaped upon his plate by his Brownies. He hardly needs more.'

Indeed, I had already seen, in the "Pall Mall Gazette" of all places, a connection made between the savagery in Whitechapel and the terrors—'precisely contemporaneous', as the paper tellingly suggested—enacted nightly upon the Lyceum stage. And Oscar Wilde, never one to miss an opportunity to inject himself into a controversy, has wondered in print 'if this is not yet another instance of Life imitating Art?'

It's a wonder the killer has not been saddled with the sobriquet of Hyde.

On the pretence of lunching with Symonds at his club, I left the house under Woggin's watchful eye, and embarked with Henley on a visit to the East End—an odyssey in itself. As anyone familiar with the city knows, there is the London of Buckingham Palace and Belgrave Square, of leafy green parks with burbling fountains and broad colonnades, of immaculate town houses with well-scrubbed steps and flowered window boxes . . . and then there is the boiling stew of Whitechapel. Even in broad daylight, as our cab made its way towards the murder site, the thoroughfares grew darker and more crooked, the throngs upon the pavements more desperate and despairing, the air itself more foetid and grey. Every stoop was cluttered with children in rags, every kerbside heaped with refuse, every shop window barred, and every pub—of which there were an inordinate number—teeming with idle and ill-tempered men. Our coach had to stop once to allow a fight that had begun inside a tavern to finish in the street. The victor, having clobbered his opponent into submission with what appeared to be a barrel stave, raised his arms in triumph and was carried on the shoulders of his supporters back into the bar.

'Achilles celebrating his triumph over Hector,' Henley said, as the cab resumed its journey. At the corner of Hanbury Street, we disembarked, and Henley, after glancing at the address of a packing case store, said, 'Number twenty-nine must be that way.'

Under any circumstances, we are a pair that draws more than a passing glance—Henley with his thick red beard, and stumping along on his crutch, me looming over him with stooped shoulders and black hair hanging to the collar of my shirt. But today, the street crowded with those who had come to gawk, we drew even more attention than usual. Plainly, we were interlopers, and the local inhabitants were trying to make out what we could be—detectives, social crusaders, sensationalist journalists? We fit no obvious category. A constable stationed outside the door of the boarding house put up a hand to block our entrance and barked, 'Move along! Nothing to see here! Move along!'

'Press!' Henley retorted, brandishing a card that identified him as the editor of the "Observer."

'Haven't you lot seen enough already?'

'This lot hasn't seen it at all,' Henley said, using his crutch as a sort of cudgel to brush past him, 'and I don't plan on coming here again.'

I followed him into the dim, narrow hallway, past a couple of open doors—in one, an old woman was crocheting intently (piecework, no doubt); in another, a sickly young man was sitting on the edge of a cot with his hands dangling between his knees—and then down two steps into a desolate back court fenced on all sides with boards. A man in a brown suit and matching bowler hat was crouching, examining something on the uneven paving stones. He turned, annoyed, at the sound of our entry.

'Who let you in?'

Henley again produced his card and handed it to him. The man read it, then glanced at the both of us, and said, 'I should have recognized you.'

'We've met?' Henley said.

'At that play.'

As the only play I had seen of late was the one based on my own book, I knew he must be referring to "Jekyll and Hyde," and that was when he fell into place for me.

'You were accompanying the prime minister,' I said.

'Inspector Frederick Abberline, Scotland Yard,' he said, though he made no motion to shake hands.

'And what were you inspecting just now?' Henley said.

Abberline, whose pinched face was bracketed by woolly mutton chops, did a poor job of concealing his disdain. 'How exactly may I help you gentlemen?'

'By giving us the facts.'

'Haven't you been reading the morning papers?'

'I never trust what I read in the press,' Henley said. 'I prefer to get it straight from the horse's mouth. And you, my good man, appear to be the horse.'

'What do you want to know?'

'Whatever you can tell me. This is the spot where the murder took place, is it not?'

'You're standing on it.'

We both stepped back, as if we had been standing on a grave. In a way, of course, we were.

'She brought her customer into that hallway—the door is never locked,' Abberline went on, 'and then out here, to conduct their business, as it were.'

An awful spot, I reflected, looking around, to have conducted anything at all, much less to have ended one's life.

'He must have taken her by the throat and pressed her up against this fence,' he said, gesturing at what I could now see were smears of blood, 'and slashed, from left to right, with a blade long enough to have nearly severed her spine.'

Henley had taken a pad and pencil from the pocket of his vest and was scribbling notes. 'Yes—and then?' he said, looking up.

Perhaps flattered by the attention to his words—a phenomenon I have observed myself in those whose views and opinions I have solicited—Abberline cleared his throat and continued. 'The neighbour, on the other side of the fence, was using the outhouse, around quarter past five, when he thought he heard a woman say one word, "no", and a bit later, the sound of something, or someone, falling softly against the fence.'

'Did he see anything?' Henley asked.

'No. It was still dark out, and the fence is just high enough to have concealed what must have happened next.'

'Which was?'

'The murderer had silenced her already, but it was then that he went to work on the dead body. She was discovered here, maybe an hour later, by another of the tenants at number twenty-nine—the young man on the first floor.'

I thought of the wan fellow on the cot.

'She was lying on her back, with her legs bent wide at the knee and her left arm thrown across her breast. She'd been sliced open, and her intestines had been ripped out and thrown back over her shoulders. Her entire abdomen had been eviscerated—he'd made brutal work of that—but he'd left her purse, with a few small things like a comb, a scrap of muslin, and a torn envelope with some pills, arranged rather neatly near her feet. Took her jewellery, though.'

'She wore jewellery?' I could not help but ask.

'If you can call it that. A few small brass rings that her friends swear she always wore.' Abberline shrugged. 'It's possible she pawned them. We're looking into that.'

To be so destitute as to pawn a couple of brass rings—what could she have conceivably received for them, a farthing or two?—was a glimpse into the abyss.

Henley, glancing up at the many windows of the tenement behind us and the buildings that were crammed all around it, said, 'And apart from the neighbour who heard her fall, no one saw or heard a thing? He must have made hasty work of it.'

Abberline sighed and said, 'That's for the doctor to determine.'

'Dr Llewellyn?' I asked, remembering the name Fanny had read to me from the paper, the one who had done the autopsy on Polly Nichols.

'We have our own expert, Dr George Bagster Phillips. At the Whitechapel workhouse mortuary.' He lifted his watch from the pocket of his vest and said, 'In fact, you have made me late for my appointment there.'

'Well, let's not be any later than we must,' Henley said, putting a full stop to his last note and ramming the pad back into his pocket. 'Lead on.'

Abberline was nonplussed.

'Well, you don't think you're getting off this easy, do you?' Henley said.

I could suddenly see how Henley had risen to the top of his profession so quickly, despite the many obstacles life had thrown in his path. He was as brisk and unrelenting as a tornado.

TOPANGA CANYON— CALIFORNIA

Present Day

"You know what that jeep was worth?" Ellen Latham was saying, and though Rafe was tempted to reply *About fifty bucks,* he didn't. "And do you know how strapped we are for funds these days?"

"I do."

"I've pulled the vehicle maintenance records—it was given a complete overhaul just two years ago and deemed perfectly safe."

"A lot can happen in two years, especially if you're driving off-road in the canyons."

"And now it's sitting under what, ten or twelve feet of water?"

"The brakes were gone," Rafe said, in as neutral a voice as he could. More than once since the accident, it had occurred to him that the brakes might not have simply malfunctioned; maybe they'd been tampered with by Roy. But without a vehicular autopsy, as it were, it was all just speculation—and speculation that would open up other questions that he did not want to address at all. "We're lucky to have escaped in one piece," he volunteered.

"Oh yes, and then there's that," Latham said, leaning back in her chair and blowing out a sigh of disgust. "Twice you take out a trainee, Heidi Graff, and twice you bring her back more dead than alive."

"She's okay," Rafe said. "Scared—we both were—but she was safely out of the jeep before it started to sink."

"You make that sound like an achievement, not a near disaster."

In a way, it was—the jeep had seemed to hang in the air longer than expected, before plunging headfirst into the black lake. It bobbed on the surface, water running in on all sides, as Rafe quickly reached over to unfasten Heidi's seat belt. She was in shock, and he had to reach across her, unlock her door, and push it open as far as he could; from that angle, it wasn't easy. Once he saw her crawling out, against the tide of rushing water, he fumbled at his own restraints and only got them loose as the jeep took on so much weight that the hood dipped down like an arrow and the whole car rapidly submerged. Pushing against his own door, he found it was too late to get it open—the pressure of the water was too great—and holding his breath, he'd had to wriggle out the open window, his backpack hastily looped over one shoulder. By the eerie glow of the headlights that were still on, he kicked toward the surface.

They were only fifteen or twenty feet from the bank. Grasping hold of Heidi's arm, he dragged her away from the sinking jeep and the suction of its descent, and toward the land. Wiping the brackish water from his eyes with the sodden sleeve of his shirt, he thought he saw someone waiting along the brush line to assist them. Someone down on all fours, perhaps urging them on, reaching out a helping hand.

He was reminded of that sensation he'd had of being followed, tracked, in their escape from the meth lab.

But if that was Roy, or Axel, waiting on the shore, they'd be better off treading water till dawn.

For a moment, he hesitated, Heidi sputtering and flailing, before the image resolved itself into something else—something even more dreadful and unexpected.

A pair of watchful eyes stared balefully from behind the broken branches and dead leaves. Its head was down and weaving slowly from side to side; its shoulders were swallowed up in the darkness. Letting go of Heidi's arm, he reached down to unbuckle his holster and remove his Smith & Wesson. He raised it, streaming water, above the surface, into full view, and clicked off the safety, but would it work at all after being underwater?

"Get out of here!" he shouted at whatever, or whoever, was lurking behind the shrubs. "That, or I'll shoot!"

There was no reply.

"You hear me?"

Praying the gun would function, he aimed at a pale clump of beech trees, pressed the trigger, and a shot—crisp and sharp and loud—echoed around the canyon.

Something bolted—big and dark and hard to discern—from the brush, and off into the night. If it was the wolf whose tracks he'd seen before, it was even bigger and huskier than he'd imagined.

But at least he'd frightened it off, and Heidi had gotten control of herself enough to strike out for the shore on her own. On all fours she clambered onto the bank and then flattened herself against the dirt, panting. He crawled up beside her, but kept his head up, surveying the surrounding area. There was no sign of movement, and when he turned back toward the lake, all he saw was a froth of bubbles, faintly illuminated by the headlights, miraculously still functioning, from the bottom of the lake.

And then they, too, went out.

"The car you've got now," Latham was saying—a beaten-up old Land Rover, abandoned and then impounded by the Kanan Road firehouse—"you can keep using for the time being." The fireman who'd helped him pry open the strongbox with the journal inside had driven it over that morning.

"It looks like a piece of shit," the firefighter had said, alluding to the faded purple paint and the Lakers decals adorning the car's dented fenders, "but it runs okay."

Rafe had stuck his head in through the open window, and quickly withdrawn it.

"Yeah," the fireman had laughed. "It smells like old bong water, but if you drive with the windows open, you get used to it."

"Unfortunately," Latham was saying, her lacquered nails flipping through another stack of official forms, "you didn't get a field sobriety test done last night, or even before coming in today."

"What, you think I was drunk?"

She shrugged. "Stoned, maybe. I'm pretty sensitive to smells, and you're giving off an odor now."

"If I am, it's because the car I'm driving was previously used as an ashtray."

"If you say so. But a clean test would have helped a lot when the whole report, including the loss of the jeep, is kicked upstairs."

Rafe had thought they were already upstairs, on the top floor of the building with the gleaming skyscrapers of downtown Los Angeles all around them, so she plainly meant it figuratively. The bureaucracy went up and up and up forever, and he was acutely aware that as an environmental science officer he was considered a lowly field hand, and one who had increasingly become a nuisance.

"Take these," she said, handing him a couple of preprinted forms on colored paper, "to the lab annex on your way out."

They were orders for a blood draw. "You're joking."

"Better late than never." Glancing at the wall clock, she said, "They close at five thirty, so hurry."

She put her head down to signal the end of the meeting, and Rafe picked up his backpack from the floor, noticing, with some satisfaction, that it had left grit on the otherwise spotless linoleum. It would probably be as close to the canyons as Latham would ever get.

As for the lab annex, he could barely remember where it was. The only time he'd been there was when he'd first been hired: state employees in every department had to have the routine tests done. He now got in barely under the wire, and while he watched his blood fill the syringes, he couldn't help but reflect on the pages of the journal that he had been reading. Blood ran through the narrative like a mountain stream. Awful experimental procedures in Swiss clinics, murders in the back alleys of London. The whole story so far read like one of Stevenson's novels, but unlike a novel, Rafe could not be sure it would come to any satisfactory conclusion. Nor, it was clear, did the famous author himself. Maybe that—in addition to the writer's obvious sympathy for animals—was why Rafe felt such a close, and growing, connection. Strange as it was, he felt like he and Stevenson would have gotten along great.

10 September, 1888

A terrible night. Coughing, sweats, disturbing dreams. My Brownies brought me nothing but ghastly images from my past—the empty chairs in the Belvédère dining room, toboggans shooting down the mountain with the dead aboard, the sack hurtling through the train window, though in the dream, it contained not the head of the wolf, but that of the dead steward Yannick.

'I told you not to go with Henley,' Fanny said, offering no sympathy when I stepped into our back garden to catch a bit of vagrant sun on my face. The heat spell had finally snapped, and autumnal weather was on its way. 'He only wants to monopolise your time, and you cannot afford it.'

In no mood for debate, I slumped into a lawn chair. The back garden was the one place to which I could repair to commune with a tiny portion of nature, a sanctuary protected from unwelcome intruders, and unstained by ink and paper.

'And it's no wonder you had nightmares. Seeing all of that blood and gore.'

I had told her some, though hardly all, of what I had seen the day before, and though she professed annoyance at my having gone,

I sensed that there was also in her a good bit of envy. Fanny has a strong stomach and is as curious as ten cats.

She was planting some vegetables now, bent over, her hands in the dirt and her skirts tied back to be out of the way. With her black hair and tawny skin, it was not hard to imagine her as a squaw in some Indian village; I know that was how Henley saw her.

'Did you see Lloyd inside?'

'No.'

She shook her head. 'You've got Henley and Lloyd's got Randolph Desmond. Bad influences all 'round.'

'I thought you liked Desmond. He's an aristocrat.'

'He's a dissolute character, and I'm afraid he's teaching Lloyd all the wrong lessons.'

'Lloyd is a quick study in that regard.'

'I won't have you criticizing my boy.'

'He's a young man now, in case you haven't noticed.'

'Stop it, Louis.'

Ah, I had forgotten the unwritten laws of our union. I put it down to my not being fully awake yet.

Straightening, she put her hands to the small of her back and stretched. 'Back in Sacramento, I had the best garden in town. So many tomatoes that we had to make ketchup out of most of them.' Surveying the sky, which was already clouding over again, she said, 'But to grow tomatoes, you need sun, and in London, sunshine is sorely lacking.' She brushed some frizzled black hairs from her brow. 'I'm going in to wake up Lloyd. Do you want anything?'

'Can you send out a pot of coffee?'

'I'll tell her to make it strong.'

At the back of the garden, no bigger than a badminton court, a pair of doves were cooing atop the iron gate. A cool breeze stirred the branches of the elm tree. I closed my eyes and tried to turn my thoughts to the manuscript still on my desk. But stubbornly, they would have their own way. It was the mention of ketchup, I think, trifling as that might seem. It conjured up the red, red scene I had encountered at the morgue.

Not much more than a brick shed, and incongruously located beside a children's playground, the workhouse mortuary was a stage set from Hell. I had barely stepped inside, behind Inspector Abberline and Henley, when I was confronted with bowls of blood and tin trays on which various organs, so violated and dissected that they were unrecognizable, were displayed, and on the long table in the centre of the room, the body of Annie Chapman, split open from the breast to the groin. Hovering over her, his sleeves rolled up to his elbows and his smock stiff with dried blood, stood a white-haired man with a pair of spectacles at the end of his nose. He glanced up at our intrusion and asked, in a perfectly congenial manner, 'And who might our guests be, Frederick?'

Abberline introduced us, and at the mention of my name, the doctor said, 'Yo ho ho and a bottle of rum.'

'You have read "Treasure Island."'

'Among other things you have written. I'd shake hands properly, but as you can see . . .' He gestured at the carnage on the table.

He was as matter-of-fact as a cobbler turning a shoe on the lathe.

'So, what can you tell me?' Abberline asked.

'I can tell you that this poor lass was not long for this world, regardless.'

'What do you mean?'

'Take a look at those lungs,' he said, lifting his chin towards a basin of mottled organs on a side table. 'Riddled with tuberculosis. No doubt spread to the membranes of the brain by now. She hadn't more than a few months at best.'

Henley, a man who had spent more time in amputation wards than anyone but Doctor Phillips, was unfazed, but I confess my stomach was taking several unwanted backflips. How, I wondered, would my own ravaged lungs look in comparison?

'For that matter,' Dr Phillips said, 'she didn't die from the severing of her carotid artery, either.'

'From the stab wounds to the abdomen, then?' Abberline hazarded.

'She was suffocated first,' the doctor said, turning her head towards us. It was a grisly sight—her eyes closed, but her mouth open, and the tongue, black and swollen, protruding from between the teeth. 'He must have choked her to death, or at least to unconsciousness, first. A blessing, of sorts.'

Henley made a note of it, which he firmly underlined in his note pad.

'Then he proceeded, in a rather deliberate and, I must say, efficient manner, not only to cut the intestines from the abdominal wall, but to remove from the pelvis the uterus and its appendages, along with the upper section of the vagina and most of the posterior section of the bladder.'

Abberline surveyed the various containers of blood and flesh and said, 'That's all this, then?'

'Quite the contrary. All of those viscera are missing.'

'What do you mean, missing?'

'He must have taken them with him.'

We all three remained silent, assimilating this additional horror, while Dr Phillips repositioned her head to face upward and said, 'Only a man with some considerable degree of anatomical knowledge could have accomplished all this without doing any damage to the rectum or the cervix uteri or other organs, and under such dangerous and exigent circumstances. Done properly, the task would take a surgeon a good hour, but from the information I've been provided, the killer could not have been about his work for anything more than ten or fifteen minutes.' There was a grudging note of respect in his voice. 'It's not some raving lunatic you are looking for, Inspector. It's a man of cool and deliberate temperament, given to episodes, such as this, when his mania overwhelms him. The ferocity is fuelled by the long-suppressed urge to commit violence, and specifically upon women—that much is plain from the concentration on the generative organs. In short, there is a method to his madness.'

'I won't be shedding any tears for him, Doctor,' Abberline said.

'No, nor should you,' Phillips replied. 'I did not mean to suggest it.'

'But if that's true,' Henley put in, 'what's to stop him?'

'Nothing, I fear. Unless and until he is caught red-handed, his mania will continue to erupt in acts of savagery. Even this murder', he said, 'is a step up, a more wanton act, than the previous one. He will only grow bolder, and bloodier, with each success.'

Henley's pencil was scribbling as fast as it could travel.

'So you think he's going to strike again?' Abberline said.

'I am a physician of the body, not the mind,' Phillips replied, 'but if my many years of practice have taught me one thing, it's that the two are inextricably entwined. Wicked thoughts can lead to wicked deeds, and wicked deeds can, in turn, poison the mind further. The man who has committed these murders is a dog chasing his own tail. He'll never catch it, try as he might, so you must catch him.'

'Easier said than done,' the detective muttered.

'I'm sure that's true,' Dr Phillips said, adjusting the glasses on his nose with a blood-besmirched knuckle. 'I wish you much luck—and speed.' And with that he went back to his sawing and stitching.

I could not gulp the air outside fast enough. Henley was fishing a fresh pencil from the pocket of his shirt, and Inspector Abberline, pensively stroking his mutton chops, looked as if his thoughts were a million miles away. My own were right there, swarming in my head like a hornet's nest. The doctor's words had struck home with me; no one knew better than I did that the maladies of the body affected the thoughts and dreams and very behaviour, or that those dark turns of mind, with which I had long been afflicted, could wreak havoc of their own. The elixir alone—the flasks securely secreted in the cabinet of my study upstairs—could alter the balance of both spirit and skin in the time it took to swallow.

'I see there's no cream for the coffee,' I heard now, though not, as expected, from Mrs Chandler. I opened my eyes to see Lloyd placing the tray upon the wrought-iron table beside my chair. 'Should I have some sent out?'

'Not for me.'

'Mother said you should eat something, too,' he said, taking a seat and starting to fill the two cups. 'The garden's nice, now that it's not so hot. Maybe I should try writing out here.'

TOPANGA CANYON— CALIFORNIA

Present Day

By the time Rafe had finished with the blood draw, he had just enough time and energy to fight his way through the rush-hour traffic to Mar Vista and say good night to Lucy at the group home. Evangelina had given her a new roommate, Amber, a teenage girl who was apparently so traumatized by whatever had happened to her that she barely spoke or looked you in the eye. Rafe did his best, but his uniform seemed to scare her; she probably thought she was about to be shuttled off to yet some other shelter or foster home. He remembered the feeling well, and was quick to compliment her on the Miley Cyrus pictures she'd taped to the wall above her bunk.

"Look what I've put up!" Lucy said, unwilling to concede any more of his attention, and he saw that she had posted a newspaper picture of a coyote loping along the side of a backyard swimming pool filled with inflatable toys. "And look at what it says underneath," she exclaimed, pointing to the caption. Rafe had to lean in to read it: *Coyote goes for a swim in Mar Vista.*

"It was only like two blocks away!" Lucy exclaimed. "Was it one of yours?"

"Nope, not one of mine," Rafe said. But it might just as well have been, and that was the problem. They were everywhere, on the prowl for a quick snack, or a handout from some homeowner who had no idea she was doing more harm than good. Once the animals got accustomed to freebies, they'd be back for more—and if a small dog or cat happened to cross their path, that would do just fine, too.

"You want something to eat?" Evangelina said, as he finished tucking Lucy in and got ready to head out. "You look like you need a decent meal, hombre."

"No, I'm fine," he said. And she replied, "Then why do you have blood on your sleeve?"

He looked and saw that a drop or two of blood had seeped through the hastily applied cotton and bandage.

"Just a routine blood test."

"I've got some turkey burgers in the fridge. You've got to put some meat on those bones."

He declined again, but by the time he was pulling his purple Land Rover out of the driveway, she'd appeared at the driver-side window with a paper plate wrapped in foil. "Cold or hot, they're good. And I mixed in some chopped jalapeno peppers."

On the way back to Topanga, he plucked open the foil with one hand and broke off pieces of the burgers. All they needed was a cold beer. He was hungrier than he realized; as he often did, he'd forgotten to stop and eat anything all day. There was always something more important on his mind. And right now, it was what had happened to the jeep—sabotage or simple decay, he still couldn't be sure—and what he had seen lurking by the lake. Was it the wolf whose tracks he'd seen?

He was just relieved Ellen Latham had asked him no further questions about the drug activity in the canyon, or if he'd come across any evidence of it. As long as he didn't have to utter a direct lie, he was okay with keeping mum. And if Axel could be believed—and this was one instance where he thought, out of the instinct for self-preservation alone, he might be—the lab was going to be dismantled forthwith, and whatever illegal activities the gang pursued next would be done far from the prying eyes of land management or park service employees. Rafe would check the place out himself, and make sure the lab was out of business. If it was closed down, then his work was done; if it wasn't, then he'd have no choice but to call in the big guns. Either way, he would not be bringing Heidi along on any further reconnaissance missions.

He was pretty sure she was going to respect her promise to keep quiet, and let him handle the whole issue. This was hardly the kind of mess that any trainee would want to get tangled up in; she just wanted credit for the necessary field hours and accreditation. And after this latest incident, he strongly doubted, in fact, that he would ever see her again. When they'd made it back to the main road and a highway patrol cruiser had picked them up, she'd jumped into the backseat and slammed the door so fast she nearly caught his fingers.

The cop had looked at him appraisingly and said, "Guess you're going to ride up front with me."

"Yeah, I think that would be best." Even in the rearview mirror, he had not been able to catch her eye. She had stared out the window all the way to the station, and when they were parting ways and he had tried to apologize for everything that had happened, she had uttered not one word. Walking away, she hadn't looked back.

Although it might have been better all around that way, it wasn't how he'd wanted it. In his heart, he'd felt that old, familiar dart of failure.

Driving past La Raza, he saw a few of the Spiritz' motorcycles outside. He wondered if they were debating their future in the canyon, wondering if it wasn't maybe time to set up shop somewhere else, someplace they were a little less conspicuous than they were now. All Rafe wanted, wrung out as he was, was to hit the sack. The Cornucopia, to his surprise, still had its lights on, and Miranda's old Subaru was parked in front, with the hatchback open. He pulled around to the side, parked the Land Rover—the Lakers fan who had owned it had even painted yellow flames around the door handles—and then walked back to the front porch of the store.

Through the screen door, he saw Miranda, in jeans and with her blond hair tied up in a do-rag, dragging the old steamer trunk out from behind the counter. For a second, he just watched, taking it all in, then rapped his knuckles on the door frame.

Miranda jumped. "Oh jeez, I didn't hear you."

"You're working late tonight," he said, stepping inside. It was only then that he noticed the destruction. Several of her paintings had been wrenched from their frames or slashed. The top of a glass cabinet was cracked, and most of the little figurines inside were toppled over or smashed. The room smelled of Pine-Sol, and the floorboards were still damp from the mop standing in the bucket in the corner.

"Don't tell me," he said. "Seth and Alfie." He went to her, intending to just wrap a consoling arm around her shoulder, but she turned into him instead, laying her cheek against his chest and accepting a full embrace. "Are you okay?"

He felt her nod.

"They were mad about the trunk?"

Now she shook her head, still not speaking. The top of the kerchief tying her hair brushed against his jaw. He had a dozen questions for her, but held off asking, letting her simply linger there in the harbor of his arms.

"It wasn't Seth and Alfie," she finally murmured.

"How do you know that?"

"They'd have taken the damn trunk."

"Then who?"

"Laszlo."

Although Rafe had never liked the guy one bit, and made no pretense of it, this still seemed out of character. "Why?"

He felt her shoulders lift in bewilderment. "He hasn't been the same since that thing was opened and he got into all that evil shit inside of it."

"What? Is he possessed?" Rafe said, half joking but half not. He glanced down at the deep green trunk, battered and corroded, squatting like an ogre on the damp floor, and wondered. He remembered dredging it out of the lake—the same lake his jeep was now sitting at the bottom of—and he had to admit, if not out loud, that a whole lot of bad *had* happened since its discovery. It was just as well that Miranda didn't yet know the other things he was learning from reading the journal.

"Did he say why?" Rafe asked.

"He didn't say anything. I didn't actually catch him doing it. But trust me, I know. I left a message on his cell, telling him he doesn't live here anymore."

Rafe felt an unexpected rise in his heart. "Okay," he said, "but what are you going to do now?"

"First, I'm going to get that thing out of the store and drive it to the dump."

"It's closed until eight tomorrow morning."

"Then I'll leave it at the gate."

"Okay, okay," he said, hoping not only to calm her down, but to forestall that plan altogether. Miranda had no idea of the significance these things might have. How could she? He was only beginning to grasp that himself. "Leave it till tomorrow."

"No—I'm doing it tonight. And then I'm going to take a long hot shower. So hot my skin scalds."

She separated herself from him, eyes downcast, and started dragging the trunk toward the door. If worse came to worst, Rafe thought, he'd get up at the crack of dawn and quietly retrieve it. For now, he recognized that Miranda was performing a necessary exorcism. He went to the other end and lifted it. Miranda then picked up her end, too, and backed toward the screen door, butting it open.

"Watch it going down the steps," Rafe said, and when they got close enough to the car, he wheeled his end around and shoved it inside. He was just making sure that it would clear the closing hatchback when he heard the unmistakable sputtering of Laszlo's ancient Vespa coming down the road.

Miranda paled, and Rafe instinctively moved closer. "You shouldn't be here for this," she said. "Seeing you here will only make him madder."

"Let it."

"No, really, he'll think it's about you."

Secretly, Rafe wished that it were.

"Go," she implored.

And in what might prove to be their first quarrel, Rafe slammed the hatchback shut, brushed the dirt off his hands, and said, "No. I'm staying put."

26 September, 1888

The killer has a name.

Not a proper one, but a name nonetheless. Self-bestowed. And one that the public has been quick to adopt.

In a taunting letter addressed to 'The Boss' at the Central News Agency in New Bridge Street, and since reprinted in both print and facsimile, he declares that 'I am down on whores and I shant quit ripping them till I do get buckled. Grand work the last job was. I gave the lady no time to squeal . . . I love my work and want to start again. I saved some of the proper red stuff in a ginger beer bottle over the last job to write with but it went thick like glue and I cant use it. Red ink is fit enough I hope ha ha. The next job I do I shall clip the ladys ears off and send to the police officers just for jolly wouldn't you . . . My knife's so nice and sharp I want to get to work right away if I get a chance. Good Luck.' The letter was signed, 'Yours truly, Jack the Ripper.'

Although the hysteria has affected the entire city, it is most notable, and logically so, in the East End, where the Ripper has struck. The local businessmen—pub owners, many of them—have seen their custom decline, and various vigilante groups have been formed to patrol the streets and, in one case, offer a reward for the arrest of the culprit. Especially subject to scrutiny are any men of a dark complexion (the Jews again), or who seem as if they might not belong there in the first place. It is in that latter net that my friend Symonds has already been snared once.

'I was simply making a visit to a certain den of iniquity off Commercial Road when I was accosted by something called the Mile End Vigilance Committee,' he told me over tea at the Athenaeum. 'It was plain that everything about me, from my manner of speech to the leather portfolio I carried, was cause for suspicion. I was rather roughly manhandled,' he said, before adding with a sly grin, 'not that I objected to that in particular.'

'How did you make your escape?'

'I might not have done,' he said. 'They had a rope and had all but hanged me when a bobby happened by and was able to calm the waters. Even so, I was made to come to the Leman Street police station and explain myself to the captain of the watch.'

'That cannot have been easy.'

'No, it was not,' he said, resting his cup back in its saucer. 'Suffice it to say, I shall limit my vices to the West End until this whole affair blows over.'

But it was showing no signs of doing so. All of London was waiting with bated breath for the next attack, and the press seemed positively hopeful—nothing sold more newspapers than a fresh rumour about the identity or whereabouts of Jack the Ripper. Fanny devoured them all, and even when I retreated to the garden to get away from her nattering on about it, what should I find but Lloyd, with a stack of writing paper on the table before him, and a copy of "Punch" in his hand.

'Look at this, Louis,' he said, showing me a cartoon that depicted a gaunt, spectral figure armed with a knife and haunting the streets of Whitechapel. 'The Nemesis of Neglect', it was entitled, as the magazine correlated the poverty and squalor of the East End with the atrocities now being committed there.

'If you reduce people to savage circumstance,' I said, 'then savagery may indeed erupt.'

'Perhaps,' he replied, 'or else the savagery is inborn.'

'Well, haven't we become the toff. Comes from hanging about with Randolph Desmond, no doubt.'

'Oh, Desmond's all right,' he said, 'but Constance and I sometimes tire of him.'

He said it in the most off-handed manner, though he must have known full well that he was firing a cannonball my way. 'Did I hear you correctly?'

'You mean about Miss Wooldridge? I expect so. We have been keeping company for some time now.'

To say I was flabbergasted would be understating the case. Flashing before my eyes were the moments in Davos when a younger Lloyd had made himself a bit of a nuisance, kissing her inappropriately on the toboggan slope or stealing a piece of her lace (Fanny told me she'd found it in his shirt drawer) from the chambermaid's basket. 'And how does Desmond feel about all this?'

'Doesn't matter; don't care,' he said, nonchalantly turning a page of the magazine. 'He treated her badly.'

'Did he now?' I was still incredulous.

'Why do you think they were at the clinic?'

'I never knew.'

'He'd got her into trouble, shall we say. And given her a dose on top of that.'

The revelations were beginning to come so thick and fast that I couldn't dodge them all. But so much, too, was suddenly falling into place—the bills from the finest restaurants and shops in town. The late nights. The unexplained absences from home.

'Does your mother know?'

'Yes.'

Another blow. 'And she approves?'

'I wouldn't go that far.'

It was fortunate that I was already sitting down. I could not have been more astonished if he had told me he'd actually written a novel and sold it to Longman's.

'Oh, and we went to the play the other night.'

'What play?'

'Yours, of course. I was sorry to have been in Paris on the night of the opening, but we finally got round to it. Mansfield, I must say, makes a great impression in the title role. Or roles,' he said, in jest.

I simply nodded in agreement. I had not yet absorbed all the more pertinent news.

'But let me ask you,' he said, slapping the magazine down onto the table as if signalling the end of idle talk. 'When you start writing one of your novels, do you already know how it will end?'

'Only in the most general sense.'

'You let your famous Brownies lead you, then?'

'Sometimes.'

Shaking his head like a man who has been wrestling long and hard with his craft, he said, 'That sort of thing won't work for me. I've tried it, to no avail.'

An errant breeze blew several pages off the stack of papers on the table.

'I work differently.'

As Lloyd and I bent to retrieve the loose pages—many of them blank, some with just a few words and all of them scratched out—I wondered what method might work for him. This one plainly did not.

TOPANGA CANYON— CALIFORNIA
Present Day

Laszlo wasted no time driving the sputtering Vespa up to the front of the store and scooting off it before it had even come to a full stop. It bumped up against the railing and teetered over. Trip raced outside to bark at all the racket.

"What the fuck?" Laszlo was saying, over and over again, as he approached Miranda. "You leave me a message on my *cell*, telling me we're done? That I've got to move out? *On my cell?* You don't even talk to me face-to-face?" Taking a breath, he said, "And what's he doing here?"

"Rafe was just helping me clean up the store."

"I'll bet he was."

"After you trashed it."

"Who says so?"

Rafe noticed that he didn't exactly deny it.

"Really, Laz? After all the other crazy crap you've been pulling—like showing up in the bedroom in those old clothes from the trunk—and getting drunk—"

"Like you don't drink."

"And stoned out of your gourd—"

"Oh, and you don't smoke weed, either."

"And just basically acting like a piece of shit all the time, you think I don't know you did this?"

"Why would I?"

"Why would you? How about because I refused to put out last night, or because I asked you to actually do some work around the place, or because our relationship has gone straight downhill ever since you found your new motorcycle buds."

"Can he leave?" Laszlo said. "Why are we arguing about our store in front of this loser?"

"First of all, it's not *our* store."

"It's Miranda's," Rafe said.

"I can handle this," Miranda said, placing a hand on Rafe's elbow, as if to forestall anyone coming to blows. "Laz, I just want you to collect your stuff and get out."

"And take it away on what? My bike? I'll need to borrow the Subaru." He glanced into the rear and saw the trunk. "Oh no you don't! You're not selling off my stuff! That trunk, and everything in it, is mine!"

"I'm not selling any of it. It's going to the dump."

"Are you crazy?"

"You can go and get it there and take it wherever you decide you want to live from now on."

"Oh, don't you worry about that, Miranda. I've got friends, plenty of 'em, and I've got a place to go."

"The Spiritz house?"

Rafe knew they maintained some kind of compound, if it could be called that, at the end of one of the dirt roads off the main canyon—he'd seen the hand-lettered sign saying "No Trespassing or You WILL Be Shot, M*F"—and like anyone else with a whit of sense, he'd steered clear.

Miranda took the car keys out of her jeans pocket and opened the driver-side door. "If you're not gone when I get back, I'll call in a domestic abuse charge."

"Bullshit you would."

But Rafe could hear a note of doubt in his voice.

"Three strikes" was all she added, portentously, before closing the door. Rafe started to get in, too—she might need some help unloading the trunk—but Miranda said, "Would you mind watching the store for me until I'm back?" The expression on her face told him that what she was really asking was, *Would you keep Laszlo from torching the place while I'm gone?* He paused—just long enough for a whining Tripod to scramble up into the passenger seat—then closed the door again, and stood there while she pulled out and onto the main road.

"That bitch," Laszlo mumbled.

"What'd you say?"

Laszlo turned toward him, his black mustache curling around the corners of his mouth, his eyes narrowed with hate. "You think you just won something?"

Though it was too soon to tell, Rafe thought that maybe he had.

"You didn't win shit. Take it from me." He stomped up onto the front porch and said, "All you just did was step into a world of pain," before the screen door banged shut behind him. "A world of pain, my friend."

Apart from the mention of *friend*, Rafe didn't doubt him. Laszlo wasn't the kind of guy to let bygones be bygones. He'd gather his belongings—something about that three strikes remark had hit home—and he'd split, but he wouldn't go far. There weren't many other places like Topanga Canyon anywhere in the world, and if you were a grifter down on your luck, it was home.

30 September, 1888

The recently installed electric lights on the marquee of the Lyceum Theatre were sputtering and frizzing in the light rain when I stepped down from the carriage. The last stragglers were leaving the theatre, opening their umbrellas and raising their collars, while an usher folded up a standing placard that announced 'Closing Soon! Get Your Tickets Now!'

Up until that moment, I had been under the impression that the play was a huge success, and would run indefinitely. My royalty of twenty pounds per month, paid by Richard Mansfield himself, had been very welcome, especially in light of the bills piling up on the hall table at home. An establishment called the Aldgate Arms Hotel, I saw, had sent something stamped Third Notice on the outer envelope, and I dared not guess what expense Lloyd had run up there, no doubt entertaining the fair Miss Constance Wooldridge.

The invitation to the theatre tonight had come not by post, but by private messenger, and even then it was marked Confidential. It was from the theatre manager, and it urged me to come backstage after the performance to see him. Going around to the stage door in the alleyway, I ducked in out of the rain, furled my umbrella, and when a passing stagehand asked me my business there, I told him I had come to see Mr Stoker.

'And you are?'

'Robert Louis Stevenson.'

'The bloke who wrote the play?'

'The book. The play is based on it.'

Hoisting a crate onto his shoulder, he said, 'Bram's in the box office, counting the receipts. Go across the stage and turn left. Can't miss it.'

'How <u>were</u> the receipts?' I could not resist asking.

'No shortage of empty seats tonight. That's all I know.'

The house lights were still on, and halfway across, I stopped and looked out at the vast and plush auditorium with its distinctive mezzanine overhanging the orchestra seats. The third-act stage set—Dr Jekyll's laboratory—had not been struck, and there was a puddle of liquid, the magic potion, on the floorboards. Overhead I saw the complex web of ropes and pulleys, lights and wires, and weighted bags common to any theatre; despite my previous forays into playwriting, how all of these are deployed, and kept untangled, remains a mystery to me. Henley always says, 'You supply the inspiration, Louis, and leave the mechanics to me.'

I could hear the sound of coins clinking before I found the actual office—a tiny, cramped cabinet where Stoker was sweeping coins and pound notes into a drawer with one hand while entering sums in a ledger with the other.

'I don't want you to lose count,' I said, hovering in the open doorway.

He held up a finger to bid me wait, finished with the money on the table, then made his final entry and stood to shake my hand.

'So glad that you could come.'

'Your note was too intriguing not to.'

'Please, have a seat,' he said, gesturing at the rickety chair on the other side of his desk. 'Can I offer you a drop of whiskey?'

Considering the chilly rain I had just come in from, I thought it was a capital idea. Producing a bottle from his drawer, Stoker poured us both a generous glass.

'To Jekyll,' he said.

'To Hyde!'

After a few pleasantries, and sips of the fine Irish whiskey, Stoker asked if I had seen the placard outside. I told him I had, and confessed my puzzlement.

'It's not just us,' he said. 'This damn Ripper has no one wanting to go out at night.'

'But surely, a play is just the sort of thing to take their minds off such a terrible subject.'

'Not this one. This one's all bound up with it in the public's mind. The play opens and, bang, Jack strikes! Not only that, Mansfield's performance as Mr Hyde is so effective that he's got half of the audience convinced that he's the Ripper himself. We get letters here every day, warning us to keep a close eye on him and report anything suspicious to the police.'

'But hasn't it occurred to them that, among other things, if Mansfield is up here on the stage every night, he can hardly be in the East End murdering people?'

Stoker took a swallow and nodded. 'The police have looked into that themselves, and a certain detective from Scotland Yard—'

'Is his name Abberline?'

'The very one. He says that there's time enough, and more, for him to finish the show and still have committed the crimes.'

'They can't seriously believe that a mere actor, particularly one as famous as Richard Mansfield, is guilty of such horrific acts.'

'They are casting, it seems, a very wide net.' Looking fixedly at me, he repeated, 'Very wide, Mr Stevenson.'

It was several seconds before I took his meaning. 'Are you suggesting that they suspect me?'

'Richard is convinced that he is being tailed everywhere he goes. I doubted him at first, but I've since confirmed it with my own eyes. I would not be at all surprised to learn that your own movements, too, were being followed.'

'Thank you for warning me,' I said, still bowled over at the news. I was suspected of being Jack the Ripper? And all for having written a horror story? It was too absurd; Fanny would either die laughing or shriek in fury. 'Thank you for having me come here so that you could tell me this.'

'It's only part of the reason I had you come,' he said. 'I also have a favour to ask.'

'Name it.'

'Richard's down in his dressing room. He stays there until midnight every night, then has a coach waiting for him in the alleyway. He is behaving like a hunted animal, which, of course, makes him look even more suspicious. He raves on about the play, about the secret truths it reveals, about his ability to physically transform—'

'Which he conveys very convincingly on stage.'

'Too convincingly, for some. I thought it might help if you could go down and talk to him—don't say that I put you up to it—and perhaps put his mind at ease. He seems to be having some trouble separating fantasy from reality. He's an actor, after all. Tell him it's just a story. Tell him you made it up and there's no truth to it. Tell him there's no such potion.'

He had no idea what he was asking of me. He had no idea that to do so, I would have to be the one telling a lie.

'If Mansfield collapses, the play, of course, closes, and we don't have anything else lined up for months. We need him to keep going, for as long as we can manage to scrounge up an audience.'

'I'll do what I can,' I said, though less out of concern for the Lyceum's finances than for the health and well-being of the suffering creature in the dressing room below. 'How do I find him?'

'Take the staircase behind you, then go to the end of the hall. His name's on the door, but it's sure to be closed. Knock. He'll be hiding.'

Draining my glass—I would need the fortifying—I followed his instructions, and saw not only his name on the door, in gilded letters, but a framed column from the "Times" that, upon closer inspection, trumpeted Mansfield as 'a great actor of our time, and let us not mince words, an actor for the ages'. Actors, in my experience, are never shy about their accomplishments.

Inside, I could hear someone rustling about and even muttering under his breath, but the moment I knocked, the sound stopped. I knocked again, and this time announced myself by name.

There was still no reply.

'I'd stopped by for a drink with Mr Stoker and thought I would take this occasion, long overdue, to meet you.'

'If you've got some opinion about my performance'—opinion said with a poisonous tang—'write a letter to the management.'

'I do have an opinion,' I said, to the closed door. 'I think it's remarkable, and only wish to congratulate you on how perfectly you have captured the very essence of the role.'

After another long pause, a bolt was thrown. 'You're alone?'

I assured him that I was.

Another lock was unlatched, and the door was opened just wide enough to allow me to slither in, then slammed shut again.

I found myself in what looked like a wardrobe closet—clothes and costumes hanging from pegs all over the walls, coats and hats on a teetering rack, a vanity table whose every square inch was covered with pots of cosmetics and brushes. An ornate mirror with a glaring lamp fixed to the wall above it reflected the entire room.

As for Mansfield himself, he was a dishevelled wreck, a dusted wig still stuck askew on his head, a dressing gown stained with rouge and powder, his pale features streaked with makeup that had only partially been removed.

'Excuse my appearance,' he said, fluttering his hand in confusion, 'but it's the devil to get this stuff off.'

'Don't let me impede you.'

He plopped back down in front of the mirror, while I propped myself, as if at a bar stool, on the end of an upright dressing case.

'You've been receiving my royalty checks?' he asked, wiping away some more of the stage paint.

'I have, and thank you.'

He snorted, relieved to know that that was no cause for the visit. 'I had intended to call on you myself,' he said, 'but it is not an easy thing for me to get around London.'

'Have you tried the new underground?' I said.

'It's not that. It's that my fame is so great, I am recognized everywhere I go. Did you know that the photograph we have done for the advertising is the most-produced picture in the land? It's up in every public house, apothecary, and tobacconist's shop in town.'

'I have even seen it in my wife's milliner's shop.'

'There you have it. When I am not being accosted by strangers, who wish to pump my hand or breathe the air of genius, I am under the surveillance of the local constabulary. Did Stoker tell you about that?'

'I don't believe he did.'

'You're a liar—a fine story-teller, Stevenson, but a bad liar.'

'Why would the police follow you?' I said, electing to stick with the lie till the end.

'Any man who can make such sudden and violent changes on stage, who can transform himself from a model of rectitude into a creature of depravity, who can ape the gestures of a monster to such startling effect, is ipso facto considered a possible, even plausible, Jack the Ripper.' He swivelled in his chair to face me and said, 'You're on the list, too.'

I pretended shock, but Mansfield went back to cleansing his face and neck and said, 'Never play poker. Your face is as transparent as a pane of glass.' Tossing the used make-up towel to the floor, he picked up a fresh one from the vanity. 'What you have written, and I have dramatised, has in it something so corrosive, but so true, that it unsettles people. It has unsettled me since the first rehearsal back in Boston.'

'How so?'

'I think I'm onto you, Stevenson,' he said, catching my eye in the mirror. 'This isn't just some story you concocted. There's a truth to it that even all your artifice can't disguise. What really happened to you? What have you discovered about the duality of man, and how precisely did you do it?'

Now we were venturing into those waters that Stoker had implied.

'You have tapped into some vein of ore, and through your story I have tapped into it, too.' He brushed the wig back off his head, revealing a pate barely covered with thinning brown hair. 'There's been many a time that I wish I hadn't. Times when I feared the police were right to trail me now. Times when I awoke in the morning in soiled clothes that I did not remember putting on. Tell me that hasn't happened to you, too.'

Perhaps I was that pane of glass, after all.

Rising from his chair, he disappeared behind a screen, the dressing gown tossed over its rim. 'For a man of words,' he said, 'I find you surprisingly taciturn.' I heard a pair of pants being pulled up and braces snapped. 'Your secret's safe with me, you know.'

'I only wish there were such a secret,' I replied, thinking, inevitably, of this journal I keep and the flasks of the elixir locked in my study. 'Because of my own ill-health, I have had a lifetime to contemplate such questions of the mind and body, of morality and mortality. You'd be amazed at the thoughts that come in the dead of night, or even the light of day, when one is confined to a room, and a sickbed, for months on end.'

'I had my own sickly youth,' he said, looking at me over the top of the screen as he buttoned his shirt. 'But my fantasies were not nearly so morbid. I dreamt of fame and fortune, and to a great extent I have realized those dreams, through industry and a God-given talent.'

'So you have.' He had no shortage of confidence, either.

Bending down apparently to buckle his shoes, his head disappeared as he said, 'We are bound together, you and I, by this business. I feel that I cannot get Mr Hyde out of my skin—he has been awakened and lives inside me now—and I fear that with each day that passes, and each performance I give, his influence grows. Do you think that's possible?' His head came up like a jack-in-the-box, his eyes, still lined with a bit of mascara, wide.

'I think a bit of Mr Hyde lives in everyone, and that's why the story resonates as it does.'

'But is it a kind of corruption, a force that, once unleashed, goes unchecked?'

'That is why we have willpower. To control the impulses and emotions that can only lead to evil.'

'Pshaw! Evil? Is indulgence evil? Is sensuality evil? I don't think you believe that, Stevenson, and I don't think your story says so. I think you hedge your bets. I think it's hypocrisy you're after. You just want an acknowledgement of how things actually stand. You want an admission of guilt from the whole human race.'

At that, I had to laugh—not only at the turn of phrase, but at the accuracy of the charge.

Mansfield, pleased that his bon mot had gone over so well, emerged, pulling on his coat and checking his pocket watch. 'I must go now.'

Opening the door, he looked down the hallway, then waved me to come on. He locked the door behind us, and, throwing up his collar and fastening a top hat onto his head, led the way back up the stairs, across the stage—all the lights extinguished now except for one, the so-called ghost light, standing on a pole centre-stage—and to the stage exit. 'I would drop you off, but it's best we not be seen together,' he said, 'lest they think we are conspiring in some fresh atrocity.' Abruptly, he turned and went out into the narrow alleyway. A cab was waiting there, the coachman holding his whip. As it left, Mansfield stuck his head out the window and said, 'Tell Stoker he doesn't need to send any more emissaries. I'm sane as the arch-bishop of Canterbury.'

TOPANGA CANYON—CALIFORNIA

Present Day

In the rearview mirror, Miranda saw the two men in a Mexican standoff, and she prayed that she'd made the right decision, leaving Rafe behind. But the dump was only a few miles up the main road, and she should be gone no more than a half hour. Trip had curled up on the passenger seat with his tail wrapped around him; he liked traveling in the car.

It was dark out now, and a cool wind was blowing through the canyon. She drove with the windows open, letting the breeze whip her hair back over her shoulders. Houses were sparse along the sides of the road, and though most of them were pretty small and run-down, every now and then there was a pair of gates, or a fancy new fence with an intercom box, to indicate that somebody had laid down a lot of money to build their dream home, secluded somewhere out of sight, up in the overgrown hills.

She drove past a couple of mechanic's shops, a hardware store, a vegan restaurant where everything was served so raw even she could barely get it down, and had to make sure she didn't hit the gas pedal too hard. Anxious as she was to get to the dump, she knew that the cops liked to lurk along the roadside at night, and spring at the last second. She'd already gotten two speeding tickets. She did not want a third.

Three strikes.

She'd thrown that little bomb at Laszlo, knowing it would hit home. He had two convictions already—one on a drug charge, one for grand theft, and God knows what else might be on his record that she wasn't aware of. What was wrong with her? What crazy, screwed-up thing in her head made her get mixed up in the first place with men like Laszlo? Maybe she thought they'd been unfairly treated by life, maybe she thought that her healing touch was all that was needed to fix them, maybe she needed a *project* . . . or maybe she was just as damaged as they were.

Trip tried to stand up and look out the windshield, but with only three legs, it was too hard for him to get his balance.

"Get down," she said. "Nothing to see. Get down."

At the next crossroad, she saw the sign, pockmarked with bullet holes, for the sanitation and recycling facility, and turned off the main road. The car jounced along on the old cracked asphalt for about another quarter mile, and when she looked back at the green trunk, she could see it rocking around as if it were alive. Christ, how she wanted to get rid of that damn thing. It was like driving with an alligator in the backseat.

As she approached the dump, a sign indicated the hours of operation—this wasn't one of them—and warned that no one, under penalty of fine, was to leave anything there unattended. A high iron fence ran all around it, with razor wire on top. Why, she wondered, did they need all that security for a dump? What was there to steal?

She stopped the car as close to the main gate as she could get it, but a chain was drawn across the driveway to impede people from doing what she was doing. She'd have to drag that trunk at least fifteen or twenty yards. Leaving the headlights on, she got out, putting a hand on Tripod to keep him from following her. "Stay."

But the minute she popped the hatchback open, he managed to scramble over the seats and jump out, landing with a splat on the dirt.

"What'd I tell you?" she said.

The trunk was at an odd angle, so she had to tug at it, this way and that, before she could get it to the edge. Damn—maybe she should have let Rafe come along, especially as the place was a hell of a lot eerier than she'd remembered. She'd only been there a few times, and always during the day. Night, it turned out, was a completely different scene.

"Watch out," she said to the dog, as she yanked the trunk over the edge of the hatchback door and it crashed onto the dirt, narrowly missing her toes.

Now what? she thought. She tried pulling it, but it was so bulky she couldn't get a good-enough grip, and it barely budged. Instead, she got behind it and started to push. Her goal had been to leave it right beside the main gate—it was the least, as a good citizen, that she could do—but the more she pushed it, the heavier it seemed to get. It was as if the thing exerted a gravitational pull of its own. Okay, she thought, if she could just get it over the speed bump in the road—again, she had to wonder, were people racing to get into the dump?—and push it to one side, she could abandon it there and no one would be the wiser.

That was when Trip let out a yelp.

She ignored it, but when it came again, and she saw his ears stand up, she said, "What?" And looked around. "What's the problem?" She just hoped it wasn't a night watchman about to catch her in the act.

But she didn't see anything, and figured with another minute or two of struggle, she'd have the trunk over the speed bump and safely out of the way; she just had to be careful not to pull it too far to the side, or it would fall into the ditch that ran along the side of the road. She could make out the rusted remains of a washing machine down there.

Trip barked—"Shh!" she said—and then barked again, this time running straight for the gate. "Stop it!" she hissed. "What are you doing?"

If there *was* a night watchman, he was sure to be awake now.

With one mighty shove, she got the trunk over the bump, and with a couple more, she had it out of the driveway. Good enough, she thought. All she wanted was to get the hell out of there.

Trip, hobbling back and forth across the front fence of the dump, was barking madly. It was astonishing how fast he could go on only three legs.

"Trip! Get back here!"

But he paid no attention at all. He was in a frenzy. Maybe he smelled a skunk; that was all she needed. Getting that stink off him, which she'd had to do more than once already, was a major hassle.

She went back to the car, got the leash out of the open hatchback, then slammed it shut. No need to be quiet now. Trip was making enough noise to wake the dead.

"Come here!" she said sternly, as she approached the gate. "Right now!"

Trip set his feet, head down, and stared through the iron bars, growling.

"Whatever it is, let it alone," she said, bending down to attach the leash to his collar.

But he kept squirming and she couldn't get hold of his collar.

Which was when she saw the other eyes—still and unblinking, a dull yellow in the faint glow of the headlights—staring right back. And heard the low, menacing growl.

"Jesus Christ," she said, backing away. "Trip, get out of there!"

The dog didn't budge, but the other animal did. She saw a blur of black and gray tear off to her left. Was it a junkyard dog? If it was, it wasn't like any dog she'd ever seen.

Trip was scrabbling frantically at the dirt below the gate, as if he could burrow under the fence. Her dog was crazy—she'd always known that—but they had to get out of there, now. If that wasn't a dog on the other side, it was something even worse—a coyote, or a pack of them.

Oh, how she wished she'd invited Rafe along on this misguided mission. He'd know just what to do.

She made a grab for Trip, snagging her fingers under his collar and lifting him up off the ground. He bucked around in her arms, trying to get loose, but she held him tight and ran back to the car. Throwing open the driver-side door, she tossed him in so hard he slid all the way across the opposite seat and down onto the floor under the dashboard.

"And stay there!" she ordered, leaping in and turning the ignition.

She wanted to gun it, but there wasn't enough room to turn around, so she had to back up. With one arm slung over the back of the seat, she drove the Subaru away from the gates, looking for a spot that might be wide enough to allow her to do a three-point turn, but there wasn't any. That damn ditch seemed to run the length of the driveway.

Trip had managed, despite his orders, to clamber back up onto the seat, and it was his barking that alerted her again. She slowed down and turned her head just in time to see something dark and powerful charging toward them. Trip had his head out the window now, yowling wildly at the creature that seemed to be aiming for that side of the car. She blasted her horn with the flat of her hand, and slapped on her brights. In the bluish glare, she saw what was either the biggest coyote that had ever lived . . . or a slavering wolf.

She hit the gas harder, squeezing the wheel with one hand, but the animal was closing in on them fast. If only she dared to go faster. She hit the button to raise the window, but like so much else in the car, it had stopped working right years ago. She had to toggle it back and forth several times before she heard the hum of the glass going up. Trip was nearly decapitated, but pulled his head back just as she felt a bump against the window and saw a furious flash of white teeth and black fur. The animal had taken a last leap at its prey, then tumbled off to the side.

She kept the car swerving backward, terrified that she would run off the road and into the ditch, and only breathed a sigh of relief when she'd bypassed all the recycling site signs and could safely turn the car around and hit the main road back. Her hands were shaking, and she realized that she probably hadn't taken a full breath in minutes.

Trip settled down again, almost as if nothing had just happened. Dogs were amazing that way.

She let out a sigh, then inhaled a deep breath of the cool night air, scented with eucalyptus and sage, attempting to calm herself. She tried to focus on her respiration, the way her yoga teachers had always taught. Inhale . . . hold it . . . exhale slowly. But what the hell had just happened? What on earth had she just seen? Wolves didn't live in the canyon. She might have doubted her senses if it weren't for the spittle still clinging to the other window, or the scratches on the glass.

The one thing she did know was that she was, finally, rid of that trunk. Even up to the last minute, it had brought her nothing but bad luck.

30 September, 1888

As I unfurled my umbrella in the alleyway, I thought that I should really have insisted on sharing Mansfield's coach. It was late, and it wouldn't be easy to get another, especially in this weather. Already I could feel the damp seeping into my lungs.

But standing about would only prolong the ordeal, so I set out for home, hoping to hail a cab somewhere along the way. I squashed my hat down firmly, pulled my head like a turtle into my upturned collar, and with some reluctance, left the shelter of the Lyceum and the electric lights of the theatre district. Now the old gas lamps, unevenly spaced and casting their warmer but more uneven glow, were all that I had to light my way. I had written a plea on their behalf—Desmond, I remembered, had commented on it when we first met in Davos—and I went now, swimming from one pool of light to the next, down the street, or around the corner. In doorways, an occasional body huddled or snored, on the avenues, a wagon, drawn by a haggard horse, trundled along like a tumbril carrying its doomed cargo to the guillotine in France.

A cough rose up in my chest like a hot bubble, and I stopped to press my handkerchief to my mouth. Before I could remove it, another cough racked me, and I had to lean in against a shop door to let it pass. I knew the symptoms well enough by now, and knew that I must find a carriage, get out of the rain and home again, soon.

Keeping close to the darkened buildings to get what protection I could, I walked along the Strand, a busier thoroughfare where my chances of finding a conveyance would be better, and towards Hyde Park. But to get there meant threading a labyrinth of smaller streets—London is a maze, even to its natives—and as I walked along these, my footsteps echoing on the wet pavement, I became aware of something—a sense that I was not alone—and I stopped, tilted my umbrella so as to look behind me, and waited for the other person to present himself.

But no one was there.

Putting it down to fancy, I huddled under the umbrella and went on, though the discomfort in my chest was growing worse by the minute. I began to amend my plan. Henley's home was on the way to my own, and if I had no luck finding a cab, then it might be wise to make the short detour and spend the rest of the night there. Arriving at someone's door at such an hour would be incontestably rude, but with Henley it would not present a problem. The man has as much trouble sleeping as I do—the pain from his phantom limb a companion to my own weakened lungs—and he often burns the midnight oil till dawn.

The high, light trot of a carriage horse came to me, though it was not clear from what direction. I paused long enough to make a determination, and hurried down to the corner, where indeed I saw it coming along at a brisk pace. I waved my umbrella and shouted to the driver as it whirled by, but in its back window I spied a woman squealing with pleasure and batting at someone with a fan.

The sudden exertion had taken its toll, however—my heart beating fast and my chest aching. The rain was coming down harder than ever, and across the square, I spotted a costermonger's arcade with empty fruit and vegetable stalls. It would have to do for my present purposes.

Stepping inside only so far as to ensure my privacy, I fumbled in the breast pocket of my coat and withdrew the tiny vial of the elixir that I carried with me always, in preparation for just such an emergency as this. I had never had to use it before under such circumstances, and hesitated even now, but the alternative was to double over in a paroxysm of pain. The coughing began again, and if I were to haemorrhage here, my obituary would note that the famous author of "Jekyll and Hyde" had died alone, under mysterious circumstances, beneath a vacant cabbage stand. I pulled the stopper with shaking fingers and put it to my lips; the taste was vile, but welcome, burning my throat as it went down. It quelled the cough, and soon I was taking the first unlaboured breaths I had enjoyed for some time. I took another sip, emptying the vial. The flask at home was nearly empty, too, and I had wondered, before filling this vial, if it was not somehow evaporating. I would need another shipment from Dr Rüedi soon.

'You wouldn't have a drop of that to spare, now, would you?' I heard from the shadows at the back of the stall, and I whipped around to see what I had at first mistaken for a bundle of rags rising up and teetering towards me. Her hands were extended, shiny but worthless rings on every finger, her hair a rat's nest. 'Not that I wouldn't make it worth your while.'

I backed away, stumbling, only then aware that my coat seemed to be hanging lower on my frame, my trousers looser.

Coming closer, but so unsteadily I feared she might tumble straight into me, she said, 'What would the gentleman say to a four-penny trembler? Just the thing on a rainy night like this.'

I put out a hand to hold her at bay, and even in the gloom I could see that my skin had acquired a more dusky hue. The nails were longer and sharper, the fingers crooked.

'The best you ever had, I can promise you that.'

I had to shove her back, but undiscouraged, she staggered forward again. 'Now, don't be like that. You're dressed like a gent, so act like one.'

I did not feel like a gent. In my breast, I felt a surging anger. I did not want her, and I did not wish to be pawed.

'Give a girl a try.'

And a laugh burst from my lips—a cruel one. A girl? This hag?

'What you laughing at?' she said, suddenly angered herself. 'You think you're too good for the likes of me?'

She came at me again, snatching at the vial, and I swatted her aside, hard, with the back of my hand. She rocked onto her heels, banging up against a stall. Pressing a hand to her wounded mouth, she said, 'For all them fine clothes, you're a right bastard, ain't you?'

'That I am,' I said, my voice—raspy and low—startling even me. 'Don't try me.'

At that moment I saw a grim realization dawn in her eyes, the anger giving way to terror. It was as if I could read the thought—Jack the Ripper—travelling through her mind. Frantically, she looked around for an avenue of escape, and God help me, a smile came to my lips. This was a kind of power—the power to instil abject fear—I had never experienced before, and I was surprised at how subtly and swiftly it had invaded my very sinews.

'Get out of my way!' she screamed, and I said, 'Now, what about that trembler?'

Letting out a shriek that reverberated around the brick walls of the arcade, she ran straight at me, arms out and shoving me, with a strength born of utter panic, out of her path. I fell back a few steps, and she was out into the rainy street, still screaming and running with her skirts held high for all she was worth. The sight, I'll admit, filled me with an uncommon mirth.

Mirth cut short by the figure of a man, in a loden coat, stepping into the shelter. A policeman? I was really in no condition to entertain such a person, but before I could even begin to make my case, he said, 'Herr Stevenson?'

Herr? This was no member of the constabulary. 'Who wants to know?'

That was when I saw, partly hidden by the sleeve of the thick green coat, the dull gleam of the knife.

TOPANGA CANYON— CALIFORNIA

Present Day

Rafe sat in a rocking chair on the porch, like a marshal in some old western guarding the jailhouse from a lynch mob, while Laszlo barged around in the apartment above the store, gathering his stuff. Every few seconds Rafe heard him let out a curse, or kick something across a room, and at one point, a beer bottle came flying out the front window and landed, with the tinkle of breaking glass and an explosion of foam, on the gravel.

Best to just let him work off steam, Rafe thought. Once Laszlo was gone, he would advise Miranda to change the locks and even put in a decent security system. She'd resist—she liked to think she lived in some enchanted valley—but Rafe knew better. It wasn't just fences, but bars in the windows, that made for better neighbors.

The screen door finally was kicked open, and Laszlo waddled out with a pair of bulging leather saddlebags slung around his neck like a poncho, and a black Hefty bag crammed with clothes and whatnot stuffed in his arms. How he was going to drive his little scooter with all that baggage eluded Rafe, but then, that wasn't his problem. If he drove off a cliff, Rafe would shed no tears.

"Tell that bitch she can keep anything I've left," Laszlo said.

"I'm sure she'll be thrilled to hear it."

"Oh, and just in case you think you're going to be the one fucking her from now on," he said as he righted his Vespa and climbed aboard, positioning the garbage bag on his lap and reaching around it to grab the handlebars, "she's a lousy lay."

Then he kicked the bike into gear, made a slow and wobbly circle toward the road, and took off. Rafe waited until his taillight and the rattle of his engine had been completely swallowed up by the night before allowing himself to believe it was true. Laszlo was gone.

Once Miranda got back safe and sound, all would be right with the world. He checked his cell phone for the time—she'd been gone almost a half hour—and unless she'd run into some problem, she should be back pretty soon. He went into the store, found a broom and dustpan, and came back out to sweep up the broken shards of glass. He didn't go upstairs to check on whatever damage Laszlo might have done—it would have felt like intruding on her privacy—but headed back to his trailer instead.

He'd seen enough drama for one day.

He took a quick shower—the water hookup in the yard supplied only so much at one time—then flopped onto his bunk in a pair of running shorts and a T-shirt. In his hands, he held the journal, but with a kind of reverence now that he had not initially felt. He hadn't known at first whose initials they were—RLS—nor had he known who Louis or Fanny were. But then he'd read and deciphered more of the text, put it all together, and discovered that the author of the book was none other than Robert Louis Stevenson. The man whose books, like *Treasure Island* and *Kidnapped* and *The Master of Ballantrae*, he'd devoured as a boy. That he should now be holding in his hands a journal that Stevenson himself had written was beyond miraculous to him.

As was its origin. How in God's name could a private journal written by a Scotsman who lived in England well over a century ago wind up in a trunk at the bottom of a lake in Topanga Canyon?

Reading the book was slow going—the ink had faded almost to the point of disappearing here and there, and he had to turn the pages with great care or they would shred and fall away from the binding. Stevenson's handwriting was very peculiar, too—angular and slanted, with a lot of what looked like hasty pen marks, swipes, and blottings. Rafe had read all the entries from the Belvédère clinic in Switzerland, and he had been especially moved by the author's attempts to protect the wolf he called Lord Grey from the cruelties of Yannick. On that score, he felt a real allegiance with Stevenson.

So it had been a hard call to watch Miranda driving off to the dump with what might have been his clothes, without saying anything to stop her. But how *could* he, without giving away what he knew from the journal? The book didn't belong to him, and he knew that; it belonged, ultimately, to the Land Management Office of the state of California. One day he'd have to give it up. But that day hadn't come yet; for now, he felt like he was in possession of something truly rare and special, something that in some weird, cosmic way (and Miranda would certainly approve of that cosmic argument) had come to him for a reason. The stories about the elixir made from wolf blood only confirmed it. He felt his own kinship with the coyotes—with any animal, for that matter, that had to struggle for its survival in a hostile world. He wouldn't keep the book forever; one day, when he had finished reading it, when he had learned all that there was to learn from it—and he had already learned a great deal about such varied things as Swiss clinics and nineteenth-century manners—he would let it go. There might or might not be some historical value in the musty old clothes that gave Miranda the creeps, but the journal, that was different.

He heard the crunch of tires on the gravel out in front of the store, and a few seconds later, the barking of Tripod and a car door slamming shut. Miranda was home, but he could only imagine what it would be like for her to go upstairs in a house where Laszlo—suddenly and effectively—no longer lived. Would she be relieved? How could she not? But would she also be happy . . . or simply so drained by the whole dreadful experience that she felt nothing? He wanted to go to her. He wanted to get up off the damn bunk and go see, but something was holding him back. Was it tact? Or cowardice? He felt like he should leave her alone—let her be. She needed to dispel a ghost, he thought, before a new suitor came knocking on her door.

He closed the journal, but went to sleep with the light still on in his trailer. He wanted her to be able to see it if she looked out the window . . . and if she needed to come to him of her own accord. The distance between her back steps and the door to his trailer was only a couple of dozen yards, but who would cross it first, he wondered, and when?

30 September, 1888

The knife was all I could focus on. It was long, a butcher's knife, and the man let it descend from the cuff of his coat only gradually.

Whatever terrible deed he was contemplating, it was not something he wanted to finish quickly.

I backed up farther into the shadows of the arcade, trying to put some distance, and market stalls, between us. Was this, then, Jack himself? And how did he know my name? I glanced around for anything that might be used as a weapon, but came up with nothing but my ivory-handled umbrella. A poor substitute for a rapier.

The man approached slowly, keeping his arms out to block me from trying to run around him and out into the street. It was so dark that I could barely discern his features—he had a heavy, squarish face, and blond hair sticking out from under a sodden deerstalker hat. He smelled of wet wool and leather.

When I made a feint to my left, he pivoted in that direction, and when I feinted right he did the same. He kept his head down, like a bull, and his eyes—cold and grey—fixed on me. I ducked behind a stall, rank from spoiled vegetables. To stay on course, he shoved a cart out of his way with one sweep of a meaty hand. In the other, his fingers kept twitching on the handle of the knife, as if the knife itself could not wait to begin its awful work. The corpse of Annie Chapman, lying on the mortuary table, came back to me in one sudden flash.

What I did not feel, and this was what astonished me even then, even in what should have been an utterly terrifying moment, was fear. I felt instead a burst of exhilaration, coupled with a sensation of freedom and power. I was not the scribbler Robert Louis Stevenson—I was the wolf Lord Grey. My blood was up, my back was up, and I all but dared the assassin to attack me.

Snorting like a bull, too, he tried to push the stall over, but all it did was keel to one side, scraps of mouldering lettuce and cucumbers sliding onto the stone floor. I made a dash for it, and he lunged, his boots slipping on the wet mess, but his blade swept through the air and caught the tail of my coat, enough to unbalance me. I stumbled towards the entrance to the arcade, where the light from the gas lamp cast a feeble glow, but to my surprise, the man scrambled to his feet and, faster than I thought he'd have been able, swung the knife again. I parried the thrust with my umbrella, which went clattering from my hand, and then he was on me, like a great clumsy bear, straddling me, trying to pin my shoulder back to the floor with one hand, while shoving my jaw up with the palm of the one holding the knife. One swipe of that blade would do the trick.

And then, as I clawed at him with my own hands and struggled to budge his ponderous weight, he paused. Studied me in the lamplight, his thick brow furrowing with confusion, his eyes uncomprehending, as if it had suddenly dawned on him that he might have mistaken his prey.

The pause was all I needed. I grabbed at the knife, the blade slicing the side of my hand, but my blood making it slick. He squeezed it harder to maintain his grip, and it twisted in his hand. Before he could gain control, a whistle blew—a policeman's whistle—and then a voice shouted, 'You there! Drop your weapon!'

'That's him! That's the one who hit me!' the old prostitute cried out.

'Police! You are under arrest!'

The beam from a bull's-eye lantern was aimed straight at us, and the man rolled to one side, lumbered up, and then charged at the constable. His lantern went flying into the air, and he went over like a bowling pin as the culprit took off down the street.

The whistle shrieked again, and the officer got up, dripping wet from the puddle he'd landed in. 'You stay right where you are!' he ordered me, before charging after the knife wielder. Several windows went up in a tenement across the way, and a curious head or two poked out.

'That's the wrong 'un!' the prostitute hollered. 'The wrong 'un!' But the copper was already in hot pursuit of Jack the Ripper and had no time for the likes of me. Suddenly, left alone at the arcade with the man who had frightened her in the first place, she kicked off her shoes and ran, barefoot and screaming like a banshee, into a side street.

Straightening my clothes, which hung on my stooped frame like loose garments on a rack, I brushed my hair back and bound my handkerchief around my wounded hand like a tourniquet. Then I sauntered out of the shelter of the arcade. The rain had stopped.

'Hey there, what you done to her?' a man called out from an upper-storey window.

I looked up at him, from beneath a gas lamp, the light falling full on my face. What exactly he saw there, I cannot say, but can well imagine.

His expression changed from indignation to confusion and then horror, a progression akin to that I had seen on the face of my would-be killer only moments before. His head went back in, the window slammed shut, and the curtains yanked closed.

In my present state, I felt it unwise, and no longer necessary, to drop in on Henley. Would he even have recognized, and admitted, me? It was an open question. Instead, I made my way, by a long and circuitous path, to the back gate of my garden—which I found locked—and scrambled over the wall like one of the captive monkeys I had befriended on my voyage to America. I found it surprisingly easy to do so.

TOPANGA CANYON— CALIFORNIA

Present Day

Balancing the Hefty bag on his lap while hanging on to the handlebars of the motorcycle was a feat Laszlo should not have even attempted. But he did things when he was pissed, and drunk, that he shouldn't have done, like trashing Miranda's shop. Now look what it had gotten him. Evicted. He'd had a pretty sweet deal there—and she was anything but a lousy lay—and now, here he was, driving all his worldly shit to the Spiritz' place—locally known as the Compound—to crash for the night. Longer than that, if Axel would let him.

But why wouldn't he? Laszlo thought. He'd done some fairly decent work for the gang, peddling meth to the occasional canyon day-tripper, and now he could do more. He'd have to sell himself when he got there—convince them that he could carry his own weight.

The Compound was up the road a few miles, around twisting turns that were poorly marked and unlighted, and more than once he almost tipped over on the bike. When his one headlight finally picked up the No Trespassing sign, he turned up the drive, bumped over the little wooden bridge that crossed what should have been a stream but was now just an empty rut in the ground, and parked outside. There was actually a hitching post, left over from the days when the Compound was owned by a movie studio and used to shoot cheapie westerns, along with several outbuildings that had once housed horses and crew. Surely the gang could make room there for one more.

The main house was a run-down adobe, but the lights were all on inside, and through the open windows, he could even hear Axel arguing with somebody.

"What is it about the words *shut down* that you don't understand?" Axel was saying.

"They're scared shitless. They're not gonna tell anybody."

"Forget it."

"It's a good lab. You know how hard it is to set up a good lab?"

"I know what it costs, that's for damn sure."

Laszlo left his bags outside the door before going in. The minute he did, all conversation stopped. Axel was sitting by the fireplace, which was filled with a plasma-screen TV. Roy—the guy who cooked the meth, so far as he knew—was sprawled out on a broken-down Barcalounger with a beer in one hand and a joint in the other, while Seth and Alfie occupied an equally dilapidated sofa. It was good that those two idiots were there; right now it felt to Laszlo like he had allies.

"Excuse me," Axel said, "but did you call for an appointment?"

Laszlo pretended to laugh, but Axel always gave him the creeps, truth be told. The guy was so sarcastic all the time.

At the far end of the room, two other guys—in Spiritz jackets with cutoff sleeves to show off their 'roided-out arms—were at the pool table, leaning on their cues and waiting to see what was going to happen next.

"I ditched my old lady," Laszlo said, and Axel looked around the room at the others as if he didn't understand what had just been said. "She's just not worth all the shit she laid down."

"Your what?"

Laszlo was confused.

"Your *old lady*?" Axel said. "What are you, a hippie?"

Laszlo laughed obligingly, and so did the others.

"So, in other words," Axel said, "she just kicked your limp dick out of bed."

The guys at the pool table grinned and clicked their cues together.

Roy looked irritated; his pitch had been interrupted, and he blamed Laszlo.

"Don't tell me," Axel said, "you want to *crash*—isn't that what you hippies like to say?—here, at my place?"

"If it's okay."

"Let's take a vote," he said, looking around the room, but they all waited, wondering which way he wanted them to vote. "A show of hands. Who's in favor?"

Laszlo looked at Seth and Alfie. Hadn't he helped them out before? Seth warily raised a hand to vote yes.

Then Alfie went along, too.

"Roy?" Axel asked.

"As long as he sleeps in the barn, why would I give a shit?" He jabbed a hand into the air. "Okay? Can we get back to business now?"

Laszlo knew enough not to push it.

"Okay, that's a quorum. You can stay. For now. Just don't piss me off."

Seth and Alfie looked vaguely pleased.

"All I need now is some more blister packs and ammonia," Roy said, trying to pick up where he'd left off, but he still hadn't recaptured Axel's attention.

"Why don't you boys show him where to bunk?" Axel said, and Seth and Alfie levered themselves up off the sagging sofa and made for the door.

Outside, Laszlo picked up his stuff and followed them around back, where he saw their truck parked at what had plainly been a stable at one time. Roy hadn't been kidding.

"This is where you guys live?" Laszlo asked, realizing only then that he had never known, or cared.

"Sometimes," Seth said.

"It's a pretty sweet deal," Alfie added, "for as long as it lasts."

An owl hooted from the gable when they opened the big wooden doors, and Alfie pulled down on a string to turn on the light.

A bare bulb hung from the rafters, and in its harsh glare Laszlo saw several ancient bunk beds—Christ, the old movie actors must have slept in these seventy years ago—and odd and ends of other furniture, including another big TV squatting on a minifridge. The wires trailed across the dirt floor.

"If the bunk's got a sheet on it," Seth said, "somebody's probably using it. If it doesn't, it's yours."

Laszlo dropped his Hefty bag between his feet. What the fuck. He knew the Compound might not be cushy, but this? At Miranda's, there were always fresh sheets on the bed, and they smelled of sunshine after drying on the line.

Now he was getting pissed all over again. How come she was still back in the apartment above the store and he was stuck in this stable? Apart from the beer bottle he'd thrown out the window, there were even a dozen more Coronas still in the fridge.

"That one's free," Alfie said, gesturing to a lower bunk with a rolled-up mattress on it.

Shit. Laszlo unfurled the mattress—it sure as hell didn't smell like sunshine—and plopped down on it. Seth and Alfie were standing around like bellhops waiting for a tip. Seth had the knife he'd taken from the trunk stuck through a belt loop. That was when it occurred to Laszlo that he might be able to stir up some trouble for the lovebirds, and maybe, if he was truly lucky, catch Miranda out in the open, alone and in the dark.

"You know that trunk you found?"

"What about it?" Alfie said.

"We can get it back."

They waited.

"It's at the dump. Right now."

"Dump's closed."

"That's right. It's outside the gate."

"Yeah?" Seth said. "It's probably empty now."

"It's not."

"How do you know?"

"I know. Miranda just drove it over there to get rid of it. Bad juju she thinks."

"What ever happened to that littler box, the one inside it?"

"Let's just say, you guys got screwed by that fucking forest ranger."

"I knew it!" Alfie exploded, smacking his own thigh. "That fucker. What was inside it?"

"Your truck running?"

"Uh-huh," Seth said.

"I'll tell you on the way to the dump."

"That fucker," Alfie muttered on his way out of the barn. "I *knew* it."

Laszlo left his stuff on the dirt floor—it looked cleaner than the striped mattress—and followed them out to the truck. The night was young, and the less of it he had to spend in that bunk, the better.

1 October, 1888

I did not dare to look at myself in the oblong cheval glass. When I had asked Chandler to bring it up to my study, months earlier, Fanny had laughed and said, 'What, you are becoming vain, at your age?'

And Lloyd had openly complained. 'I use that mirror myself.'

'Too much,' his mother said.

On that, we could agree. Lloyd had taken an increasingly time-consuming and expensive interest in his appearance ever since beginning his amour fou with Constance Wooldridge. Once or twice, I had tried to engage Fanny in a discussion of it, but she either brushed it aside—'puppy love, leave it alone'—or cut me off abruptly. 'I know your opinion, Louis, before you even say it, so what's the point of having an argument?'

The glass, tall and brightly polished, stands in the far corner of the room so that my back is to it when I sit at my desk. I don't want to be reminded that it is there . . . or why.

But today I needed it. I had managed to come in from the garden unobserved, but nearly bumped into Sally Chandler in the kitchen, setting out the breakfast dishes. I did not know she rose so early. I had to duck into the pantry, wait until she stepped outside to the coal bin, and then dash up the back stairs, the cuffs of my trousers snagging on my wet shoes, and breathed a sigh of relief only when the door was closed and locked behind me.

Unfortunately, old Woggin had chosen to spend the night in my study, and looked up with cloudy eyes at the figure in ill-fitting clothes, with dusky skin and stunted posture, leaning back against the door frame. He struggled to get to his feet, a low growl in his throat, before I could reassure him, in a soft voice, that it was his master.

'Down, Woggin, down. It's only me.' But even my voice was altered, and Woggin came closer, head down, still wary. 'Smell me, then. Smell me.'

A sniff or two, and the touch of my hand, even with its gnarled fingers, scratching the back of his head, and he relaxed enough to return to his rug.

I hastily removed my wet coat and hat, tossed them on the rack, and opened the locked cabinet in which I kept the elixir concealed behind some books and bottles of liquor. I threw down a generous shot of whiskey, feeling the smoky burn travel all the way down into my hollow chest, before carefully, painfully, unwinding the handkerchief from my hand. The bleeding had stopped, but the wound was deep. His knife must have been very sharp. Soaking a corner of the handkerchief in the whiskey, I daubed at the cut, cleaning it as best I could, before falling back into my desk chair. The mirror above the desk, the one in which I had first seen my hideous reflection, I have had replaced with a small watercolour Symonds gave me, painted by one of his acolytes.

'The boy is no Corot,' he said, 'but he captures clouds nicely.'

A bluish light was filtering into the room; birds were chirping on the boughs of the elm outside the window. Exhaustion was overtaking me. Had it not been for the vial I had brought with me that night, I might well have died beneath that cabbage stand. Of course, had it not been for that vial, I might not now have found myself imprisoned in the skin, and soul, of this alien creature. The elixir is a blessing—the one thing that can stop the galloping consumption in its tracks—and a curse—the one thing that can overtake and transform me physically and spiritually. I could not forget the vigour I had felt in my limbs, or the glee I'd felt at the woman's terror.

Turning, I looked at the cheval glass across the room. A misshapen thing, with drooping arms and jutting jaw, sat in my chair, in soaked trousers and a bloodstained shirt. It was at once the most appalling sight I had ever seen, and the most entrancing. If I chose to raise my arm, this creature's arm went up. If I yawned, it yawned. If I stretched my back, it stretched its own. I was reminded once more of those poor caged apes aboard ship, and the one whose fingers—remarkably like my own—had been extended in mournful friendship through the bars. What separated our natures now?

A church bell tolled an early hour, and before it had stopped, my chin had fallen to my chest in slumber. I dreamt I was a wolf, hunted by men in deerstalker hats, calling me by name. What was it the villainous Jack had said in his letter to the news agency? 'I shan't stop ripping till I do get buckled.' Something like that.

Well, buckled he had not been, and it appeared that he was the hunter now. And I his quarry.

TOPANGA CANYON— CALIFORNIA

Present Day

"You don't think it's too yellow, do you?" Miranda asked, and Rafe, standing on the ladder with the paintbrush in hand, debated how to answer that.

"I mean, when I wake up on a sunny morning, it isn't going to blind me, is it?"

"There's always that possibility," he replied.

She puckered her lips, reassessing the section of wall he had already painted, while Rafe held his fire. He did think the yellow was awfully bright, but he also understood exactly why she'd chosen it in the first place. She was determined to exorcize all trace and memory of Laszlo from the place, to make it seem new and fresh, and so she'd decided to change everything from the drapes to the paint. He had accompanied her to the Topanga Hardware and Locks shop, and from the limited selection of paint colors they offered, she had chosen the brightest one. Sunshine Gold.

And then, with some more of the small bequest she had just inherited from her great-aunt Gladys—"Now I feel bad that I only visited her once in that nursing home in Pasadena," she confessed—she had stopped in at the Canyon Quilt Shoppe and bought an equally colorful bedspread—big squares of yellow and red and orange—with pillow cases and curtains to match. Personally, Rafe thought it would all be enough to give him a headache.

"Should I keep going?" he asked.

"Yes, go on. I like it."

He dipped the brush in the bucket again, and started making long, even strokes on the wall, while Miranda fussed with a box of clothes she had decided to donate to Goodwill. It had only been a week since she broke it off with Laszlo, but already Rafe could see a change in her. On the whole, she seemed lighter, and more buoyant, though he could also see that there were times when, all of a sudden, she went into a tailspin, everything about her—from her eyes to her shoulders—falling. "What is it?" he'd asked the last time it had happened. "Please don't tell me you're missing him."

"No, it's not that," she said. "I just feel like . . . I failed somehow."

"Laszlo was not some kind of school project. You didn't fail at anything."

"I wonder where he went."

"He's fine, trust me."

"You know that?"

Rafe was reluctant to get into it, but hoping to put her mind at ease, he said, "He's living at the Compound now."

"No," she said, incredulously. "He's joined the Spiritz?"

"Not until he gets a decent motorcycle. But I saw him arriving at La Raza with a bunch of them, and leave with them later." He didn't tell her that on the way out, Laszlo had passed Rafe at the bar and whispered, "You getting any yet?"

Downstairs, he could hear his sister calling for Miranda. "There's a customer," she called out, and Miranda dropped a scarf into the box and said, "I'm coming!"

Lucy wasn't getting along with her new roommate any better than she had the previous one, and Evangelina was getting increasingly frustrated. It was clear that Lucy just didn't want to live there anymore; she wanted to live with her older brother, and even though that was not going to work, Rafe had volunteered to keep her at his place for the weekend, and as often as he could otherwise. Miranda was fine with it, and she was the one who suggested that Lucy could mind the store while she and Rafe painted the apartment. "I think she'll like being in charge of something for a change."

"Just don't let her *make* change," Rafe said. "Her math is as bad as mine."

Rafe stepped down from the ladder and moved it to the other side of the window. From here, he commanded an unimpeded view of the scruffy backyard and his even scruffier trailer. Some of Laszlo's old clothes, also on their way to Goodwill, hung on the clothesline, the same one under which he had found the Asprey gold watch. The initials in it weren't Stevenson's, nor did it work anymore, but it was the only thing, besides the journal, that remained from the trunk he'd recovered from the lake.

When he'd gone to retrieve the trunk from the dump, it was already gone. Nothing in Topanga ever went to waste, and he wouldn't be surprised to see someone come into the Cornucopia one day wearing the top hat or the opera cape.

Scraping away at a stubborn spot of the old paint still showing through the primer, he thought about how it wasn't only Miranda who'd changed since Laszlo's sudden exit. He'd changed, too. He hadn't realized how deeply he'd disliked seeing Laszlo's Vespa parked outside the house, or watching the lights go on—and more important, off—in their bedroom at night. He also hadn't realized how often it had kept him from stopping inside the store to see Miranda: there was always the chance that a snarky Laszlo would be lurking there. Now, he looked forward to returning from his solitary work in the canyon and popping into the shop.

Miranda came back into the room, laughing and fanning herself with a bunch of bills. "Check it out!" she said. "I just sold three paintings to a couple of German tourists."

"You're kidding."

"Don't act so surprised," she said with mock indignation.

"I didn't mean it that way."

"Lucy's a good-luck charm."

"I hope you told her that."

"As a matter of fact, smarty-pants, I did."

A lot was going right in his world just now. Miranda was happy, Lucy was happy, and he figured he'd even reached a kind of détente with the troublemakers in the canyon. He'd paid a visit to the scene of the former meth lab, and apart from some dusty beakers and supplies, it looked pretty much abandoned now. The Potheads said they'd seen nobody coming or going. All Rafe wanted was to be able to go about his own business and complete his coyote studies, without any interference from the locals, or, ideally, the Land Management office downtown.

"Miranda!" he heard Lucy calling again. "There's another customer!"

"You see what I'm saying?" Miranda said, heading back downstairs. "By the way, I'm buying dinner tonight, anywhere except La Raza."

Rafe went back to painting. In the yard, he heard Tripod barking, no doubt in futile pursuit of a squirrel or a lizard; you had to give him points for trying. The ladder rocked on its base, and he had to step down for a second to reposition it. The floors in this old building were as uneven and bumpy as the walls. Trip was still at it, and he glanced out the window to see what was up.

That was when he saw Alfie, in his backward baseball cap, snooping around the trailer. He stuck the paintbrush in the can, wiped his hands on a rag, and hurried down the stairs. But before he could even go outside, he heard Miranda in the store, saying, "That is not what he told Rafe. He told him that anything he left here, I could toss."

"Well, what we must have here is a failure to communicate." Seth was standing on one side of the counter, with Miranda on the other, shielding Lucy.

"What do you want?" Rafe said.

"Laszlo's shit."

"He took it with him."

"That's not what he said. He said he left some stuff behind."

Rafe knew what Seth was doing—he was creating a distraction, hoping no one would notice Alfie was out back. "Fine," Rafe said. "What's left is hanging on the clothesline. Let's go get it."

He banged out the screen door to the yard so loudly Alfie spun around.

"You want Laszlo's shit?" Rafe said, striding to the clothesline and ripping down the clothes that Miranda had put out to air before donating them. "That's why you're here, right?" He wadded them up into a big ball and shoved them into Alfie's arms.

Seth had come out behind him, and Miranda and Lucy had followed, too. He wished they hadn't.

"Anything else," Rafe said, "or are you done here?"

Alfie looked at Seth for further instruction.

"We want our own stuff, too," Seth said.

"What stuff is that?"

"The stuff from the trunk."

"Not that again. It wasn't yours, and there was nothing else in it, anyway. You already got the knife," Rafe said, noticing that it was prominently displayed through the belt loop of Seth's baggy jeans.

"No, we mean the stuff from the littler box," Alfie said.

"There was nothing it but some old useless papers."

"Then give us those," Alfie insisted, dumping the clothes on the ground.

"They're gone. Thrown out."

Seth and Alfie exchanged a mutinous look.

"That's not what Laszlo says," Seth said.

Ah, now it all made sense. The bitter and evicted Laszlo was trying to stir up some trouble by planting these ideas in their heads.

"Maybe we should look around in that shitty little trailer you live in just to make sure," Alfie said.

"Maybe you should pick up those clothes and get out of here instead."

It was starting to feel more and more like some schoolyard dispute, charges flying back and forth, only this one, Rafe knew, could turn ugly any time. He thought of the Smith & Wesson locked in the safe inside the trailer and wondered if he would need to get at it.

"Who's the girl?" Alfie said, out of the blue.

"Nobody you need to know."

"I'm his sister," she said proudly. "Lucy."

Alfie smiled, revealing a big gap in his front teeth. "Nice to meet you, Lucy." Alfie looked at Rafe. "She living in the canyon, too, now?"

"No." He had to put a stop to this. "Miranda, why don't you two go back inside?"

Looping an arm around Lucy's shoulders, she shepherded her back toward the house. Glancing back, Miranda said, "You coming, Rafe?"

"In a minute."

The three men stood in a circle no more than ten feet apart until Seth said, "Pick up the damn clothes." Alfie said, "I'm not carrying his fuckin' pants around." And to make the point, he kicked the heap, scattering them around the ground.

"Come on, then," Seth said, one hand resting obtrusively on the handle of the knife.

"We ain't done with you, Salazar," Alfie said, as he sauntered off behind Seth. "We know when we been screwed."

Rafe felt his hand clench, and it was all he could do not to slug him. But he waited and watched as they got into their old truck, revved the engine defiantly, and backed up onto the main road. He knew things had been going too well. Now, unfortunately, they were right back to normal.

1 October, 1888

'Louis!'

There was a knock on the door. It felt as if someone were banging on my very skull.

'Louis! Are you in there?' It was Lloyd.

The door handle jiggled. The knocking got louder.

'Are you asleep? Wake up.'

My chin rose from my chest, my shoulders aching—everything aching.

'There's a detective here, from Scotland Yard. He says he needs to speak with you.'

The room was flooded with light. Woggin was standing by the door, whining to go out.

In the cheval glass, I saw myself again, a haunted, haggard creature, but mine own.

'What should I tell him?'

'Tell him', I croaked, 'to go away.'

'I don't think I can tell him that. Shall I tell him you'll be down in a few minutes?'

I didn't reply. I was testing my legs to see if I could stand.

'I'll tell him that,' Lloyd decided.

Yes, I thought, tell him anything. All I wanted right now was a hot bath and a deep sleep in a long bed. I settled, however, for a good, hard scrub with a basin of fresh cold water, a hasty shave, and a new suit of clothes. I was hardly the picture of health, but presentable enough to go downstairs. As I passed the grandfather clock on the landing, I saw that it was already half past four. I had had a long, if uncomfortable, sleep. In the parlour, I heard Fanny's voice.

'I'm sure I don't know, Inspector. He keeps his own hours. Great artists are like that.'

'But you don't know what time he came to bed?'

'Our sleeping arrangements are our own affair.'

'Pardon me,' Abberline apologised. 'Let me rephrase the question—do you know what time your husband retired that night, wherever in the house he might have been?'

'He often falls asleep at his desk.'

'And wakes there, too,' I said, entering the room, 'with a stiff back.'

Abberline, in his usual brown suit, was standing between the front windows, holding a note pad and pencil. Lloyd lounged beside his mother on the sofa.

'Mr Stevenson,' the detective said, nodding his head.

'To what do we owe the honour of this visit?'

'There was a double murder last night,' Fanny interjected. 'You have not yet seen the papers.'

Several of them, from the most staid to the most lurid, were fanned out on the sofa between herself and her son. They were late editions, the ink still wet, as it were.

'Two more ladies of the evening', Fanny said, 'slaughtered even worse than the ones before.'

'Perhaps it would be best if we spoke in private,' the detective said, but I had already deposited myself in one of the wing chairs and had no desire to be interrogated privately, or otherwise. All things considered, it seemed wise to have Fanny there, acting as my advocate, if need be.

'You can speak freely,' I said. If I banished Lloyd, he would only linger at the keyhole, anyway.

Clearing his throat, Abberline said, 'What your wife has said is true. You know nothing of this?'

'I was working late into the night. I saw the dawn from my study window.'

'Surely you didn't work all night,' he said. 'Didn't you go anywhere earlier in the evening?'

It was a leading question, if ever there was one, and my answer would establish, or destroy, my veracity in whatever else was to come.

'I did go out earlier last night.'

'Where?'

I knew he had the answer already. If Mansfield was under surveillance, as even Stoker admitted, then the operative must have seen me enter and leave the theatre. 'I went to the Lyceum.'

'To what purpose?'

'Can't I go to see my own play without arousing suspicion?'

'The play was over when you arrived.'

At least he had shown that card.

'I came at the request of the manager, Bram Stoker. You may corroborate that with him. He wanted to consult with me on some artistic questions.'

'With him alone?'

'And with the lead actor, Mr Mansfield.'

Under questioning, it is always best to share as much of the truth as possible, not only to display cooperation, but to obfuscate whatever portion of the tale you are hoping to conceal. A simple lesson of the storyteller's art.

'What were Mr Mansfield's artistic problems about, then?'

'Nothing much. He wondered if he was remaining true to the original text, and I assured him he had the greatest latitude to bring to the role whatever he chose.'

Abberline look unpersuaded. 'And after your consultation?' He said that last word with the utmost suspicion.

'I left Mr Mansfield at the stage door, and tried to get a cab home. It was raining quite hard last night, as I hardly need to remind you.'

The corollary is to offer up nothing you don't absolutely have to.

'Have any luck?'

'No.'

'So you walked all the way back? In the rain?'

'Apparently so,' I said. 'I know I was thoroughly soaked when I got here.'

'Did you, by any chance, take Wellington Street in the direction of the Strand?'

The very route I had taken. 'Yes, I believe I did.' So that sense I had had of being followed was not altogether wrong. I had attributed it, in hindsight, to being stalked by the man with the knife. Jack. But could it have been a policeman? Could it have been the same one who intervened in the attack, though almost too late to have saved me?

The detective waited, as if giving me time to sort through my own questions.

'There was an altercation in a costermonger's arcade,' he finally said. 'A man with a knife.'

'Was it Jack?'

'Unlikely, but possible. The other murders occurred close to the same time, but all the way over in Whitechapel again.'

'Who was the victim of this incident in the arcade?'

'None, fortunately. A woman escaped clean, but the men got into a bit of a brawl.'

'Men?' I asked innocently. 'There were more than one?'

'Yes.'

'Did the policeman get a good look at them?'

'Good enough. The one with the knife was big and blond, the other was a queer-looking gent.' He studied me oddly. 'Shorter than you, and rather twisted in both his frame and features.' It looked as if he were trying to puzzle something out.

'So you now have two Rippers?' Fanny said, as if that prospect held some grim sort of satisfaction. Lloyd, a young man whose interest in anything but Constance Wooldridge was lackadaisical at best, looked positively riveted at receiving this privileged information.

'Possibly. But knife attacks in London are not as uncommon as some people might think. What distinguishes Jack the Ripper, as he fashions himself, is the savagery and cunning. This morning, we got the following, delivered in the Central News Agency's morning post.' He took from his pocket, as gently as if it were a piece of a papyrus scroll, a postal card. 'Might I ask a small favour of you, Mr Stevenson?'

'If it is in my power to grant.'

'Oh, it is.' Abberline handed me his pencil and his note pad, turned to a blank page, and said, 'Could you write down the following words?'

I took the pad and pencil, and as he dictated, I wrote down, 'I was not codding, dear old boss, when I gave you the tip.' Then he said, 'Thank you, that's enough.'

As he accepted the pad from my hand, his eye fell on the gash to my wrist. 'That's a nasty cut, and looks fresh,' he said. 'How did you get that?'

'Unwisely, climbing over my garden wall. The gate was locked, and I didn't want to wake the house when I came in late.'

'So that's from last night?'

'Louis, let me look at that,' Fanny said, bustling up from the sofa, turning my wrist to get a better look. 'Why didn't you call me? I could have dressed that properly.'

Lloyd, meanwhile, showed no concern whatsoever; his eyes were fixed on Abberline, who was now comparing the words I had written to the postal card.

'What's the rest of the card say?' Lloyd asked eagerly, all but trying to snatch it from the detective's hand. 'You know it will be printed in tomorrow's paper, anyway.'

Having done with his comparison, he gave it to Lloyd, who read it aloud. 'I was not codding dear old Boss when I gave you the tip, you'll hear about Saucy Jack's work tomorrow double event this time number one squealed a bit couldn't finish straight off. had not the time to get ears for police. thanks for keeping last letter back till I got to work again. Jack the Ripper.'

I had never heard Lloyd read with such facility, or enthusiasm. 'Dare I ask,' he said to Abberline, 'is this red ink, or blood, that it's written in?'

'Ink, like the first.'

'But the handwriting is nothing like Louis's, is it?'

Dryly, the detective admitted, 'No, it is not.'

Fanny whirled around, exclaiming, 'Is that what this is all about? You actually suspected my husband of being this foul creature?'

'At the Yard, I'm afraid we rule nothing out until we have proof to the contrary.'

'Then it's no wonder you haven't caught this monster, and probably never will. How dare you even think to accuse my husband?'

'We have accused him of nothing,' he said, slipping the papers and pencil into his pocket.

'I'll thank you to leave the house right now,' Fanny said.

At the door, to which I escorted him with Fanny, lest she give him a slap, Abberline put his brown bowler hat back on, and said, 'Thank you for your time.'

'Don't forget this,' Fanny said, smacking an ivory-handled umbrella into his hand.

'Oh no,' Abberline said, though looking straight at me, 'that isn't mine.'

'You brought it.'

'You must be mistaken,' he said, still holding my gaze. Then, he touched the brim of his hat, and went down the steps to the street.

TOPANGA CANYON— CALIFORNIA

Present Day

Although it was the kind of event Rafe dreaded with every fiber of his being, he couldn't refuse Miranda.

When she'd held out the engraved card, he'd read it—at two p.m. that Sunday, there was to be a memorial service commemorating the life of Mrs. Gladys Ashcroft, at a private home in the posh suburb of San Marino—and handed it back to her, uncomprehending.

"That's my great-aunt Gladys, the one who left me the money."

"Oh, right."

"And the house is my mother's."

Now he could see where this was heading.

"I can't face it alone. Will you go with me?"

Even without that pleading look in her beautiful blue eyes, he could not have turned her down. There were a couple of sticking points, though.

"I don't own a suit." That was the first.

"I'll buy you one, with Gladys's money."

"No way. She shouldn't have to pay for clothes for people coming to her funeral."

"It's not a funeral. She's already been cremated, per her instructions, and she's in an urn in the family mausoleum at Forest Lawn."

"I do have a sport coat. Can I just wear that?"

"You can wear your ranger duds, for all I care. Just come."

"And what about Lucy?" That was the second.

"She can come, too, if she feels up to it."

But when Sunday came, Rafe wasn't so sure she did. She was staying in the canyon because she'd come down with an awful flu, and Evangelina had been thrilled to have her out of the group home for a few days. "Once a bug starts going around here," Evangelina had said, "it's like I'm running a hospice."

When Rafe popped his head into the trailer to ask her, Lucy took out her earbuds, put down her magazine, and said, "Eww. A funeral?" Tripod was lying beside her on the bunk, on his back with his paws in the air.

"It's not a funeral," he said, echoing Miranda. "And it's supposed to be at a really pretty house."

"I'm too sick," she said, sniffling for fuller effect. "Do I have to?"

"No, you don't have to," he said, still debating the wisdom of leaving her alone in the trailer. "We'll only be gone for about three hours, max."

"I want to go to sleep," she said.

"You'll do that?"

"Uh-huh."

With some reluctance, he said, "Okay, then. Just stay in the trailer, with the door locked, until we get back."

"Then can we go out for some ice cream?" Trip's tail thumped. Certain words he knew.

"Sure. And I'll tell Miranda to leave the new key to the back door under the mat, so if you want anything from the fridge, you can have it."

Lucy didn't exactly jump for joy. She was already acquainted with the contents of Miranda's fridge—fruits, veggies, unsweetened juice, nonfat yogurt.

"Call me on my cell if there's any problem."

"Okay, okay," she said, sticking her earbuds back in. "I'm not a baby."

Miranda came out of the house in a dress he'd never seen her in before—dark blue with a prim white collar—a short string of pearls, and pointy, high-heeled shoes. Suddenly, he could see what she had been brought up to be, the Miranda Willoughby of the Marlborough School, the one whose mother had expected her to go on to Wellesley and then marry a Princeton banker and raise three perfect children. A far cry from the Topanga Canyon Miranda, with her long loose skirts and sandals, and a shop filled with massage oils and homemade jam.

But that was the one he'd fallen in love with.

At least he'd stopped kidding himself. He hadn't actually said the words—he'd have sooner stuck his hand in a beehive—but every night, the last thing he thought about, lying on his bunk, was Miranda, and the first thing he looked forward to in the morning was catching a glimpse of her passing the window in her apartment upstairs, or maybe popping open the screen door on the store. Any other guy would have made his move by now—even Rafe was disappointed in himself—but he knew that once he did, there was no going back. If she wasn't receptive, he'd be so humiliated he'd have to find some other place to live.

But if she *was* receptive—and he had every reason to believe that that was the case—then that posed a whole other set of questions. What about his work? What about the fact that he had no money? That the Land Management office could cut off his funding any day? Or that Lucy could finally try Evangelina's patience to the point where she was no longer welcome in the group home? She was aging out of the home as it was, and Evangelina had dropped a hint or two already. What kind of life could he and Miranda construct, when he brought nothing but poverty and family complications to it?

In the back of the cramped compartment that passed for a closet, he'd found his sport coat; it was still in the plastic from the dry cleaner's, where he'd taken it after wearing it to the induction ceremony for new environmental science field officers. That had been four years ago. He put it on over a fresh white shirt and a pair of khakis he'd smoothed out by slipping them under the mattress while he'd slept.

He'd even played a hose over the purple-and-gold Land Rover to get some of the dust off it—the soil in the canyon was so parched from the drought that the slightest breeze lifted it up and deposited it like a fine silt on everything—and put extra air in its worn tires. Miranda had hinted at taking her Subaru, but Rafe liked to be behind the wheel of his own car—even this one.

Driving the length of the main road, with Miranda in the passenger seat, he felt as self-conscious as some kid on prom night. There wasn't much traffic in either direction, but the hairpin turns and steep cliffs to one side or the other meant he had to keep his eyes on the road, much as they would have liked to stray to his beautiful companion.

On the way, Miranda explained the cast of characters he was going to meet, most notably her mother, with whom he already knew she did not get along, and her mother's third husband, Bentley. "I think I told you about him—the retired curator from the Huntington, which pretty much adjoins my mother's backyard."

"But a curator? Not a millionaire?"

"She's already married, and buried, two of those. This time she could just marry someone she felt like having around the house. If she doesn't have a husband, she feels off-kilter."

Her recitation of the rest of the family quickly became a blur, and his attention wandered. As they passed the turnoff to the sanitation and recycling center, Rafe thought of the trunk, and the horrendous story Miranda had told him about the night she'd dropped it off there.

"I know you think I'm nuts," she'd said, "but that was no coyote. That was a wolf that tried to eat Trip."

When he told her wolves were not seen this far south in the state, she'd looked straight at him and said, "Say that again, only try to make it believable this time."

He'd laughed, and let it go. Secretly, of course, he didn't doubt her, but he also didn't want to give any credence to the story. If word of the wolf reached the Land Management office, his fieldwork would be overwhelmed by outside experts; and even worse, numbskull hunters, eager to bag a renegade unwanted wolf, would descend en masse on the canyon.

The drive from Topanga to San Marino, just south of Pasadena, was a little over an hour, but the two worlds could not have been farther apart. The streets of San Marino were wide and quiet, lined with stately homes and estates, many of them built for captains of industry and local movers and shakers back in the 1920s and '30s. Glancing over, he could see Miranda visibly stiffening in her seat as she gave him directions for the final few turns to her mother's home.

"You want me to drop you off and then go park this heap a block away?" he asked, only half facetiously, but she shook her head and said, "There's an auto court. You can leave it there."

She might as well have said a parking lot. Just past a pair of wrought-iron gates that stood ten feet high, there was a broad, flagstone courtyard with a guy in a red jacket guiding cars into nice neat lines. Rafe was pointed to a spot between a Lexus and a Mercedes, and when they got out of the purple SUV, the valet gave him a wary look.

The house itself, a pale yellow stone, was only two stories high, but spread out behind a perfectly manicured line of cypress trees. The towering oak doors stood open, and a young woman in a gray suit was checking off names as the guests entered. When Miranda announced herself, the woman looked up and said, "Oh yes, your mother said to keep an eye out for you and to tell you she would be in her bedroom before the ceremony begins. You can go right up if you want."

Miranda looked at Rafe. "Will you be okay?"

Though he wasn't sure he would be, he said, "Of course. You go."

"The rose garden is where the ceremony is being held," the woman said. "It's straight out back, through the library."

"That would be the room with all the books in it?" Rafe joked, but the woman didn't catch on.

"Yes, it's on the left," she said, "just off this main hallway."

Rafe followed an elderly couple down the hallway, passing rooms filled with heavy dark furniture under coffered ceilings. The library, though, was flooded with light from the French doors that opened onto a lush, flower-filled garden. No water conservation measures enacted here, Rafe thought. One server held a tray of lemonade glasses, another a tray of bubbling champagne flutes. The other guests each took a glass and stepped out into the garden, but knowing no one, Rafe lingered in the library with his lemonade, studying the beautifully bound leather sets that lined the floor-to-ceiling shelves. These were the sorts of books that he'd found on the back shelves and in the storage closets of the facilities he'd grown up in, though by the time they got to him they were in terrible condition. Standing here now, he felt like he'd discovered the source of the Nile.

There were books by Melville and Conrad and Dickens and Kipling, but he had other game in mind, and with his head cocked to one side to better read the spines, roamed the room, intently looking. So far as he could tell, there was no organizing principle to the library—no alphabetical arrangements—but he was sure he'd eventually get lucky.

"Anything in particular you're looking for?" a voice asked, and when he turned, he saw a smiling, white-haired man in horn-rimmed glasses and a business suit. "I get lost in here myself sometimes," he said, extending his hand. "Not that I mind one bit. I'm Bentley Wright."

Rafe introduced himself and said he'd come with Miranda, and the man's eyebrows went up. "So she's upstairs with her mother right now? Alone?"

"As far as I know."

Bentley cocked his head as if listening for something. "No gunfire so far," he said with a smile. "That's good news. I know her mother would like to see more of Miranda than she does."

Rafe shrugged as if he wouldn't know about any of that, and Bentley discreetly changed the subject. "Some of these books are so valuable," he said, waving a hand at the elegant ranks, "they belong next door, on the shelves of the Huntington."

"Miranda said you're on the staff there."

"Retired now. I was curator of incunabula, also known as very old books. *Were* you actually looking for a particular book or author?"

"Yes," Rafe admitted. "Robert Louis Stevenson."

"Ah, then, come right this way," he said, crooking a finger and leading Rafe across the Persian carpet to the other side of the room. Running a hand across a red leather-bound set, he said, "Everything from his essays to his novels." Scanning the shelf, Rafe quickly spotted the most famous titles, from *Treasure Island* to *The Master of Ballantrae*. "This was the comprehensive Edinburgh edition begun by Longmans Green in 1894," Bentley explained, "along with the two concluding volumes of Stevensoniana published after his death."

Apart from some cracks in the binding, they looked to Rafe like they'd never even been opened.

"Are you a fan of his?" Bentley asked.

Rafe nodded, wondering what in the world this guy would think if he knew what he was keeping in his trailer.

"Go ahead—take one down."

Rafe picked *The Strange Case of Dr Jekyll and Mr Hyde*, as he had been reading in the journal about the opening of the play in London and how, once Jack the Ripper had appeared, suspicion had fallen on the lead actor and even on Stevenson himself. Holding the old book, he felt a lot like he did when reading the journal—as if he were in close personal communion with the author.

"His wife, Fanny, as you may know, hated the first draft of that one," Bentley said. "He was so upset at her reaction that he burned it, then wrote it all over again. His stepson, Lloyd, claimed he did it in three days, but I think that must be an exaggeration."

Rafe nodded, carefully turning the gilt-edged pages.

"She was a Californian, by the way."

Rafe nodded again. It was mentioned several times in the journal.

"And her son, Lloyd Osbourne, lived for a few years not that far from here. Wrote a few books of his own, but nothing very good."

This he did not know.

"In fact, he died in Glendale, of all the unlikely places, at a ripe old age. Isn't that strange?"

The revelation caught Rafe so much by surprise that his hand clenched for a second on the book. Suddenly, he saw a connection—however fragile, however attenuated—between Stevenson and a remote lake in Topanga Canyon. It was as if a rickety bridge, made of ropes and planks, had just been thrown across a deep ravine. It would take a lot of work to trace any actual nexus between the two, but he'd known that there had to be one. Had the trunk come to the region with Lloyd? Was he the one who had buried it in the lake? And if so, why? Before he could follow up with any questions, however, Miranda came in and said, "Hello, Bentley. I'm glad you two found each other."

"So am I," Bentley said, kissing her cheek. "I miss showing off rare books to people who appreciate them."

"Mother's coming down in a minute. We should grab a seat in the shade if they're not all taken."

Outside, a white canopy had been set up over forty or fifty chairs, and Rafe and Miranda found two at the end of an aisle.

"It's nice that your mother wanted to see you as soon as you got here," Rafe said. "It's a good sign, right?"

"Not really. She just wanted to make sure I hadn't shown up in a paisley skirt and flip-flops. She actually had a replacement outfit on the bed for me."

When her mother did appear—hair tinted the color of the gilt bindings on the books, and wearing an ivory suit that matched her shoes—she wafted down the center aisle, graciously acknowledging the family and friends in attendance, and took her place behind a walnut music stand that was serving as a lectern. Rafe could see where Miranda got her looks. By her mother's side, a table had been set up, with flowers and silver-framed photos of Gladys Ashcroft at various ages of her life.

After the general request to turn off any cell phones, which Rafe obligingly did—"Gladys called them the end of civilization," Mrs. Wright joked, "and sometimes I agree"—he did his best to pay attention, but since all the names and stories and anecdotes meant nothing to him, and the people who stood up to speak were all strangers, his mind wandered off, out over the green lawn—Jesus, he thought, what were her water bills?—and past the brilliant red rosebushes and the bees that buzzed around them. He couldn't get out of his head what Bentley had said about Lloyd living in nearby Glendale at one time. He was dying to get back to the journal and see what happened next, and in Bentley he thought he might have found someone to advise him on what to do once he decided to come forward and give the journal up.

When the last eulogy had been made and the guests stood up to mingle again, Miranda was quickly surrounded by some cousins who, judging from the warmth of their greetings, hadn't seen her in years. Rafe took the opportunity to seek out Bentley again, hoping to find out more. But now he was at his wife's side, and before Rafe knew it, he was being introduced to Miranda's mom, who took his hand and gave him a bright, beaming smile.

"I'm so glad you could join us today," she said. "Was it Mr. Sandoval?"

"Salazar. Rafael Salazar."

The smile didn't so much as waver. "Bentley tells me you're a book lover."

"You have a pretty spectacular library."

"That we do. My late husband Oscar was a bibliophile."

Rafe was beginning to wonder what Miranda was making all the fuss about—her mother seemed perfectly nice to him.

"I gather you drove Miranda here today."

"Yes."

"That was so kind of you. How do you know my daughter?"

"I'm her tenant. In Topanga."

"Of course. And do you drive for a living?"

"Um, no, I don't. I do environmental work, for the state."

Leaning in, Bentley said, "Rafael and Miranda are seeing each other. I told you that."

For a second, her eyes went downcast, the smile frozen. Then she looked at Rafe again and said, "I don't know where my head is at today. You'll have to forgive me. But I do wish my daughter would share more of her life with me." Then, hailing a couple on their way out of the garden, she said, "Please excuse me. It's been lovely to meet you."

Bentley tried to make up for the awkwardness of the encounter with a very hearty handshake and a promise to show him around the library. "Either the one here at the house, or the collection at my old stomping grounds, the Huntington, next door. I'm always looking for an excuse."

But Rafe knew when he'd been dissed.

As soon as Miranda had escaped from her cousins, he took hold of her hand, entwining their fingers—Miranda seemed as pleased as she was surprised at the gesture—in the hopes that her mother would spot them leaving together. If she also saw them getting into the purple Land Rover, with the gold flames painted on the door handles, she'd probably faint away on the spot. Truth be told, he'd have kind of liked to see that.

10 November, 1888

For weeks now, the city has been like a powder keg, just waiting for Jack to touch a flame to its fuse with another murder. The divide between East and West, between the dismal, impoverished slums of Whitechapel and Spitalfields, where the Ripper has committed his foul deeds, and the West End, where the gentry have so far been spared all but the ominous sense of dread, has never been greater. Leaders of the various social movements—the Social Democratic Federation, the Fabians, the International Working Men's Educational Society, the Fair Trade League, the Metropolitan Federation of Radical Clubs—have set aside their differences and banded together to call for a mass demonstration in Trafalgar Square, to protest the widespread unemployment and squalid living conditions that foster criminality and have given rise, in their view, to a creature as vile and depraved as Jack. The square was chosen not only because it affords the organizers ample space for the thousands of struggling workers they expect to turn up, but because it is, both symbolically and geographically, the precise point at which the East and West ends met.

'Are you sure you must attend this dinner?' Fanny said, reaching up to help fasten my silk tie. (Symonds had warned me not to turn up at his club, the very fashionable Athenaeum, in one of my more bohemian costumes.) 'The streets', she warned, 'aren't safe.'

'I shall be fine,' I said, with a certainty I did not feel in the slightest. I had never told Fanny, or anyone, about the attack from the man who spoke German—there was enough suspicion hanging about me already—but I had taken from its velvet-lined box a Colt two-shot derringer that I had purchased on impulse from a saloon owner in San Francisco, examined it to make sure it was in perfect working order, and made plans to carry it in the pocket of my suit jacket, under my long overcoat.

'Who else is going to be there?'

'Only Henley.'

'Why would anyone want to dine with Henley?'

'Because Symonds's essay, which we are celebrating tonight, appeared in the pages of the "National Observer." Henley paid him handsomely for it.'

'Well, be careful, Louis,' she advised, smoothing the satin lapels of the jacket. 'Stick to the main thoroughfares and stay well clear of the rally. They always end in violence.'

'Yes, Mother,' I chided her.

The fog that had enveloped the city for several nights had lifted, and so I decided to take advantage of the clear weather and walk all the way to Pall Mall. In the precincts of Cavendish Square, all seemed orderly and ordinary, but as I travelled east, I could not fail to notice the occasional storefront that had been boarded up; the Metropolitan Police, who had lost control of the streets in the infamous 'Bloody Sunday' demonstrations the year before, had issued a warning to shopkeepers. Loiterers, in more than the usual numbers, were hanging about outside the public houses. One of them complimented me on my fine clothes as I passed by, and though I thanked him, I knew full well the spirit in which the comment had been made. The sound of his friends' laughter followed me up the street.

Perhaps that's why I was especially aware of a footfall behind me, and at the next corner, ducked into a doorway to wait and see who was on my heels. I was becoming quite an adept at this procedure. A moment later, the footfall increased in speed, and a woman, with flaming red hair and carrying a black lace parasol, hurried by, scanning the streets ahead.

'Looking for someone?' I said, and she whipped around, blushing furiously. I found myself confronting no more frightening an assailant than Constance Wooldridge.

'Oh, I am so embarrassed,' she said, hiding behind the parasol. 'I had so hoped to make our encounter appear accidental.'

'Why? It's a pleasure to see you.'

'And you, too, Mr Stevenson.'

'Louis—call me Louis. Where are you heading?'

'Wherever you are.'

Now I was truly puzzled.

'I have needed to speak to you,' she said. 'I went to your house, but lacked the courage.'

'To knock on my door?'

'I can explain. Shall we walk?'

'Of course.'

Taking my arm, her eyes downcast, she said, 'I could not risk it. It might have made the situation only worse.'

My puzzlement turned to consternation. 'What situation?'

As we walked, she began to pour out her heart. 'I doubt I could have spoken of this in front of his mother, and if Lloyd had been home, it would have been utterly impossible.'

'If you are going to tell me that you and Lloyd have been keeping company,' I said, patting the back of her hand, 'I know all about it.'

Her face, when she turned it to me, was stricken. 'Is that what he has told you?'

'More than once. He's quite proud of himself, as well he should be.'

She all but groaned. 'I don't know how to express it, but your stepson has brought nothing but fear into my life.'

It was as if she had stabbed me with an ice pick. 'Fear? How?'

And so she explained. Lloyd, quite unbidden and, as she assured me repeatedly, with no encouragement, had manufactured a romance where there was none. Had begun to send her love letters two and three times a day. Had sent her lavish gifts (I thought of the bills piling up on the hall table). Had taken to ringing her bell at all hours, and shouting up at her windows. 'I live with a maiden aunt, and she is quite beside herself. She has spoken to the police, but he is never there when they come round, and she is, to be candid, a somewhat eccentric character herself. I think they find her accounts unreliable.'

'You should have written to me,' I said.

'I did.'

'I never received it.'

'I know,' she replied. 'Lloyd intercepted it and left it crumpled in my post box. He had scrawled on it in red ink, "I love you, and you WILL love me."'

The ice pick stabbed again.

'And what about Desmond? Lloyd said you two had had a falling out.'

'Over this, in large measure. Randolph thinks I have instigated it somehow.'

'How could he think such a thing?'

'But he does. And frankly, I think he is afraid of Lloyd.'

Afraid of Lloyd? I had known people to be annoyed with Lloyd, I had known them to grow bored with his self-admiration, I had even known them to be irked by his arrogance. But afraid? This was altogether new.

We turned down a side street, and then into a quiet mews. Constance pointed her parasol at a somber town house with a fanlight above the door and barren window boxes. 'That is my aunt's house,' she said, 'where I live. Lloyd wrote to tell me I should not leave the house today because of the demonstration, and that he would check up on me after it was done. To make sure that I was safely at home.'

I walked her to the front steps and said, 'Leave it to me. I will speak to him at the earliest opportunity, and do whatever is necessary to set him straight.'

To my own embarrassment now, she clutched my hands and, with tears welling in her beautiful green eyes, thanked me. 'I knew that you would be the one to understand.' And then she fled up the stairs and into the house so swiftly, I was left wondering if the whole conversation had not been a figment of my own imagination.

All the way to Pall Mall, I turned it over in my mind, resolving, once the dinner and the contemporaneous demonstration were over, to return and keep watch on her house.

The avenue on which the prominent and powerful men's clubs were lined up, shoulder to shoulder like a row of limestone dominoes, was broad and clean, unlike so much of the city. But even in that panoply of rich and aristocratic institutions, the Athenaeum stood out. Known for the Greek frieze, which was based on the Elgin Marbles, that ran like a ribbon below its outside balustrade, as well as for the intellectual rigour of its illustrious membership (Dickens had ended his feud with Thackeray on its grand staircase; Darwin was often seen scratching his beard in the well-stocked library; Michael Faraday had once served as the club's secretary), the Athenaeum exuded an effortless superiority over its neighbours and peers. The moment I passed under its Doric portico, with its row of twinned columns, I felt myself embraced by its cool and soothing atmosphere. Trafalgar Square could be in turmoil, the streets could be a battlefield, but here . . . peace and civility reign.

Leaving my hat and coat with the hall porter, I ascended to the Smoking Room, where, through the low burble of men's voices and wreaths of smoke, I found Symonds and Henley already ensconced in deeply creased leather chairs, glasses of sherry at their elbows.

'What, you've left the rally so soon?' Henley boomed, in a voice that caused several of the other members to glance our way in disapproval. 'Did your speech whip them up to a frenzy?'

'William, please,' Symonds admonished him. 'Your jokes could cost me my membership.'

'For such a small offence?' Henley countered.

Before I could draw up a chair, a white-gloved servant had already done so, while also proffering the sherry decanter, which I declined. 'An Irish whiskey, please.' And when Henley heard that, he said, 'Make that two. Sorry, Symonds, but this sherry is like gargling gumdrops.'

Symonds had the look on his long face of a missionary failing to civilise the natives.

'What's it like out there?' Henley asked. 'I attended the rally for an hour or two, and it was all very merry, but when one of the revellers questioned my note-taking—I think he suspected I was from Scotland Yard—I had the impression that the mob was about to crack me over the head with my own wooden leg.'

'The mobile vulgus,' Symonds put in, 'from the Latin for "mob". Employed to describe the labouring poor. But I think a closer translation might be "movement", as it also encapsulates the element of protest.'

'Well, when it comes to that, they've got good reason,' Henley said, taking a whiskey from the servant's silver tray and leaving the other to me. 'Plenty of it.'

'To John's essay,' I said, raising my glass in an effort to divert the conversation into safer channels, 'a work both bold in conception and brilliant in execution.' We toasted, Symonds dipped his head in acknowledgement, and then Henley went right on with his disquisition.

'Walk the streets of Whitechapel, as Louis and I did not long ago, and what do you see? An utter indifference to life, of any sort. For amusement, the children cling to the iron railings of the open slaughterhouses and watch the animals having their throats cut. The lack of proper mortuaries means the dead are kept in the kitchen until a shallow grave can be dug somewhere. The water, what there is of it, is filthy and undependable. You've got more brothels than you've got schools, more pubs than you've got shops, and the common lodging houses are nothing but breeding grounds for vice of every stripe.'

'But didn't the government do what it could, in respect to those lodging houses?' Symonds said. 'The Artizans and Labourers Dwellings Improvements Act demolished the worst of the lot, did it not?'

'Oh, that it did,' Henley said, as if rolling up his sleeves to continue a blistering editorial. 'It knocked 'em down all right, but what happened to the rest of the scheme? The doss-houses were supposed to be replaced with new housing, along with the brothels that were blown down with the same breath—but were they? They were not. And who do you think wound up living rough on the street as a result? The very women that Jack the Ripper now preys upon.'

'Please,' Symonds said, leaning forward, 'lower your voice, Henley, or we'll all be taken for revolutionaries.'

Henley signalled the servant for another whiskey, but Symonds forestalled him by recommending we go in to dinner.

'A capital suggestion,' I remarked, as I had eaten little that day and the walk had been a long one.

In the dining room, a vast wainscotted room whose walls were adorned, in keeping with the Greek motif and title of the club, with gloomy neoclassical paintings—the one above our table showed Socrates holding aloft the cup of hemlock—we were served bloody roast beef, boiled potatoes, and broiled tomatoes. French windows ran the length of the room, opening onto the balustrade, and through them I could see the tops of the gas lamps flickering. The club had outfitted itself, under the direction of Faraday's successor, with electric lights only a year or two before, but I still found dining by their harsh illumination uncongenial. A candlelit chandelier could make the simplest repast appear a banquet, while electricity rendered everything unappetizingly vivid.

'Is it true', Symonds said over the trifle that followed, 'that there was some writing on a brick wall not far from the body of the Ripper's last victim?'

'Where did you hear that?' Henley said, though not, I noted, denying it. 'And why would you, of all people, take an interest?'

'You mistake me, Henley—I do not live entirely in the Renaissance,' he said, dabbing at his pale lips with his napkin. 'And as for where I heard it,' he added, inclining his head towards a distinguished-looking man at a corner table, 'Sir Charles Warren. He's been a member for many years, and he indicated something to that effect over dinner last week.'

'So that's the bumbling fool,' Henley said.

'Please,' Symonds begged again.

'There <u>was</u> chalk writing, presumably in the Ripper's own hand, on Goulston Street, and, in his capacity as commissioner of the Metropolitan Police, Warren had it expunged.'

'Why would he do that?' I said, already stowing this information away for Fanny's delectation. She especially enjoyed tales of professional incompetence.

'Because he thought it might ignite an anti-Semitic riot.'

'What did it say?' Symonds asked. 'I was never told.'

'According to PC Alfred Long, one of my more reliable informants, it said, "The Juwes—spelled j-u-w-e-s, incidentally—are not the men who will be blamed for nothing."'

'That makes no sense,' I said.

'Be that as it may. The handwriting alone might have proved a clue. Was it the same as the writing on the notecards sent to the news agency? Now we'll never know.'

'Surely his motives were good,' Symonds said. 'The prejudice against the flood of immigrants from Germany and Poland and Russia is already at a fever pitch. Another mention of the Hebrews in this connection and a riot might well indeed have swept the city.'

As if all the talk of riots had given rise to one, we heard in the distance a low swell of noise—a murmur of many voices, the tramping of many feet. Several heads were turned towards the French windows, including that of the police commissioner.

'What's that?' Symonds said.

'The symphony of insurrection, if I'm not mistaken,' Henley said, tossing his napkin on the table and tucking his crutch under his arm.

The servants were already attempting to draw the draperies, but Henley brushed one of them aside, threw open the windows, and stepped out onto the balcony overlooking Pall Mall. Others quickly followed, until even Symonds and I had left our chairs.

I can only compare the sound to the rumble of distant thunder. The club members, some with brandy glasses in their hands, bent their heads towards each other, muttering of rebellion and foreign influences, Marxists and Irish malcontents. Even George Bernard Shaw, a noted Fabian, was singled out for calumny.

But the rumble grew louder, and though nothing could yet be seen, Sir Charles Warren advised that all the electric lights in the club be extinguished. 'Turn them off!' he cried to the staff. 'And tell everyone to stand clear of the windows.'

In the Bloody Sunday riot the year before, all the windows in Mansion House and other fine homes along the route of the rioters had been smashed by bricks and stones.

Henley had his note pad out and was already scribbling in it when the first wave came into view, surging around the corner with bullhorns blaring, banners waving, posters jabbing at the sky like lances.

'Inside, all of you!' Warren called out. 'You'll only serve as a further provocation.' But the curiosity was too great, the spectacle too mesmerizing. A few cowards scurried back into the dining room, but the rest of us stayed on the balcony to watch the tide of history come on. In a darkened doorway across the street, I glimpsed what might have been a forward scout—a burly fellow in a deerstalker hat—lurking.

Could it possibly be?

'We've got ringside seats!' Henley exulted, clapping Symonds on the shoulder. 'And we've got you to thank!'

'It was not a planned entertainment,' he said.

I craned my neck to catch another glimpse of the scout, but that doorway—indeed, the whole of Pall Mall—was eclipsed by the vanguard shouting slogans and epithets and brandishing fists at the façade of the Athenaeum. When they realized its members were observing them from behind the balustrade, the shouts grew louder and the curses more colourful. Four or five of them, in tattered jackets and caps, stretched out a banner that read, 'We want jobs—not Jack!'

Henley jotted it down. 'Not bad, that.'

A younger member of the club, plainly in his cups, staggered to the front of the balcony, and after surveying the mob, ostentatiously pinched his fingers to his nose as if smelling something unbearable.

The brick that came flying up at him hit with deadly accuracy. The man went down on the flagstones like a poleaxed cow, a huge cheer went up from the crowd, and within seconds a barrage of bricks and rocks and bottles had thoroughly demolished every window in the club.

TOPANGA CANYON— CALIFORNIA

Present Day

For the tenth time, Laszlo rummaged through the old clothes in the trunk—the battered top hat, the black cape, cotton gloves, a leather satchel like a doctor might carry, looking for something of any value. Axel had told him he'd have to pay rent for the privilege of living at the Compound, and Laszlo had almost laughed in his face. Rent, to live in this fucking barn and sleep on a stained mattress on a rotting old bunk bed? With Seth and Alfie snoring six feet away? Axel should have been paying *him*.

Still, he did need to raise some dough fast. He had his own little habits to feed—mostly liquor, with drugs a close second—and the only thing in this trunk that could conceivably have any value was a tarnished and dented old flask. It took a while to get the lid unscrewed, but the minute he did, the smell of alcohol was so strong it was like he'd been punched in the face. Phew! He sniffed at it, and the closest he could guess was brandy. Very old brandy. Brandy that had been aging for an eternity. Laszlo had always been told that the older it was, the better and more potent it would be. By that standard, this stuff had to be dynamite.

"I thought I'd find you in here, dipshit," Roy said, barging through the door of the barn. Laszlo quickly screwed the top back on the flask and stuck it in the back pocket of his jeans.

Seth and Alfie were loitering behind Roy as he said, "Guess what? You're coming with us."

"Where?"

"On a nature walk."

Even if it was a joke, Laszlo didn't like the sound of that. "I don't think so."

"Oh, I do," Roy said, running one hand over his shaved head, "because if you don't, I will have to beat the living shit out of you, right here. Now, put your boots on and get out to the truck."

Roy went back outside, leaving Seth and Alfie smirking in the doorway. "You don't get no free rides from Axel," Alfie said, turning the brim of his baseball cap backward. "And you better bring some water—it's a bitch of a walk."

"And wear some work gloves, if you've got 'em," Seth said. "You're gonna get your hands dirty."

Now Laszlo was even more pissed off. What the hell was he being recruited for? But since he knew it wouldn't be a good idea to cross Roy—the guy was not only nuts, but Axel's right-hand man—he put on his boots and fished the fancy white gloves from the trunk. Although thin and worn, they were a perfect fit.

Outside, Seth was in the driver's seat of the truck, and Roy and Alfie were crammed in the front beside him. There was no backseat—only the open flatbed. Maybe that was why they were laughing.

"Get in," Seth called out his window.

"Screw you," Laszlo said.

"Then try to keep up with us on your tricycle," Roy shouted. "We're heading north on Topanga Road."

They pulled out of the yard, dirt and dust kicking up from the tires. Laszlo looked at his pathetic little Vespa, and then at the big gleaming Harley, with saddlebags and upright ape handlebars, parked next to it. The key was still in the ignition—the Spiritz knew no one would be dumb enough to come onto the Compound and steal one of their bikes—and the silver helmet was resting on the black leather seat.

Getting on, he revved the throttle once or twice, and tore out of the Compound before whoever owned it could catch on; he was probably in the adobe house with Axel, getting stoned. It was a little hard to handle—so much faster and more powerful than the Vespa—but man, it felt good to have a real machine between his legs. In no time, he caught sight of the back of the old red truck, plodding up the two-lane blacktop with its bald tires and dragging tailpipe. He'd have raced right past it, but he didn't want Roy to see him on the borrowed bike yet. Christ, he thought, what if it was Roy's?

Instead, he dawdled behind, getting used to the raised grips and riding with his butt so far back on the curved seat. Once he had enough money together, he would get himself a Harley just like this one. He passed La Raza, keeping his head down in case some other biker spotted him riding a stolen motorcycle, and slowed down when he saw the sign for the Cornucopia coming into view. At the thought of Rafe fucking Miranda, *his* woman, a surge of anger rose in his throat like a hot bubble, and he wished he had a weapon, like that knife Seth always wore, stuck through his own belt.

But he saw no sign of either one of them. Even that purple piece of shit Rafe drove lately was nowhere around. What he *did* see in the side yard was Tripod running around in circles and that fat girl—Rafe's sister, Lucy—chasing after it. As if the bike had a will of its own, it did an immediate wheelie and jolted to a stop in front of the store. The Closed sign was hanging on the door, which meant Miranda was probably away. This was getting better all the time.

Still wearing his shades and helmet, he walked around to the side. Trip recognized him and didn't bark. But the girl just said, "Sorry, sir, the store's closed." She sounded like she had a bad cold.

He tried the back door, but sonofabitch, Miranda had already changed the locks.

"That's too bad," he said, not even breaking stride as he turned around and walked toward the trailer instead. Its door was hanging wide open.

"You can't go in there," Lucy cried.

He stepped up into it, taking off his shades. Jesus, what a pit. This guy was such a loser. No way Miranda could be doing him. Not after Laszlo. He took a quick look around and spotted a small floor safe tucked beside the fridge, but it was locked. When he tried to lift the whole thing free, he discovered that it had been bolted down.

"You can't be in here," Lucy said from the door, her voice, between coughs, trembling with fear.

"Almost done," he said, giving up on the safe. He'd need a jackhammer to get it loose. What could a guy like Rafe have in it, anyway? Then, on the bed, half-hidden by the pillow, he saw the corner of a green book. He pulled it out. It looked more like a diary. Handwritten, with a funky old smell to it. It dawned on him that it was probably another item from that damn trunk. It didn't look like much to him, but if Rafe had hung on to it, that was a good enough reason to steal it now. He took it, and Lucy dropped away from the door.

"You can't have that," she cried out, as he walked away. "That belongs to my brother."

He kept on walking, but she ran up behind him and tried to pry the book out from under his arm. He turned just enough to smack her across the face with the back of his gloved hand. She fell back, stunned.

"You tell that asshole brother of yours that if he wants it back, he should call Laszlo. Can you handle that?"

She didn't answer.

"Tell him it'll cost him five hundred bucks." It was a wild guess, but why not start out high?

He unfastened the saddlebags to toss the book inside, and was very happily surprised to find that the owner had supplied him with the necessities of biker life—a half pack of beef jerky sticks, some loose joints, brass knuckles, a length of chain suitable for swinging, and, incongruously enough, a dozen boxes of pseudoephedrine. Tucking the fattest joint into his shirt pocket, he climbed back onto the seat and maneuvered the bike around toward the road. Those ape handlebars really took some getting used to, and the front wheel wobbled until he'd picked up enough speed and momentum. Still, he was more than satisfied with the fruits of his little detour.

Gunning the engine, and learning to weave in and out of traffic using the opposite lane, he soon caught up to the back of the truck, and followed them another few miles. The left side of the roadway was mostly scrubby brush and stunted trees, but the other side often gave way to steep cliffs and deep gullies. Laszlo had heard stories about the bodies of Spiritz' enemies getting rolled down into those ravines, stripped naked and coated with grease and honey, to be pulled apart and picked clean by wild animals and insects. It certainly looked like an easy way to dispose of your unwanted visitors.

The truck waited in its lane for a passing camper van, then drove into and up a short turnoff. Laszlo followed them, and parked the bike off to one side. Roy, fortunately, was already plowing up into the woods, with a big empty net thrown over his shoulder, while Seth and Alfie unloaded a couple of low, flat carts on wheels from the back of the truck.

"Is that Jake's bike you're riding?" Seth said.

"Yeah," Laszlo said, having no idea which one of the gang was Jake. "He's cool with it."

Seth and Alfie exchanged a look of sly amusement. "Yeah, I'm sure he's *cool* with it," Alfie said, and Seth laughed.

"You drag one of these," Seth said, throwing a rope, attached to one of the carts, on the ground. "We'll take the other."

"Where?"

They didn't answer, just turned toward the rough chaparral and started dragging their dolly behind them. It bumped and rattled along, but the wheels were big enough to keep it moving most of the time. Laszlo's own cart kept getting snagged on the undergrowth, and he had to keep stopping to kick one corner or another loose. Bad as it was, it occurred to him it was going to be a lot worse coming back, when the carts were loaded with whatever they were planning to haul back.

He'd never actually spent much time up in the wilderness of the canyon; what interested him most were the margaritas and the waitresses down on the main drag at La Raza. But he had to admit that out here the air smelled different—there was the scent of dry grass and wildflowers, of soil and sun, cactus and eucalyptus leaves. The sky, often obscured by overhanging trees and cliff walls down by the road, was wide open here, and as blue as a robin's egg. For ten or fifteen minutes, the canyon worked its magic on him, but then he got bored and tired of dragging the cart.

The other three were usually about fifty yards ahead of him, but he still couldn't see where they were going. At one point, he saw a ramshackle hut, the kind of place where some witch might live, but then he spotted that forlorn pair of potheads who occasionally ate at La Raza standing outside, holding hoes and silently watching as they all marched by. Christ, why didn't that woman cover her boobs? They were way past their sell date.

No words were exchanged as Laszlo hauled his empty cart, sweating like a mule, past the two mute witnesses, then up over a ridge, down another, and finally, toward what looked like a cement bunker, almost level with the land, its roof tangled with rusty antennae. *This* was their destination?

Even the ground around it was desiccated—stained weird colors and littered with used batteries and empty blister packs for pills. The door was a few feet lower than the ground, and when Laszlo left his cart outside and went down the steps, he found Seth and Alfie already starting to wrap up lab gear in old newspapers and pack them into cardboard boxes. Roy had gone to the far end of the room, put a face mask over his nose and mouth, and was tinkering with some dusty beakers and tubes.

Although he'd sold plenty of meth in his time, Laszlo had never been in a lab before. He sure as hell knew he was in one now, however.

"Start taking these boxes outside," Seth said, and Laszlo picked up the one closest to the door and carried it out. The old white gloves he was wearing weren't exactly tailor-made for the job, but they fit him like a second skin. By the time he went back inside, two or three more boxes had been packed up, filled with everything from bottles of drain cleaner and antifreeze to table salt and matchboxes with those long red strike pads along one side.

After a few runs, he was sick of it, remembered the joint in his pocket, and striking one of the long matches, lit up. He took a heavy drag, waited a few seconds to gauge the effects, and blew out the smoke. Oh man, he thought, this was high-grade stuff. The Spiritz did not mess around. He took another hit or two, feeling lighter and mellower all the time.

In fact, as a peace offering, he thought it might be nice to share this premium weed, even if it wasn't exactly his own, with his fellow workers. It made him feel not only happy, but magnanimous, and the work might go a whole lot better if everybody was getting along. He stacked a couple more of the boxes on the carts, then went inside, the glowing joint between his lips.

Seth looked up at him, smacked Alfie on the shoulder, and then without a word, they both crashed into each other, bolting for the door and knocking over anything in their path. What the fuck? A bottle of something smashed on the floor, emitting a harsh chemical smell, and a box toppled onto its side, spilling other glassware onto the rough cement. With the joint extended like a peace pipe, Laszlo wandered a few steps closer to Roy, who whipped around, his eyes wide over the face mask, staring at his gloved fingers. Laszlo heard some muffled words that sounded like *stupid motherfucker!* before the explosion ripped up from the floor, turning Roy into a burning matchstick from the soles of his feet to the bald dome of his head, and rocketing Laszlo backward so fast he landed with a thud on the outside steps, the wind completely knocked out of him.

For some reason, his shirt and his shoes were gone. His face felt hot, and when he ran his fingers over the skin, it felt like his eyebrows were missing, too. So were the tips of the gloves.

The lab was an inferno, and he scuttled on all fours away from the belching flames and poisonous smoke. That euphoria he'd felt just thirty seconds before had been knocked out of him, too. Leaning back on his elbows, trying to come to his senses and figure out what came next, he felt a hard rock under his butt and scooted back another foot, only to realize the lump was still there, and it wasn't a rock. It was that metal flask from the trunk.

His throat felt like it had been scorched, too, and as he unscrewed the lid, he noticed that his fingernails were black. He tilted the flask to his lips, and the drink went down. It might not have been brandy after all—Laszlo wasn't exactly a connoisseur of fine liqueurs—but it had a bite like nothing else he'd ever tasted. After a slug or two, it suddenly threatened to come up on him, like lava about to spew from a volcano, but he swallowed hard and it went back down, soothing his ragged throat and settling like a glowing coal.

He moved back some more, looking around now for Seth and Alfie, but they must have hightailed it back toward their truck. All the salvaged supplies were still stacked on the dollies, and it dawned on him that if the flames got close enough, those carts were going to go off like nuclear bombs. He wasn't completely sure he could get up and walk, but he knew that staying put was a very bad idea.

10 November, 1888

'You're mad, the both of you,' Symonds said, when first Henley, and then I, said we were leaving. 'The streets are uncontrolled. The police have only the most tenuous hold on them.'

'That's precisely why I must go,' Henley said, waving his note pad. 'First-hand news for the next issue of the "Observer."'

'But Louis, you have no such excuse. Stay at least until all the protests have ended.'

'We won't know that until tomorrow's papers come out,' I said. 'For now, I really must go.'

My real reasons I could not confess, but a short time before, a squadron of mounted policemen had appeared at the top of Pall Mall, and backed by truncheon-wielding constables on foot, had beaten back the protesters, channelling the unruly mob towards their lawful meeting place in Trafalgar Square. After the mêlée subsided, they had left guards at the front of the club, and cleared away, among others, the man in the deerstalker hat. If there was ever a time for me to make a clean getaway, this was it.

Leaving the club, my boots crunched on the carpet of broken glass littering the front steps.

'You'll be going straight home, I hope, sir,' the constable said. 'It's not a fit night to be out and about.'

'Yes,' I lied, 'straight home.' Then I set my course for the town house where Constance Wooldridge lived with her maiden aunt. At the corner of every major avenue, a policeman stood guard, whistle around his neck, truncheon hanging from his belt and bull's-eye lantern in hand. My formal dress and top hat put me above suspicion, and the most I received was another warning to stay clear of the East End.

By the time I arrived at the house, all I could hear, and it depended entirely on the direction of the wind, was an occasional dull roar, like the sound of the heavy waves crashing on the rocks of the Skerryvore lighthouse. Nowhere along the way had I seen any sign of the man in the deerstalker hat. The derringer, however, was still neatly nestled in my pocket.

The fog, which had abated earlier, was now returning with a vengeance, and so I had to remain closer than I would have liked to Constance's door if I hoped to keep watch. Lloyd, she said, had planned to come by once the demonstration was over, but was it officially done yet? It didn't sound so. I took out my cigar case, and sheltered in the doorway of a closed tailor's shop, struck a lucifer against the brick to light a cigar. Dr Rüedi would no doubt have had a seizure at the very sight of a pulmonary patient putting a rum-soaked crook to his lips, but regardless of his constitution, a man needs his whiskey and his cigars, or what's the point of living at all?

The fanlight above the town house door was illuminated, as was a single window on the second storey. Once or twice, I thought I detected a silhouette moving behind it. My coat kept me reasonably warm, but with tendrils of fog creeping up the street, it wouldn't be long before the chill had settled in my chest and set off a volley of coughs that would be sure to give me away to anyone with ears to hear.

And Lloyd had ears. It had long struck me that he had a marked propensity to peep through keyholes, listen through walls, prowl about the house at all hours, and, in general, stick his nose in where it did not belong. More than once, I'd found him in my study, ostensibly looking for a new nib for his pen, or, more recently, claiming he needed the cheval glass to assess his attire. 'There are other mirrors in this house,' I'd said.

'Not so good as this one. This one provides the full effect.'

That much I could vouch for, in a way he would never understand. When I am under the influence of the elixir, it seems to be an enchanted glass, the only one in which I am able to capture a true reflection of my basest self and corrupted nature. The cheval glass does not lie, much as one might wish it to do so.

I was nearly done with the cigar when I perceived, through the growing fog, a man moving slowly, and in a rather cautious fashion, towards the town house. His back was to me, and he had a bouquet of flowers in his arms. But unless Lloyd had gained in height and trimmed his figure, this was someone else. I waited to see if he would approach a neighbouring door, but he stopped, instead, in front of the Wooldridge house, straightening his collar. Was this some new suitor, unaware of the fraught situation into which he was entering? I instantly dropped the glowing cigar behind me and crushed it underfoot.

He put one foot on the lowest step, his eyes fixed on the fanlight, then paused, looking up and down the street. Such timidity never won a lady's heart. He went up another, adjusting the flowers he carried, his head down as if rehearsing some lines. By the time he got to the top step and raised his hand to knock on the door, I was prepared, if necessary, to intervene, even if it meant posing as some bibulous uncle paying an unexpected call.

But I was stunned instead at the sudden appearance of a cloaked figure in a top hat—had he materialized from the fog

itself?—vaulting up the steps behind him and knocking the bouquet loose with his cane. The flowers scattered as the suitor, who
could never have even seen his assailant, raised his hands to defend
himself. But the cane came down relentlessly, again and again, on
his head, his arms, his shoulders. The interior lamp illuminating the
fanlight was abruptly extinguished. The suitor rolled to the stair railing, used it to lift himself up, and then, propelled by a swift kick to
his rear, stumbled the rest of the way down the steps and ran blindly
in my direction. As he came close to the tailor shop, I whispered,
'Here, come in here!'

In his panic, he could barely see me, and I had to grab him by
the elbow and pull him out of sight. His attacker was not in pursuit.
He crumpled over, his shaking hands on his unsteady knees, and it
was only when he caught his breath enough to say, 'Thank you, sir.
I'm in your debt,' that I recognized his voice.

'Desmond?'

His head snapped up, and with an equal measure of surprise,
he said, 'Stevenson?'

'My God, are you all right?' There was a gash over his right eye,
and he would be sure to show some bruises the next day, but he
seemed otherwise intact.

'Hardly. But at least I'm alive.'

'Who was it that attacked you?' I asked, dreading the answer I
nonetheless expected.

'Who do you think?' he said. 'You wouldn't be here, would you,
if you didn't know.'

Now I did. Every word Constance had told me was true, and the
proof was right there, trembling beside me in the darkened doorway.

'I've got to go and find him,' I said. 'Will you help?'

'Help find him? Have you lost your mind? I don't want to clap
eyes on him ever again.'

'He has to be stopped.'

'That's what solicitors are for. I'll be swearing out a complaint for assault first thing tomorrow.'

But there was no time to waste if I hoped to catch up to him, and clapping Desmond on the back, I left him cowering there in the tailor's entryway.

Lloyd was gone, but as he had not passed us, he must have gone in the other direction. Sticking close to the shadows, I hurried along, and at the corner I looked both ways. A few doors down to my left, a pawnbroker was standing in front of his broken windows, assessing the damage.

'Excuse me,' I said, 'but did you see a man run by here in the last minute or two?'

He looked me up and down, as if I were a dolt, and said, 'I saw a lot of men tonight—louts and thieves and sons of whores.'

'A gentleman', I said, 'in an opera cape and a top hat, carrying a cane?'

'Gentlemen don't do this,' he said, gesturing at the ruined shop, and turning away in dismissal.

I ran the other way, holding my handkerchief to my mouth to warm the air entering my feeble lungs. I could not keep this up for very long, especially as the fog was growing thicker with every step I took towards the East End. The aura of menace was still in the air, a faint glow in the sky where a fire was raging unchecked, an angry shout carried on the vagrant wind, the shrill blast of a police whistle. When I heard the rattle of carriage wheels, I swiftly hailed the passing brougham—the faint trace of the original owner's coat of arms still visible under a lacquer of black paint—and told the elderly coachman whom to look for as we made our way down the street.

'Keep the horse to a slow trot,' I said, stepping off the footplate into the compartment, and latching the door behind me.

I kept my head out the little window as we headed in the direction of Whitechapel, staring into every nook and alleyway.

'You're sure you don't want me to turn around and head back towards Mayfair?' the coachman called down from his dicky box, but I instructed him to hold his course. 'In this direction it's going to be double the fare,' he warned.

'Steady on.'

But what was I going to do even if I found Lloyd? Could I persuade him to come home with me? Could he be reasoned with? Who was this creature of such unbridled malevolence?

The fog was denser than ever, and we hadn't gone another half mile before the carriage slowed, and I heard the driver call out, 'Make way, or you'll be run over!'

But whomever he was addressing must not have complied, because the coachman was pulling back even harder on the reins, the carriage was grinding to a halt, and though I was craning my head out the window, I could not see past the flanks of the horse.

'What's going on?' I demanded.

'Let go of those!' I heard the coachman exclaim, and then there was the sound of a scuffle. Shifting to the opposite window, I saw the back of the old man as he was hauled down from his seat and cast aside as if he were no more than a worn-out shoe.

I drew my head back just as the door was unlatched, and a devil of fury leapt inside. All I could see in the gloom of the interior was a deerstalker hat and loden coat, a thatch of blond hair, and a knife blade slashing at the air. The springs of the carriage jounced, the horse whinnied, and with no one holding the reins, it bolted down the cobblestoned street.

The German and I were rolled about like marbles in a jar, the knife tearing at the buttoned upholstery, my boots kicking out at him, as the panic-stricken horse dragged the carriage at a terrifying rate of speed, the wheels banging over every loose stone in the road, the cabin tilting wildly from one side to the other.

'Ich bin der Sohn von Yannick!' he hissed, and even with the rudimentary German I had picked up in Davos, I could understand that much of what he was saying. He was declaring himself the son of Yannick—I had a flash of the wolf's head, flying through the window of the rail car—come to London, all these years later, no doubt to avenge his father's death.

Though he was much stronger and younger than I, there is something about fighting for one's life that provides extraordinary energy. I held tenaciously to the arm holding the knife, even as the runaway carriage teetered and rocked and threatened at any second to turn over entirely.

'Ich bin Josef!' he snarled, his face so close to mine that his hot spittle stained my cheeks.

With a sudden yank, he got his arm free, but as he reared back to strike the fatal blow, my fumbling fingers found the derringer in my pocket, and without so much as removing it, I fired through the fabric. The bullet struck him close to the shoulder, and I think it was the shock more than the shot that knocked him to the floor.

The horse, reacting to the explosion, tore off even faster—I could hear voices shouting at us in alarm—and then, the carriage crashed over a kerb, the axle snapping, and the whole world went topsy-turvy, end over end, before we all went sliding into the side of a building.

I was too stunned to move at first, but Josef was somehow pinned by the splintered floorboards and seat backs. I groped for a door handle before realizing that the entire door had been wrenched loose. Slithering like an eel, I extricated myself from the wreckage as several hands slipped under my arms to hoist me to my feet.

'You're all right now,' someone said. 'Can you walk?' another asked.

When I stood, I saw that we had smashed into the brick wall of a lodging house, and two men on the other side of the carriage were dragging Yannick's son out, while another struggled to free the rearing horse from its tangled harness.

'Where's the coachman?' someone asked.

But then they saw the knife, still clutched in Josef's hand, and backed away.

Shouting something else in German—I heard the word 'Vater', or father—he tried to clamber over the ruined carriage to get at me, but between the knife and the outburst in that foreign tongue, the crowd thought that they had at last brought their quarry to ground.

'It's Jack!'

'It's the Ripper!'

One of the onlookers jerked a broken spoke loose from the wheel, said 'Now you're done for,' and swiped at him with the jagged tip.

Josef knocked the spar aside, but a man in a blue conductor's uniform jumped at his back and tried to pin his arms to his sides. Even with a bullet in his shoulder, the Swiss peasant was able to shake him off. Sweeping the knife in a circle, he held the others at bay as he backed up. A woman screamed from the lodging-house window and threw a flower pot down at him, a boy hurled an empty bottle, several men tried to surround him, hunched over like wrestlers entering the ring; but he broke through and took to his heels.

'Stop him!' the woman cried.

'It's the Ripper!' the man with the spoke hollered at some men down the street.

But they ducked out of his path, as if he were a rabid dog running their way, and the ones chasing him were soon as lost in the fog as he was.

'You've had a narrow escape, you have,' one man said, brushing at my shoulder, as another one held out my crumpled hat, salvaged from the ruins, and said, 'He won't get far. They'll catch that bastard and string him up from a lamp post!" He spat on the pavement to emphasize his point.

'There's a bar round the corner', the conductor said, 'in the Aldgate Arms. I expect you'll be wanting a glass of gin to calm your nerves.'

On that, he was correct, though it was more than a drink I wanted. I doubted a whole bottle would do the trick. I allowed him to steer me towards the bar, but it was only as I passed through its double doors that the name of the place tolled some distant bell in my head.

'That's a story to tell your grandchildren," the conductor said, settling me onto a stool, "how you took a ride with the Ripper and lived to tell the tale.'

But the Aldgate Arms – why was it familiar to me?

TOPANGA CANYON— CALIFORNIA

Present Day

As if walking through the woods in boots wasn't bad enough, walking in bare burned feet was agony. Every time Laszlo took a step, something stung his soles. When the Potheads' place showed up, he saw his salvation on their clothesline: an old blue work shirt, and just under them a pair of neon-green Crocs. He was putting them on when Mr. Pothead crept out of the hovel, like a mole, and without commenting on the clothes heist, said, "I smell smoke."

"Yeah, and where there's smoke, there's fire," Laszlo said.

Mrs. Pothead emerged—pulling on a blouse, thank God—and carrying a plastic crate containing a yowling cat.

"What happened?" Mr. Pothead asked, his eyes anxiously scanning the horizon.

"An accident. I'd get out of here fast if I were you."

Three squirrels went scampering past, and a flock of crows overhead flew toward the other side of the canyon.

Laszlo was searching for buttons on the shirt—it appeared to have only one left—when there was a loud explosion, and a plume of noxious black smoke suddenly shot up into the sky like a geyser. A few seconds later, it was followed by a second explosion. Both carts now accounted for.

Laszlo wasn't about to wait for the wildfire to go out of control. He scampered across the open chaparral, the rubber Crocs slapping the bottom of his feet, the open shirt flapping. He just hoped he could follow the path back out of there. It wasn't like he was some woodsman, like that asshole Rafe. But he figured if he just kept going over one slope, then down the next, he'd eventually come out at the main road. With any luck, he'd be close to the spot where he'd parked Jake's motorcycle.

As he ran, the image of Roy, roasting like a pig on an upright spit, kept popping into his mind. Was he alive while on fire? He had the discomfiting idea that he had been. True, he'd never liked the guy, but the look on his face, even after the flames had enveloped it, was one of shock. Not so much pain. Shock. Like he was stuck behind a waterfall of fire and didn't know how he'd wound up there.

It was a miracle that Laszlo had been thrown clear. Eyebrows would grow back. The only pain he was feeling now was in his gut—a slow, but growing, wrenching sensation. He put it down to being winded, from running so hard, for so long, and he slackened his pace to let it pass—but it didn't let up. He felt like the pain was bending him over. His shoulders were drooping, his arms swinging at his sides like he was some monkey in the zoo. He couldn't keep the shoes on at all anymore, and when they fell off, he finally didn't care. It actually felt better to be moving along without them. He didn't even feel like he was running anymore—he was loping like a wolf. He was half-inclined to drop to all fours.

A helicopter swooped by, so close to the ground that he could see the wraparound shades on the pilot as he looked for the source of the smoke. You could say one thing for a meth lab explosion—it sure as hell wouldn't leave much evidence behind. Roy was no more than a bunch of charred bones by now, and even his teeth had probably been reduced to cinders and ash.

Panting like a dog, his tongue hanging out of his mouth, Laszlo eventually broke free of the scraggly brush and trees and saw a slice of the Topanga blacktop. He ran down to the edge of the road, and already cars were zipping by on their way out of the canyon. Locals, who knew what might be coming, had piled their kids and pets into their cars and split before the fire engines came and the road closings and detours began.

But he couldn't see the truck or the motorcycle and he couldn't tell if he was too far up the road or down it. He tried to flag a passing dune buggy down, but the girl in the passenger seat looked at him like he was something from a freak show. The hell with her, he thought. Just because he was missing some facial hair and wearing rags, that was no reason to cop such an attitude. He felt his hands, still in the tattered remnants of the gloves, clench as if they were around her throat, and he flashed on an image of her terrified open mouth, silently screaming.

His hand fumbled at the back pocket of his jeans, and, unscrewing the flask, he took another swig. The stuff was kind of foul, all in all, but it was wet, he'd say that much for it, and damn if it didn't pack a wallop! It was like getting a punch in the stomach and a jolt of electricity all at one time.

He decided to take a chance and trot south, and around the next bend he was rewarded with the sight of Seth and Alfie, huffing and puffing and climbing into their old red truck.

"Wait up!" he shouted at them, waving his arms. He really didn't feel like riding Jake's Harley right now; the road was getting congested and his arms felt too weird to hang on to the raised handlebars. "I'm coming with you!"

Alfie, at the passenger side, stared at him like he wasn't even sure who it was, said something to Seth across the hood, and they both jumped in and locked their doors. By the time Laszlo had staggered to the turnoff, they were backing out so fast they were burning rubber.

"Hold up!" Laszlo shouted, banging one hand on the rear wheel cover as they pulled away. The last button popped off his shirt, and now his whole chest was exposed—darker, and weirdly hairier, than usual. Just what had all those chemicals in that explosion done to him?

The bike was still right where he'd left it, though, and now he had no choice but to ride it back to the Compound. Unless that guy Jake was stoned into oblivion, by now he had come to and figured out his bike had been stolen, and when Laszlo showed up with it, he'd be in the mood for murder. But instead of worrying about it at all, which he might have done at one time, Laszlo thought it was simply funny. He looked forward to a confrontation, something he'd never have done in the past, except on those rare occasions when he knew he was bigger, stronger, or better armed than his opponent. Now he didn't care anymore. He felt powerful, impervious, and itching for a fight.

He pulled on the silver helmet—it felt like it didn't sit quite right on his skull anymore—slithered onto the leather saddle, booted the kickstand up with his bare foot, and revved the throttle. True, his arms felt oddly cocked and it wasn't easy to grab the handlebars, but he also felt stronger than usual, and it was as if the massive horsepower of the Harley was channeling itself right up into his body. He leaned back on the seat, his grimy soles stuck on the footpegs, the hems of his jeans dragging on the dirt, and shot into the passing stream of cars and vans and campers. He was king of the road, lord of all he surveyed, and all these other people were just peasants passing through his world. And he was okay with that, really . . . just so long as they didn't cross him.

10 November, 1888

I had downed several glasses of the finest whiskey the Aldgate Arms had on hand before my nerves calmed enough from the attack in the coach to allow my faculties to return. I was looking at the peculiar font used to inscribe the hotel name above the back mirror of the bar (writers are perhaps the only creatures besides typesetters to take note of such things) when it came to me. I had seen it on my own hall table, imprinted on the envelopes marked Second and then Third Notice, and addressed to one Mr Osbourne.

A few of the men who had attempted to capture and chase Josef had filtered back into the bar, despondent at allowing the notorious Jack the Ripper to slip from their grasp. 'It's like 'e just melted into the damn fog,' one of them remarked.

'But at least we've all got a good look at 'im now,' another commented. 'He'll know not to show his face around Whitechapel any more.'

'Or talk that German. He won't dare do that, neither.'

'It's just like the papers said all along. A foreigner. No Englishman would ever do such things.'

And perhaps they were right, I thought—not about the relative barbarity of various nationalities (I have seen enough of the world to know that vice and virtue are evenly distributed)—but in concluding that Yannick's son was indeed the infamous killer. Did he not fit the description in some of its most salient aspects? Had he not appeared in London, with murder on his mind, during the dread epoch of Jack's emergence? Was a butcher's knife not his choice of weapon? While I might have been the ultimate target—and for that I began to feel a crushing burden of guilt—who was to say that he did not keep his blade sharp in the meantime by whetting it on the necks of the slaughtered women?

'Can I get you another, sir?' the proprietor said from behind the bar. 'This one's on the house. You helped us almost nab him.'

'Thank you, but no. You can do me one other service, however.'

'Name it.'

'Do you, by any chance, have a hotel guest named Lloyd Osbourne?'

The proprietor put the bottle down on the bar. 'We have a Samuel Osbourne by that last name. But why would you be asking that?'

My guess had been correct.

The man leaned in closer, and lowering his voice, said, 'Are you a friend of the gentleman?'

'I have reason to believe that he is behind on his bill.'

At this, he perked up considerably, and extended his hand. 'Donohue's the name. And you?'

'Stevenson.' I left it at that. 'He keeps a room here, then?'

'That he does.'

'May I see it?'

'Well, now,' he said, rubbing his stubbly jowls, 'I don't know that that would be quite right.'

I took two ten-pound notes from my wallet and slid them across the bar. 'Does that settle his account?'

'If you will just follow me,' he said, drying his hands on a bar cloth and slapping it over his shoulder.

We went up a back stairway on a worn carpet runner, and down a hall to a room at the farthest end and around a sharp corner. 'Professor Osbourne, he likes his privacy. Comes and goes at all hours. Most of the time, I don't see no more of him than the back of his coat.'

'Professor?'

'He's a gentleman, with a house on Cavendish Square, but a scholar by trade. Teaches at Oxford, I believe he said, but does good works at the Whitechapel Union infirmary on Charles Street, not more than a mile from here.' He stopped before unlocking the door and said, 'If you're a friend of his, why don't you know that?'

'I simply thought he kept his charitable work a secret.'

Donohue snorted—the ten-pound notes were still having their effect—and turned the lock. He lit the gaslight just inside the room, and once he'd gone, I leaned back against the door, surveying Lloyd's private sanctuary.

Like the rest of the Aldgate Arms, the room showed signs of having once been more respectable. There was an intricate William Morris wallpaper—the trellis pattern in pink and green—but patches of it were missing. The washstand in the corner was sturdily made, though nicked and scratched, and the basin atop it needed a thorough scrubbing. The canopied bed, like the seat of the wing chair by the casement window, sagged. Of Lloyd himself, there were few indications—just a spare shirt and trousers hanging in the wardrobe, a pair of velvet slippers that I remembered seeing him wear at home, a few books by Wilkie Collins and Thomas De Quincey, both of whom I knew he admired. I tried the bottom drawer of the wardrobe, but found it securely locked.

The only thing that looked new was a mirror, much like the cheval glass in my study. It stood beside a writing desk on which I saw a stack of papers and blank postal notes, a clutch of pens, and bottles of ink.

Sitting in the chair, which creaked even beneath my insubstantial weight, I picked up the top pages of the stack and quickly saw that it was a novel in progress—a farcical story involving some complicated scheme to win a fortune in a tontine. So he was writing something, after all. Its theme was no surprise—Lloyd's thoughts never strayed far from fortune and fame.

I had read no more than a few pages before the events of the day, and the night, took their toll. My eyes closed, and I drifted into sleep. My Brownies slumbered, too, leaving me to dream of nothing more than men in deerstalker hats, skulking through fog-bound streets and alleyways, in search of easy prey. I awoke with a start when a key turned in the lock, and in the flickering light of the gas lamp, I saw a figure in a top hat and black cloak, the collar turned up all around the face, slipping into the room. He did not see me at first, but stood, as if puzzled, before the burning light.

'I fell asleep with it on,' I said, and he whipped around so hastily his cape swirled like a matador's.

In his hand, he held a leather satchel, just like one a teacher might carry to hold his books and papers.

'Were you giving a late lecture, Professor?'

His head remained buried in the folds of the cape, his hat was squashed down low on his brow—all I could see were his eyes, dark and angry, as he took in the sight of me.

But it was enough. It was then that I suddenly realized the truth.

'My God, Lloyd. My God.'

I heard a grunt of acknowledgement.

'You have broken into my cabinet.'

'Hardly a challenge.'

'You have drunk the elixir.'

'What's good for the goose,' he said, his voice hoarse but recognizable.

'Let me look at you.'

'So you can gloat?'

'So I can pity.'

'There's no cause for that,' he retorted, dropping the satchel onto the bed. 'I like it.' Opening the wardrobe doors, he hung his hat on a hook, then his cloak, straightened his vest, and turned to me, arms akimbo, legs spread. 'Ecce homo.'

The sight was almost more than I could bear. His features were contorted into a hateful mask, his body was misshapen and stunted. Even the curls of hair on his head, matted down from the top hat, seemed coiled like snakes. And all I could think was that I—in the desperate search for my own cure—had brought this about. This was all my doing.

'You must have settled my bill with Donohue, or he wouldn't have let you in. I don't even allow the maid. He knows that only Constance is to be admitted in my absence.'

'That's a lie.'

He sat on the edge of the bed, taken aback by my rejoinder. 'Is it?'

'I have spoken to Constance.'

'What won't a woman say?'

'I have seen you assault Desmond.'

'Have you now.' He studied the tips of his wet boots. 'Seems you've been acting the sleuth. What else do you know?'

'I know that before dawn breaks, you will undergo another agonizing metamorphosis. Don't forget, I have lived through it myself. I was its reluctant pioneer.'

'Ah, but there's the difference between us. You regret the change; I regret the return.'

'You can't mean that.'

'Wait and see,' he sneered.

I had every intention of doing so. 'What do you do here?' I asked, taking in the four tattered walls of the room.

'Live,' he retorted. 'My own life, my own way. Without my mother snooping into my affairs, asking if I've had my breakfast yet or how I slept or where I went the night before. Without you forever asking how my work is progressing.' He jutted his sharp chin at the pages on the table. 'That's how it's going, by the way; you can see for yourself.'

'I read a bit. It's good.'

'I don't care if it is, or isn't. I don't care what you think, Louis. I'm my own man now—Samuel Lloyd Osbourne. I'm not some worthless fop like Desmond, from some godforsaken shire in the middle of nowhere. I'm an American', he said proudly, 'from California. It's time I acknowledged as much.'

'Is that where you want to go, then?'

'In due time.'

Though I would not have missed the burden of Lloyd, I knew full well that his mother would feel compelled to follow him anywhere he chose to go, and I wondered at what hard choice this might present for me. Without Fanny, I would feel as bereft as Robinson Crusoe.

His voice, as he had been speaking, had grown more strained, his words slurred, and I knew that the transformation was beginning to take place. The cords in his neck had begun to bulge, and it was almost as if one could see the blood pumping through the arterial passageways. His head drooped; his eyes became unfocussed.

'Take some water,' I said, filling a cracked teacup from the pitcher beside the basin and bringing it to him.

He took the cup and slurped at it, as an animal might do. Water ran down his chin and onto his waistcoat, spotted with dirt and gravy and red wine.

'Lie down,' I said, lifting his legs onto the bed and plumping a dilapidated pillow under his head. He did not resist. A palsy appeared to be taking over his limbs, a slight shiver that gradually became more and more pronounced and uncontrollable. I remembered an occasion when I had experienced a seizure so violent that I had bitten my tongue raw. I looked for something now to wedge between Lloyd's teeth, but all I saw was a bit of embroidered lace on the bed stand. I quickly rolled it into the shape of a horse's bit, and tucked it firmly between his jaws. The protruding end bore the distinct initials CW.

His trophy from Constance's laundry basket at the Belvédère Hotel.

The shaking became so powerful that the entire bed rocked on its spindly legs. I dipped my handkerchief in the water basin and mopped his brow with it. Sweat glistened on his skin, still dusky from the effects of the elixir, and his eyes rolled up so far into his head that only the whites—bearing a yellowish cast of their own—showed. His jaws clamped down on the lacy cylinder so hard that, without it, I feared his teeth might have broken. How often had he taken the drug? How had I been so blind to the theft of it? More than once, I had noted that the amount seemed unduly diminished, but I had always put it down to my own immoderation. Under its influence, I assumed that I had lost any sense of my own actions and intent.

I heard the church bells toll five and then six o'clock before the change had been completed. Lloyd, restored to himself, lay on the bed, sleeping the sleep of the dead. His skin was white again, his features recognizable. I went back to the armchair and fell into it, exhausted beyond words. Dawn was breaking, its feeble light bathing the dismal room and its even more dismal tableau in a pale blue wash, the same blue light of an Edinburgh morn. But oh, what a vast chasm yawned between those days and this. What, in God's name, I wondered, had I done?

TOPANGA CANYON— CALIFORNIA

Present Day

Even from a distance, Rafe had noticed the helicopters heading toward Topanga Canyon. At first he thought it might just be part of a police chase—every few weeks one of them was caught on tape and endlessly replayed on the evening news—but then he saw that at least one of them was traveling from the west with a full bucket of ocean water, up to twenty-six hundred gallons suspended from a cable, and he knew it spelled trouble.

His first thought was of Lucy, alone at the trailer, and he told Miranda to fish his cell phone out of the pocket of his sport coat and check it for messages.

It was an older model, and she had to fumble with it for a second.

"Sorry," she said, extending it to him, "it might be time for an upgrade. Now it's on again."

"It was off?" he said, suddenly remembering the admonition to do so at the memorial service. Ever since, he'd been totally absorbed in what Bentley had told him about the Stevenson family connection to this very part of the world, and as a result he'd forgotten to turn it back on.

"Check the messages for me," he said, keeping both hands on the wheel of the Land Rover and both eyes on the road. Already, twenty minutes from the Cornucopia, the two lanes were getting snarled, and a flood of animals—always the most reliable harbingers of trouble—were scampering or scooting south across the road. Raccoons, skunks, rabbits, opossums, deer—he'd already seen more sad roadkill in an afternoon than he had all year.

"You have five texts, all from Lucy," she said.

"What do they say?" he asked, trying to quell the panic rising in his chest. He should never have left her alone there. What had he been thinking? "Did she get sicker?"

Miranda was uncharacteristically silent as she read them, and it was only after Rafe pressed her again that she said, "It sounds like she had a visit from Laszlo."

"She says that?"

"She says it was the man who used to live here with me. She can't remember his name."

"What happened?"

"Well, I think it's all okay in the end," she said, still studying the messages.

"For God's sake, Miranda, what happened?"

"He went into your trailer. She couldn't stop him. He took a book from the bed. The old book, she says."

"The journal."

"And he said you could have it back if you gave him some money."

"Where is he now? Is he gone? Is she okay?"

"Yes," but there was a tiny note of reservation in her voice.

"Miranda," he repeated, "is Lucy okay?"

"She says he hit her."

And for a second Rafe saw red—a flash as bright as a traffic light.

"But she seems like she's okay now," Miranda said, laying a hand on his arm to calm him. "I mean, she's texting, isn't she? And he's definitely gone."

He grabbed the phone from her hand and hit the speed dial. But as expected, the call did not go through. The canyon was always bad, but with all the choppers overhead, the police and fire engines starting to emerge, plus the fact that everyone in the canyon was trying to make or take a call of their own, it was impossible. All Rafe could do was step on the gas—to make matters worse, the low-fuel light had just gone on—and try to weave around the slowest-moving vehicles in his way. Normally, they'd have slowed down or pulled over to let him pass— it was canyon etiquette—but today they weren't doing the courteous thing and edging into the turnoffs—probably because they knew no one would ever let them back onto the road again.

Rafe's fingers were clutching the wheel so hard they'd turned white.

"Rafe," Miranda said, "it's going to be okay. Really. It won't do any good if we get into an accident trying to get there. It's only another ten minutes. She'll be fine."

But she hadn't been fine—she hadn't been fine that day he left her—for only ten minutes—at that community pool. He had the awful sensation that he had done the same thing, all over again. He'd failed her, even if the repercussions this time were not nearly as bad. He'd left her alone, and now look what had happened. Given the chaos in the canyon, look at what could *still* happen.

He blasted the horn—it made a trumpeting sound—and then swerved around the U-Haul truck ahead of them, then back into the proper lane.

Miranda held her tongue.

And he did it again, leapfrogging and hopscotching through the traffic, gaining whatever time he could.

He poked his head out the window to look ahead at the unending cavalcade of cars and other vehicles snaking their way around the perilous turns and switchbacks of Topanga Canyon Road. The air was noticeably more acrid. It carried the smell of burning sage and chaparral, dried cactus, and parched soil, and under it all, a tinge of something foreign, and chemical in nature. The smoke was drifting overhead from a northerly direction—the direction of the derelict meth lab . . . though maybe not as derelict as he'd thought.

Dusk was falling, the smoke darkening the sky even further. There was a constant whirring from the helicopters flying overhead, some of them dropping tons of water, some no doubt just reporting on the wildfire. A coyote skipped across the road, its tail and head down, barely missed by a passing SUV. Diego and Frida were somewhere in there, too. Along with the first wolf to have made it this far south.

He saw a tiny opening and jerked the wheel to the left, got around a station wagon packed with barking dogs, and settled in again behind a truck—a red one, with a dragging tailpipe.

"Is that Seth and Alfie's truck?" Miranda said.

It was. And maybe their buddy Laszlo was with them.

"Can you see who's in it?" Rafe said, quickly speeding up to close the gap between them.

"Rafe, you're going to run into them!"

Before doing just that, he swung to their left, and drew abreast of them long enough to look into the cab. Seth was driving, and when he saw who was in the Land Rover, he gave them the finger. Alfie hollered something Rafe couldn't hear over the long shriek of the air horn on the semi barreling his way.

Miranda shouted "Watch out!" And he pulled back behind the truck in the nick of time. "Rafe, come on—you're going to get us killed."

But Rafe's blood was up, and he could swear the truck was deliberately slowing down, just to impede his progress. Did they know something he didn't about what had happened back at the store, or what might be awaiting him there?

He hit the horn and signaled that he wanted to pass, but if anything the truck slowed down more and even edged a bit onto the center line, blocking his view of what was coming.

"Let it go, Rafe. We'll be home in a few minutes no matter what."

Taking advantage of their slowed speed, he shot the Rover into the left lane, but as soon as he had, Seth steered the truck left, too, and when Rafe fell back, and then tried again, Seth actually jerked his truck so hard it banged into the side of the Rover and knocked it farther toward the cliff running along the south side of the road.

Miranda screamed, and Rafe was barely able to wrestle the Rover back toward the land side. Alfie had turned around in his seat and was staring back, laughing like a maniac. They were coming up on Topanga Hardware and Locks, and Rafe knew that on the right-hand side of the road there was a wide and long turnoff for weight-bearing trucks that wanted to slow the momentum of their descent. He could use that to swing around them on the right. When he saw the sign for it, he gunned ahead, and skidded off the asphalt and into the dirt and grit of the turnoff.

"What are you doing?" Miranda asked in alarm.

Rafe just hit the gas harder, gaining on the truck, but he knew he had to get past them before the turnoff ended. Alfie in the passenger seat looked startled to see him coming up on the right, quickly said something to Seth, and the truck sped up, too, not enough to pull away—Rafe doubted it had the horsepower—but enough to keep him hemmed in. Rafe swung his own wheel to the left, hoping to sneak in ahead of them, and managed to make it with only inches to spare. But Seth wasn't about to give up; he drove his front bumper into the back of the Rover, sending its back tires fishtailing on the road. Rafe was barely able to maintain control of the car. Miranda braced her hands against the dashboard.

Seth, however, had overcorrected, and his truck drifted out of the right lane and then into the left just as the turnoff was ending and a hairpin turn was coming up.

Rafe sped up to give the truck room to get back into the right lane, just as he heard a siren blaring and a horn blasting. Before Seth could get out of its way, a fire engine with a long ladder, making a wide turn, emerged like a monster from its lair. Its front grille smacked straight into the truck, pushing it back up the road so hard the old red flatbed went up on its back tires, like a stallion rearing, before twisting to the side and tumbling over a low white guardrail.

"Oh my God!" Miranda screamed, but Rafe could only catch a glimpse of what had happened in the rearview mirror. He was desperately trying to pilot the Rover down the incline and through the gaggle of cars that had already paused to make way for the fire engine.

"Rafe, they went over the cliff!"

He nodded. He knew.

"What should we do?"

But what could they do? Already the traffic behind him was piling up—there was a Hummer riding his back bumper—and the firemen would know better than anyone else what needed to be done to rescue them . . . if rescue was even possible.

The only thing Rafe could think of doing was getting back to the house. "Try Lucy on the cell again!"

"It won't work," she said. "You know that."

"Keep trying anyway!"

A bobcat shot across the road, dodging between the cars and shooting under the guardrail.

Rafe wiped his sweaty hands, one at a time, on the fabric seats, and deliberately putting all other thoughts out of his mind, focused his attention entirely on the road ahead. And Lucy.

11 November, 1888

It was perhaps a matter of my heritage, but I could not take my eyes off the silver-plated lamp mounted inside the commissioner's carriage. No son and grandson of lighthouse builders could help but be fascinated by the ingenuity of its design. What might have originated as a hearse lamp mounted on the outside of a funeral carriage had been modified to sit firmly atop a fixed desk, impervious to the joltings of the carriage by virtue of a spring-loaded base, and offering a quartet of bevelled glass ports and interior mirrors that at once emitted and magnified the candlelight from within. Putting my hand over its crown, I felt the narrow vent through which the heat was allowed to escape from the mechanism, lest the glass crack or the brass fittings become too hot to touch.

'When you are quite done . . .' Inspector Abberline said dryly.

'Yes,' I said, withdrawing my hand. 'I've never seen a lamp quite like this.' It made the cabin of the carriage feel as if one were sitting inside a hearth.

'The commissioner had it specially made for his coach so that he could continue his work even after dark.'

But Sir Charles Warren, whose insignia as head of the police force was proudly emblazoned on the doors of the coach, was absent. He had lent the carriage to Abberline in an attempt, I could only surmise, to show his flag in the precincts of the city most affected by the Ripper's most recent crime . . . for another crime, perfectly in keeping with the modus operandi of its predecessors, had been committed.

This time, a young prostitute, Mary Jane Kelly, had been discovered by the landlord's agent, dispatched to collect the overdue rent on her hovel off Dorset Street in Whitechapel. But if the early accounts in the penny press were true, and Abberline had so far said nothing to deny it, there were but two new wrinkles in this instance.

'He did his work indoors this time, and not out on the street or in some alleyway,' he said, unsealing an envelope bearing the Scotland Yard address. 'Which may account for his—what shall we call it—thoroughness.'

He slipped from the envelope three or four photographs and laid them out on the carriage desk before us. Inured as I should have been to these horrors, having attended the autopsy of Annie Chapman, I was nonetheless appalled at the images taken by the Criminal Investigation Department's official photographer. The victim—a twenty-five-year-old from Limerick, given to singing, and reputedly so pretty that she had once been a wealthy gentleman's consort in France—had been reduced to a mangled pile of flesh and bones. She was splayed on her bed, legs spread, abdominal cavity eviscerated, and all of her internal organs placed willy-nilly, as other photographs showed, around her on the blood-soaked bed or elsewhere in the tiny room. Her kidneys rested under her head, her liver between her feet. Her intestines were thrown to the right, her spleen to the left, and portions of her thighs, stripped of skin, had been placed on the bedside table, beside the lone candle protruding from the neck of a wine bottle that had once provided the sole illumination.

'He was in no hurry,' Abberline said. 'It was if he finally had acquired the proper laboratory for his atrocious procedures.'

Methodical he had been, most particularly when it had come to the poor girl's face. It was turned to the left, towards the camera, and the Ripper had carved away the nose, cheeks, and even the eyebrows; the ears had been partially severed, and the lips had been slashed. It was as if, in his frenzy, he had tried to do nothing less than utterly obliterate the girl.

What remained unclear, however, was exactly why Inspector Abberline had appeared at my house with two constables in tow, to enlist me on this mission. Fanny had been quite hysterical when I was escorted out.

'What do you want my husband for? Haven't you troubled him enough already?'

But Abberline had explained that I was not under arrest. 'We are simply seeking his advice and counsel.'

'I am sending word to our solicitor!' she cried out as I stepped up into the coach.

Another lawyer, I thought. Only that morning, I had written a note to Randolph Desmond begging him to abstain from legal action against Lloyd. 'I will recompense you for damages you have received, and take strong measures to ensure that no such incident recurs.' I counted, too, upon his reluctance to become the subject of public notice, and even perhaps ridicule. (Should not men in a romantic imbroglio be able to settle the matter with their own wits, or fists, without recourse to the law courts?)

As the police carriage made its way towards the East End, I heard, through the closed windows, muffled catcalls from passers-by.

'Too little, too late, Sir Charles!'

'What took you so long?'

'If this had been Mayfair, Jack would be hanged by now!'

Sentiment in the street had never been more volatile. For months, the public had been demanding that a reward be offered for the capture and conviction of Jack the Ripper, but the official government stance had been unyielding. They did not offer rewards to people for doing what must only be construed as their civic duty. Others had stepped forward, however, to fill the gap, including Sir Samuel Montagu, the Hebrew businessman who had been elected to Parliament to represent Whitechapel in 1885. The Whitechapel Vigilance Committee was raising its own funds for another reward. In a grudging concession to the mounting pressure, Sir Charles had declared that a murder pardon would be issued by the secretary of state to 'any accomplice not being a person who contrived or actually committed the murder who shall give such information and evidence as shall lead to the discovery and conviction of the person or persons who committed the murder' of Mary Janet (as she was inscribed in the document) Kelly. It was unlikely in itself to quell the unrest.

'As you can see,' Abberline said, gathering up the photos and replacing them in the envelope, 'the madman is becoming, if anything, more emboldened, and his butchery, if it is even considered possible, more savage.' Turning down the lamp and taking a pipe from his pocket, he said, 'The German who attacked you in the coach—and let's not have any folderol about you not being the gentleman in the coach, I have your name from the publican at the Aldgate Arms—did you know him?'

He had been doing his work. 'No, not exactly.'

'Did you, or didn't you?'

'Although I have never met him, in the usual manner of speaking, I do believe I know who he is. He is the son of a man who worked at a clinic in Switzerland. His name is Josef.'

'Josef what?'

'That I don't know. But he blames me for his father's death.'

'_Were_ you responsible?'

Was I? It was a question I had been known to wrestle with myself. 'From his perspective, yes.'

Lighting his pipe, he said, rather sharply, 'I must ask you, why did you not come forward with this information on your own? Why have I had to come to you?'

It was a fair question. But between the vigil I had had to keep by the bedside of my stepson—a matter I did not wish to bring up—and the fact that Josef's salient characteristics, from his knife to his attire, had already been confirmed by the onlookers, I did not have much more to offer. I could not even guess where he might be hiding. 'I have not been well,' I said, 'but would have done so shortly. In light of this new crime, I regret the delay.'

'Yes, well, regret it all you like, but without the cooperation of people such as yourself—people intimately involved in some way with the killer—we shall forever be one step behind.'

At this, I took umbrage. 'I would hardly call myself intimately involved.'

'Choose your own words, then. But let me be frank with you, Mr Stevenson.'

When had he not? I thought.

'I do not understand you.'

'In what way may I enlighten you?'

'I do not understand the impulse that causes you to create what you do. The world is filled with horrors enough; I see them every day—babies thrown into dust bins, wives beaten senseless by their husbands, children left to starve—and I do not see the point, any point at all, in imagining even more of such stuff. The fact is, your play opened at the Lyceum and all hell broke loose in the city that very night. Not only the fires at the docks, but the first of these murders. I do not read your books, and I have forbidden my wife to do so either, but from your success, I gather that you are not without ability.'

From Abberline, I took that as a ringing endorsement.

'Why would you not put such abilities as you have towards the writing of works meant to elevate the soul, to teach morality, and to raise the spirits of your audience? If you have it within your powers to summon the devil, why not summon angels instead?'

Though Abberline had put it well, he was hardly the first to do so. My father had often taken me to task for not bending my efforts in a direction more consonant with his Covenanter faith, and in an effort to please him, I had ameliorated certain effects in my early work. (Later, I had always been sorry.) 'I do not believe a story like "Jekyll and Hyde" depresses the spirits', I now replied, 'or contributes to immorality. If anything, it is a tale designed to throw some light on what it is that makes a man good, or bad. Are we born with a single nature that drives us on, or are we cursed with a duality of purpose? Are we not, all of us, amalgams? Free will would have no resonance, would it, if that will was forever and already ordained to the good?'

There was a splat as a piece of rotten fruit struck the window of the carriage. 'Catch the bastard!' a man shouted.

'You there,' the police driver shouted, 'no more of that!'

The man shouted something else in reply, but the carriage had already rattled on. While I had initially assumed that we were on our way to the headquarters of the Metropolitan Police on Whitehall Place for a more formal interview, somewhere along the way we had bypassed that destination and continued towards the East End. Glancing out the window, I saw a sign for Dorset Street, and a number of people hanging about the lamp posts and loitering on the pavement.

'Miller's Court, sir,' the driver called out, pulling on the reins. Plainly, I had been taken to the scene of the murder. Another constable opened the door on Abberline's side and said, 'This way, sir. They're all waiting.'

Who was waiting? I hoped not the coroner—I had no wish to see the mutilated corpse. Surely, it had been removed by now.

Abberline, his pipe stuck between his teeth, tamped his brown bowler hat down on his head and stepped out. I followed, keeping an eye out for flying fruit. We stood before a darkened passageway, flanked by a Cart Hire on one side and a forlorn shop advertising everything from stovepipe varnish to Dartnell's ginger beer on the other.

The detective strode into the tunnel, and I, feeling like Dante led by Virgil into Hell, stayed close behind. We emerged into a small and dank courtyard, lit by a single gas lamp suspended from a crooked pole. A policeman stood at attention before a broken window, beside a door that had been reduced to splinters by an axe. Not Jack's work, that was for sure; he was a good deal stealthier than that.

Abberline engaged another officer in a private conversation, while I stood about awkwardly, wondering what my role in this could be. Why bring me here? An oil lantern had been left burning in the little room behind the guard, and in its light I could see the remains of the carnage. The body was gone, but the sheets, saturated in blood, still lay on the mattress, and even the walls glistened with crimson streaks. This room, where Mary Jane Kelly had breathed her last—a newspaper account had said she was heard singing a French tune not long before her death—looked now like an abattoir.

It was then that I noticed, lurking in the shadows, four or five men and women, like animals being kept in a pen, under the watchful eye of another constable. Were they the other residents of the court? Abberline gestured that I should meet him under the crooked pole. A policeman prodded me in the back with his truncheon. I went to him, and he took several seconds to relight his pipe. Then, he said, 'The door we had to chop down ourselves.'

'So I surmised. But how did Jack leave, then?'

'Must have taken her key', he said, 'and locked up after. He likes his souvenirs.'

I remembered that.

'The morgue tells me he took the heart, too, this time.'

The residents had been allowed to come rather close, and when I glanced their way, I saw one or two of them shaking their heads, and I heard a woman in a threadbare shawl say to the policeman, 'Never seen 'im before.' A man in a fish market apron seconded her, muttering, 'Not around here.'

Abberline's gaze shifted to the constable, who shook his head at the results of their little experiment. Its purpose had become clear to me. I had been brought here to be inspected, and possibly identified, by the local denizens, who, of course, had never clapped eyes on me until this night.

'All right, you lot can go now,' the policeman said.

One of the men asked if there wasn't to be any compensation for aiding in the investigation, but a poke from the baton squelched his request.

'A clever ploy,' I conceded to Abberline, 'but now that I have passed my examination, am I allowed to exercise my free will and go?'

'Just one more thing, Mr Stevenson. The Aldgate Arms. You paid the bill for a certain professor, affiliated with the union infirmary. We cannot confirm his identity or whereabouts now. Can you?'

It occurred to me that Abberline would not necessarily know Lloyd—or "Samuel" as he had been known at the hotel—was my stepson, particularly as he bore a different surname.

'He was a friend, in dire straits.'

'A friend whose room we have searched thoroughly.'

'Did you find anything of interest?' I thought of the locked drawer in the wardrobe.

'Nothing. It had been quite stripped of any personal effects.'

I had wondered what Lloyd had been up to all day, and now I knew.

'I suppose you have no more information as to his whereabouts as you do of this fellow Josef.'

'Not at present.'

'Don't make me come to you again, Mr Stevenson. You do yourself no service.' At this, he turned away and I felt myself dismissed. It was plain that I would not be ferried home again in the commissioner's coach. On the street outside, I drew many long, hard stares, and hailed the first hansom cab I could find. Huddled inside, I felt like an animal that can sense the snare being closed, that knows it has only seconds to escape, but cannot fathom how.

TOPANGA CANYON— CALIFORNIA

Present Day

Before he could make the turn into the Cornucopia, Rafe had to wait for several creaking motorhomes to lumber by.

"Come on, come on already!"

There was no sign of Lucy or, for that matter, Trip.

"I'll check in the house," Miranda said, "you go out back."

Jolting the Rover to a stop next to Miranda's little Subaru hatchback, he jumped out and ran to the yard. The items on the clothesline were dancing in the wind that had sprung up in the canyon. There wasn't any light on in his trailer, and the door was shut.

"Lucy!" he shouted. "Are you in there?" He stuck his key in the lock, but it still wouldn't open. The dead bolt had been thrown inside.

"Lucy! It's me!"

He heard Tripod barking and scratching at the door, and then Lucy saying "Rafe? Rafe?"

The bolt was yanked back, and when the door opened, she threw herself into his arms, sniffling, and said, "Why didn't you call me? I kept sending you texts! Why didn't you answer me?"

"My phone was off, Luce—I'm so sorry. And then I couldn't get through. For all I know, the towers might be down from the fire."

"I didn't know what to do! I was afraid that that man would come by and hit me in the face again."

"That man," Rafe said, "is never going to hit you again. Trust me." Her nose was red, but only, he knew, from blowing it. "Come on, grab your stuff, we're getting out of here."

Lucy stuffed some things into her backpack, and by the time they got outside, Miranda was racing out the back of the store, kicking off her high heels and letting them fly. Trip hobbled up to her, tail going a mile a minute, and she scooped him up in her arms.

"Into the car!" Rafe said, yanking open the back passenger door of the Rover.

But Miranda said, "No, let's take my car."

"The Rover's bigger, safer."

"And it's almost out of gas. I've got a full tank." She had already opened the side door and tossed Tripod onto the seat. "Get in, Lucy!"

But Lucy was frozen solid, looking at the road, where a biker in a silver helmet and shades, his arms clinging to upright handlebars, was roaring past. "That's him!" she cried.

Rafe shot another glance at the motorcyclist as he zoomed away.

"That's the man who hit you?"

"And stole the book!"

Laszlo must have somehow acquired, or swiped, a real motorcycle. It wasn't hard to guess where he was going.

Rafe urged Lucy into the backseat of the Subaru, and then said to Miranda, "Get going!"

"What do you mean?" she said, the car keys still dangling in her fingers.

"I've got something I need to do."

"Oh no, Rafe, let that go! Do not try to settle that score now."

But Rafe was already running back toward the trailer.

"Rafe, Laszlo's not worth it!"

"He is to me! Now get going!"

Whipping off his sport coat, he went straight to the safe, but he was in such a hurry that he put in the combination wrong, then had to spin the dial and do it again. He grabbed the Smith & Wesson, loaded it, and strapped the holster around his waist. He had little to no intention of firing it—besides the shot at the lake, he'd only used it at the training range—but it seemed like a good idea to have it along if he was planning to enter the lion's den.

By the time he got out front, there was no sign of the hatchback, which was a relief. He did not have time for further debate. He tore out of the parking area and headed straight for the Compound. In the twilight, he could see the rosy glow of the wildfires off to the east, and a flock of helicopters circling above it, dropping water and foam fire retardant, as the pilots monitored its lethal progress.

He passed La Raza—the owners were out front, hosing down the roof—his eyes peeled for the Compound's dirt road and the sign saying "No Trespassing or You WILL Be Shot, M*F." When he spotted it, he drove up onto the shoulder and parked the Land Rover under the cover of some trees. No use announcing his arrival. He wished he'd thought of changing out of his white shirt and into something darker, but it was too late to do anything about that now.

He hustled down the driveway and across the little bridge over the dried-out stream, sticking to the shadows, and hunched down behind an old Dumpster when he spotted an adobe house, the lights on in the windows, and heard raised voices outside of it. Two men were really going at it, and one of them, he could see, was his quarry. The Harley was lying flat on its side in the dirt, and the other guy, in a denim vest and jeans, was shouting and brandishing a fist. He had the pumped-up arms and thick neck of a serious steroid user.

But Laszlo wasn't backing down. He still had the helmet on, although he was barefoot and wearing an old work shirt that looked like it had been rescued from a rag bin, along with some shreds of what might have once been white gloves. For some reason he just looked different, even from this distance.

The other guy took a step closer, shouting, "Pick it up, asshole! Pick! It! Up!"

Laszlo must have refused, because the guy repeated it, and this time he shoved Laszlo's shoulder hard enough to make him stumble backward.

Laszlo said, "Don't do that again." And the guy said, "Then pick it up."

He punched him in the other shoulder, and Laszlo spun to one side. Rafe expected to see him back down or run for it; that would be the Laszlo he'd always known—a bully whenever he could get away with it, but a coward underneath it all.

This time, however, he acted out of character. To Rafe's surprise, he sprang at his attacker like a cougar leaping from a branch, landing on him with such force that the guy was bowled over, toppling backward onto his own motorcycle. Nor was that the end of it—Laszlo rained a hail of blows on him, his arms swinging like pistons, over and over again. The guy tried to roll off the bike and crawl to his feet, but Laszlo jumped on his back, arms tightly wrapped around his throat, choking him and dropping him to his knees. With his arms bent back and fingers struggling to pry the arms loose, the guy tried to throw his head back, tried to butt Laszlo in the face, but he missed, and Laszlo held on, and on, like a cowboy riding a bucking bronco, choking him harder and harder, until the guy went from his knees to flat on the ground, and then lay still.

Was he playing dead, Rafe wondered . . . or was he?

When Laszlo finally let go and stood up, he brushed at his ragged clothes, spit on the guy still lying in the dirt, and walked away. Judging from his gait, however, he wasn't unhurt himself. His hands were clutching at his stomach, and he was walking like a seasick sailor.

Rafe, crouching low, followed him. There was a barn, or maybe it had been a stable, out back, and Laszlo threw open the big doors and disappeared inside. A few moments later, the lights went on.

Who was this guy, Rafe wondered, so altered from the Laszlo he thought he knew? When he got to the open doors and peered inside, he saw a Formica table with chairs, some bunk beds, a huge TV sitting on a minifridge, wires trailing across a dirt floor. It looked like the worst frat house in the world. Way in the back, harsh fluorescent light spilled from what must be the bathroom.

This could be his best chance to get the book.

He crept into the barn, looking for any clue, and saw it when he spotted the big black Hefty bag crammed under a bunk to his left. The shredded work shirt and scorched gloves were lying on the mattress. He glanced in the direction of the bathroom and heard water running, but couldn't see anything more than a rack with some dingy towels hanging from it.

He went to the bunk first, lifting the pillow, checking under the blanket, scanning the wooden shelf next to it, where he saw a pair of shades, some loose coins and pills, an old whiskey flask that might have come from the trunk. But no book. He'd have to go through the garbage bag, and fast.

On top he found nothing but a pile of shirts and pants, and sticking his arms to the very bottom, only some heavier items like a leather jacket and boots and shoes. He rooted around, but came across nothing even resembling the journal. Damn. Now what? He would absolutely have to confront Laszlo, and having seen the fight over the motorcycle, he was glad he'd brought the Smith & Wesson after all.

The water stopped running, and Laszlo came out of the bathroom wearing only a pair of jeans and rubbing a towel over his wet hair and pressing it to his face. His chest and shoulders were much hairier than Rafe would have guessed. When he put the towel down and saw Rafe holding the gun, he stopped, and smiled.

Since when had his teeth become so prominent? Rafe wondered.

"What are you supposed to be? The sheriff?"

The voice was Laszlo's, but raspier. Probably from all the smoke in the air. But the face . . . it wasn't really his anymore. The jaw stuck out, the eyes were sunken beneath a bulging forehead. Rafe's first thought was of steroids again, but he'd seen Laszlo so recently this change couldn't have happened that quickly. Or so extremely. The man had turned into a gargoyle.

"Where's the book?"

"Huh. I thought you were here because I slugged your fat sister."

"We'll get to that. Where's the book?"

"Where's the five hundred bucks? Or was she too retarded to mention that?"

Rafe suddenly understood what it was to have a twitchy trigger finger.

"Just give it to me."

The rafters shook with the roar of a helicopter passing low overhead, and Laszlo glanced up.

"There goes the store." He twiddled his fingers. "All up in smoke. All those shitty paintings and macramé."

Rafe wasn't sure what to do next. He wasn't about to shoot him, and what made it worse was that Laszlo undoubtedly knew it. He'd played his ace and they were at a standstill.

Laszlo tossed the towel onto his bunk, as casually as if he were at some health club, then picked up the old flask and put it to his lips. He turned it completely upside down, even shook it, but it seemed it was empty. He plopped down on the edge of the bunk, one hand rubbing his gut, the other clutching the flask. "You try this shit?"

"No."

He grunted. "I was just checking myself out in the mirror."

Rafe suddenly understood. He remembered reading Stevenson's horrified reaction to his own image in the mirror. Until this second it had seemed like some sort of fiction or hallucination. Something those Brownies he talked about might have concocted. Rafe hadn't believed it was actually true.

But now he did.

"It's worse than coke. You gotta have it, but look what happens."

There was a crackling sound as brush and twigs outside began to catch fire from the blowing sparks. Fire engine sirens blared.

"It's getting close," Rafe said. "We've got to get out of here." Even the journal wasn't worth dying for.

"Yeah, I guess you've got a point."

Rafe lowered the gun a notch, and the second he did, the flask came flying, cracking him in the eye like a hardball. He dropped back, stunned, and before he could recover, a fist punched him in the stomach. He reeled back, dropping the gun, and Laszlo hit him again, catching him under the chin. He went down on his back and Laszlo leaped onto him, perching on his chest like a malevolent spirit, leering into his face. "But come on, Salazar—who's afraid of a little fire?"

Rafe groped for the gun.

"You looking for this?" he said, lifting it and pointing the barrel at Rafe's mouth.

Laszlo just smiled, enjoying the moment. Blood was running down into Rafe's left eye, tinting his vision, but with his other he saw the timbers of the barn turning red, too, then bursting into flame. Laszlo turned to look, and Rafe bucked his legs into Laszlo's back, knocking him forward and pushing the gun away from his mouth. The shot was deafening and kicked a fountain of dirt into the air, but rolling away, Rafe was able to get out from under before Laszlo could take any better aim. The second shot grazed his shoulder before shattering the TV screen, and the next one ripped into the fridge with the clang of a bell. Rafe ducked behind the table as another round splintered the chair beside him. Laszlo was standing, laughing, lit by the glow of the fire surrounding the barn and shouting over the roar of a hovering chopper. "How many shots do I get with this thing?"

Rafe wasn't sure.

And then the roof caved in, the old shingles and boards and rafters collapsing under the weight of the bucket drop. All Rafe could see, between the blood from his eye and the water gushing down, was Laszlo looking up in surprise as the flood of liquid and debris came crashing down on him. Rafe hurtled over a still-sizzling timber and stumbled, half-blind and -deaf from the gunshot, toward the open doors of the barn. Outside, the Compound looked like an immense bed of coals, every branch and twig and leaf burning on the ground, the trees like torches. He ran toward the adobe house, and when he saw the biker still lying beside his motorcycle, made a sudden detour. He rolled him over, felt for a heartbeat or a pulse, any sign of life, but the guy was gone. His eye fell on the overturned bike—the gas tank had been punctured and a thin trickle of fuel snaked along the soil, past the saddlebags and exhaust pipe.

Was it in there, he thought? Was the journal in the saddlebags?

On all fours, he scrambled across the dirt, but when he fumbled at the latch, the heat of the red-hot metal seared his fingers. He blew on the tips, licked them with his dry tongue, but before he could try again, the limb of an ancient oak crashed down in flames, bouncing on the dirt beside him, throwing a shower of sparks everywhere . . . and igniting the trail of gasoline.

The flame raced toward the bike, enveloping it in a halo of fire as Rafe scuttled backward. He kept going, and was only a few yards away when the whole motorcycle went off like a hand grenade, shrapnel flying into the air.

If the journal was in there, it was hard to believe that anything but cinders could have survived.

The fire was swiftly encircling the whole compound. Before he was completely cut off from the road, Rafe got up and raced over the little bridge and toward the Land Rover, ducking inside just as another burning branch slammed onto the windshield. The car was as hot as an oven, but the engine turned over, and once an emergency vehicle and an ambulance had zoomed past, he pulled out, heading west and praying he had enough gas to get out of the danger zone. It was only when he'd zigged and zagged his way down to Pacific Coast Highway that he hit Empty, and coasting on fumes alone, managed to guide the Rover into the gravel bed of a plant nursery across from the beach.

He slumped back in his seat, his ears still ringing, and wiped the blood from his eye. Wincing as he felt the burn from the bullet that had grazed his shoulder, he stared out at the ocean, glimmering pink in the reflected glow of the encroaching flames, the blue and white lights of the helicopters darting above the water like fireflies against an inky-black sky. Clouds of smoke and ash, looking like rosy swirls of cotton candy, drifted out over the open sea. It was a weirdly mesmerizing scene, an awful beauty born out of fire and death and destruction. Rafe had to hand it to Mother Nature—she could sure as hell paint a picture when she wanted to . . . a picture he knew he would never forget.

12 November, 1888

Fanny, in an old sweater, was down on her hands and knees, digging in the dirt, ripping out weeds, and flinging them over her shoulder as if each one had offered a personal affront to her dignity. 'English gardens,' she said. 'All weeds and no flowers.' She threw another one, so angrily it landed on the table atop the latest instalment of the serialized novel I had been slaving over. "The Master of Ballantrae" it was called, a title that even Henley had not mocked.

'It's late fall,' I offered, brushing the weed from the page. 'An unlikely time of year for flowers.'

'Not in California.'

Had she been talking to her son? Did they hanker, after all, for their native land? Was there some plot afoot? 'Where has Lloyd been all day?' I asked in a tone of voice meant to disguise my growing concern. 'I haven't seen a trace of the boy.'

'You know Lloyd; he comes and goes as he pleases,' she said, leaning back on her haunches and wiping her brow with the back of one wrist. It was an unusually temperate day for autumn. 'Off chasing Constance Wooldridge, unless I miss my guess.'

That was my fear. Despite all that had happened, and all that had passed between us, he remained a wild card, in part because of his unruly nature, and in part because he had drunk the powerful elixir. No one knew better than I that, once taken, its effects could be felt immediately, or, as I had learned to my own shock, at a later and less predictable time—an Alpine peak, or a costermonger's arcade. To my knowledge, all that was needed was some sufficient stimulation—whether it be emotion or incident—to bring on the dreadful change—a change that was in some ineffable way as welcome as it was horrific.

'Will he be joining us for dinner?'

'Why this sudden interest?' she said, turning to face me. Her face was smudged with dirt, and her black hair clung like tendrils to her cheeks. To some men, she would have appeared no more than some humble and hardy native worker; to me, and even at her age, she was an exotic, like some tawny-skinned creature of a faraway isle.

'I just wondered. I was writing and skipped tea.'

'Then go ask Mrs Chandler to get a move on. I'll go and wash up.'

First taking the manuscript back up to my study, a bit of damp weed still clinging to the page, I paused at the door of Lloyd's room, listened for a sound, then knocked. When I got no answer, I went in.

Sally Chandler must have tidied it up. The bed was neatly made, the carpet swept, the slippers by the bedside—the slippers I had last seen in the Aldgate Arms. On the bedstead, I saw a volume of De Quincey's perverse and satirical essays; it was bookmarked, I discovered, with the final bill from the Aldgate Arms, stamped Paid In Full. At least he hadn't set up camp somewhere else. I stuck the bill in the pocket of my coat, lest there be any dispute from the hotel regarding further charges. I looked around for the satchel but didn't see it anywhere. I opened the wardrobe, peered under the bed, and even behind the curtains. I was about to leave when I had an intuition and looked in the wardrobe again. Parting the clothes, I found the satchel, hanging flat, by a crooked nail—a sure sign of Lloyd's own handiwork.

I put it on the bed, where I had laid my stack of papers, and opened it, wondering what books or papers I might find inside. But there were none. Still, it did give off an unpleasant odour, and its inside was encrusted as if with old blood. Had the bag belonged to a doctor at one time? Tilting it towards the last light of day coming through the windows, I saw the oddest assortment of things—brass rings, an amber comb missing several teeth, a torn envelope, a rusty key. I took the key out—it was nothing like the keys to this house. Was it the key to his room at the Aldgate Arms? Surely he should have returned that to Mr Donohue.

But another thought also flitted ignobly through my mind, a thought too terrible to entertain, and it was abruptly dispatched.

Packing the satchel away again so as to leave no sign of my snooping, I went to my study, where I happened upon Sally cleaning out the fire grate. 'Oh, sir, I didn't think you'd be in here,' she said, gathering up her rags and pail.

'No, no, that's all right,' I said, 'pay me no mind—I'm just passing through.'

She chuckled. 'That's exactly what Lloyd said.'

'Lloyd was in here?'

'Yes, sir. Not twenty minutes ago.'

'What was he doing?'

'Using the mirror,' she said, gesturing at the cheval glass. 'He looked right smart. All dressed up, and smelling of the nicest cologne.'

Mine. Its scent still lingered in the air.

'Did he say where he was going?'

'Oh no, sir, and I wouldn't ask him no such thing.'

I would have asked, though the answer, I feared, was plain.

'Please tell your mother I won't be dining at home tonight,' I said. 'Something's come up.'

'What about the mistress?'

'No, my wife will be dining here. But tell her, too, that I'll be out.'

I ducked into the master bedroom while Fanny was in the bath, grabbed my hat, and, noting the hole in the pocket through which I had shot the derringer at Josef, pulled on my coat; one chamber of the gun would still be loaded and he was still out there, somewhere, his mission not yet fulfilled. I was beginning to feel, however unwillingly, quite like a character from one of my own novels.

Outside, it took me several blocks before I could catch a cab, and all I could think of was the twenty-minute advantage Lloyd had over me. The horse seemed as lethargic as the coachman, who replied to my every entreaty to hurry by touching the brim of his cap and saying, 'Whatever you wish, your lordship,' before proceeding at the same slow pace. I got the distinct impression that he was drunk.

In my mind's eye, I pictured Lloyd knocking, and then importunately banging, on the door of the Wooldridge house, and her aunt quaking on the other side. Desmond, I was confident, would be nowhere in the vicinity. But what would I say, what could I do, to dissuade Lloyd from further pursuit? He had always been a fickle lad, his attention wandering from one servant girl to another (thank goodness Sally was so plain), or from one female acquaintance to the next. I had noted, however, that he was almost invariably rebuffed, as there was something in his manner, something too hasty, too odd, that put off the objects of his desire. I had not only seen it in Davos, with his amour fou for Constance, but in Torquay with an innkeeper's daughter, and on a cruise down the Rhine, with the captain's young niece. On that last occasion, the situation had become so fraught that I deemed it best for us all to disembark in Koblenz, from which we took the land route back to France.

When I saw the tailor shop where I had taken refuge on my first visit here, I banged on the lid of the cab with my walking stick and got out. I paid the driver, who was slumped forward as if he'd been dozing, and the cab plodded on, as I held back. From here, the brown-brick town house looked as quiet as its neighbours, the walls of which nearly touched it on either side. The gas lamps were on in the street, a thin scrim of fog gathered about each beacon, and in the house, a yellow glow emanated from the fanlight above the door and from several windows on the third storey. To my relief, there was no sign of Lloyd or a commotion of any kind.

Perhaps I'd been wrong, and he was merely out on the town, bathed in my cologne and pretending to be . . . what, this time? Not a professor. An author, no doubt!

A constable wandered past on his nightly rounds, swinging his lantern, and lest I look suspicious by loitering in a doorway, I coughed conspicuously, strode to the town house, and mounted the front steps. Having come this far, I thought Constance might be glad to see me, and to have my assurance that the problem was now well in hand.

But when I came to the door and lifted the knocker, I paused. The door was already open, though just off the latch, and the brass plate around the knob looked damaged. Looking down, I saw fine splinters of wood on the step.

And my heart took a sudden beat.

Rather than announcing myself with a knock or a shout, I pushed the door open with the tip of my cane, and stepped into the foyer. The gold pendulum of an imposing grandfather clock ticked back and forth, a dour portrait of an old bewigged judge hung on the wall, a hall table held a vase of silk flowers. All was otherwise still.

Before me, a narrow staircase, the runner a faded purple, rose to a landing, and even though I went up as gently as I could, each step emitted its own distinctive creak or groan. Rounding the corner, I stopped, thinking a rug had been rolled up and left there for removal. It was only on second glance that I saw it was a woman—small and elderly—fast asleep . . . or something worse. I bent down, quickly determined that she was alive and breathing, and lifted her onto the window seat. There was a bruise on her forehead where she had clearly received a blow, and though she remained unconscious, she appeared in no other immediate danger.

That, I now knew, lay somewhere else in the house.

I went up the next flight, and heard voices from a bedroom towards the back. They were not raised in agitation, or argument. It all sounded quite subdued, even amiable, and as I approached, I detected the unmistakable scent of my cologne.

The door was ajar, and pressing myself against one wall, I could see into the room. Constance, her red hair spread across the shoulders of a long white dressing gown, was standing with her back to me, and I could hear Lloyd's voice saying, 'It could always have been like this. Don't you find this nice?'

He was off to one side and out of sight. Constance was pouring brandy into a glass.

'Well, isn't it?' he said when she didn't answer.

'Very,' she said softly, bringing him the glass and thus passing from my view.

'That's better,' I heard him say, and then in a slurred tone, 'More.'

'More brandy?'

'Don't be daft. More. You know what I like.'

Several seconds passed—what was happening?—and then he said, 'Get rid of it.'

'Please, why are you—'

'Entirely.'

'But I cannot—'

'I told you, get rid of it!'

Silence again.

Was now the optimal moment? I had hoped to catch a glimpse of Lloyd and get a better idea of the lay of the land before taking any action, but things were progressing rapidly. I reached down into the bottom of my coat pocket to fetch the derringer—I had felt its bulk against my thigh the whole way in the coach—but discovered now that it wasn't the gun at all. It was a pair of leather gloves, lined with rabbit fur and wadded tight. I examined them with horror; they weren't even mine. They belonged to Lloyd.

Did he have the gun with him then? Was he holding it now? And was he even Lloyd—or was he that foul, Hyde-like creature he could become?

The ticking of the clock below was all I could hear above the beating of my heart and the mounting urge in my throat to cough. What now? I had my walking stick, but, should it come to a fight, it would be little defence against the derringer. I could only hope that if the shot went off, it would go awry.

There was the rustle of clothing, and the silk dressing gown flew into view, puddling on the floor.

'Now, welcome me,' he said.

'How?'

'Good God, do I have to do everything for you?'

'I only meant—'

'Over there.'

'Please, you know I—'

'Over . . . there.'

I heard the sound of bedclothes being turned back, and a mattress squeaking.

'Invite me,' he said. 'And make it convincing.'

Her voice, all but trembling, said, 'Come to me.'

'Come to me, my what?'

'My . . . darling.'

When I pushed the door back with my cane and stepped into the room, Constance was lying naked on the bed, and Lloyd, his braces hanging and trousers undone, was stripping off his shirt. Her eyes widened, and even before turning around to see who had entered, he said, 'If it's you, Louis, you've come at a very inopportune time.'

'I'd say I've come in the nick of time. Constance, you may cover yourself.'

'Ever the gallant knight.'

She dragged the corners of the coverlet around her and shrank into the bed.

And then he turned towards me in the lamplight. He wasn't quite Lloyd, and he wasn't quite not. The features were his, but the malevolent glint in his eyes, like the sneer on his lips, was pure Hyde. 'We could share, you know.'

'You disgust me.'

'That seems unfair,' he complained. 'You made me what I am.'

'For that, I will be forever remorseful. Now, get out.'

As languidly as if he were removing his handkerchief, he took from his pants pocket the derringer and squinted at it from several angles before saying, 'Look what I've found.' He glanced up at me. 'What have you got? Gloves?'

He raised the gun and pointed it at my chest. 'Time to leave, Louis.'

My name came out as a hiss.

From the landing, there was a moan. The old woman was reviving.

Lloyd's ears pricked up as markedly as a wolf's might, and his eyes momentarily shifted focus. It was my best chance, and I leapt forward, lashing my cane at his outstretched arm. I caught him at the elbow, knocking the muzzle downward, but he held onto it and swept his arm back up, catching me off-balance. I crashed against the window, shattering the glass, and Constance screamed, her cry echoing out into the night.

'Damn you!' Lloyd shouted, and when I raised the cane to strike him, he fired the derringer wildly, the bullet ricocheting off the armoire and demolishing the perfume bottles on the vanity.

I struck him on the collar of his shirt, and he pulled the trigger again, only to find it was spent.

Constance screamed even louder, and in a fury, he hurled the gun at my head, narrowly missing, and then, at the sound of a policeman's whistle on the street outside, ran to the window, and to my shock, jumped out. I looked outside, thinking to see that he had fallen to his death, but instead I saw him scrambling across the roof of the town house next door, as agile as an ape, braces still dangling as he dodged among the chimney stacks. The whistle came closer and footsteps echoed on the pavement. Constance, wrapped in the quilt, slithered to the floor, and I slumped down beside her, my breath gone, coughing, knowing that my life, as I had lived it until then, was at an end.

TOPANGA CANYON—CALIFORNIA

Present Day

Wildfires are like tornadoes, Rafe reflected. They jumped all over the place, destroying one thing and leaving another, right beside it, intact. The Compound had been razed, but La Raza had been spared. So had his trailer. Apart from a thick layer of ash lying all over it like black icing on a cake, it had withstood the blaze.

The Cornucopia, however, had not been so lucky.

When the fire crossed the road, it had consumed the porch and was well on its way to devouring the whole building when a helicopter dropped a couple of thousand gallons of water on, and through, its roof. Foam retardant had followed. Traipsing through the wreckage now, Miranda said, "They might as well have let the fire have it. At least the sandalwood and incense would have made the canyon smell nice. Now it's just this unholy pile of junk."

As far as Rafe could tell, there was nothing left to salvage. The fire department had left red tape around the outside to warn that the structure was off-limits and unsafe to enter, but he and Miranda had ducked under it, and even taken a chance on going upstairs. The wood was still damp and squished underfoot, and the walls reeked of smoke. The bedroom that they had just finished painting Sunshine Gold was the color of a battleship, and the fancy new quilt and curtains were a sodden mess. The windows were all blown out. Miranda went to the closet to gather some clothes, but after prying open the door that had swollen shut, simply stood there, silent. Rafe handed her the linen laundry bag they had brought along to retrieve a few of her belongings, but she just let it dangle from her hand.

"What was I thinking?" she said, and peering over her shoulder, Rafe could see that the interior of the closet, too, looked as if it had been hit by a bomb. She took a blouse that had been hanging on the back of the door, smelled it, and tossed it back in again. "A total loss."

Rafe didn't know what to say. He stood back and let her roam around the room, looking for anything she might want. She found her jewelry box on the floor, put it in the bag along with some clogs that had survived under the bed, and said, "That's it. Let's just get out of here. I can't stand it."

Outside, she threw the almost-empty bag into the backseat of her Subaru, where Tripod gave it a good sniffing before losing interest.

"How's your mom adjusting to the dog?" Rafe asked.

"She's calling the American Kennel Club to see if she can get a three-legged dog an emergency pedigree."

Rafe laughed. "And how about you?"

"Listen—as halfway houses go, San Marino isn't half bad. I've got a two-room suite overlooking the rose garden. And it helps having Bentley there. Turns out he's a pretty nice guy."

"I liked him."

"He liked you, too. In fact, I hope you don't mind, but I told him you'd salvaged an old book in the canyon and might like his opinion sometime."

Rafe looked down at his shoes. He'd known this question was pending, but in all the confusion since the fire, it had not directly come up.

"I mean, you got it back, right? The night you went after Laszlo?"

"I did not."

"What happened to it?"

"The best I can tell, it was destroyed in the fire."

"Oh no. It's gone?"

He nodded.

"Did you ever even get to the end?"

"Yes," he replied, though he did not reveal the shocking conclusion to a narrative that had already been incredible enough. "I'm going to go back and take one more look around the Compound. But I'm not holding out any great hope."

"Maybe Laszlo's still got it, wherever he is."

How could he tell her that that was impossible?

"That night," she said hesitantly, "you're sure you didn't see any sign of him?"

"Nope. I told you—the place was abandoned when I got there. Even the Spiritz aren't dumb enough to hang around in a wildfire." He didn't dare look up and meet her eye.

"Okay," she said. "I suppose he'll turn up one day. The bad penny always does."

He could tell she was torn between never wanting to see the man again and making sure that he was at least alive. Old habits die hard.

"But let me know when you—and Lucy—would like to come out to the Casa San Marino," she said. "We've got a tennis court."

"I'm not sure we've got the proper attire."

"For you two, we'll make an exception. Just be sure my mother doesn't spot you."

She got into the car, pushing Tripod's snout away from the steering wheel, and said, "Don't forget to put Polysporin on that cut."

He touched the spot over his eye where the metal flask had hit him. "Or that scrape on your shoulder."

He hadn't mentioned it was actually from a bullet. "You don't want me to use some all-natural unguent?" he kidded her.

She shrugged, pulling her seat belt over her shoulder. "Sometimes I cave in to modern medicine. Call me later?"

"For sure."

And then, he leaned into her open window and kissed her. Although it wasn't the first time, it still had the virtue of feeling that way. He could taste one of her flavored lip balms and guessed, "Strawberry?"

"Nope," she said, keeping her face tilted up toward his. "Try again."

He did, and guessed raspberry.

"Wrong again."

When he'd run out of fruits, she laughed and said, "You were right the first time." And then she waved one hand and pulled out of the lot.

Going back inside the store and picking through the wreckage, he found one painting, upside down below the empty cash register, that had been miraculously spared. It was a waterfall, all blue and green and silvery lines, with the silhouettes of a couple, about to embrace, in a secret grotto behind it. He took it as a sign, and stuck it in the backseat of his Rover before heading out.

Driving down the main road, the canyon still smelled like a barbecue, but the weather had changed at last. It was cool and gray outside, and the forecast had even included the possibility of light showers in the next day or two. The classic definition of too little, too late. But he'd take it. The land was so parched, and denuded of ground cover now, it needed any drop of rain it could get.

From force of habit, he'd propped his antenna out the side window of the car. Although he'd already tried to pick up a signal from his coyotes, to no avail, he wasn't ready to give up. Not yet. The thought that they might have been trapped by the fire was just unbearable to him; he prayed that they'd been able to make it across the main road and down the cliffs and into the ravine where the fire department had managed to hold the line.

There wasn't much traffic—just a few cars and pickups here and there, people coming back to assess the damage, recover what they could, or, in some of the rare cases, rejoice at the discovery that the flames had somehow bypassed their homes. As he passed La Raza, he saw that a few of the outdoor tables were occupied, one of them by the Potheads. He tooted the horn of the Land Rover and waved, and though they looked up from their meal, they didn't wave back. He realized that they probably hadn't had time to recognize him behind his shades, and the purple-and-gold car must have stumped them. But he was awfully glad to see that they were okay.

Seth and Alfie, he'd heard, had been lucky, too. True, they were both in the hospital, listed in stable condition, but they'd miraculously survived that end-over-end crash through the guardrail. Couldn't have happened to two nicer guys.

It was only when Rafe got within a few hundred yards of his destination that he slowed down. He had hoped to get in and out of the Compound unobserved, but a red-and-white van, marked Department of Medical Examiner–Coroner, was pulling out of the driveway, and a squad car was parked by the side of the road. Was he too late? He parked behind the cruiser and got out, then reached back inside and retrieved his broad-brimmed khaki hat. For this, the more official he looked, the better.

15 November, 1888

The hackney coach made slow progress through the mêlée that was the London docks. A world of its own, the quayside was populated with the most disparate cast of characters imaginable, from Jamaicans to lascars, Levantines to Chinamen, butchers in blue aprons swinging pigs' heads by the ears, clerks in black toting up bales of tobacco and barrels of wine only now disgorged from the holds of hundreds of ships, drunken sailors still finding their land legs, apprehensive emigrants sitting atop their lone sack of possessions, spooning the last scraps of meat from a tin of boiled beef or salted pork.

And bobbing on the water, as far as the eye could see, a thicket of masts and ropes and bunting, clippers and schooners and steamships, flying flags from every corner of the earth, all come here to trade at the greatest emporium of nations ever assembled.

On most such days as this, I'd have been transported by the spectacle and clamour, but today I had my eye out for only one thing—Henley.

'Where is the man?' Fanny said, as I glanced out the window again. 'Did you tell the coachman he's hard to miss, with that filthy red beard and wooden crutch?'

Even now, when Henley was proving instrumental in our plans, she could not spare him a kind word. Perhaps that was the very reason, I thought, for her lack of charity—she was now beholden, forever, to a man she despised, and she hated him all the more for it.

'We're not even close to the Victoria docks yet,' I said. 'Have patience.'

The quays were enormous, stretching out over more than six hundred acres and encompassing innumerable piers and jetties, warehouses and customs offices, taverns and tenements, granaries, and even a subterranean vault capable of holding thousands of casks of rum; these were deliberately stored there in a Stygian gloom, with no source of artificial illumination, or the accompanying risk of fire. The workers navigated among the barrels by the artful manipulation of bright tin reflectors held in their hands.

Fanny settled back in her seat with a nervous sigh, her luggage all around her; Woggin, whose ancient bones always sought the softest spot now, lay in her lap.

As we made our way past the older St. Katharine's and Millwall docks, and approached the East and West India Company's territory, I kept my eyes peeled even more closely for the newer docks named for the Queen. It was there that we were to rendezvous with Henley and board the Yankee ship, the Mercury, bound for Boston. It was the best berth we could get on such short notice, and the first ship to be leaving England for America. I had told Henley to buy passage no matter what the cost . . . and for three.

When the coachman pulled on the reins and the carriage stopped, I heard Henley shouting, 'That you, Stevenson?'

'Is he alone?' Fanny asked anxiously.

He was, though I had expected no less. 'Wait here.'

Getting out, I greeted Henley, and we both looked about in every direction, for any sign of imminent apprehension. He pressed the necessary travel papers into my hands—'You've got a first-class cabin on a third-class ship, I'm afraid'—and I assured him it made no difference to me.

'It might to her ladyship.'

'Not under circumstances like these.'

'True.'

He pointed to a weather-beaten boat, flying the American flag, where a string of stragglers, seaman's bags slung over their shoulders, were already boarding. 'There, that's him now,' Henley said, and I saw a figure dressed like a lowly deckhand, kerchief tied around his brow, slouching up the gangway. 'Travelling as Samuel Smith. Steerage all the way.'

'He can't have been happy about that.'

'He's lucky to be out of it at all. I still can't tell you the shock I had when he turned up at the "Observer." He looked like he'd been through one of those riots over near Shadwell, where they're roughing up the foreign workers.'

Although I still hadn't told Henley the true story, I thought he might have found it out anyway; no one had his ear to the ground in London more than Henley. Constance's aunt had sworn out a complaint for assault and battery, and Abberline had put out a warrant for Lloyd's arrest. Constance, fearing for her reputation if the whole tale were made public, had allowed it to rest at that.

More resourceful than I might have expected, Lloyd had run to the offices of the "National Observer," knowing that they remained open around the clock and that he would not be turned away. Henley—no great admirer of Lloyd's to begin with—had, out of loyalty to me, dutifully hidden him there.

'He'll be a burden to you wherever you go, Louis. You know that, don't you?'

I nodded, thinking that he knew only the half of it. Had the derringer carried another bullet, I might not have been standing there at all.

Fanny, whose patience had evaporated, was supervising the unloading of the trunks and bags that had been so hastily packed. I had given her a full accounting of our predicament in London—both Lloyd's transgressions and the attacks upon my person from the still missing Josef—and she had agreed that an immediate departure was the safest bet all around. In her heart, I believe she was secretly relieved. This was not how she had planned to leave London, but at least she was leaving. Somewhere, she might yet have a flourishing garden.

'Henley, old man,' I said, clasping his hand, 'I cannot thank you enough.'

He started to reply, but for the first time in his life faltered. No joke could spring to his lips.

Fanny had commandeered a porter and called out, 'What ship is it?'

'The Mercury,' I said, pointing.

'And what about . . . our friend?'

'Already aboard,' Henley answered.

She put a hand to her heart to signal her relief, and even went so far as to mouth the words, 'Bless you, sir.' Never in my life had I imagined such a thing.

'Well now,' Henley said, 'miracles abound today.' Then, straightening himself up on his crutch and clearing his throat, he said, 'You'd best be on your way, or the ship will set sail without you.'

'Yes, I should be going.'

But neither one of us moved as Fanny and the porter trundled down the dock. We both knew that this might well be the last time we saw each other. I was bound for the most remote and tropical port of call I could find—somewhere to nurse my ravaged lungs for the rest of my days, while keeping my dangerous ward under the closest supervision—and Henley, as much a fixture of London as the Tower Bridge, was highly unlikely to pay me a call there. 'I will write and tell you where we've finally alighted.'

'Yes, of course, do,' he said, avoiding my eyes. 'Perhaps I can assign you some travel pieces. But promise you won't use the money for something frivolous—use it to pay for some fine Irish whiskey.'

'Agreed.' I turned away and followed Fanny past the sagging bowsprit of the Mercury, then up onto its deck, where I stayed for the next hour. When we raised anchor and caught the sluggish current of the Thames, I saw that Henley, perched on a keg of rum, was still keeping vigil, a cigar between his lips and the crutch across his lap. All he lacked was a parrot on his shoulder.

My own Long John Silver.

TOPANGA CANYON— CALIFORNIA

Present Day

Crossing the dry gully between the road and the Compound, Rafe prayed that he could get to the remains of the Harley without being spotted. If there was any chance of the journal surviving the fire, it would be in those metallic saddlebags on the back of the bike.

The adobe house had been reduced to a pile of rubble. The motorcycle still lay in the dirt, a tangle of scorched and blasted metal, but the body of its owner was gone. Rafe assumed it was in the back of that coroner's van. He was moving swiftly toward the ruined bike when he heard a noise coming from the barn—all that remained of the structure were a few upright timbers and interior walls—and then a shout.

"Hey, who are you? This is off-limits!"

Damn. Rafe adjusted his course and announced himself. The guy was wearing an open yellow slicker that read Fire Marshal, over street clothes, and poking at the ruins with a piece of rebar in one hand and a flashlight, even though it was broad daylight, in the other.

After giving Rafe, and his uniform, the once-over, the marshal said, "You know who lived here?"

"A motorcycle club," Rafe said. "They called themselves the Spiritz. This was their hangout. I saw the coroner's van leaving just now."

"Yeah, we found one of them."

"The guy with the bike out front."

"No," the marshal said, "we found him yesterday." He stopped and gave Rafe a look. "How'd you know about that guy?"

Damn, Rafe thought; he shouldn't have opened his mouth so soon. "On my way out of the canyon, I swung in here to warn them all to evacuate immediately, and the guy who owned that bike gave me some grief. Said he wasn't going anywhere."

The marshal looked dubious, but said, "Well, he should have taken your advice. You know his name?"

"I'm afraid not."

"Just to be on the safe side, we came back for one more look." He returned to poking at the wreckage and pointing his flashlight beam under the fallen timbers. "And what do you know—we found another victim. White guy, tall, stringy—can't say much more about him than that. There wasn't much left. Any idea who he might be?"

A terrible thought suddenly dawned on Rafe. Now that they had found Laszlo's body, they were also likely to find the gun—*his* gun, and traceable, through Land Management records, back to him—unless he found it first. Why hadn't this occurred to him before?

"Nope—I didn't really know these guys by name."

As casually as he could, he worked his way over toward what had been the center of the barn, trying to judge where he had last seen Laszlo standing before the roof had caved in on him.

"Careful where you step," the marshal said. "That's about where we found that last guy."

"Yeah, sorry," Rafe said, hunching down to look under some burned furniture—the remains of what had been the bunk beds?—"just thought I could help."

The marshal turned and drifted off in the direction of the demolished bathroom, and Rafe took the opportunity to thoroughly reorient himself, to replay the final fight and figure out just exactly where the gun might have landed.

"Something tells me this place was a dump even before it burned down," the marshal called from behind a partial wall. "Am I right?"

"Yep," Rafe called back, not wanting to offer any more precise knowledge than that. He flipped over the spindly legs of the old Formica table, and instantly some little woodland creature scrambled for new cover. Plainly, Laszlo had lost his grip on the gun, or it would have been found when his body was. Rafe dug deeper.

Hearing the noise, the marshal called out, "I told you, you don't have to do that. It's more dangerous than you think."

"Okay, gotcha," Rafe called back, lifting a burned board and shifting it quietly to one side; under it, he saw a scorched mattress and splintered bedpost. Then, moving another, he spotted beneath it some smashed plates, charred pillows, and, barely visible, the dull glint of a Smith & Wesson muzzle.

"Nothing in there, thank God," the marshal said, coming out of the bathroom. "I guess the rest of 'em got out in time."

"Looks that way."

The marshal wiped his hands on his slicker and looked up at the sullen sky. "You think it'll ever rain in this town again?"

"The park service forecast says it might, later this week."

"Yeah," he said, clambering over some debris and passing Rafe on his way out. "And then again, I wouldn't bet on it."

Rafe quickly stuck a hand under the board, grabbed the gun, and shoved it under the back of his shirt.

"Come on out of there," the marshal said without turning around. "You're gonna get hurt. Leave it to the bulldozer."

"You're right," Rafe replied, watching him go. The gun was cold and hard and grimy against the small of his back, but he left it where it was. Lodged there, it felt like a little bit of penance.

When he heard the squad car driving off, he returned to the burned bike in the yard and knelt down beside the rear compartments. The saddlebag latches had been twisted into curlicues, and when he pried open the one on top, he found nothing but some rags and a melted tin of chrome polish.

Wrestling the remains of the bike onto its other side took a few minutes of hard labor, but when he was done, he was able to pop open the compartment and reach inside. What he pulled out was a molten mess, an amalgam of fried jerky strips, pills, chains, candy bars, cigarettes . . . and something else.

The journal.

Everything had congealed into one lump. The mottled shagreen covers of the book had been burned to a crisp, and once Rafe had managed to separate them from all the rest, he opened the book to find that the few pages left intact were entirely black. The rest were nothing but cinders, scattering the moment they were exposed to the sunlight. He watched the ashes rise up in the morning breeze and disperse like dandelion seeds into the canyon air. Even if he had ever been able to convince anyone of what he'd recovered from the bottom of the lake, he'd now have no proof of it at all. And if he tried to tell anyone the astonishing story he'd read, they'd have looked at him like he was crazy. What he held in his hands—the seared covers and a handful of dust— was all he had to show for the last words of Robert Louis Stevenson.

PART III

25 November, 1894

Samoa

Vailima.

That is the name we have given to our plantation.

Good Lord, who would ever have thought it possible that I, a son of Edinburgh, writer of stories and verse, scion of lighthouse engineers, should one day rule as master of a tropical paradise?

A native Samoan word, it means 'the place of five waters'. Waterfalls cascade from the surrounding slopes, streams and creeks abound, the jungle, green and glittering as an emerald necklace, embraces us on all sides.

It is here, after wandering the world, and in particular the South Pacific, that Fanny and I have fetched up and built, over these past six years, a comfortable and secluded life for ourselves, high atop the slopes of Mount Vaea, overlooking the harbour of Apia far below. By day we watch the trading vessels come and go, and gaze off at the hazy blue splendour of the mountains of Atua to the east. At night we sleep to the booming of the surf and the rustle of the broad flat leaves of the banyan trees outside the verandah.

It has been a long and oftentimes hazardous journey to this lofty haven.

Although we knew that Lloyd—Samuel Smith to all aboard—was below deck much of the time, we made the voyage to Boston Harbor without attempting any contact. It was best, I thought, to keep up the masquerade, lest any connection later be made by Inspector Abberline. Truth be told, I enjoyed the respite. Even Fanny seemed reconciled to it, or at least incapable of altering it, as she spent most of the ten-day passage sick from the pitching of the ship and the wretched food served up by the galley.

Still, the moment we disembarked, she eagerly scanned the other passengers coming ashore, waiting to catch her first glimpse of her errant son. But even after the flood had abated and the last stragglers had ambled down the gangway with their rucksacks, she had not seen him. Grabbing a ship's mate by the elbow, she said, 'Is that all of them?'

Glancing back, and seeing only porters climbing up the plank and no one else coming down, he said, 'Looks that way, ma'am.'

'Lloyd Osb—I mean, Samuel Smith. Do you know him?'

'Sammy? Sure I do,' he said, brightening up. 'The young doctor, come back to finish his studies at Harvard? Told some fine stories about the ladies of London,' he said, laughing, then catching himself. 'Though nothing too, well, improper, you might say.'

It surprised me not one whit that Lloyd had lacked the sense to keep a low profile, or that he had once again concocted an identity for himself. What did surprise me, however, was that he had indeed gone missing. Fanny bustled back aboard, and only after the first mate himself had given her a guided tour of the empty berths above and below, did she grasp that Lloyd had somehow slipped ashore before we had done so ourselves, and was now making his own way through the streets of Boston. Snow was falling from a leaden sky, and a cold wind was blowing, and I wondered how he hoped to fend for himself. Then it dawned on me.

'You gave him money?' I said to Fanny, and she replied, 'Some, before we left.' Turning on me, she said, 'The boy had to have something to call his own. And it's not so much he can live on it long.' I dreaded asking how much of our travel account she had shared with him before setting sail.

We stayed in Boston for a week, Fanny hoping that Lloyd would turn up any day, but he did not. After an article about our arrival had appeared in the "Boston Globe," and I had given an interview about my impressions of the city, she received a brief letter from Samuel Smith at our hotel—saying he was off on his own now 'to make my fortune or be made a fool', and declaring that 'though Louis has done me wrong, I forgive him—tell him so.' It cost me the better part of an hour to defend myself against that calumny.

Making stops in Chicago and Denver and Salt Lake City—at all of which I was able to offer impromptu lectures and earn generous honorariums—we journeyed westward, finally arriving in San Francisco, where we booked a private schooner, the "Casco"—seventy tons, ninety-five feet long, white sails and decks, polished brass, and a cockpit fitted out with cushioned seats surrounding the wheel and compass, as if one were in a drawing room on dry land. Like the Flying Dutchman forever fleeing before the gale, we crisscrossed the islands and atolls and archipelagos of the South Pacific, searching for the place we might call home. The place where the long arm of the law might never again reach out to interrogate me about certain events in London. The place where my lungs might function untroubled. The warm and humid climate proved a boon to my health, and although we were reconciled to our exile from England, we knew that we must choose somewhere that provided one more thing in addition—a sufficient link to the civilized world that I could continue in my career. In all this vast region, there are only four such places that afford fast mail-ship service—Papeete and Honolulu, which are already poisoned by the tide of French and Americans; Suva in Fiji, where the Melanesians have earned a rather unsavoury reputation for themselves; and finally, Apia in Samoa. If all goes well, a letter or manuscript can arrive in London in a month's time, a telegram in only a week—and the Polynesians are a friendly, if feckless, race. Furthermore, there are no malaria-bearing mosquitoes anywhere on the island. No snakes, either, for that matter. Did Saint Patrick sojourn here?

I contribute letters and essays from exotic ports-of-call for several publications, most notably the "New York Sun," which deposits twenty pounds to my accounts in London and two hundred dollars to my bank in San Francisco for each one. In Hawaii, I came across a local legend that, in a few days of sustained work, I managed to turn into a popular and much-translated tale. 'The Bottle Imp', it is called, and it tells the story of a demon that would give its owner anything he desired in return for his soul. Once it was produced in the Samoan language in a sort of cartoon form, it answered many questions that had perplexed the minds of the locals. Seeing the grand house that I have built, on more than three hundred acres, filled with mahogany furniture imported from Sydney, Oriental rugs on the floors, and a liquor cabinet well stocked with Irish whiskey and French cognac in crystal decanters, the natives had wondered how a man who sits about in his pajamas all day, scribbling, could accumulate such riches. Now they knew. I had sold my soul to a bottle imp! From that day forward, I have been known on the island (and, to some small extent, feared there) as Tusitala, or 'teller of tales'. Some of the islanders can occasionally be found snooping about the house, trying to find the magic bottle.

It was only a matter of time, I always suspected, before the prodigal stepson would reappear. Letters came to his mother from far-flung spots, filled with stories of high promise and imminent success, though never failing to appeal in the end for additional funds. One afternoon, as I sat at my desk in the library, the trade winds sifting through the open room, I saw a lone figure in a straw sun hat, a battered brown suitcase clutched in one hand, ambling up the path to the house. He stopped to catch his breath and put his bag down—it was a long climb—and his head went back to take in the peacock blue of the house, the red roof, the native tapas floating in the wide windows like tapestries. He trudged on, and soon I heard a cry of joy from below. Before descending, I left Fanny a few minutes to revel in the unexpected reunion.

'Look who's come home!' she exclaimed, though it was hard to imagine how this eyrie, which he had never before seen, could be considered his home.

Odd as it may seem, I, too, was glad to see Lloyd—a singular reaction, I know, in a man once shot at—but I could not fail to recall the boy he had once been, hunched over the rudimentary map we had drawn of Treasure Island, or gambolling with the late Woggin in the snow of Davos. (The dog's humble grave lies beneath a tree outside my study window.) Nor could I forget my role in the terrible changes that had overtaken him. We shook hands in a manly fashion, and then under Fanny's approving eye, embraced. In my heart, I have always felt a powerful urge towards forgiveness, coupled with the conviction that time can alter anyone, for good or ill. I was prepared to believe that the Lloyd I knew, serial impostor and unwanted suitor, was a new and different man.

He certainly looked it.

His hair had turned darker, his frame had filled out even more, and his face bore the telltale lines of battle. There was a deep furrow in his brow, a droop to the corner of his lip, a faint scar on one cheek. He wore the loose white shirt and dungarees common to most travellers in these regions, along with a necklace of shells whose clacketing I would come to know well. He was given spacious quarters in an upstairs corner of the house, and readily made himself at home there (some skills are never lost), sleeping late into the day, helping himself to the liquor cabinet, and mysteriously disappearing whenever the prospect of plantation work arose. Nights he spent carousing in the harbour bars, which were always packed with the usual assortment of beachcombers, seamen, and native girls. Because the German government had designs upon monopolizing the Samoan trade, there was a heavily Teutonic contingent along the waterfront, most of them in the employ of the so-called Long Handle firm—Deutsche Handels und Plantagen Gesellschaft der Südsee Inseln zu Hamburg—backed by Bismarck himself. Beer hall songs, more commonly heard in the streets of Heidelberg, often rang out across the piers and customs houses, sometimes carrying, if the wind was just right, all the way up to Vailima.

Indeed, I had caught a snatch of a tune one night while relaxing on the verandah with a glass of whiskey and a cigar, admiring how the moonlight lent the jungle surrounding the house a silvery sheen. Insects chittered, the occasional monkey howled, the banyan leaves flapped like elephant ears in the night breeze. All was right with the world . . . until, like a thunderclap, all went wrong.

Malaki, my head houseboy, came racing up the jungle path from the harbour, crying out for me, and though I moved to hush him lest he wake Fanny and everyone else in the house, he insisted that I take my gun and follow him back down the mountain. The blood on his pareu made the case more imperative, and by the time I had loaded my rifle and come back outside, he was waiting with my horse saddled. I offered him a hand up to ride behind me on the horse, but he shook his head. Not only would it be a breach of decorum, but he believed, and rightly so, that he could keep pace on foot as well as my horse would be able to pick its way down the zigzagging trail.

When we got down to the beach and I had dismounted, he led the way, with a torch held aloft, along the waterfront. It was very late, and even the German sailors of the Long Handle firm had ended their revelries.

We followed the footprints in the sand for several hundred yards. One pair, small and dainty, most probably belonged to a bare-foot girl, the other to a man in hobnail boots.

'Here, Tusitala, here!' Malaki urged as we approached a tide pool. Lowering the torch, he said 'See,' and see I did.

I remember confusing the long black hair for seaweed, the pink hibiscus blossom for a sand crab—my eyes again refusing to accept what lay before them. It was a girl—I'd seen her selling woven baskets to tourists—

And she was lying in the water, her face down. 'Quickly,' I said, 'we must get her out.' But Malaki would not touch her or help. I soon saw why. Once I had dragged her body above the tideline and turned her over, I saw that her throat had been cut, and her dress sliced open from top to bottom. Someone had gone at her with a knife, slashing and ripping in a frenzy of bloodlust.

My mind reeled, as well as my body, transporting me back to the Whitechapel mortuary and the remains of Annie Chapman, to the squalid quarters at 13 Miller's Court, to the fog-bound streets of London and the Swiss assassin, Josef. But fast upon those reflections came another, nipping at their heels—a thought that was suddenly as inescapable as it was horrific.

Closing up the torn halves of her dress and leaving Malaki to watch over the corpse, I traced the footprints of the hobnail boots, seldom worn in these climes, towards the customs house, mounted on caissons, its decks cluttered with casks of copra and coffee beans. I climbed the stairs and, inside, heard the grunts of a struggling beast. I unslung the rifle from my back and, looking through the quarter-panes of the window, saw the figure of a man, with hunched shoulders and bandy legs, shimmying open the cash drawer. Cocking the rifle, I positioned myself outside the warped wooden door, only to have it flung open so violently that I fell back, the gun exploding in an orange blast of smoke and fire as I toppled over the railing and down onto the sand. The culprit leapt down beside me, his boots nearly thumping on my chest, and then, before I could recover my breath or senses, he escaped into the labyrinth of docks and empty stalls.

How long I lay there, stunned, I do not know, but Malaki, having heard the gunshot, hurried to my side and urged me to my feet. 'We must go, Master! We must go!' And with his strong arm around my waist, he guided me back to the horse.

'But the girl,' I said, and he shook his head.

'It is the work of the imp,' he said. 'Maybe you can get him back in the bottle!' He slapped the horse on the rump and sent me on my way.

The imp. If only it had been so . . .

The horse knew its way back, which was just as well, as my head was filled to bursting with other thoughts and fears. Conclusions that were all but impossible to deny crowded my mind. What course of action could I possibly take? What could I prove—and was I willing to prove it, knowing that I would be sending one man to the gallows and his mother into a despair from which she would never recover? Was I prepared to admit, to myself and the world, that I had carried this thing, like a contagion, from one continent to another? Or to accept that all I had done in my career, all my work and toil, would be forever after eclipsed by this one awful and overarching calamity of my life?

At Vailima, I stabled the horse and surveyed the house for any sign of wakefulness, but there was none. The lights were out; all was quiet. I knew where I needed to go, and mounted the staircase to the second floor with my heart pounding. Did I hope to find Lloyd fast asleep, unsullied with blood, snoring from too much drink? Even then, I did harbour such a hope—quickly dashed when I parted the curtain and saw the bed unoccupied. Still, my mind searched for some way out, some answer that would be more acceptable than the one I knew. I lit the oil lamp and looked about the room. Only once or twice had I ever ventured in here, and Lloyd had made loud complaint about the intrusion on his privacy.

'It's bad enough that the damn place has no proper doors,' he'd said, 'but if I cannot trust everyone to stay out, I shall have to move down into Apia.'

There was little chance of that—Lloyd enjoyed his status, and his comforts, at Vailima far too much to trade them for a waterfront room above a brothel. His slippers lay beside the bed, his books on the night table, his brush and comb and mirror on the dresser. I opened the drawers, rummaged through his clothes, unsure of what I was even looking for. Then, I was reminded of the armoire in his room at Cavendish Square, and how he had hung the satchel sideways behind his clothes. In this armoire, too, I found the satchel, similarly concealed, and opened it once more.

On this occasion, however, the assortment of oddities assumed a newfound, and long-denied, clarity. The mind is a curious thing, able to suppress whatever it must, for some time. But observing the contents, I knew that the last redoubt had been breached.

The brass rings.

Polly Nichols, the first of the Ripper's victims, had worn such rings.

The torn envelope. A scrap, no doubt its mate, had been found in Annie Chapman's purse.

The rusty key.

The killer who left Mary Jane Kelly's room had locked the door behind him, and the key was never found.

Was there a similar connection for the amber comb with the broken teeth? Had it belonged to Elizabeth Stride?

Or the loose buttons at the bottom of the bag? Were they torn from the dress of Catherine Eddowes?

Souvenirs, all?

And what of the folded paper I found there now, a paper that I did not remember from before?

I opened it and saw that it was the bill from the Aldgate Arms. I had not seen it in years. Was he so sentimental about his tenancy there that he had found it among my papers and made off with it? Studying it by the flickering light of the lamp, I noted only one thing that had escaped my attention before. The date on which the room had been taken.

It was on the thirty-first of August. In 1888.

The date rang a bell because it was the night of the London premiere of "The Strange Case of Dr Jekyll and Mr Hyde." Lloyd had not attended because he was off in Paris at the Folies Bergère with his erstwhile friend Randolph Desmond. Or so Fanny and I had been led to believe.

It was also the night that Jack the Ripper had claimed his first victim.

The bill still in my hand, I sat down on the edge of the bed. It was as if I had just suffered the coup de grâce. The Ripper had not struck even once since my family and I had boarded the boat to Boston. Henley's letters had kept me informed on that score, and on the rest of the London news. 'The bastard seems to have vanished into thin air,' Henley wrote, 'and we can only hope that he is roasting in some peculiarly hot corner of Hell.'

How could I ever tell him—though Henley would be the one to whom I must reveal it—that Jack had materialized again, six years later and ten thousand miles away?

And that I had been his author, in both a fictional and actual sense? I had proved to be the real Dr Jekyll—and what I had conjured was a genuine Mr Hyde.

30 November, 1894

Lloyd did not come home that night. Or the next. Or the next.

When word of the murder got around the island, suspicion fell everywhere—on the German sailors who got drunk and rowdy in the harbour bars, on the local pimps and publicans who used the native girls as bait and chum, on the crew of a French trawler that had upped anchor and left at the first crack of dawn for an unknown destination—but none fell on Tusitala or his household. I was considered above reproach, a cross between a mighty chieftain and a shaman. If anything, I was expected to employ my occult powers to sort it out.

Malaki, I believe, assumed that I had promptly done that very thing by recapturing the imp and sealing him up again in his bottle.

Fanny, however, was beside herself, not because she suspected her son of any such crime—she was quite capable of watching him shoot someone before her very eyes and blaming only the bullet—but because she feared the murderer might have done some harm to her son, too. It wasn't unlike Lloyd to miss the occasional night at Vailima—he was a man of robust vices—but several in a row became cause for concern, especially as there had been a mighty storm uprooting trees and blowing the roof off many of the native huts. Fanny wanted to send Malaki down to Apia to ask around, but I warned her that doing so might have unintended consequences. She gave me a long look, but took my advice, held her tongue, and waited.

Meanwhile, I had hatched my own plan for his return. The last of the elixir I had secreted in an iron safe with a combination lock, purchased in town for just that purpose; if the elixir alone was what brought on the murderous madness, then never again would he have access to it. I had felt its effects myself, the brutal physical transformation, the almost ungovernable impulses, but I could only surmise that it worked hand in hand with some natural propensity—that where the urge to malevolence already existed, the conjunction led to murder and mayhem; but that in a higher nature, its influence could be controlled, or even quelled. I, too, had experienced the quickening of the blood, the sensation of sudden strength and, in my case, an exalted constitution, but I had committed no murders under its sway.

Regardless, I had determined to confront Lloyd upon his return and tell him that I now knew all. All. Once we were done with what were sure to be his furious denials, we could move on to the more practical questions. I would have to make quite clear to him that his secret was safe only so long as no further monstrous acts occurred; if one did—before I could put a stop it—the full account of his crimes, along with the evidence (from combs to keys, buttons to brass rings) would be given up against him.

Privately, I had made another decision, one that I could not share with anyone. At the first sign of a descent, I had decided I would take matters into my own hands, but in such a way that neither Fanny nor the authorities could ever hold me responsible for his demise.

By the end of the week, however, I felt I could no longer postpone a trip to the neighbouring island of Savai'i, from which I had promised "McClure's Magazine" one of my regular dispatches. The Samoan nation was being torn in every direction by the great colonial powers—England, France, and Germany—and in my reports I have attempted to describe the ruthless machinations of the Europeans against the weaker and unsophisticated islanders, who are no match for them in cunning, duplicity, or greed. In acting on their behalf, I feel myself compensating in some small way for all the grief I have brought into the world.

Grief that I have confessed in a letter to Henley, the only man who would fully understand, and left in the postal basket on the hall table, along with a short story I hope he might be able to sell for me, days earlier. The story, like 'The Bottle Imp', is based on one of the ingenious local legends.

Malaki kept a small fishing boat in the harbour, no more than twenty-five feet long, with a double hull and half-claw rig. Known in the islands as an alia, the boat and its single triangular sail is as nimble as it is fast, remarkable for its windward performance free of heeling force. In true Polynesian fashion, two big eyes have been painted on its prow, so that the alia, as primitive as it is unsinkable, can see where it is going. Even so, Malaki was reluctant to take it out to sea. The cyclone had passed, but the weather was still changeable and uncertain.

'We wait, Master. Maybe tomorrow, better.'

'No, today we go,' I said. I needed to be away from Apia, away from Fanny, away from the whole business. 'We can beat the weather.'

The strait between the islands was only eight or nine miles wide, and if a storm struck, there were two smaller islands—Apolima and Manono—where we could put in. 'You are a great sailor, Malaki, and I have every faith in you.'

Grumbling, though unwilling to offer further resistance, Malaki made the boat ready, stowing the fishing nets in the tiny cabin and freeing the sail from its resting place in the fork at the top of the mast. We were just passing the end of the dock when I heard thundering footsteps on the planks and saw Lloyd, in straw hat and soiled clothes, leap into the air and land full square on the deck of the boat. Malaki looked at me in astonishment, wondering what to do and whether to turn back, but I was nonplussed myself.

Lloyd, straightening, said, 'A fine day for a sail, don't you think?'

He was unshaven and sunburned, and gave every impression of having roughed it in the jungle, or on the beach. He also looked slightly different . . . his brow more pronounced, his jaw more jutting. Around his neck he wore the familiar necklace of bleached shells, his good-luck charm.

I waved a hand at Malaki to indicate that he should keep to his course, and soon we were well past the breakers and reef and out in the open sea. The storm the day before had dropped pieces of the village huts and the fronds of palm trees into the water all around us. I even saw the painted placard of a French café, the Coq D'Or, bobbing among the waves.

'I hope you don't mind,' Lloyd said, helping himself to a hunk of cheese and a slab of bread from the basket that Fanny had packed, 'but I'm famished.' He had lost weight, and I could not help but wonder what weapon he might be concealing under the loose and untucked tails of his long white shirt.

'How is my mother?' he asked, eating with such gusto that crumbs fell from his mouth.

'She is well,' I replied, 'but, of course, concerned about your absence.'

He nodded, as if that was only to be expected, and said, 'You can tell her I'm fine.'

'Why not do that yourself?'

He gave me a long, level stare. 'Do I need to dignify that question with a reply?'

'You do. No suspicion has fallen on you, or anyone in my household.'

'Oh, that's right—the mighty Tusitala! Lord of all he surveys!' He bowed his head three times. 'Forgive me, Your Highness, for my presumption!'

Rooting around in the basket, he took out a ripe coconut and then, reaching under his shirt, withdrew a long and evil-looking blade with a bamboo handle. He thwacked the top off the coconut and tilted it back to drink the milk. Was that the very knife used on the girl in Apia? I did not doubt it.

'Then what are your plans?' I asked. 'To hide out in the jungle, or sleep on the beach, forever?'

'You should try it sometime. It's not bad at all.'

I let that pass. Malaki threw me another glance; had he surmised that it might have been this dishevelled creature on the boat—a Lloyd unlike any he might have seen lounging about Vailima—and not the bottle imp at all, who had committed the abomination in the tide pool? I signalled, with a raised palm, that all was under control, and he returned to his piloting. The alia, heeling only a few degrees, skimmed along the water like a skater on smooth ice, sending up a fine but cold salt spray.

'I have given it some serious thought,' Lloyd said, carving out chunks of coconut, 'and I've decided that it's too difficult to maintain a proper literary career from this godforsaken place. I need the stimulation of my peers.'

What he needed was talent, and the industry to use it. But what would be the use in saying so?

'London isn't for me—too snobbish, and I'm an American, after all. I don't like New York, either—too noisy, too dirty. Coconut?' he said, holding up a white chunk, and before I could decline it, chucking it to me. Considering the knife that had cut it, I could not eat it.

'No, I think California's the coming place,' he continued. 'San Francisco, or even perhaps Los Angeles. It's still a little rough around the edges right now, but it will clean up nicely over the coming years. Mark my words.'

I knew where this was going. Every conversation with Lloyd inevitably went in the same direction.

'Of course, it may take some time for me to establish my reputation.'

'And in the meantime, you will need an allowance.'

'You always were a quick study, Louis.'

A sudden surge sent the coconut rolling against the bulwark, and I put out a hand to brace myself against the stern. Malaki looked off to the northwest, where the blue volcanic peaks of Savai'i were being obscured by a rapidly approaching bank of clouds.

'But what assurance would I have that you had not returned to your old ways?' I asked. 'Once you were beyond my purview, how could I be sure you had not succumbed to the same savage impulses?'

'What assurance do you have right now?'

There he was correct. What had I done to protect the people of Apia from this monster of my own creation? Even now, it looked as if the elixir was having some residual effect. His jaws, when he chewed, did not neatly align.

A powerful gust of wind billowed out the sail, and Malaki, legs spread wide to keep his balance on the sloping deck, hauled in on the line.

'Master, maybe we go Manono instead. More closer.'

The cloud had already turned a darker shade of grey. Squalls in these seas can come out of nowhere, and dissipate just as abruptly.

'Can't we outrun it?'

Malaki shrugged, his bare brown shoulders straining at the line.

'I'd say five hundred a month,' Lloyd suggested, oblivious to the growing danger. 'Dollars, of course, not pounds.'

'Of course.'

'And it wouldn't hurt if you wrote a few letters of introduction to your various editors in the States. Just to make them aware of my availability.'

I agreed to this, too.

'Scribner's, in particular. I think I have an idea for a book they'd like.'

I nodded, humouring him for want of any better strategy, but he seemed to have guessed as much. 'Why do I doubt your sincerity, Louis?'

The boat was buffeted again, and a surge of water washed across the small deck and into the tiny cabin where the fishing nets and emergency provisions were kept.

'Master, too far! Must go Manono instead!'

'Then do!' I shouted back, over the rising wind. Malaki was one of the most renowned sailors on the island, but even distracted as I was by the colloquy with Lloyd, I heard a note of alarm in his voice that could not be denied.

Malaki braced himself hard, and held tight to the sail. The boat tacked sharply to the east, where I could just make out the waves crashing on the coral reefs of the nearby island.

'Bloody hell,' Lloyd said, his brow furrowing with anger, and one hand groping for purchase on the cabin door. The other still clutched the knife. 'What have you got me into now?'

I gripped the handle of the tiller and flattened my sandals against the deck.

Moments later, the squall had descended upon us in all its fury. It was as if we had just stepped under the falls at Niagara, a wall of white water whipped to a frenzy by a lashing wind, wrapping the alia in a cocoon of pounding waves and stinging spray. Catching a breath was nearly impossible, and squinting my eyes against the salt and mist, I could barely discern Malaki, clinging to the line, his feet swinging free above the tilted deck, and Lloyd, the knife clutched between his teeth like a buccaneer, crawling towards me along the length of the rope.

The sail swung across the boat as swiftly as a cricket bat, back and then forth, with Malaki struggling to keep some hold on it. The boat heeled and ducked and dodged among the waves, the eyes on its painted prow no doubt as blinded by the storm as our own. Lloyd was close enough now that he could grab at my ankle, and did, but I pulled it back. His face was more contorted than it had been, the look in his eyes more malignant, and it came to me that he had suddenly gone beyond reason, that the monster in him—perhaps aroused by the storm, finding in the tempest a kindred spirit—had swallowed whole the rational man. One hand was grasping at me, but the other now gripped the gleaming knife. There was no question in my mind that he had set aside all practical advantages to my continued life—that his intellect had been subsumed by base animal instinct—and that he meant instead to settle all his scores with me then and there. Hang the reference letters to Scribner's—with me gone, his mother would freely dispense as much money to him as he could spend.

I drew my legs back as far as I could, and when he jabbed the knife, I swivelled my body to one side, the tiller nestled in my armpit, and then, when he thrust again, twisted the other way. A wave crashed down like a sledgehammer, sending him skittering back down the deck towards the cabin.

Malaki shouted something in his native tongue—a plea to some Polynesian deity?—all the while wrestling with the flapping triangle of sail.

Lloyd dragged himself back towards me, clinging to the rope like a man climbing a mountain, his murderous intent confirmed by the strange grin on his face and the obsidian glint in his eyes. His hair was plastered to his skull, his shirt ripped open by the wind to reveal a mass of curls so dense as to constitute fur.

The boat bucketed through a trough in the waves, and when it rose again on the next crest, Lloyd rose with it, staggering to his bare feet, one hand braced against the mast, the other brandishing the knife aloft, like one of great Caesar's assassins.

'The whole world', he bellowed, 'is my Whitechapel!'—before plunging towards the stern, where he was met by the soles of my feet on his chest. My knees were crushed by the weight of him, and though his face came so close that the necklace of shells dangled against my lips, I was able to lever him back before the knife could swipe again. He stumbled towards the cabin, and then, when the alia pitched again, he used its momentum to rush at me once more.

I readied myself for the onslaught, and caught hold of the arm wielding the knife only when the tip of the blade was inches from my throat. I squirmed to one side, the knife propelling itself deep into the wood of the stern. As he struggled to free it, I scrambled towards the bow, nearly colliding with Malaki, whose battle with the boat had rendered him oblivious to everything transpiring behind him. But now he turned, astonished, as Lloyd trudged after me, and when he had come close enough to deal another blow, I shoved Malaki to the deck, hard enough to send him sprawling halfway into the cabin and safely out of reach of the knife and the errant sail. The sail swung wildly, its wet canvas wrapping itself like a shroud around the flailing Lloyd, who tried to slash his way free. He had almost managed it when the howling wind lifted the boat, and I threw myself at the rope, yanking it with all my might. The shredded sail carried Lloyd over the bulwark, and before swinging back the other way, it dropped him, arms and legs thrashing like a lobster in the pot, into the churning ocean.

I banged down hard on the deck, and let go of the rope only long enough to throw my arms around the creaking mast. All I could see of Malaki were some fingers tenaciously gripping the cabin door. The boat rocketed this way and that, a bucking bronco with no one holding the reins, and every moment I was sure would be my last. There was a splintering judder that ran all the way down its shaft as the mast snapped in two, the upper portion splashing into the sea, and then a grinding noise from below. The boat wrenched itself to a stop, waves sluicing over the deck, the winds still swirling, until, almost as suddenly as it had come on, the squall passed, and the ocean slowed to a ponderous roll.

Minutes later, the sun broke through, and I wiped the salt from my eyes. The alia was perched, like a seabird, atop a coral reef, its painted eyes staring straight at the strip of beach not a quarter mile away. Head down, Malaki emerged from the cabin on hands and knees. He saw me clinging to the stump of the mast and looked around for the missing Lloyd, but neither of us saw him, and by mutual assent neither of us said a word about it. Providence, I could not help but feel, had lent a righteous hand.

2 December, 1894

The strip of sand that I could see from the stranded boat was littered with seaweed and debris from the storm.

After several hours of teetering atop the reef, Malaki and I were rescued in a war canoe sent by the natives of Manono, and though we told them that we had lost a man at sea, they said none had been found, nor did they appear to believe anyone could have survived the squall.

I prayed that they were right.

After spending a night ashore, we were carried back home in the same canoe—these are made to hold as many as twenty men and to travel swiftly among the many islands that dot the Polynesian archipelago—and once we had put in at the harbour at Apia, I rewarded our saviours by telling the proprietor of the Coq D'Or, whose sign I had seen floating out to sea, to give them all the food and drink they desired, and send me the bill. They were eager to have me join them—Tusitala is a name to conjure with on all the islands of Samoa—but I was anxious to return to Vailima, where Fanny would be awaiting my return. All the way up the mountain trail, I wondered how I would be able to break the news to her. She had no idea that Lloyd had leapt onto the boat, much less that he had been swept overboard in a squall.

When Malaki and I came into the clearing, I saw her on the verandah, slicing breadfruit into a bowl for our customary after-noon tea. 'When do we start calling it afternoon coffee?' she often remarked, as both of us preferred the stronger brew. She beamed at our approach.

'I wasn't sure what day you'd be home,' she called out. 'But I made the snack anyway. Malaki, you're welcome to have some.'

But there must have been something in the set of our shoulders and heads that told her something was amiss.

'Louis, is everything all right? Did you get a good story on Savai'i?'

'I never made it there,' I replied, slowly mounting the steps to the rocking chair next to her own. Malaki, knowing that this needed to be a private conversation, veered off to the stable to tend to the horse.

'Why not?'

'We encountered a sudden storm at sea.'

'Oh, that's too bad,' she said, 'but you both look like you made it through all right.'

'Not entirely.'

'What happened? Did the boat sink? If it did, we'll have to make it up to Malaki.'

And then, in halting words, leaning forward to take her hand in my own, I told her that her son had unexpectedly joined us. She stiffened immediately. I told her that Lloyd had been in good spir-its and was helping us to untangle the fishing nets when a squall descended out of nowhere. Her eyes were retreating into their sock-ets; her lips grew thin and bloodless. When I told her how heroically he had attempted to help hold the sail, even after the mast had begun to break, she had already grasped the full import. The bowl of breadfruit slid off her lap, spilling onto the verandah. I did not need to concoct anything more; she could read it in my eyes. Nor would she have heard me, anyway, over her anguished cries.

'Fanny, what can I do?' I implored, still clutching her hand, which had turned to ice. 'What can I do?'

But she could not stop the howls of pain, slumping from the chair and deliquescing onto the rough planks of the verandah. Her cries came so unceasingly that I feared for her breath. All I could think to do was to race upstairs to my medicine cabinet, prepare a syringe of morphine, and hurtle back down again, by which time Malaki had come to her side. As he held an arm steady, I injected the drug, and in no more than a minute or two, she had slipped into a stupor.

Carefully, we carried her up the stairs to the bedroom, where we laid her on the bed, her eyes vague and unfocussed, her tongue lolling from the corner of her mouth. Much as I had dreaded the paroxysm of grief, this preternatural stillness I found equally disquieting. It was as if she were voluntarily departing the shores of life. I stayed by her bedside for the next several hours, stroking her hands and arms, occasionally whispering some words of comfort or endearment. Once or twice, I was rewarded with a yes, or a sigh to indicate agreement, but by the dead of night, she had escaped into a sleep forty fathoms deep. The trade winds that blew through the wide-open spaces of the house, billowing out the tapas, had chilled me to the bone, and I felt a coughing fit arising from my chest. Not wanting to disturb her slumbers, I gently disengaged and went to my study for my robe and a glass of whiskey.

I dropped into my chair, a handkerchief pressed to my lips to muffle the eruption of coughs, and reached for the cut-glass decanter, glimmering in the moonlight. But my fingers encountered something brittle, dangling from its top, and when, puzzled, I lit the oil lamp to get a better look, I saw a strand of bleached shells draped like a necklace around its stopper.

TOPANGA CANYON— CALIFORNIA

Present Day

There was just one more thing Rafe needed to do before saying good-bye to the canyon.

The day before, he'd been officially relieved of his duties by a plainly pleased Ellen Latham. By then, she'd heard reports of everything from meth labs in the hills to motorcycle gangs and missing coyotes. "I can't see that there's anything left for you to accomplish there," she said, requesting that he surrender his badge and his gun on the spot—man, was he glad he had retrieved the weapon—and handing him instead a bunch of termination forms to fill out and return at his leisure. He'd stood in the concrete plaza outside, feeling everything from mild shock to a sneaking sense of relief. He'd been waiting for this shoe to drop for so long, it was strangely comforting to have gotten it over with. What he would do next wasn't clear, but he wouldn't miss the bureaucracy of the Land Management office. That was for sure.

Driving home, he was just glad that she'd forgotten to requisition the purple Land Rover. Or maybe she just didn't care.

This morning, he'd awakened on top of his trailer with the sun in his eyes and a bee buzzing around his nose. Leaving his khakis in the closet, he put on a pair of jeans and sneakers, drove to the trailhead, and hiked into the canyon. No antenna this time, or heavy backpack. Just a canteen slung over one shoulder and, tucked into his pants pocket, something that he meant to return to where it belonged.

The air was fresh and sweet and scented with the wild chaparral. Grouse scurried into the brush, lizards darted, and insects buzzed. Whatever problems there were in the world—and there were plenty— they were nowhere in sight. Not here, not now. Even the land was starting to show signs of rejuvenation. Already, sprigs of grass and clumps of mushrooms were popping up among the coastal sage. Sparrows and white-throated swifts flitted overhead. It was paradise . . . even if it had once harbored something terrible.

He crested the hill, and saw just below him the lake. A light breeze stirred the water, and the sunshine gave its pale-green surface a silvery sheen. To think that here, in this unlikely place, a dreadful secret had long been buried. A secret that no one else would ever know . . . or believe. There was just one piece of proof left, and striding down to the bank, he took it out of his pocket. Though dented and dull, the gold watchcase still glittered in the morning light. Rafe popped it open and looked one last time at the initials—SLO. Samuel Lloyd Osbourne. His last claim to fame.

As if he were skipping a stone, Rafe cocked his arm back and shot the watch at the lake, where it took one, two, three leaps before sinking to the bottom. That was where it belonged, along with everything else that had ever belonged to its long-forgotten owner.

Once the ripples had stopped, Rafe turned to go, but not before something else caught his eye. On the opposite shore, he thought he saw some movement—an animal, head down, cautiously approaching the water. He raised a hand to block out some of the sun. It came down to the waterline and bowed its head to drink. Rafe didn't move a muscle. From here, he could tell it wasn't his beloved Diego or Frida; they were both smaller. It looked like either the biggest coyote he'd ever seen in these parts . . . or a wolf.

A big gray one.

Although wolves generally met their water requirements through eating the flesh of their prey—most of the meat was water—in warmer weather like this, and in conditions where prey was scarce, they were known to drink for thermoregulation. When this one had finished lapping at the water, it raised its head and looked straight at him. Its ears went up, though one was bent, and then, unperturbed, it turned away and loped off to the south.

"Hey, stranger," Rafe said softly. "Welcome to Topanga."

5 December, 1894

Vailima

Indistinguishable, don't you think?

My handwriting, and Louis's?

If I had not admitted to my imposture just now, wouldn't you have thought it was still Louis making this entry? How fortunate that over the years I spent many an hour mastering his distinctive scrawl—so useful when forging bank cheques or IOUs.

I had never expected, however, to employ it to this purpose . . . setting the record straight in the final pages of this, his private diary.

True, I enjoyed toying with him in other ways. I thought looping the shells around his whiskey decanter, for instance, was a deliciously sly means of announcing my return to Vailima. Given the man's weak constitution, I didn't want to give him a seizure by simply showing up at the house.

Not that I should have given it so much concern. Louis cared not a whit about me! Once I'd been plunged into the storm-tossed ocean, he assumed me dead, and no doubt wished it so. These pages, which I have just read, make that plain. Such a want of faith on his part! Using the torn sail to bind myself to the broken mast, I rode it all the way to the shores of Savai'i, where some natives plucked me from the beach and transported me in one of their alias back to Apia. As they consider me the son of the great Tusitala, they could not have been more obliging.

But I knew my welcome home would be problematic, to say the least. Louis had tumbled to the truth—only someone as blinded by proximity as he was could have taken so long to do so—and even gone so far as to share the news of his discovery in a letter to his old chum, Henley. I know this for a fact because, as it was a frequent custom of mine, I had purloined the letter from the postal basket.

It wasn't until the next night that I allowed him to see me. He was in the kitchen with my mother. Poor woman, she looked like she had died a thousand deaths; how comforting it was to know how much she might mourn my real loss one day, should some strange accident befall me. I was sorry she'd been put through this ordeal, but consoled myself with knowing how much greater her joy would now be at my salvation.

As for Louis, slicing a pile of taro roots on the cutting board, he looked distracted. I was standing silently just outside on the verandah, concealed in the dark. The kitchen was well lit by several oil lamps. I could understand the consternation on his face, and, frankly, revelled in it. Who would argue that the anguish of others is not in some way delightful to apprehend? He was trying to draw my mother out, hovering over her like a benevolent stork, but she was having none of it. Good for her.

Timing my entrance was critical. I waited until he had put the carving knife down and raised a glass of his precious Irish whiskey to his lips before I stepped close enough to the open window to be seen. Even before I'd uttered my opening line—'What are we having for dinner?'—Louis saw me take shape there, like a ghost in one of his bogey tales, dropped the glass, and clapped his hands like cymbals to the sides of his head. Down he went, in a jumble of bony elbows and knees, groaning as if his head had been split with an axe, and Fanny had no sooner taken that in than she saw me. She was torn between screaming in horror and shouting in joy!

The exultation was deep, but momentary, superseded by the need to immediately tend to her supine husband. Malaki was summoned to help carry him upstairs—oh, what a pleasure it was to see the surprise on that one's face, too!—while another houseboy was dispatched to town to fetch a doctor. Louis did indeed look gravely ill, and despite the many injuries he had done me, I felt a pang of conscience. It is simply my nature.

He lay still, eyes staring, unable to speak, while my mother attempted to revive him by rubbing brandy into his skeletal arms. When Malaki tried to remove his boots, I warned him not to do so: 'Louis once told me he hoped to die with his boots on.' My mother flashed an impatient look, perhaps at my lack of diplomacy, but honestly, the outcome was clear. As soon as the doctor arrived—the ship's surgeon from HMS Wallaroo, anchored in the harbour—he confirmed my importunate diagnosis.

'I fear he has had a cerebral haemorrhage', he said, 'brought on, perhaps, by some sudden shock to the system.'

Another pang.

'But they can come on out of nowhere, too,' he added, 'like a comet streaking across the night sky.'

I remember the comet remark because it recalled a line from Louis's morbid poem 'Requiem': 'Under the wide and starry sky, Dig the grave and let me lie.' Louis had spent a good deal of time studying the heavens, either out on that verandah, or up among the snowy peaks of Davos. (In London, it was hopeless—the fog and chimney smoke were thick enough to obscure even the lamp posts.)

My mother often remarked that the man lived with his head in the clouds.

'But what do we do now?' she said. 'How do we help him?'

The doctor looked quite baffled and had nothing more to suggest than keeping a close watch and answering any need he might find it possible to express. Small chance of that. The light in his bulging dark eyes was already flickering like a candle caught in a draft, his long face going slack. Whether he registered my presence at all, I cannot say.

Over the next hour or so, several of the native servants crept into the room and sat cross-legged in a circle around the bed; under their breath they hummed some mournful island dirge. At some unnoticed point, between one shallow breath and another, Louis shuffled off this mortal coil. My mother remained beside him on the bed, while Malaki crumpled forward in a heap on the floor. Stepping round the mourners, I went into the study, and using the combination to the safe that I had divined with ease (Louis always used some iteration of his birthday, forty-four years earlier), I opened it and removed the flasks from Dr Rüedi. Using my unique penmanship skills to impersonate Louis, I would urge the good doctor to find some way to manufacture, and send, more, but the prospects of success were dubious. Henceforth, conservation would have to be my watchword.

That, and discretion. I have grown too bold and incautious, I will admit, a change that I attribute in part to the powerful effects of the elixir, and in part to the predilections of my own character. From what secret source these impulses arise remains a mystery to me. But governable, they are not. All I can do is indulge them in as clever and masterful a manner as practicable. My success in that respect has been indisputable. Apart from Louis—and even he kept his own counsel—no one has publicly accused me of a worse impropriety than booting that dullard Randolph Desmond down some steps. The brilliantly executed crimes of Jack the Ripper have been laid at a dozen doorsteps, but none of them mine. Nor will they be—not so long as I am alive to be called to account for them.

No, I mean to keep this journal, and my souvenirs, intact and unknown. They shall travel with me wherever I go (at this moment, my native California is again striking my fancy), and when, many years from now, my end draws near, I shall consign them to some appropriate grave. An unmarked spot where, in the fullness of time, posterity shall rediscover—and perhaps reassess—them. I leave that to Fate. Like Thomas De Quincey, I contend that there is an artistry in any pursuit—be it literature, or murder—and as someone who expects to rank high in the annals of both, I wish to be assured one day of the proper recognition. I've earned my laurels, and what's fair is fair. On that much, I believe, as reasonable people, we can all agree. Can we not?

AUTHOR'S NOTE

As someone who writes books in which history and fiction get all tangled up, I'm often asked how I go about it, what the rules are, and occasionally why I do things this way at all.

First off, let me say that I do it because the real characters I find—Benvenuto Cellini and Count Cagliostro in *The Medusa Amulet*, Rasputin and the Russian royal family in *The Romanov Cross*, Florence Nightingale in *Blood and Ice*, Einstein in *The Einstein Prophecy*—are so much richer and better than any I could ever have imagined, it seems crazy not to just pick them up and use them.

Also, I'm something of a history buff. I love reading it, which means that when I'm researching one of my novels, I get to sit around and read lots of biographies and historical texts and tell myself I'm working. I am, but it's fun, too.

You might also have heard that old line about truth being stranger than fiction—I'm here to tell you it's true. My storytelling abilities pale in comparison to true events and twists of fate. *The Jekyll Revelation* came about, in fact, because of something I happened to read in a book about Victorian London. It was while the stage play of *The Strange Case of Dr Jekyll and Mr Hyde* was playing in the West End that Jack the

Ripper first struck, and official suspicion briefly fell on Robert Louis Stevenson and on the actor who played the dual title role. That started the wheels turning, and led, in the fullness of time, to this very book.

But here comes the caveat. Don't treat everything I say as gospel. When someone at a reading asks me if everything in my book is true (and someone always does), I reply that ninety percent of the historical stuff is correct; I do my best to keep it so. But I also bend events and chronologies and even family relationships all the time in order to better and more sleekly service the story I'm trying to tell. In other words, if you can enjoy the book, and it sends you back to reading the primary historical sources, then that's great. However, do not, under any circumstances, write your term paper based on facts you find in one of my novels. I just might have made them up—or dispatched my little Brownies to do it.

Now *that's* a good example of everything I've just been saying. I was delighted to discover, while reading Stevenson's letters, that when he closed his eyes at night, he believed that a troop of tiny imaginary creatures—his Brownies, he called them—went to work, coming up with stories and ideas and plots for his work, and that when he woke up in the morning, if they'd done their job, he'd be able to go straight to his desk and start writing. These Brownies are mentioned throughout this book, as is his friendship with the poet and editor W. E. Henley. Robert Louis Stevenson and Henley, the model for the one-legged pirate Long John Silver in *Treasure Island*, were indeed the best of friends—until they were not. In later years, a feud broke out, and though I do not get into that in this book, Stevenson died, to his immense regret, with it unmended.

If you want to learn more about the life of Robert Louis Stevenson, I can highly recommend Frank McLynn's eponymous biography of the author (published by Random House), and for more information on Jack the Ripper, I'd suggest a beautifully illustrated volume entitled *Jack the Ripper—CSI: Whitechapel*, by the noted Ripperologists (yes, that's a real term) Paul Begg and John Bennett (André Deutsch/Carlton Publishing Group). For those of you with a more academic bent, there's a harrowing look at the London of this era in a book entitled *East End 1888* by W. J. Fishman, published by the Temple University Press in Philadelphia. All these books, and others too numerous to mention, were indispensable to me. To all their authors, I send my gratitude.

ACKNOWLEDGMENTS

It has become standard operating procedure among authors to thank their agents, but in this instance it is especially meaningful. I had struggled for some time with the idea of writing a book about Robert Louis Stevenson, and even taken a couple of stabs at it, before throwing in the towel. But Cynthia Manson insisted I give it one more shot, and for better or worse, you hold the results in your hand. I am forever in her debt.

I also wish to thank my assiduous editor, Caitlin Alexander, and my publisher, Jason Kirk, at 47North; even when he was bugging me about the deadlines that I kept missing, he managed to keep a lid on his panic, and as a consequence, on mine.

Although I take the blame for any mistakes in the book, I do want to acknowledge my cousin Robert J. Masiello (yes, he spells the family name differently; my father abbreviated it) of bucolic Roseland, New Jersey, for his help with all things mechanical—from firearms to motorcycles. My thanks, too, to my nephew, the rugged outdoorsman and environmental scientist Daniel "Hawkeye" Masello, for his help with wilderness and camping matters, and to Hannah Hoch, of Whitefish

Bay, Wisconsin, for addressing questions about teenage life and the current music scene.

Finally, I extend my gratitude to you, the readers, who took the time to come along on this trip. We authors really and truly do appreciate the company; we'd be nowhere without you.

ABOUT THE AUTHOR

Robert Masello is an award-winning journalist, a television writer, and the bestselling author of many novels and nonfiction books. His most recent novels, published in more than a dozen languages, include *The Einstein Prophecy*, *The Romanov Cross*, *The Medusa Amulet*, and *Blood and Ice*. His guide to composition, *Robert's Rules of Writing*, has been adopted in many college classrooms. His articles, essays, and reviews have appeared in such prominent publications as the *Los Angeles Times*, *New York* magazine, *People*, *Newsday*, and the *Washington Post*. A long-standing member of the Writers Guild of America, he has taught and lectured at colleges and universities nationwide, including the Columbia University Graduate School of Journalism. He also served as visiting lecturer in literature at Claremont McKenna College for six years. A native of Evanston, Illinois, Masello now lives and works in Santa Monica, California.